W9-COH-684

THE MELODRAMATISTS

Books by Howard Nemerov

THE IMAGE AND THE LAW
(poems)

THE MELODRAMATISTS

The
MELODRAMATISTS

BY HOWARD NEMEROV

If I should vndertake to wryte in prayse of a gentlewoman, I would neither prayse hir christal eye, nor hir cherrie lippe, etc. For these things are *trita et obuia*. But I would either finde some supernaturall cause wherby my penne might walke in the superlatiue degree, or els I would vndertake to aunswere for any imperfection that shee hath, and therevpon rayse the prayse of hir commendacion.

—George Gascoigne

RANDOM HOUSE · NEW YORK

COPYRIGHT, 1949, BY HOWARD NEMEROV

All rights reserved under International and Pan-American Conventions

Published in New York by Random House, Inc., and simultaneously in Toronto, Canada, by Random House of Canada, Limited.

The quotation on pages 210-11 is from A Vision, by William Butler Yeats, copyright, 1938, by William Butler Yeats. Used by permission of The Macmillan Company.

DESIGNED BY MAURICE SERLE KAPLAN
MANUFACTURED IN THE UNITED STATES OF AMERICA
BY THE HADDON CRAFTSMEN, INC., SCRANTON, PA.

for
MARGARET

The action takes place in
Boston, from the winter of
1940 to the autumn of 1941

BOOK · ONE

HERE was to Claire something invincibly embarrassing about the sight of misery coupled with riches, bringing momentarily to the surface a childhood memory of the parental retreat behind closed doors, whence issued the confused, unlikely noise of sobbing and recrimination. When her mother wept, as she did now, all the jewels on her fingers and at her throat winked in sparkling connivance as at a joke which, they seemed to say, you too might appreciate, were you as detached as a stone—cold as this sapphire, hard and cutting as this diamond. Mrs Boyne's tears fell heedlessly where they might, into her coffee, over the bright little spoons and dessert knives, stained the damask cloth. Her back rose and fell in genteel, choking spasms, the little jewels caught the light and flashed with a terrible brilliancy.

The worst of it, Claire thought, was that nothing could be said, done; people are not equipped to handle dinner parties and outraged emotion at once; they sit like a community stricken with paralysis, or as the disciples must have sat, thunderstruck, when Judas had the bad grace to ask, "Lord, is it I?" She looked at her sister.

But Susan, though she sat with abased eyes, seemed undeceived and apart. Claire thought she could detect com-

3

placency even to contempt, to the trace of a smile. This was
infuriating, for Claire realized her own embarrassment to be
the function of her identification with the milieu: she was
ashamed not even for her mother's sake, but for the betrayal
(as she felt) of this material environment, these rich and old
things which existed, so far as concerned her conscience, to
give happiness to whoever could afford it. But Susan patently
felt no such allegiance to the perfectly genuine George III
silver, the Caravaggio above the oaken sideboard, or even to
the butler, Hogan, who imitated now almost to parody the
perfect servant, seeing, hearing nothing. For Claire, Susan was
almost disgracefully at ease where anxiety would have been
respectful and even appropriate; she had the self-sufficiency
of a cat, regarding with dour amusement the improbably genuine tears of some ophidian monster.

As was not unusual in this family, the occasion was somewhat trivial and the scene semi-public. Besides Mr and Mrs
Boyne and the three children, Roger, Claire and Susan, there
were present Uncle and Aunt Fred Seely and a lawyer, a not
very intimate associate of Uncle Fred Seely's, who had been
invited at the last moment because he was in town just for the
night. This lawyer, named Barspaw, was naturally not pleased
to find himself in the midst of a family quarrel. He did not
know these people, he told himself; he found them rude; he
did not like quarrels; surely they might have chosen a more
appropriate time. To relieve his embarrassment, he tried to
derive a civilized entertainment from the dispute, stating dryly
to himself the rights and wrongs of the matter, drawing up for
practice a brief for both sides at once. To aid his thinking he
drew little marks on the cloth with the tines of a dirty fork
which he had unwittingly concealed when the main course was
cleared away. He began by making a mark for each reason, to
the right, to the left; but as his attention began to wander he

4

became attracted by the designs it was possible to make by using all four tines simultaneously. In the vast backwoods of his mind, a child pretended to be plowing a snow-covered field. . . . While the ploughman neer at hand Whistles o'er the furrowed land, he cried silently, feeling the cool wind on his cheek, and was content.

But by words, by tears the debate raged. The substance of it was this: that Roger intended to divorce Lee. Since he had married her two years before, against the wishes of his parents, it might be thought that his present decision would evoke at most a mild rebuke along the lines of, "Perhaps you'll listen to your poor stupid parents next time, eh?" and even a secret jubilation over the fact that "in the long run" (which is always exactly as long as time requires to prove something) their calamitous prophecies and threatful warnings had been entirely justified. But this would be to reckon without the special characteristics of the people involved: so that for Mrs Boyne the crux of the matter was Roger's "leaving that poor helpless girl without a word of explanation"; Mr Boyne saw the public scandal reflected from the shameful and private weakness; Uncle Fred Seely (who wished to become state senator in the next year) saw simply the public scandal. Susan was distantly amused, though she found the concentrated venom of the charges on both sides unclean, like the sudden eruption of an established disease to the surface of the skin; and Claire, in scrupulous anguish, saw a collapse of the glittering surface of things and, beneath, the abyss boiling with tribal savageries. As for Roger, possessed as he was of a callowness too natural to be outgrown, he had chosen the worst possible moment for his revelation: unable to contain himself for five minutes, he had come out, while the soup was being served, with possibly the last dispassionate statement he was to make that evening.

"Mother, I have decided to divorce Leonora."

5

To Claire the quavering stiffness apparent in his posture and voice at once emphasized the comic period-piece aspect of the matter; his little speech, so obviously prepared in just this formula, parodied the righteousness it was supposed to contain and called in question the scene itself. As though the fourth wall had folded back they were exposed to the obscene laughter of an audience; as certainly as on a stage, they sat in a room where such things are said. But Susan laughed outright, causing Mrs Boyne to say in a sharp voice which trembled slightly, "I don't see anything to laugh about, Susan." And Mr Boyne said, with a wealth of squirine authority, "We will discuss this after dinner, Roger. It is not a matter for the table."

So Hogan continued to serve the soup, which was vichyssoise, and they began the meal in a kind of dry anger, all of them, mitigated only by the admiration of each for his own tact. Mr Boyne, like most men who appreciate fully the sound of their own voices, quite looked forward to having a "man-to-man talk" with his son; particularly he intended, when he should have learned the grounds for divorce (if they were what he felt they must be) to establish himself on a firm footing of masculine and adult superiority with his son, whom he regarded not without reason as a child: "I do not want to hear your confessions," he fancied himself as saying, with a wry, ironical smile, "but you must know I'll get to the bottom of this thing one way or another, so we may as well be reasonable." Being reasonable, in the family vocabulary, covered a number of devices of discourse, none of them distinguished by logic. Meanwhile, as he quite well knew, every moment that delayed the interview made more improbable this rounded and on the whole literary approach, replacing it by the automatic anger that he felt both as abhorring divorce and more particularly as hating any disturbance, especially if it involved problems of a sexual nature: his contempt for what he called "smut" was compulsive and, in its way, salacious.

Mrs Boyne, for her part, could not bear the realization that her husband intended to exclude her from the reasonings, diplomacies, causeries that would attend upon the "discussion," and she wished desperately to be able to say something, now, that would show her complete understanding and command, and thus prevent all interested parties from leaving her out of their calculations. Something, it had to be, that would place her clearly where she belonged, at the center of things, meting a matriarchal justice. Silently, while she chewed her food, she searched her mind for an entrance and a cue.

Mr Barspaw, the lawyer, felt the terrible hostility around him and tried to consider whether he might not have given cause for displeasure. Mention of the divorce had not at once struck him as a sufficient reason for the sullenness of his hosts—divorce, marriage, death, he thought: a will, a litigation, an appearance in church or in court; and his mind moved gently over stacks of yellowing paper with which he was perfectly familiar—so he examined his clothing to make sure it was completely buttoned, ascertained that his hat was not still on his head, that he had not spilled anything, that his napkin was on his lap. When, after making this check, he looked at Susan, he saw that she was smiling straight at or through him, and he became quite flustered indeed—so much so that when the main course was cleared he found himself with one dirty fork left over.

It was just at this time that Mrs Boyne leaned over her plate and began to sob.

"You see," Mr Boyne said to Roger. "You have upset your mother so she cannot eat." This was not true, for Mrs Boyne's plate was not only empty but very nearly clean; nevertheless, as no one dared mention this fact, the point was scored.

"I can't help it," said Roger. "But I can't go on like this."

"Don't be melodramatic with me, young man," cried the father, half rising from his chair as Roger too threatened to break into tears. From childhood Roger had cried when reproached, easily and automatically, as a defense and a gesture of obedience which often saved him the worst part of punishment. Now he said, his voice tremulous with self-pity:

"If you knew all the facts, maybe you wouldn't be so anxious to blame me."

Mr Barspaw made a line with his fork, on Roger's side this time. Mrs Boyne wept while her plate was taken away.

"Come, come," said Uncle Fred Seely. "It's few of these lovers' quarrels can't be patched up somehow."

"Many perfect matches go on the rocks after a year," said Mr Barspaw, as though with statistical accuracy. He was using all four tines now, far away on the snowy hills—where the milk-maid singeth blythe. Hogan began now to bring in the dessert— *baba au rhum*, in little individual saucers—and coffee.

"There was no warning," Mrs Boyne gasped between sobs. "We thought you were so perfectly happy."

"The facts . . ." Roger said again, and paused suggestively on the edge of this timorous threat. The silence was marked metronomically by Mrs Boyne's emotion: sob—snuffle, sob— snuffle. It was, Claire thought, the operatic moment: the recitative stops, the orchestra goes tum-tim-tim, tum-tim-tim; and in a moment the tenor will begin with the obvious reflection, *"La donna è mobile."* Enter the Facts, dressed like Furies. They dance.

"Hogan," said Mr Boyne, "that will be all for now."

"Sir?" Hogan looked inquiringly at his employer, and held up ritually, as though in symbol of his office and obedience, the little instrument used for scraping crumbs. "Sir?"

"I mean, go into the kitchen. I shall ring when you're needed again."

"But the dessert, sir, and the coffee? Two people, sir, including Miss Susan . . ."

8

"I said: go into the kitchen!" In silence all watched Hogan turn smartly about and march into the kitchen. Before the swinging door settled to behind him, "My Christ," they heard him say to Mrs Purse, the cook; and heard also her reply: "Shut up and listen. I've got the oven to do."

"Needs discipline, that man of yours," said Uncle Fred Seely.

"What do you suggest—the whip?" Susan asked.

"I must apologize," Mr Boyne began in his most signorial tone, bending courteously toward Mr Barspaw, "for having subjected you, in my house . . ."

"Ah?" Mr Barspaw, startled, recalled himself and put down the fork. "Ah. It is nothing, sir, nothing. Pray do not—that is to say, I was about to suggest, myself, that I withdraw until a more"—he got up and edged, bowing, toward the door, throwing them easily the glib and final phrase—"propitious moment."

"Wait, please." Roger got up too. "You're a lawyer. You must know: how long will it take me to get a divorce?"

Mr Barspaw stopped. "Well," he replied with clarity and precision, "that depends. You have grounds, of course?"

We have grounds fine, medium and coarse, thought Susan in a momentary collapse of perspective. Percolate, drip, silex.

"Of course I have grounds," said Roger. "Goddamn good grounds." He felt, obscurely and correctly, that anger might improve his position; and certainly it did wonders for his tone. Mr Barspaw sidled gently back toward the table, where he gripped devoutly the back of his chair, and, with head bowed, seemed ready to recite a grace.

"Now, Roger!" Mr Boyne prepared to make a diversion by noise alone; but too late. Roger had already said the word.

"Adultery—precisely." Mr Barspaw was playing on his home grounds now. He picked up a dessert spoon and twiddled it as expertly as if it had been a pencil. "Adultery. Yes." He gave the

9

impression of musing, priestlike, upon frailty. Now, as though to elicit a confession by shock, he raised his head and said crisply, "Whose?"

"Why, hers, of course, Leonora's."

It was, Susan felt, like a desperately bad movie in which the actors do not respond to a situation until it has been six ways made clear to the audience. Now Mrs Boyne caught her breath, choked momentarily, then wept with renewed vigor; Uncle Fred Seely allowed his orator's smooth face to express astonishment and his orator's mouth to hang limply open, while Aunt Emma Seely, who was deaf and a little feeble in the head, smiled in her most charming manner.

Mr Boyne stood up. "I think," he said, "you will excuse Roger and myself if we go upstairs."

As they pushed back their chairs they heard Hogan, like a chorus leader, speak behind the kitchen door: "This is *only the beginning*," he intoned. "Only The Beginning. They're going upstairs now."

"Good night, all," said Mr Barspaw in a cheery, professional voice, like that of a doctor leaving a house of mortal sickness. "Good night." And like a doctor, too, he gave a final word to the patient to speed him on his journey. "Good night, young man," he said to Roger, just one whole tone lower.

2

AFTER MR BOYNE had followed Roger upstairs, Mrs Boyne, like a commander left in charge of garrison while the crack squadron goes forth to battle, led her remaining cohorts, the aged, the infirm, women and children, through the *seicento* plaza (with the fountain that did not work) into the library-cum-parlor.

This was a massive, overbearing room, paneled in walnut stained almost to black and insufficiently illuminated by lights set in gilded wooden sconces along the wall, so that the ceiling (which was quite low) received the best part of the light, while the habitable part of the room rested under the bulging shadows of scrolled woodwork. The furniture was a hotch-potch of styles and degrees of comfort: slim chairs, that would not bear the weight of Uncle Fred Seely, bespoke the room of some great courtesan, or her maid; but this impression was contradicted by other chairs, enormous, deep and heavily stuffed, and a fat sofa covered in heavy purple velvet. Many of the pieces, moreover, seemed to have been practice fields for the mythological fancies of their creators; on them fertile invention had entwined maidens with serpents, with vines, had set warriors fully armed, had in a multitude of ways advantaged itself of the one constant fashion of making things resemble what they are not; so that the unwary visitor, throwing himself back in a chair, was liable to severe damage from the keen aquiline nose of a nymph or helmeted Amazon, designed perhaps with the sinister intention of being tipped with poison and penetrating the base of the skull. Every so often Mrs Boyne decided that this room should be made "more gay," and in consequence had several pieces re-covered in brightly striped or patterned silks: the resulting gaiety always proved discouraging enough to cause the idea to be dropped, the bright little chairs against the heavy panelling producing an effect at once fey and unwholesome. Several bookcases, filled with leather-bound standard editions of the best authors, were let into the panelling at equal intervals along the walls. In one corner there stood a harpsichord, lacquered in red and black. Alert and delicate on spindly legs, this instrument supported two things: a silver peacock with tail upspread, and a cast of the bust of Plato in the Vatican. The philosopher's brow was ever so slightly creased, his mouth turned ever so little down at the corners, into the stylized mustache which flowed past his chin to the tip of the beard.

Mrs Boyne, as leaning on Claire's arm she directed the seating of the company, was thinking that perhaps some decision might yet be reached without the aid of the principal parties. It may be possible, thought she, to present if not a *fait accompli*, at least the decision of a large part of the family—without knowing very many of the facts, to be sure, but then, facts were so seldom important, she found, compared to an innate predisposition to "do the right thing." First, however, she must allow herself time, time to develop the adequate appearance of one who recovers by simple strength from a grievous blow.

"Claire," she said, disengaging herself and sitting down, heavily, in an armchair, "Claire, play something for us, something nice." There was a dutiful fidgeting, then a devout or uninterested silence on Uncle Fred Seely's part, as Claire sat down at the harpsichord. Mrs Boyne sighed loudly, almost a groan, above the music.

The only person who listened to Claire while she played, competently, the B-flat Partita, was Aunt Emma Seely; and curiously, Claire was the only person who thought at the time of this old lady, who sat stiffly upright in the uncomfortable chair assigned to her—not listening, perhaps, so much as attentive with her whole being, attentive in more than the poise of her small head on her gross, shapeless body, in more than the vacant fixture of her alert, meaningless eyes. The clangor of the instrument might have meant for her the noise of men rattling garbage cans, in some street where she had lived; or the tinkle of many silver spoons being cleaned and put away. For Claire she represented one of the worst of life's many dangers, something hard to name but which she called "the obesity of utter disappointment." It was as though she had said to her body, "Come, there's nothing else for us, let us grow, let us triumph at any rate over space." In her all capacity had been strangled, save the vegetative, which by some impertinent freakishness had allowed to remain uncamouflaged by fat the birdlike, unhappy features which, some said, had once been handsome and more than handsome.

Occasionally it was remarked that Uncle Fred had been "a little heavy-handed" with her in their first years of marriage; originally Claire had thought this meant to beat her, but she soon learned from Susan (who had a way of picking up the oddest confidences about the family from comparative strangers) that with a subtlety unlooked for in a man of his size and habits Uncle Fred had simply insisted on her drinking much more than was good for her. By conviviality, prescriptions of port for health, pretending offense if she did not drink with himself glass for glass, he had kept her in a state of moderate alcoholic stupidity accompanied by diarrhoea until, when one day he turned on her and diagnosed her case as "feeble-mindedness," her fuddled brain took the suggestion and progressively relaxed its control to meet her lord and master's description. No one knew why Uncle Fred had behaved this way in his youth; now, in public at least, he was careful and considerate of the silly old woman.

Much in the world frightened Claire, but most of all the contemplation of the number of wicked things people might do and still not merely live on, but preserve as well their social position and the esteem in which they were held among their acquaintance. Sometimes she was frightened of Susan for this cause: Susan seemed to understand so well about time and its modifying effect on action—how time was a desert, in which the lineaments of decisive acts crumbled or got covered, lost, in sand—and seemed ready to accept this, even take it for granted: a concession which Claire could not by any means make. Sometimes she felt that one's potential for disaster grew with one, or grew even faster, far faster; and when she looked into the future she saw but two alternatives: a strict negative volition, a will-not-to-do, or swift catastrophe, not killing at once but leaving her to the quiet, often offensively humorous depredations of time, while there grew up a new, cruel generation that would not understand.

She had reached the Sarabande, which she played well indeed. The two clear levels of music, of elegant, melancholy rhetoric, rose into the room with a splendid metallic resonance. It seemed the purest emotion of the storyteller, the crisp rendering into the present, into the moment, of a sad tale from the past.

"Very nice, Claire," said Mrs Boyne, before the second repeat could be played. "Very nice indeed." She clapped her hands delicately.

"I don't know why you don't get a piano," said Uncle Fred Seely. "That thing there—every time I hear it I think it's a pretty expensive get-up for something that sounds like a banjo."

"It is a harpsichord, Fred," said Mrs Boyne, as she had said many times before. "It is very old." Now her bland expression, suitable for music, became a bleak, forbidding mask, and she said: "I must apologize to you all for my—my slight lapse, in there." She motioned toward the dining room. "But I was, excusably I think, overcome by shock. Now I have recovered sufficiently to consider with you what must be done."

"Really, Mother," Susan said. "I think Roger has decided pretty definitely what must be done."

"Susan, I must ask you not to take sides with Roger. That's the trouble with you young people, you have not the slightest sense of responsibility. You like to be considered, yes, but you do not consider others. Your family means nothing to you, nothing whatever, you have very little regard for a reputation built up over a century and a quarter. . . ."

There is no telling how long this might have continued, had not Mrs Boyne realized herself to have been entrapped in a filibuster. She stopped, and after a moment resumed from her beginning, in the tones of authentic, impartial justice.

"Whatever is being decided upstairs," she said, "need not be taken as final. You will admit, Fred, that you men will always join forces against a woman. . . ."

"She should be spanked," said Uncle Fred Seely suddenly, referring presumably to Leonora. He finished with an abrupt laugh, as he saw Susan flash him a glance which said quite clearly: "I'd like to see you try it, too." His face reddened slightly, and he tried without success to stare the girl down. "After all," he said with dignity, "misbehaving is misbehaving."

"Exactly," said Mrs Boyne. "Now, I say—even if Roger is my own son—that whatever Leonora did, she had a good reason, or else she was driven to it." She presented these alternatives with an air of finality, like the salesman who asks whether you will have the large or the small package. The curious feature of her attitude was an apparently complete forgetfulness of the fact that she had always disliked Leonora; and until now, a grudging element had always been foremost in her acceptance of the marriage. Inasmuch as she acted reasonably, two reasons might be found: first, because of a strong tension between herself and her children, any stick would do to beat any of them; and second, whatever happened in the end, Roger would remain to be beaten, while Leonora quite possibly would not. If there were no divorce, on the other hand, if all were forgiven, Mrs Boyne would commend her own fairmindedness in shifting a large part of the blame to Leonora simply because she had again become accessible.

Now, as she developed her thesis, she claimed that Roger's unfortunate financial dependence on his parents must prove irksome to a girl of Leonora's spirit (which previously she had called "the impudence of that girl"), that her discontent might easily have led to some harmless indiscretion ("she's still just a girl, marriage or no marriage"), that whatever she might have done had been intended merely as a criticism of Roger; and in short, before concluding her exposition, she had made of the adultery ("if there was any such thing"—this with all the propriety of great doubt—"which I don't for a moment admit") a mere spur to Roger's pride, a way of making him a great success by simple compensation, which success once made, Leonora would live safe again at home, never more to roam from beside her industrious and suddenly mature, important husband, a lay figure in which no trace was to be found of Roger in his proper person as he was.

What nonsense, Claire thought, what precious nonsense. She looked at her watch, then up at Susan, and shook her head very slightly toward the door. Susan, with an expression of the gravest interest in what was going on, affected not to notice.

"We must do everything we can to keep them together," concluded Mrs Boyne, looking triumphantly and challengingly at Uncle Fred Seely. "What do you think?" she wanted to know.

Uncle Fred, for his part, was torn by two desires. The wish not to give in to any woman in her slightest request was balanced by the wish to prevent, if he could, the publicity attendant on a divorce in the family; one had, he put it to himself, a position to keep up, the respect of the community . . .

While he considered how to phrase acceptably these sentiments he salt bolt upright in a judicial posture, with his arms extended on the carved arms of a dignified oak chair. For some time he had been tracing with his fingertips the lineaments of the carvings, and now, looking curiously down, he discovered himself to have been fondling all this while the round breast and sharply erected nipple of a nymph. With a sudden movement he dropped both hands in his lap and looked quickly and furtively about him. Obviously, he saw, Susan had been watching him for some time: a slight, contemptuous smile played on her lips, and Uncle Fred felt himself shaken by a remote, entirely sexual thrill of hatred. He would like, he thought, to "paddle her bottom for her"; yes, that was it: to "paddle her bottom." The fine old manly phrase barely served to cover, in Uncle Fred's mind, Caligulan dreamlike lecheries that made sleep so attractive to him.

He was roused from a consideration of these practices upon Susan's remarkably nubile body by the voice of Mrs Boyne, who demanded to know, for the third time, what he thought. Nervously weakened by the diversion of his strongest emotions into such distant ways, Uncle Fred answered briefly and absently that he thought that what she said was fine, fine. He agreed perfectly, and he was sure Emma did too. For emphasis he looked his wife straight in the eyes and shook his head slowly up and down. Emma, still more slowly, imitated this movement. She found herself in agreement.

Claire asked to be excused. She felt she could not bear to be present when Roger and her father came downstairs, when in all probability the ridiculous and pompous attitudes already developed in both camps would compound to form a little drama, militant and absurd.

"Where are you going, dear?" Mrs Boyne asked.

"I may go out. I'm not sure."

"Ah. Out." The two syllables followed Claire in vague protest and reproach. "Out" was, in Mrs Boyne's opinion, already and without further specification a dubious, questionable place.

Susan, who did not ask to be excused, simply left the room and caught up with Claire on the first landing.

"Silly," she said. "Why didn't you stay around? It was just getting funny."

"Why didn't you?" asked Claire sullenly.

"I didn't want to stay without you," Susan said. "Come on up to my room and let's talk."

"Aren't you going out tonight?"

"Not for an hour or so. Somebody is calling for me. A Dr Einman, whom I've never met."

"Not met? Isn't that slightly unusual?"

"Not in these parlous times," said Susan. "People depute people to take people to parties—it's a shorthand symbol for the disintegration of all the better customs of society. We move toward anonymous vulgarity, lechery in blackouts and so on. Civilization, war and death." She pirouetted neatly on the top step.

"Well, are you coming?" she demanded then.

Claire considered for a moment. "All right," she said finally. "But only for a few minutes."

As they passed the closed door of their father's "den" they heard tones of reproach, subdued shouts of anger, contrition, the unmistakable sound of a fist hitting a table.

"Gawd," said Susan, with a sweeping gesture towards the door. "They ain't done right by our Nell."

3

As THEY ENTERED the den, Mr Boyne closed the door and settled himself in the leather chair. By affixing his gaze squarely on Roger's eyes he gained what he conceived to be the advantage of keeping his son standing before him; the premium placed by amateur psychologists on superior height in such an interview was here outweighed by the fact that patience lasts longer sitting down. Mr Boyne searched for a way to begin. He was not entirely certain as to what would be, for him, a desirable outcome of the interview, but he treated it from the first as a passage at arms in which his opponent (so he referred to his son) must be "made to see the right thing"; which meant that Roger after being defeated must be slightly humiliated as well.

"The Lord knows," he began at last, "if I'd known what a lot of trouble it would be I never would have had a family."

The mildly humorous entrance to the subject was lost on Roger, because of his own tension and because, as he was perfectly aware, his father resented "trouble" more than anything else; and perhaps, as well, he did resent having a family and looked upon it as one of the trials that gave his Episcopalian universe a faintly Calvinistic tinge.

"Now I want you to know, Roger, before we begin," said Mr Boyne, "that I'm not inclined to treat this matter lightly, whatever the right and wrong of it. Divorce is a serious thing. There has never been a divorce in my family before, or anything remotely like it—no scandal, no really unhappy marriages." This was not true, but Roger in his present position could scarcely make policy of it. Mr Boyne continued:

"I have always been strict with myself, Roger, very strict—in an ethical sense, I mean. I have taken care to be always honorable. I am a respected member of this community."

He paused, and Roger said, "Yes, sir," in a low voice.

"As for you, I have always allowed you more latitude, more freedom, than I had myself. I did not want to play the heavy father with my children, although make no mistake, I would if it became necessary—I will if it does become necessary."

This had, so far as Roger could remember, formed the invariable prologue to these "man-to-man talks" that had marked like irritants and poultices the eruptive crises of his life. But in his boredom it never occurred to him—he was in this way quite like his father—that this preamble took no account of the facts, never even asked for the facts of this particular case: Roger felt himself to be in the situation of a man who, on trial for his life on a murder charge, finds himself about to be convicted of the terrible crime of having presumed to be born at all. Heavily, Mr Boyne followed the worn path.

"I cannot conceal from you, Roger, that you have been a disappointment to me in many ways. I have wanted to talk to you for some time past; this business of the divorce is serious, yes, but it isn't the only thing that leads me to find fault with you. There is, to begin with, your treatment of your mother and myself, which has been careless and inconsiderate to say the least. How do you think you made your mother feel when you spoke up before everyone about your wife's supposed or real infidelity? A matter that you should be almost ashamed to mention to me alone, and should not whisper in your mother's hearing. Not only as your father, but simply as one man to another, let me tell you I resent your manner in speaking to her."

"I thought it was my duty to tell you, sir," mumbled Roger, conscious that it was a weak reply. Like a student who has tried to outguess the examiner, he had come prepared for catechising on the subject of divorce and that alone. Now he realized the futility of this preparation against a sneak attack on the irrelevant foundations of his being.

"It's rather late in the day for remembering your duty," said Mr Boyne with broad sarcasm, "considering that you practically eloped in defiance of your mother's wishes, two years ago."

"No such thing, sir. We merely assumed your permission from what was said, and got married quietly." With a fierceness close-allied to tears Roger took a stand on this open point.

"Now, Roger," Mr Boyne made a temple of his fingers, rubbed their tips slowly together, "I do not wish to drive you into a lie. To me a lie is a serious offense."

"I was twenty-one when I married. I am twenty-three now. There is no law that permits you to dictate to me, sir. I can be free of you if I wish."

"I do not want to embarrass you, Roger, by raising the question of your financial position. It is easy to talk about being free of me after taking my money. We will not mention that, however. I give you money freely, of my own volition, you do not force me, I could hardly say it is your fault."

Roger was silent. Relentlessly Mr Boyne continued.

"I do not pretend ever to have expected great things from you. When you left college, for the sole reason, apparently, that you fancied doing so, or did so out of a fear of expulsion if you remained, I said to myself: 'Well now, wait and see; perhaps he wants to get into the world, get to work.' I could not have been more mistaken. But I let you go on, I gave you enough rope and more than enough: now your life is a wreck, it's nobody's fault but your own, and you come to us expecting not only to be set on your feet, but to hear nothing about it afterwards, not one word of reproach." He rose to his feet and commenced to walk about. "Have you ever put yourself out for me? Have I ever heard one word that would show me you appreciate what has been done for you, often at great expense and personal inconvenience? You have been, in my estimation, a ne'er-do-well, a spendthrift, and a wiseacre. You don't know how serious life is." He sat down again, allowed a judicious silence, then went on.

"But you're going to find out. You got married, and you'll stay married. You want a divorce, but no money will be forthcoming from this house. For a while I thought the country might go to war to help Britain. That would have been a horrible mistake, a direct contravention of the Monroe Doctrine. But you would have been in the army. In the army they would have smartened you up, I'll say. But there'll be no war for us; we learned last time when we're well out of a thing. Perhaps you'll still get a year of it in the draft, and I tell you I'll see to it there's no deferment in your case. Now crying will get you nowhere!" This last remark, uttered in a tone of the most compulsive temper, was the only uncalculated statement of the speech.

The factors that caused Roger to begin to cry have about

them an interesting complicity. Tears were, in the first place, his only way of being heard: to have opposed his father with reasons, even had he any, would have invited the reproach of stubbornness. Having tried it he knew that Mr Boyne would simply say: "Very well. You are not amenable to reason, then I'll talk in a language you do understand." And he would proceed to list again, in a louder voice and at greater length, the same catalogue of sins he had just finished reading. So even boredom was, in its way, a contributing cause to his tears. Then, as has been suggested, an emotional breakdown at this point amounted to a formal submission, a gesture of obedience which would make things easier from this point on, in this sense a dangerous kind of shortcut to the crisis and subsequent conciliation. Also, the years had established a pattern for these interviews, which were like a folk-drama in having been worn into shape by repetition, so that they illustrated not the oppositions and antagonisms of the moment, of the particular question, but more importantly and artistically the tensions and conflicts that were permanently characteristic of the relation between father and son: it will be recalled that nothing of any practical significance had yet been said about the divorce.

As for Mr Boyne, this was to him as well the most difficult moment. All his efforts thus far had been directed simply at the result now achieved. To what extent consciously or unconsciously it would be impossible to say, his object had been to bring his son to the humiliation implicit in their relationship as both conceived it. But this submission had a double effect. Recognizing that he could now make unopposed any point he found desirable in particular, he was nevertheless shocked and embarrassed by his son's tears. A part of himself demanded and found them, as a tribute, pleasant and ordinate; but another part insisted on rejecting these feelings as proper only to a certain low and bestial envy, as not superior or judicious. There was something terribly, mysteriously womanish about their effect on one another, a conflict which was the other aspect of a slavery to love and fear, so that in the motions of the one, the other felt a physical pull, a resistance that tore himself. In its practical conclusion this climax always set in operation some law of diminishing returns: Mr Boyne could never resist advantaging himself of his total victory by keeping Roger in tears for some time, but this inevitably meant that he must restore the boy's self to him by a capitulation on the practical point at issue.

For a while longer, then, he kept his son there, crying quietly and saying yes to everything, while he went over in detail the list of life's crimes. Roger kept blubbering that he was sorry, which was perfectly true at the time, until Mr Boyne felt a disgust and loathing for both of them that caused him to conclude the matter as rapidly as possible. The danger in this, he had found, was that he could, by generosity, by the reasonableness that followed on the collapse of his emotions, raise his son again to the point at which he could be respected; but for himself, no such thing, he left himself under an inexpiable and increasing burden of worry. Had he behaved bestially? What should he have done? Why did he always insist on this token victory that afterwards became so repellent to himself? He was convinced that there was some fundamental error in his ways, but he could not make it out by any means.

In short, the doubly explosive capacities of the interview's first part had really the effect of reducing the difference between the parties to a readiness for agreement to almost anything; and the decision that finally would be made had already been prepared by the completest irrelevance.

Now, the critical point over, they were able to discuss the question of divorce in the most dispassionate, if not actually divorce. You've made your bed, now lie in it." The aptness of the metaphor struck him just after he had made it, and he coughed slightly. "I mean," he went on, "that I cannot support you in it, because it doesn't seem worth it to disgrace your whole family, in yourself, by dragging all this out in the open. And then again," he said vaguely, "there's Uncle Fred . . ."

With this, the discussion was over, though both felt that more might have been said. Particularly Mr Boyne remarked that he had in a way commended murder, and wondered what his son thought. In point of fact, there had been a gun in the desk drawer until two years ago, when Mr Boyne had sold it by way of capitulating to old age, and also perhaps in recognition of the safety conferred by the same.

4

THE TWO GIRLS were comfortably disposed in Susan's room, which was furnished, like the rest of the house, in a dark and saturnine fashion. Susan lay across the high, canopied bed, almost concealed by maroon-velvet hangings. Why a canopied bed in this room? No one knew. It had always been there.

Claire sat in the only chair, which was, like herself, prim, straight-backed and uneasy. The curtains, also of maroon velvet, were withdrawn, disclosing the narrow, lonely street at the corner of which a street lamp reflected brilliantly on a heap of dirty snow. Beyond, one could see a small part of the Charles River and, on the farther shore above the dark arc of the railway bridge, an illuminated sign advertising Carter's Ink.

Claire was twenty-one, two years older than her sister. She was tall, with heavy pale-blonde hair which she braided and coiled on her head. In repose she was beautiful in that pre-Raphaelite conception of beauty that could be called by choice ethereal or bovine. It was statuesque, it was "admirable" (the fashionable word at the time), but one could not imagine it capable of warmth or of great mobility: at best an awkward, shy affection was predictable, and even this, concealed though it might be by good, even grand manners and a certain poise belonging to always threatened innocence, would be a source of self-torment and anxiety. Already she had developed a spinsterish asperity of voice and, on occasion, the primness of a young dowager.

But Susan was small, not fat but not thin either, beautifully well-formed, in fact, with black hair that she swept behind her ears and tied loosely at the nape of her neck. Her face was not beautiful, being too gross of feature, with somewhat thick lips, but her skin was pale and very white, shining like a light in bloodless wax, or with the waxen quality of flowers.

"Poor Roger," Susan said now. "What a beating he takes being the scion of the Boynes."

"What do you suppose the real trouble is?" asked Claire.

"Something sexual, I suppose." Susan said it carelessly, yet with a slight emphasis on the fact of saying the word, of introducing a potent theme.

"What do you mean?"

"Well, Roger gave it a name. I suppose, maybe, that they just can't stand each other. . . . How should I know? It all seems very disagreeable somehow."

"But why does it have to be that especially?"

"Well," Susan said dully, "Leonora's such a bitch, for one thing. Imagine how embarrassed Father must be. Have you noticed how he hates just the idea of sex? Uncle Fred would be the boy to enjoy himself, though—lecherous old Uncle Fred that he is."

"Really, Susan, why do you have to make these judgments, especially on your own family? People are the way they are."

"I suppose so," Susan said. "But I feel resentful."

"Resentful—about what?"

"Well, call it about 'education.' Doesn't it occur to you, that all this—your intellectual qualities, Roger's drinking, even the way Fred treated Emma—that all this begins in bed, and this is the one thing we are supposed never to mention?"

"That seems," Claire said, "sufficiently obvious. And so?"

"So it seems to me we're all being victimized by our own pretenses. Pretending that we can do this, and keep from doing that, and that it's all a matter of will power and, well, education, when really we may be just blind activities started by two other blind activities having what they call fun."

"But that would be just to deny yourself all individuality," Claire said excitedly. "You would be just living in a dream."

"Maybe I like it that way," said Susan with a teasing smile. "Maybe I'm better off blind. And as for a dream, what do you call the other, this perpetual mooning about noble motives, when really—do you know," she asked suddenly, "that we have a relative in the state asylum?"

"No."

"Fred's brother. He tried to kill his wife, long ago. He was a prime example. She died the year after he was put away, and they still keep telling each other she died of a broken heart because she couldn't live without him. Whether her heart was broken or not she did it with a rope."

"Suicide."

"Yes."

"How did you find out?"

"Leonora told me, and I put it up to Roger. He said he'd gotten it from someone he'd met at the Napoleon Club. That doesn't matter, the point is there's something so nasty and attractive about the idea of killing yourself because your husband can't murder you."

"I don't see it," Claire said. She stood up and said angrily,

"Why can't we keep our lives clean? Why is there this perpetual making of dirty jokes running like a sound-track beside us, as though some—some horrible little toadstools were leaning together and whispering about us?"

"Maybe it's just built that way from the beginning," Susan said gravely. "Built like a trap. But I don't know."

"But why do we have to talk about it, why do we have to admit it all the time?" Claire put up her hand to the window and felt the wonderful coldness, looked out at the river, the intermittent gleaming in its blackness: her mind was full of images of coldness, of the magnificent vaulted solemnity of churches; convents, white stiff robes, coldness, centuries cold as the tomb devoted to denouncing warmth, intimacy. Even sweat might turn into ice, into sharp delicate crystal spines.

"It's life," Susan said, with a large gesture that seemed to add, 'Take it or leave it.'

"Life!" Claire laughed shortly and turned to her sister. "You know all about it." She surprised herself with boldness, and said: "Have you ever slept with anyone?"

"No," Susan said. "No, I haven't."

"Then don't sound so horribly clever. 'Life.' "

"You mean you have?"

"Yes." Claire had not meant to say this much, but now she continued. "I didn't like it. I wouldn't do it again, ever. Maybe it would be different for you."

"Ah, Claire, I'm sorry." Susan came over and touched her sister's shoulder. "I'm sorry," she said again. "I was just talking."

They stood together at the window. A man and a woman were advancing up the street, leaning against the wind. In the shadows they stopped to kiss briefly, then she pushed him away, or so it seemed, and they walked on, disappearing under the window.

A knock sounded at the door. Hogan's voice said that a Dr Einman was waiting for Miss Susan.

"He has a taxi waiting, Miss," Hogan added with respectful urgency.

<h1 style="text-align:center">5</h1>

AFTER ALL, Roger thought, it could have been worse. He meant only that it could have gone on for another hour. Returning with his father to the living room and knowing what was expected of him, he had gone at once up to his mother and, in stilted, formal phrases, apologized for any trouble he might at any time have caused her, and made renewed promises of filial duty and obligation. It was unbelievable, he was forced to admit, but his mother seemed to find a mysterious delight in his professions, forced and academic as they sounded to him: almost he felt the vocational pride of a diplomat empowered to lie by superior authority. His relief, when the reconciliation had been made, his gratified sense of a newly constituted equilibrium that would last for possibly a month, was so strong that he was almost able to mistake it for love, even while he realized himself to be, like a dog whose master projects into it his own moral sense, grateful for a deserved thrashing.

At the same time, in a distant way, he knew that nothing had been settled: the problem of the divorce, for instance, had simply been referred a step back, he was on his own. He was honest enough to admit that he felt no pride, no family pride especially, merely because it was inconvenient for him to feel any, a strong sense of a link with the generations preceding and proceeding being immediately referable to a more specifically sexual pride: which last he had not got. Try as he might to feel ashamed of the fact, he could not. Unconditionally he accepted himself as he was, with a tolerant sympathy that he would extend to no one else. In a queer way this made him invulnerable with the proof of diffidence: except by his parents he could not even be challenged in his self-sufficiency. Moreover, he felt the oncoming of war; for him it was already something possible; and the final spine of his creation lay in his almost automatic, involuntary power, when a purely personal life should have become too difficult, to identify his disaster with that of the world.

Now, as he sat on the harpsichord bench while his family talked about other matters (even the emptiest triumph at once leaves people free to talk about other matters), he thought: so we learn about life, which proves always to be surprising in minor ways, the point being that (contrary to his father's belief) there is always an out, always a step back and a further resignation. He saw even the possibility of life's being a test set by invisible powers, in which weakness might prove a satisfactory reply, and the kind of strength that stakes all on one last throw might receive a failing mark, with a sarcastic note in red pencil attached: "Life is the test, not death," or "Why do you panic just at the last question?" Love of weakness, detestation of strength—*heureux sont les debonnaires, car ils heriteront la terre.* But he recognized this for a parable: the earth was precisely not inherited by *les debonnaires,* who, when one came to think of it, were taking the most desperate chance, which they only partly concealed by wearing ordinary clothes and drinking in commonplace bars.

On the other hand, a jejune saint, who fought his family for the dubious privilege of marrying, and fought again for divorce, was not easily to be imagined.

The doorbell rang and Hogan, answering, admitted Leonora and Gerry Landis, who without taking off their coats entered the living room. Wind-disheveled and ruddy of cheek from the cold, they made, Roger thought, a handsome pair. Leonora was small, daintily made—"petite" was the word which, with all its implications of laciness and frailty, described her ambition in life: simply to be, and to go on being, "petite." Her hair was shining blonde, her features had the thinness and elegant peaked quality of an aging film star's, though as a matter of fact she was twenty-three. Gerry was robust or even stout, and somewhat older than Roger. He dressed carelessly in tweeds and wore a loosely knotted red tie; at the moment there was a set smile, probably meant in a conciliatory sense, on his round face.

After a moment of stupefaction the same disastrous lack of family balance that had acted against Roger before, now moved with equal clumsiness in his favor.

"What do you mean by coming here?" asked Mr Boyne aggressively, and Uncle Fred Seely added in a sullen voice, as though it doubled the charge, "At this time of night, too." They looked quickly from Leonora to Gerry and back, then Uncle Fred Seely looked only at Leonora.

"Leonora," cried Mrs Boyne. "I'm glad you've come. I wanted to talk to you." Looking at Gerry she said: "You should not have entered this house, young man."

Gerry, embarrassed, made a meaningless gesture. It looked as though, by way of reparation, he wished to give Mrs Boyne his hat. The stupid smile, dehydrated, prepared, what you will, but lifeless, remained on his face.

"If you don't mind, sir," Roger said to his father, "I'll take care of this." And before anyone could object he had backed the visitors into the entrance hall.

"Now what is it?" he said abruptly.

"We've come to apologize," Gerry said, twisting the brim of his hat.

"We haven't done anything wrong," said Leonora. "In fact we thought you had a damn filthy mind."

3 2

"But when Leonora told me you wanted a divorce I said to myself . . ."

"Let's never mind," said Leonora, "what you said to yourself."

"I said, 'Hey, wait a minute, that's too much of a good thing'—I mean, that is, it would be a hell of a mess all about, well, nothing."

"So we thought rather than have you go on believing what you do, we'd apologize," Leonora said, "and try not to see each other again, if that's what you want."

Roger thought, as he had before, that there is always a step back, there is always a further retreat to be made, nothing final need ever be done. He assumed rather than knew they were lying, but he saw that Gerry was even more anxious to straighten things away without a fight than he was. And it was funny to see that they were both offering up Leonora on the altars of an armed truce: rather, he thought, like Munich, except that in Leonora one did not deal with a helpless Czechoslovakia. She was perfectly able to take care of herself, this had probably been her plan, and in her eyes what was being sacrificed was their masculinity. If it were possible for her to conceive, he thought, how little it mattered.

"That would probably be best," he assured them gravely; and to Gerry he said, "I quite understand, and I feel no spite whatever about it, but surely you can realize this sort of thing causes talk." Brazenly he put between them a public reason, one that could be acknowledged utterly without embarrassment.

"I'm sure glad you feel that way, old man," said Gerry, and shook Roger's hand. The smile on his face, though probably the same smile in every physical respect, seemed to combine in a barely perceptible way relief and triumph. Where will they meet from now on? thought Roger, and smiled too, considering the dingy hotels, the brass bedsteads . . . Of course she probably gave him money from her allowance.

"Now I'll take you home, Lee," he said. "I think we can consider the matter closed." Leonora smiled too. Everyone smiled. It was a brilliant and perfect rehearsal of smiles all around.

"That will be fine, darling," she said.

The elders heard this conversation through the open doors. They were puzzled. They had won, there would be no divorce. But they too realized that something had been sacrificed. They had been presented with a puppet performance, cheated of the life. Among the random images that went through Nicholas Boyne's mind was one of some Roman general who had ordered the execution of his own son on a battlefield; and another, more vaguely recalled, of a Roman—was it ambassador?—who for some reason had stuck his hand in a pot of fire and seen it consumed. To prove something, was it?

*S*USAN stepped into the taxi without assistance of any kind from the dark bundle that was presumably Dr Einman. As they started off, passing beneath a street lamp, she saw a flash of white silk scarf, a glint possibly from a gold tooth; for the rest the bundle was as unknown as it had been silent. She felt the slightest suggestion of fear. After all, one couldn't know. The bundle here reached out an arm, and a gloved hand patted her knee.

"Don't worry," the bundle said with great assurance and in sepulchral tones. "I am Dr Einman."

"How reassuring," Susan replied; but she moved nevertheless as far as possible to her side of the cab. That pat on the knee, she thought, reflected a confidence that could bear considerable diminution without ever approaching modesty.

"We have so many kinds of doctor these days," she said. "And what kind are you?"

"I am a psychoanalyst," he answered. "Or, more precisely, an analytic psychologist."

"The distinction quite escapes me."

"Ah." Silence. "Hum."

And that was all, for it was a short distance they had to go, and even now the cab drew up before Abel Hanway's studio apartment on the hill. As Einman turned to pay the driver Susan saw his face. He's quite old, she thought with some little surprise; and became quite offended with herself for her delicacy. The pat on the knee had represented not insolence but, more likely, an aged erotic courtesy. How funny. She made amends by taking his arm on the way upstairs.

Mr Hanway met them at the door, instructed them where to dispose of their coats, met them again after this with cups of a pale, lemony punch, which tasted somehow vicious and medicinal—nastier than it need, Susan thought.

She and Dr Einman now settled themselves in one of the few available places, one of two facing couches at either side of the fireplace. They did not immediately begin to talk, indeed they paid each other little enough attention at first. There was something about a party, it seemed, which required the newcomer to acclimatize himself, to listen, to take up finally the exact tone of his neighbors. At Abel Hanway's parties this tone had always to do with the minor arts: interior decorating, incidental music to some or other script, amateur dramatics, museum lectures, etc.

Hanway was rich, likable and not untalented, though it would have been hard to say just what it was at which he was not untalented. At the present moment his rather original hand-painted cellophane doilies were very fashionable on and around Beacon Street and the Hill. These sets were of two main kinds, with many variations: the first worked out abstract designs on Christian symbols—the cross, the five wounds, the magical pentagram of Joseph of Arimathea, the Holy Grail; while the other kind similarly exploited the Orient and showed, over the lotus lying on the eternal waters, the tree of the world, the vajra, the Buddha, various minor deities dancing. But this, as has been said, was of the moment. Next week it might be something else, Mayan ash trays or pipe-racks in the shape of a prie-

dieu. The best thing about the doilies was that being cellophane they were washable, and this made them very useful.

So the guests, in deference as much to their own as to Abel Hanway's wishes, discussed art and many things that went with art, while Susan and her escort simply listened, alert for that moment when at last they should have caught the tempo and style and be able thus to step out into conversation themselves. Susan heard Freddy Paisley say that someone, or something, migrated from Canarsie on or around the first of June; and Theo Sulka replied yes, that it was all in a rather profound little book by a man named Morkwal—few had ever heard of him.

"I met him last year," said Matilde Fairisle. "A Buddhist priest, I think. And a dreadful social climber."

"But he writes *well*," insisted Theo with a toss of the head. "You must admit that."

"Oh, yes. Very well indeed."

Dr Einman now arose as though on the light end of a balance, bowed slightly and went across the room to fetch two more cups of punch. When he sat down again he seemed disposed to conversation, and began to ask Susan about one or another of the people near them. Susan answered with a distant agreeableness, naming the person and reciting several of his or her connections. "That is Arthur Charvet. He paints slightly, and lives in Needham with his mother. I think she is paralytic. Her people were Benhafts, from Lynn." She saw, however, that it was impossible to make a satisfactory identification of anyone, for Dr Einman was obviously the most perfect of strangers in this group, and even when he nodded quickly and said "Ah, yes," or "I see," it was evident that he did nothing of the kind: in fact he asked about the same person twice. It was with some exasperation that she asked, finally, if he had lived in Boston long.

"Not long, no." And that was that. He pointed across the

3 7

other couch. "Can you tell me who is that interesting person over there?"

"That is Ingrid Argyle. She models."

"Ah. Thank you."

After some time this game began to pall even upon Dr Einman, or he felt suddenly its unsuccess, for he turned to Susan and asked in the coy fashion considered so appropriate by middle-aged gentlemen in addressing young ladies, if she were not "in love" with any of the young men she had pointed out.

"No, certainly not," said Susan.

"And in love with no one?"

"With no one."

"Admirable. Admirable. Your independence does you credit."

She looked sharply at him, concerned to detect wherein lay the mockery she thought she felt; but could find only the smooth surface of the words, which were rather conventionally well chosen than particularly meaningful; the gravity of his face (in which she suspected impudence) attached no second significance to his remarks.

This face of his was worth inspection. One would not begin, certainly, by calling it handsome; not that it was so very ugly, but its category was the farcical, not the heroic. There was so much life in it: not one feature seeemed unblemished, unturned by experience, there were no blanks in the face. The nose, first, had been broken and had knit ever so slightly to the left of center. Though he was not a very stout person, his face was fleshy and high in color; his eyes, black and meaningless in the ruddy cushions of his cheeks, stared out exotically like a serpent from a rose bush. His hair was a stiff brush, graying slightly from black, and his eyebrows, teetering out on a massive frontal structure, were still black. The mouth, though full-lipped, seemed yet tight and drawn, as though closed over possible grimaces or cries of a painful yet comic sort. The set of the jaw suggested that Dr Einman's forehead might be glistening with sweat. A Rouault clown, Susan thought; but the epithet did not seem adequate for the face.

When he left her side in order to get another round of drinks she remained where she was and inspected the young faces, familiar bland fronts of lives not yet properly in the weather. She found them by contrast somewhat less satisfying, less provocative than the face of Dr Einman, which was, in this gathering at least, something of a mask, a curiosity, almost an artistic production to which the years, chipping and scarring and blemishing, beyond the intention of the maker had added the grotesque accidental beauty of life, the full evidence of a continuing destruction.

She felt slightly handicapped in his presence by her youth and her acquaintance with youth alone, and apologetic for her society, which seemed to her for the moment given entirely to inane pleasures not even to be dignified with the name and gross weight of sensuality: pleasures without issue, without consequence, without liability and so, essentially, without pleasure.

"To be young is in a way rather terrifying," she said to herself. "And really somewhat fake."

In consequence of this new uncertainty, she spoke to Dr Einman, on his return, with less reticence than before, with a delicate antagonism vaguely felt proper as between innocence and age, but at the same time with some realization of the entirely incidental quality of innocence. Soon they were talking with relative intimacy, while about them ranged the public voices that discoursed in loud fragments of art, of war, of love, of reputation and next Saturday night.

"This life, this death, that dinner at the Ritz," said Susan, quoting in fact an epigram quite common in this group.

"Indeed?" Dr Einman smiled gently. "You must not be so

harsh. It is a question what would be a relevant thing to talk about. And at a party. What is a party?" He spread wide his hands in doubt, and seemed not disposed to answer his question.

"I suppose," Susan said, "we must seem rather inconsequential to you." She was not ready, she felt, to ask why he came to such a gathering, frequented as it was for the most part by people so much younger.

"No, why?" He seemed more surprised than offended. "I find it good to watch—these young pushing their heads into the sun, learning the words for things, entering the dance. It is very healthy, I think, to watch beauty and strength even while beauty and strength are pushing oneself nearer and nearer to the shadows. And it would be a mistake to say, I believe, that life in the shadows has not its own callowness, its own—adolescence." He smiled and took her hand, which she at once withdrew.

She had a remote idea of urgency from his words, as though he were inviting, soliciting, as though he expected of her a less than conscious acquiescence to she knew not what.

"You are a beautiful girl," he said. "And virgin too, yes?"

Far from clarifying the position, the directness of this little speech had the opposite effect. Unlike the moonstruck advances which, coming from one of her own age, she would have known quite easily how to defeat, there was here a baffling quality of things unarguable and assumed, of everything and at the same time nothing having been said. Susan found in herself an unexpected though entirely theoretical receptivity to the outrageous calm and utter lack of embarrassment with which Dr Einman announced the intention of laying siege to her virtue.

"I hope you won't try to build too heavily on the simple chance of our meeting," she said.

"Simple chance, yes," Dr Einman replied, "as long as we had

not met in fact. But now—the particular carries with it an irresistible power, simply by occurring."

"The simple occurrence of this particular does not, my dear Doctor, indicate its concurrence in just anything at all." God, she thought, how helplessly clever all this is.

"What do you want me to do—become importunate? I'm telling you nothing that you are not ready to be told."

This at any rate was true. While she did not for a moment conceive of herself as submitting to any proposal of Dr. Einman's, Susan admitted she had been ready to hear it; and its freedom from the conventional protestations, of love, of fidelity, and pretensions to doing one good andsoforth, had served to discountenance in advance the equally conventional countermeasures that might otherwise have been employed. The idea itself opened out in her a sense of the possible that was agreeable to consider, and in her reply she admitted sufficiently, she thought, to a certain theoretical charm:

"I must of course give you a categorical refusal."

"Of course."

"If I do not seem angry, I am temperate with you on account of your age."

"Naturally."

"I take your presumption as a compliment."

"Thank you."

"And now I think we might talk of something else."

"Certainly."

2

THE MAILBOXES, in a shiny panel, gave away nothing but names, which told nothing. Slivos, Bahlman, Green, who were they, who marked their residences so clearly and meaninglessly? And he, John Averist? And Edmond Einman, whose name was on the same mailbox? The linkages of choice and chance . . . He was somewhat drunk. The mailbox had been empty when he went out for supper, it would necessarily be empty now. By stooping to peer inside the scrolled grating it was possible to see that the mailbox was empty.

He opened it anyhow. A clean golden color outside, it inwardly resembled a cage in the zoo, dirty and bare, when the animal, whose droppings are dust, has gone out to the admiration of others. Hope, or Tomorrow, the animal is called: it feeds on the white envelopes of electric-light bills, on circulars from book clubs, on the mournful letter of a friend teaching at a Western college, on the invitation, the sharp reply, the last word, the notice of weddings or deaths, or equally well on nothing, on air. And of this it leaves dust, of its relentless and shy pacing, condemned on the outside to wear your name, there remain when you look the pure excrements of time itself.

So he passed upstairs, to the glass-paneled door upon which was lettered EDMOND EINMAN MD, *analyst*; and in smaller letters on the lower corner JOHN AVERIST, *private tutor*. The door was on the latch, and he pushed through to the consulting room beyond the little antechamber. The couch on which he sat to smoke a cigarette was of red leather, cold under the hand. It had witnessed, as had the whole room, too many tedious triumphs of science or sensuality, too many contortions of body and mind: the place stank, he thought, with repulsive memories and *odor di femina*. He noticed a light under the door to his own room.

Angel did not wake up when he came in. It was a little like tracing a smell to a dead rat in the back of a cupboard. Her mouth was open, and a tendril of hair curled gently over her tongue. Her stockings had slipped their points and wrinkled disgustingly, and her dress, hitched up over one naked thigh, disclosed thereon a tattooed red heart pierced by a tattooed blue arrow.

4 2

Averist shook her by the shoulder. Angel sat suddenly upright and blew the hair out of her mouth.

"All right," he said. "Out."

"Don't rush me. Where's Edmond?"

"He's out."

She put her hands to her face, then scrabbled rather vaguely through her blonde hair. "Christ," she said. "I must have fallen asleep. Honestly, I don't know where I'm at any more. I haven't slept for two nights. I've got to see Edmond, Johnny."

"He's out. He won't be back till late. Also he doesn't want to see you." This was the wrong thing to have said.

"Don't want to see me?" she said in a loud voice. "I'm his patient, he's got to see me. A helluva doctor he is—could die sitting right in his office. . . ."

"This isn't his office, Angel. This is my room. My only room. His office is in there. Anyhow you're not going to die until paresis sets in." She was on her feet now, and he emphasized each remark by backing her toward the door. "Also Edmond is a very queer man, Angel. Things are quite confused around here, and it is getting quite difficult to tell who is patients and who is whores. At fifteen bucks an hour incoming for the one and outgoing for the other he is barely breaking even. If you have to wait"—here he edged her through the door—"wait out here."

"He's got to see me," he heard her say, without much conviction, as he closed the door. "I say the most awful things to myself at night. Over and over."

Averist lit a cigarette, sat down at his desk and listened to Angel as she began to cry. She did not cry loudly, for though the door was thin he found himself straining to catch the sound, choked and liquid whimpering, as of blood filling the mouth.

"Shut up," he called. "Shut up. Don't be silly." But the little

4 3

gasps and chuckles of grief—for what cause, for what reason?—continued.

Yes, definitely, he thought, shutting his eyes as though that would help, definitely this man Einman is too much and too queer. Instructive, but how long could one go on with the instruction? One could of course walk out, though Einman did after all pay the rent—as one had not, oneself, any money for rent. And this raised again that other question: himself, John Averist, what part did he serve in this rented asylum, this priest's hole? Disciple? Secretary? Conniver? Mere companion? Like a registered and scientifical Leporello he could hold up the thick file of case histories . . . *In Italia seicenti quaranta.*

It had been, on a drunken evening, a linkage of choice and chance. Edmond bit and spat the end of a small cigar, Edmond said, "Of course you could live with me—if you would not be inconvenienced by my patients—my women . . . I also sing, sometimes. I deny myself very little, very little. I learn. You would have, of course, to listen to my conversation. . . . You might be interested to read my book. *Eros and Agape,* I call it. It is not finished. It will possibly not be finished. . . . I have not begun to draw conclusions, but merely I record the facts."

The facts were recorded over a thousand sheets of paper in Edmond's neat scrawl, in black ink, green ink, red ink, diagnosis, prognosis, treatment, cure, silence, error, correction, theory. . . . "There is of course more *eros* than *agape,*" said Edmond. The facts went on being recorded: *Miss L remembers having been extremely frightened at the age of six in the Women's Lavatory of the Boylston Street Station. . . . She relates the following dream. . . . Felt extreme remorse over the death of her elder brother, who had . . .* ("Silly boy," Miss L had drawled finally, "silly old Ed." Giggles. Flushing, in the distance, of a toilet.) "There is much suffering, much," said Edmond, bending under the green eyeshade he wore when he recorded facts.

He lifted the eyeshade momentarily. "Of course," he said seriously, "it's not without its funny side." And, a second later, "Remind me to tell you some time how I left Toledo. Ha-hm." On other occasions, though, Toledo was erased, for Edmond was a refugee. Auschwitz.

"Don't ask me how I lived through it," he said with a deprecating wave of the hand. "That Hitler—a maniac." The hand moved over the page, now with the red fountain pen, now with the green, with the black. "So much unhappiness in the world." Often when he said this Edmond spat on the floor. No one cleaned the flat, unless as occasionally happened Averist could definitely not stand another minute, in which case after an argument—they had had several—he took a rag, since they had no broom, wet it and went on his knees over the stained and splintered boards.

Somehow in this way they became friends. "Do you want Miss R?" Edmond said. "I am quite finished with her. It's a duodenal ulcer, but she won't believe it." Averist politely declined. On another occasion, drunk, he had accepted the offer of a Mrs T, who metamorphosed behind his locked door and on his bed as a fat, motherly person named Birdie who told him a good deal about the Seventh Day Adventists.

How Edmond recruited his patients, or for that matter his mistresses, was unknown. "They are valuable primarily for the research," he said once, "and only secondarily for the cure. It's all in the mind anyhow," he finished cryptically. "They don't care if they live or die." This seemed true in numbers of cases, and was the only general conclusion John Averist had ever heard his room-mate reach; but it never got put down on the records.

Not all the patients were women; numbers of men came also for whatever it was that Einman did for people. And, quite apart from his sexual proclivities, he seemed in fact to do some-

4 5

thing extraordinary: there had been what appeared to be relief if not actual cure with astonishing frequency. To take the case of Angel: *Miss M came to us* (sic) *with an entire paralysis of the left side of the cheek, for which her doctor* (i.e., a clinic) *had done nothing. This condition yielded to treatment in three weeks.* This was, so far as it went, utterly true. *By that time, symptoms had manifested themselves of a deeper dislocation.* This also, true.

The weeping in the next room had stopped. Averist stepped to the door and opened it. The girl was looking at herself in a pocket glass.

"Repair your ravaged face," he said to her. "I'll take you to a party."

"I'll wait for Edmond—if you don't mind," Angel replied.

"But Edmond is at the party," he said patiently.

While she put on her lipstick—using a paintbrush fully a foot long, which she fished from the terrible mess in her bag— Averist considered, with a slight smile, what it was he proposed doing. Whatever happened, he felt, his relation with Edmond, if it survived, would be clarified extremely. It would be as much as to say: "The apprenticeship is over, I wish to become a partner." And how Edmond would take that would be sufficiently amusing if, for example, he had overlooked in John Averist the idea that a rather hopeless person becomes, if he lives, a bit of a humorist. Or, as it might be put in the records, *Symptoms had manifested themselves of a deeper dislocation.*

He felt so amused—despite a certain apprehension which ran parallel to the amusement—that he gave Angel, before they left, a short slug of Old Grand Dad from a bottle he carried in his coat pocket. He took some himself.

"Thank you, sir," Angel said coyly. She seemed to have put on spirit with as much ease—or as many pains—as cosmetics. She looked very attractive, and he told her so.

4 6

"You could pass for thirty anywhere," he said.

She smiled, demurely insolent. "Silly Johnny," she said, and tipped his chin with her gloves.

They went down into the street.

3

THE PARTY had rather rapidly changed its quality. The proximate cause of the change was evidently alcohol. The formal cause was Arthur Charvet, and the material cause lay perhaps far back and forgotten, somewhere in the tangled mess of relations in space and time that was so glibly referred to as Arthur Charvet. The final cause, however, seemed to be Dr Einman. The entire event, at least, had referred itself to him, established his credit; and now, an hour later, he was still talking.

Drink, he explained carefully and with a multitude of odd, foreign gestures of the hands—drink was interesting and attractive, from the experiential point of view, because it offered to our gaze a brief, partly controlled replica and analogue of life itself, in all its mystery. Dr Einman was not afraid of the word *life*, nor even of the word *Life*; he used it again and again, in a monologue mystagogical and scientific; he spoke of Life with the tongues of the priest, the doctor, the scoutmaster, the man of experience.

He held Susan's hand intermittently during his lecture— picked it up, dropped it to illustrate largely this or that subtlety—and she permitted this as part of the general triumph, for it was a triumph.

Here is a bottle, the doctor explained. It holds, say, ninety proof Life, and we will pour some into several people. They are quiet people, like dust in the earth, or like vegetables, capable at most of a rather vague turning sunwards, an opening by day and a closing at night. Observe: it is, with all these people, the same bottle that we employ. We tip it up so; they drink; they drink a little more. So. Soon we begin to get results. But why are not the results similar, even identical, considering the same fluid was combined with the same dust? For observe again: here is A who begins to dance, B who looks around for a fight, C who thinks dark thoughts, and D who spews over the front steps. X has great ambitions. . . . Y knows that he is being terribly clever. . . . Z will enter a monastery.

Or drink, if you like, is the stain in whose contrast life becomes supremely visible. Take, for example, this Arthur—Arthur Charvet.

But Arthur Charvet had been taken home an hour or so before.

This was what had happened.

After Susan had suggested to Dr Einman that they talk of other things, they had done more: they had also talked to other people. The party became more free and more general. Mr Hanway proclaimed loudly that the fruit juice had run out; the punch from then on was composed of brandy, rum, bitters, thinly diluted by a momentary contact with the ice in the bowl. Conversation and behavior ran to different extremes, becoming here louder and more convivial, there quieter, darker-toned, more serious. Groups formed and dissolved, lights were turned off only to be snapped angrily on. Everyone was sufficiently drunk to find everyone else not quite drunk but only charming.

"Susan, you are so beautiful," said Arthur Charvet. His white and serious face bent down to her. "I don't know if I ever told you—so—so pale and . . ." he twisted his hand in a creative, molding way, and was whirled by, out of reach, replaced by a stranger who said four serious sentences about the nature of lust. Matilde Fairisle came then, and briefly mentioned Ronald Firbank. "He's so—so passionately trivial," she said, twisting her hand up in an illustrative way. Eileen Bluenose came up and mentioned Roger and Leonora. "I had so hoped they'd hit it off," she whispered. "Of course I haven't said a word to anyone. It may still work out, don't you think?" "I don't know, Eileen," Susan said. "But I'm naturally glad to have an expert opinion." Eileen Bluenose frowned and rushed away crabwise.

"I'd like to paint you." This was a tall arrogant-looking person with a crew cut. "You're not much, but at least you're not magazine cover. See what I mean?" With his thumb he traced sweepingly the curve of Susan's cheek. "The kind of ugliness I really admire," he said. Then he too was gone.

Dr Einman did not neglect her. With astonishing regularity he appeared to take her glass and hand her a full one. "Prosit," he would remark on each of these occasions, raising his drink to her. Then he went away; Susan saw him talking, at odd moments, with numbers of different people in different parts of the room.

Once she had some conversation with Abel Hanway, whom she asked about Dr Einman. The reply was vague. "A refugee. Trying to set up his practice again, you know. I was asked to introduce him around. I think one should do everything one can to help." It amused Susan to be able to think of her new acquaintance as combining business with pleasure—he did seem to be enjoying himself—and prospecting, behind the smooth façade and the glib talk, for the soft vein of decay, the foul abscess that ticked like a bomb through every gesture. What had he found, she wondered, in herself?

In all, she realized at this time, this was not a very amusing party, nor did the people—her set, as they called it—particularly interest her. It was the first time, though, that Susan generalized this not seldom felt sentiment, to discover that it might apply, for her, to all parties and gatherings of this sort, of which the acknowledged purpose was to have a "good time." What is a party? Dr Einman had asked, but had supplied no answer. It

49

seemed now to Susan that a party might be a kind of playful limiting of the possible, an experiment carried on unfortunately without the attention of the observer. She felt, all at once, exhibited and under glass. In the way she stood alone, the way she held her drink—the defiant sullenness with which she refused to thrust into any group, or to appropriate anyone's conversation—she must look obviously misfit here. She felt like the still center of a trivial and filthy storm: one of those cyclones that arise for no apparent reason in vacant lots. The voices all around, whatsoever they might be saying, had the sound of voices engaged in bitter harryings, desperate and querulous debates about something that was never mentioned in the words. This nagging and insistent tone, surely it meant more than the words themselves. It seemed to say: time is running out. Another evening disappears, and the brilliant seduction is not, will not be, accomplished; the divine lust, of splendid and unfailing powers, will be reduced again to sick, lonely fumbling in alleys, doorways, taxis. The installments are more than half paid, we already own tomorrow's headache. Is there no hope, and no chance? And are we alone? finally, furtively, inadmissibly crawling away from all impossible heroisms?

And truly a second change was affecting the party. So suddenly that you might put your hand to your sleeve, pull it up to show the watch and say, Now! a certain urgency dominated the variousness. The members of the party were like spirits that knew they must vanish at an hour, undetermined beforehand but very soon. The not uncharming license granted earlier to superficial sensualities had now become swift, brutal: in part an effect of drink, in part of time. A coarse joviality seemed now to drop the mask, so friendly and so rowdy; the center of the room was all but vacated in favor of the corners, where (for example) Theo Sulka, Matilde Fairisle, Flagg Lauder, Alison Meese, were conglomerate. Susan heard a severe-looking gray-haired woman explaining at large: "Life is nothing but fornication and don't let anyone tell you anything different. If I've had nothing else out of my life," she cried loudly, "I've had that." No one paid her much attention.

Einman came up to Susan and in the most friendly and sober way put his arm about her shoulder and asked how she was feeling. She allowed herself to be led over to the couch and submitted to being kissed, with permission, once. She felt a terrible contempt for Einman and for everyone. It was not the contempt of the master, the one above; but the sneer of the servant who caters to lecheries he does not share.

There had been some embarrassment over the fact that the bathroom door had no lock. The solution was to leave the bathroom door open, and now it was possible to watch the guests relieving themselves. A small group had collected about the door for this purpose. "Bravo," they cried. "Bravo." Arthur Charvet, pale, resolute, slammed the door in their faces. "Bravo," they cried.

"I think you might take me home," said Susan.

"If that is your wish," replied Dr Einman, removing his hand and preparing to rise.

But at this moment the bathroom door opened and Arthur Charvet came out. He was in his shirt sleeves, and the expression on his face compelled silence. He came toward the center of the room slowly, his arms stretched forward in a gesture of patient and domestic supplication. From his left wrist blood flowed, very dark red and surprising, over his hand.

"He's bleeding," said Hanway.

"That seems obvious," came from someone in a corner. Someone else, behind Susan, began to vomit. No one moved. Charvet came to the center of the room and then, as if foresight and plan had taken him this far and then abdicated their function, stood there. The blood dripped rapidly to the carpet.

A voice, sobbing, said: "Please do something. He's bleeding."

Dr Einman got up, without haste, took Charvet's wrist and looked at it, then at Susan. He led the boy to the couch and laid him down so that his head was in Susan's lap. A handkerchief and pipestem served him for a tourniquet, and while he applied this he spoke in a low voice, more amused than anything, to his patient.

"Unhappy, yes? Very unhappy? Dramatic, too. You make us such inconvenience, with blood on the nice rug. . . . You're not going to die, you know. That fading sensation is not what you think, you're coming back to us. How cruel we all are, how unkind. But you weren't going anyhow, you know, even if we let you alone. You hardly scratched the artery. This is not big blood, important blood, this is only little blood. You are a very stupid, nice boy," he said in a caressing tone.

Hanway brought a first-aid kit and a bowl of water.

"You see, your friends all want you to live," said Einman. "To live." As he washed out the wound and began to dress it his voice continued, soothing and addressed to the sufferer, but presently increasing in volume and expanding his theme until he was, properly, lecturing.

"It is very instructive," he said. "Very enlightening. Did he want to die? Did you want to die? Is life so terrible in Needham? The paralytic mother such a waste of your time?" Dr Einman's memory, whatever it might normally be, seemed, Susan thought, to be unobtrusively ready in emergencies. She noted, too, the little comedy that went on as Einman casually dropped the bloody swabs of cotton to the floor and Hanway, with a polite effect of not noticing, nevertheless picked up each swab and put it into a silent butler. Charvet's eyes were closed, his face very smooth and white, his head heavy on her legs.

"He tried it last year, with about forty aspirins," said Eileen Bluenose.

"You are unhappy, so what?" inquired Dr Einman with a curiously foreign inflection of the "so what." He turned around to the others. "You are so young. You should be happier. I have seen so much of it since I have come to America, so many romantics. Try to be happier." His voice was between pleading and commanding; in any case, final.

"Hell, it's not our fault," Lauder said.

"Yah, fault fault fault, that is all I hear. Somebody is dying, immediately comes somebody to say who will pay for it, where is the money coming from, will there be an investigation, who will pay me the money he owes? Fault. Yah. Go 'way with your fault." His job done, Dr Einman rose up from his knees. "Listen to me what I am saying." Susan remarked that his accent had developed a thickness and strangeness both surprising and impressive. "Listen: everything is fault. Nothing is fault. There is only suffering and we are all to blame. Don't think I haven't seen it. It is written also in the Bible, the damn trouble with you all. You don't love one another enough."

Susan asked herself from what depth came this speech. What did the man mean, intend, want? With a faint shiver, not entirely of revulsion, she envisioned the word, the idea, Love, coiling in the gray of the brain, spewing up the complicated words, subtleties of tone, charming overtures, vicious practices, the first prayerful tentative motions and the ultimate lewdness.

"You can take this one home now," Einman said, and went to wash his hands.

After some fretful talk, that led and was intended to lead to no action, several commanding persons decided that an ambulance was unnecessary. Flagg Lauder and Matilde Fairisle agreed to take Arthur Charvet back to Needham. The wounded Charvet was carried down to Lauder's car.

Then Einman returned, sat down at Susan's side, took her hand and, in expectant silence, began to speak. Why this silence? It was inexplicable. He was not, surely, an inordinately impressive person, nor had what he had just done been, for a doctor, anything extraordinary. Nevertheless, after Abel Hanway had unnecessarily and not a little theatrically apologized, after the windows were opened, the vomit and blood cleaned up a bit, there seemed a general expectation that Dr Einman—a small, middle-aged man unknown to most of them, and given unexpectedly to grinning in a way both satiric and tormented—should begin to speak.

The attention they accorded him showed outwardly in that glazed earnestness that people so often display late at night after having had much to drink: a state of superficial resignation in which the mind becomes as clear as it is empty, and disturbing symptoms make themselves felt of the oncoming of tomorrow: nausea, a slight headache, the blood beating in the ears. It was as if, having seen a tragi-comic action, they now sullenly and passively awaited the interpretations of the critic.

Einman's manner of speech was not direct. Now, knowing the floor was his, he proceeded in an almost musical manner, hammering alternately two notes: life, death, life, death: making a sudden incursion into these tonalities—"Metempsychosis is by all odds the most attractive, logically satisfactory and, in the West, least considered of all the eschatologies"—meandering then down esoteric by-paths with the vague enthusiasm of the scholar (The *Bardo Thodol*, the *Timaeus*, the *Signatura Rerum Omnium*), returning to repeat: life, death, life, death.

Yet from the detail, from the massive allocation of terms, the elaboration—how far from Arthur Charvet—of ornament, theme and design began surely to emerge. His subject was, in conscience, large enough; he had already stated it: life and death. Life, death, and the will; that would be another way of putting it; order, disorder and the will. What was the living substance, or energy, or power? What put—he grinned disturbingly—the fire in the fat? Again, what was the code-script writ so plain in the chromosome fibers? So plain as a directive, it seemed, yet so thoroughly obscure to the mere reader. How far was it determinative, in what detail? Did it suggest, command, inspire? Had it—this little scribe-god in the cell—had it arranged personally and in particular for the suicide attempted by Arthur Charvet? Even down to the fact that this suicide was doomed from its conception to be the purest sort of hysterical fake? Or was there instead the mere provision and prevision of dominant possibilities?

The definition, the essence, of life, look, is this: not that it moves, no. But that it continues to move, it keeps going—so far as we can see, at any rate; though we must never overlook the possibility, the rarest joke of all, that what we live in is not life at all, but simply the vast motion of a mechanical energy to the largest scale, like a rock falling from the highest mountain, like a ship—with its gods and emperors, crew and passengers, its fine foods and economic problems—sinking slowly down the height of an incredibly deep ocean.

He took them, he tried to take them, he explained, back to the beginning. "To that primal love which was before the stars," he said. The journey from life to death we were accustomed to think of as proceeding from order to disorder. Very well. But otherwise considered (and how easy it was, and how relieving, to consider things otherwise) the procession was reversed. There was much disorder in life; and in the equal distribution, the equilibrium which was death, there was much order. What then was this transaction between, from which our late departed guest tried to abdicate? Was there not an extremely romantic relation between order and disorder? Entropy, according to Boltzmann and Gibbs, was composed of just such a flirtation—the liaison between a constant and disorder.

This kind of talk, far out as it was on the frontier marches of knowledge, this sleight-of-hand which so liberally shuffled the literal and the allegorical, had the normal effect on the lay minds of Dr Einman's hearers. They were attentive, they were becoming slightly nervous, both elated and apprehensive, Susan with the rest. Will it be solved? they half dared to ask themselves. Will it be solved here, in our presence, tonight? Can there be some question, some loophole through which the spirit can slip, a way out of the vast down-falling exchange of all things? Perhaps in our time death will yield. They exchanged glances, furtively.

But Dr Einman seemed to know when he had secured his effect, seemed to know how their hardly admitted hopes hung upon the oracle of sciences yet unborn, for here he graciously turned his mute supplicants away, deftly entering variations which successively digressed from the theme even while they appeared to lead back. And back, in a way, they did lead, but not to the main subject; rather they led back to this evening, to this world, to what we saw in it, to that life which was full of commonplace pain, and was ended—how often he had seen it—by commonplace death: to suffering, which was the penance and the prerogative of us all, no one knew why. He spoke of that spirit of inquiry which uses no laboratory but goes into the town and goes into the country and watches; he measured life on the ground of its accessibility to one's observation. For example, drink. Drink was interesting and attractive, from the experiential point of view, because it offered to our gaze a brief, partly controlled replica and analogue of life itself. . . .

Susan was at once fascinated and bored. She acknowledged the man's skill, and admitted that it might be something incredibly more than skill—that he might be, in fact, one of those rare learners, corrupted saints of this world, of whom one hears occasionally, or reads accounts, blatant and empty, in the papers —yet she felt acutely the deliberate charlatanism, the stage-direction, the impression that if the rabbit were to be folded back into the hat it would simply cease to exist. Her feet, also, were getting cold, and her face felt tired.

"Or drink, if you like, is the stain in whose contrast life becomes supremely visible. Take, for example, this Arthur—Arthur Charvet."

Steps were heard on the stair. Susan hoped they would make an interruption. The steps stopped, giggled loudly outside the door, hush-hushed one another, and knocked.

4

JOHN AVERIST and Angel had not come directly to Abel Hanway's, but by a circuitous route that included a place called the Private Club. Angel had supplied, unexpectedly, five dollars. "My drinking fund," she explained. They had got a little tight on that, and then some kind of argument seemed to have started. There was a blonde sitting in the next booth, and her escort seemed to know, or want to know, Angel. A question of propriety was involved, as Angel sat very still, looking at her drink, while the blonde tugged at the escort's coat, somewhat ineffectually.

"Darling, don't you remember me?" he kept on saying. Angel did not, apparently, remember him, and in the solution of the contretemps the escort, a fairly stocky man, threw John downstairs. Angel caught up with him on the sidewalk.

"You were sweet, Johnny," she said. "I knew him, but I didn't want to get mixed up with him again. The cheap little bastard."

"Thank you so much," he said. Then Angel wanted to know what did that tone mean? And he told her, straight. And she said that was a nice thing to say. And he said that if she didn't like it she could find a place for it.

On the stairs to Hanway's flat they forgave each other liberally and munificently: "Aren't we a couple of funnies?" Angel said, when they had kissed.

The door was opened by a blank-looking man who said that he was Abel Hanway, and they were drawn into the room.

"What do we know of Charvet?" Dr Einman said. "We see him; we say, that is Charvet, he paints a little, he lives in Needham, he is a part of Life . . ." He caught sight of Angel and John Averist. "Children!" he cried, springing up. "Come in. How glad I am to see you."

"Doctor," said John Averist. "Here is your patient." This remark, whatever he had planned for it, got no refutation whatever in the confusion of welcome and introduction that Edmond achieved.

Susan was presented to a tall young man with black hair. He wore a baggy gray tweed jacket and gray slacks, a maroon shirt and a black knitted tie, sufficiently shabby. His lower lip was cut, and the skin under his right eye contused. She understood his name to be John Averist. "My assistant," said Dr Einman, "and my friend." Of Angel, Susan was given to understand considerably less; she was shuffled past the introduction as glibly as from the bottom of the deck. Susan realized that we have a general impression from the word "patient." Angel, or "Miss Mmmm" as she seemed to be called, bore no resemblance to this abstract picture of delicately "mental" suffering. Angel was robust, blonde, handsome, aged perhaps twenty-five.

"Well," said Dr Einman heartily. "Time for us to be leaving you. A pleasant conversation, I wish we could continue, but"— elaborately he yawned—"getting late." To Susan he whispered: "The girl, my patient. She must be got out of here at once, and as quietly as possible. Don't, please, pay too much attention to whatever she may say—agree with her if possible." Then began the Thank yous, the Good nights.

For a moment after, everyone stood about looking rather bewildered. For most of the guests the party had broken up not perhaps too soon, but all soo suddenly. They blinked as Hanway turned on the hall light. Susan felt cold, tired. It was about three o'clock.

The night was quiet and star-lit, and their heels echoed loudly in the narrow street. They had to walk some distance for a cab. When they had found one, and got into it, Angel began to weep but no one said anything or gave any sign of noticing.

"Judas. Judas," Angel said several times, but it was unclear whom she meant.

"I hope I may see you again," Dr Einman said softly to Susan. "I will call."

In his corner of the cab John Averist sat up straight and said in a funny tone, "Why don't we all resign? You especially, Doctor. Why don't you spit yourself out of your own mouth and die?" His tone attached, it seemed, no animus to this recommendation, nor did Dr Einman appear to feel any.

"We are all tired," he said quietly. "Tired and a little cold. At this time of morning everyone catches a metaphysical chill. Death is near enough. Here, children, love one another." He took Susan's hand and put it in Averist's. "Now kiss," he said, "but chastely." He laughed. "So, you won't. Very well then, you won't." As he laughed again, Averist brought Susan's hand to his lips and kissed it. It was a rather drunken and brutal gesture, pulling Susan over against Angel, who continued to weep.

"And here is Miss Boyne's house," Einman said. "And it is over, it is over."

They said their good nights politely and with a large indifference; then Susan got out and stood for a moment on her doorstep, watching the tail-light of the taxi as it went to the end of the street, turned and disappeared.

It was already, in its very beginnings, an old morning.

CHAPTER THREE

*E*VEN the most well-balanced equation will lose its stability if one of the terms, acting in entirely liberal and un-term-like fashion, deserts its fellows for foreign parts; and the precarious equilibrium set up so recently, and with such a deal of humbug and tribulation, collapsed upon Roger's disappearance.

"Really," Leonora said to Susan and Claire, "he might have said where he was going. Not that I'd chase after him, but really, there is such a thing as loyalty."

It was late afternoon, three weeks after the *settlement* of the divorce issue. Susan and Claire had been having tea in the living room. Entered to them Leonora, excited, with for some reason Gerry in tow, whom she caused unceremoniously to be dropped, like an overcoat, into an armchair somewhat apart from the arena of conversation. Mrs Boyne the elder, having a headache, took tea in her room.

Leonora was so habituated to gossip, about everything, that she could not begin even this conversation, serious as it might presumably be, without having first said conspiratorially, "Wait till you've heard *this*," and when she had finished her recital she said, "Isn't that amazing, though? Isn't it *amazing*?" It was as though she were linguistically incapable of being anything but a spectator.

Roger, it seemed, had gone that morning, leaving a curt note to say that he did not intend coming back, that for himself he considered their marriage at an end; he requested Leonora not to try to communicate with him, when he was settled she might learn his whereabouts from his sisters. Since she did not rise until noon, Leonora had not discovered the note until nearly one, after which she ". . . called Gerry, threw some clothes on, and came over."

"I don't know where he could have gone," she said. "But it couldn't be far, he didn't take any clothes. I hope he doesn't expect me to run after him shrieking 'Darling, your tweeds.'" She smiled brilliantly and nervously to show that she at any rate could survive, that she viewed the catastrophe in proportion, in very small proportion at that, and to let the sisters know that their silence—which had up to this instant been complete, and gave an air of being judicious without being discourteous or more than attentive—could not unsettle her in the least, since it was after all she who dispensed the favor by bringing them her news.

Now Susan said, "It doesn't worry you, make you sad, at all?"

And Claire said, "It makes one feel the world is so large. He might be anywhere."

"Oh, he'll be all right," Gerry put in from his corner. "Probably he's just out on a drunk some place." Gerry sounded unhappy, and as though he wanted very much to believe in his own assurance, but found it hard.

"Oh, yes, he'll be all right," Leonora said sharply. "What about me? Why couldn't he say something definite? I don't want to go ahead and make plans and then have him barge back into my midst again."

"I don't see how he could have been more definite about that," said Susan. "He wrote, you say, that he wasn't coming back."

6 1

"Yes, you don't know Roger," Leonora said. "Do you think this is the first time I've had something like this happen?" In fact it was, but having made her effect she would not easily relinquish it.

"What plans do you mean?" Claire asked, handling the word "plans" as one might carry excrement on a newspaper.

"Well," Leonora grew thoughtful. "Just plans, you know, for my future. Listen: one thing you can do. Don't tell your folks about it yet—I mean, suppose he comes flying back tomorrow, they'd have all that worry for nothing. I expect I should hear from him anyhow. If you get word, let me know before you do anything else." She rose to her feet and said, with a gracious gesture, "Tell you what. If you'll do that for me, I'll take on the job of breaking it to the folks. There's no point in your getting mixed up in this thing; you know how hysterical they'll get. I'll tell them as soon as I hear definitely what's happened. And another thing: better not say Gerry was here with me, there'll be enough hysteria without that."

"I must say," Susan remarked, "I'd feel better about all this if you worried a little more about Roger and less about yourself."

"Don't tell me, dear," Leonora said in a disagreeable way. "I'm his wife, you know, in spite of everything." She put her hand on Susan's shoulder. "We just want to make sure, don't we, that I don't get thrown out in the street and forgotten."

"Take your hand off my shoulder, Lee," Susan said, getting up. "I'll do what you say, but the first nonsense I hear from you about money, I'll—I'll stop it."

"Stop what, dear?" asked Leonora. "What is there to stop? After all, I am his wife, he does have a legal responsibility. He's not free to run off where he pleases."

"Don't you worry, Lee. I'll stop it somehow."

6 2

"Susan!" Claire stepped past her sister and faced Leonora. "I think you'd better leave, Lee," she said. "We'll do as you say, at least until we hear from Roger, then we'll see. But now I think we've talked about it enough."

"Gerry," Leonora called, and Gerry got himself up. "We were just going. It's sweet of you both to help. These damn family crises . . . 'Bye." Preciously she waved her gloved hand. Gerry opened the street door and escorted her into the cold, early darkness.

"So that was Gerry Landis," Susan said. "Repulsive, isn't he?"

"Oh, stop it, Susan! You hardly spoke to him. He may really be quite nice. And none of this is his fault, he can't help it if he loves her."

"Ah love love love. I should think I could help it. What a dreadful woman she is. Do you think we ought to open a window?"

"Be serious a minute, Susan. Do you think something could have—happened to Roger?"

Susan looked at her sister for a long moment, and began to laugh.

"You mean, did Lee murder him this morning and hide the body in the closet?"

"I don't see what's so funny. Things like that do happen, and she's perfectly capable of anything."

"Leonora? Oh, Claire! And then she called Gerry and said in a hoarse whisper, 'Bring your car right round, Aegisthus, we've got a body to dump in the Charles'?"

"If you want to clown about it, go ahead. I'm worried about Roger, and I don't mind how ridiculous I sound. What do you think we ought to do?"

"Do?" Susan spread her hands. "Wait, I suppose. We promised Leonora, at least you did."

This, in the end, was what they did. Simply to have waited,

6 3

Claire thought, would have been reprehensible; but there was a reassurance in making out a policy on those lines, in making the decision to carry out a program of waiting. The next day, and the day after, there came no post, no call from Leonora.

"Tomorrow night," Claire said, "is their night for coming to supper. Suppose there's no mail by then?"

"That's up to Lee; I suppose she'll phone Mother and say they can't come. Or maybe she'll explain."

"I really think about calling the police if there's nothing by tomorrow morning."

"Well, wait till then anyhow," Susan said irritably, "then we'll decide."

2

WHEN CLAIRE and Susan appeared at breakfast next morning Mrs Boyne was weeping bitterly over a letter. It was from Roger, and was addressed to his sisters. Mr and Mrs Boyne tacitly reserved the privilege of opening their children's mail. Since in open argument this could not possibly be made to stick, what they really reserved was the privilege of opening their children's mail by accident, and even of reading it by accident. "There's nothing here you'd be ashamed to have me see, is there?" Mr Boyne had asked on several occasions. "Then why are you making such a fuss?" This was unanswerable except by a plea for privacy, which would provoke a quarrel too tedious and bitter to describe.

The letter, when at last they were permitted to see it, bore a Montreal postmark and read, in part:

"I have joined the Royal Canadian Air Force, for various reasons some of which you doubtless know. I'd rather you didn't tell Leonora unless you have to, but do as you think best. I put down that I'm single, and listed you both as my next-of-kin so

6 4

that if anything happens there'll be, as they say, something in it for you. I am going in for pilot, and think I have a reasonable chance. I got my uniforms this afternoon, tomorrow I start to learn things—just how to walk at first—and I feel comfortably mechanical and, curiously, quite free. I'll write from time to time, not often."

After her first fit of tears Mrs Boyne accused her daughters of conspiracy, to do what was never made clear. "Wait till I tell your father," she kept saying. They stood by while she did call Mr Boyne at his office, but the metallic little voice that came over the wires, completely incomprehensible to them, did not sound so much angry as bewildered, defeated and as though lost in the course of some large impersonal change. Mrs Boyne cried again and called Leonora.

"Poor, dear child," she said to the phone. "Why ever didn't you tell me?" The voice at the other end expostulated briefly, and Mrs Boyne went "cluck-cluck" through her tears and said, "That's the way it is—without a word, just as you think everything's all right." She turned away from the phone at last to say, in the voice of a staff commander outlining an operation, "Leonora is going to Montreal to bring him back."

"But Mother," Claire said. "He's in the war now, it isn't that easy."

"Anyhow," Susan said, "Leonora's going to Montreal to see if she can attach his pay."

Two nights later, a family meeting with the forsaken Leonora. She had been to Montreal, where she spoke with three people: the sentry at the gate, the chaplain, a finance officer. The first had said, "If he don't want to see you he don't want to see you, but you can make him wish he had, that is, if you're really married." The Padre was pleasant and vague: "We have a lot of that sort of trouble here," he said. "I often think that if people would talk things over more first. . . ." The finance officer was pleasant but less vague: "AC/2 Boyne enlisted as a single man; as long as he's doing his work I don't want to stir him up any trouble. Of course if you were to bring suit for non-support, or something like that, we'd have to ship him back for the hearing. But as it is, why, what he's getting is chicken feed anyhow. If I can be of any service while you're in Montreal . . . ?" Leonora included this last with a mincing shamelessness designed to accent her desirability, fidelity, etc., etc.

After supper that evening it was determined to exclude from the parley both Claire and Susan, as subversive elements. Leonora was of course entirely agreeable to this, feeling a vague resentment over the fact that Mrs Boyne should have opened the letter, but a far stronger resentment that the letter should have been addressed to Roger's sisters.

The act of exclusion was, however, quite unnecessary, as both daughters had made their own arrangements for the evening, enabling them to reply to a direct question that they were going "out." This right to being noncommittal had been gained only after a long battle during which Mr and Mrs Boyne had contended for more precise information (which being received had somehow never pleased them) and from which they had withdrawn grudgingly upon perceiving that they forced their children to the wildest evasions and innovations. Not that, they felt, the children "did anything wrong" when they went "out"; but that they had reached an age at which a certain privacy was correct. Thus the granting of the obstinately withheld concession became a point for the other side. "I never," Mrs Boyne would say to friends, "ask my children where they are going."

In fact Claire's destination would have caused a certain amount of comment: she was to attend the weekly meeting of the Catholic Poetry Society. Catholicism, the elder Boynes felt, was dangerous. Roman Catholicism alone was bad enough, but the inevitable social complication of Irish Catholicism was also unclean, and had an odor of the wrong sort of politics. Mrs Boyne happened to know (she had got it from Uncle Fred Seely, to whom it was a well-known fact) that if you examined the figures of saints and angels in Catholic churches around Boston you would detect facial resemblances to various municipal officers, district bosses, wardheelers. Mrs Boyne never having entered a Catholic church any more than she had ever questioned this notion, she had developed an interior picture of the Roman God that must inevitably have satisfied a Melanesian.

Claire herself felt vaguely ashamed of the group—the girls wore too much perfume, as if staving off mortality, the men had red faces and an appearance of just having gone on the wagon—and did not even tell Susan where she was going.

For her own part Susan had not spoken to Claire of Dr Einman, with whom she was going out tonight. If there was between the sisters less confidence, less exchange, than previously there had been, this was because both felt that they were entering now upon paths darker, more serious and conclusive (as well as more obscure) than any they had yet traveled. Neither suspected the other of similar turnings away from the home and family which had until now served effectively as the center and gathering-point of their lives, with the result that neither knew how any discussion of the subject might be entered on.

The family, withdrawn, heard them depart within a few moments of one another.

3

MR AND MRS BOYNE and Leonora sat in the living room. Uncle Fred Seely was also present, for no apparent reason unless to act as the reverse of a publicity agent, in the interest of prudence and security. The discussion was conducted in what might be called a "reasonable" manner, not in the sense that reason was employed exclusively or even very extensively as the instrument of decision, but rather in that negative, modern sense that speaks of the absence of strong emotion as reasonable. In truth there were few strong emotions left to command, the Boynes being in the famous position of a nation which, having waged a successful war in defense of vague ideals, finds itself too exhausted to cope with the purely material depredations of a small barbarian tribe. Then too, that reflexive similarity of blood, which made discussions with Roger so fully predictable, limited as they were to the brief repeated platitudes of loyalty and rebellion, was absent in Leonora's relation to the family, and the talk, revolving around extended appreciations of "the situation" and determining factors of a possible "settlement," might have been held with a lawyer instead of a daughter-in-law, so impersonal and seeming-judicious were the terms used. In short, Mr and Mrs Boyne, finding themselves so placed as not to care to invoke the domestic proprieties and allegiances, and having as it were already driven the scapegoat into the wilderness, placed themselves willingly at the disadvantage of behaving in an entirely civilized, not to say sophisticated or sporting manner. The result was that in a short time they were excusing Roger to Leonora, witnessing in extenuation his "flightiness," and realizing their responsibilities all over the place, until they reached the extreme at which Mrs Boyne was ready to say "I feel we have lost a son only to gain a daughter." (The point had been mooted but not pressed against Leonora's obvious unwillingness, that she come to live in the Boynes' house.)

There occurred, of course, moments of tension, but these were, to borrow the term, purely surface tension. Questions were asked Leonora that could have proved embarrassing, were it not that the manner of the asking proved them to be simply formalities, a matter of satisfying the inquisitors by round and full professions. Mrs Boyne asked Leonora, coyly, if she could be certain she had not at some time given her husband good cause for his strange behavior; but upon Leonora's becoming somewhat flushed and at a loss for a ready answer, Mrs Boyne took up her own question, sighing and murmuring, "As I thought—capriciousness. He was so young." It was already the custom to use the past tense in speaking of Roger. What he had done was so unprecedented to them—its only equivalent in their minds being to join the Foreign Legion—that they found it impossible to orient his act in relation to Roger, or themselves in relation to either Roger or his act; and the point that, from their perspective, his whole motive had been to escape a difficult situation at home, enabled them to discredit the act itself from every side and on every count. In a brief interlude to the discussion of the allowance Leonora was to get, in one of those doldrums that occur, right in the middle of the conversational trades, at such functions as funerals and bereavements, the family talked for a few moments of this.

"He was always in favor of peace," Mrs Boyne said sighing. "I cannot understand his running to the war."

"What beats me," the father said, "is what's wrong with the United States Army if he had to go and enlist?"

"As I see it, Nicholas," Uncle Fred Seely replied, "it's simply a way of dodging the draft, nothing more. If I was the government I wouldn't allow it, running over the border like that."

"Ah, but after all, Fred, they are at war, you know."

"Yes, yes, I know. But that doesn't alter the fact, does it? If we went to war with Japan, God forbid, why, your son'd be no better than a deserter."

"Now I think you're putting it a little too strongly, Fred."

So it went on, until Leonora felt moved to defend her husband's name, slightly, by saying that after all he was going to kill Germans. To which Uncle Fred Seely answered abruptly that it wasn't the Germans we had to fear so much as it was those damn Soviets.

On the whole, however, the evening passed successfully enough, and fulfilled its purpose of giving everyone concerned a somewhat higher idea than he had previously possessed of his own charity, acumen, self-sacrifice and businesslike goodness. When Leonora left, to join Gerry at the Napoleon Club, she was in possession of Roger's monthly allowance. Uncle Fred Seely, with his overcoat collar closely drawn about his ears, went to an address he knew on Commonwealth Avenue, having previously informed his wife that he would stay the night at the Harvard Club which, by way of palliating the offense, had the good manners also to be on Commonwealth Avenue. The silence of the bank-vault, like that of the grave, had descended over the possibility (for the moment anyhow) of divorce, of suit, of trial, of publicity. At one point on his way he almost considered sharing Leonora's allowance with Nicholas. But in twenty steps more he concluded that the expense, in this instance, far outweighed the slight erotic frisson of giving money to a woman other than one's wife.

"I don't see what else we could have done," Mr Boyne said to his wife when they had been left alone.

"At least," that lady replied, "there has been some sort of arrangement. It isn't as though we had just let things slide."

In these remarks they expressed to the limit of their verbal understandings the complex dissatisfactions they felt. Saying their good nights briefly they parted at the top of the stairs and went to their rooms.

Alone in the silence of the house Mr Boyne began to be deeply impressed with his son's action. He felt somewhat as Claire had when she said, "He might be anywhere in the world," that is, the possible expanded, broke out of the pre-figured limits set by a life conceived and lived in Boston; he might indeed be anywhere in the world.

Instead of going to bed, he sat down at his writing table and drew to him a sheet of notepaper and a pen; but undecided as to whether he should write to his son or make instead some general confessional or testament about his life, he wrote nothing, simply stared in anxious uncertainty at the white paper and moved the pen above it so that quick, vanishing and changing shadows were made on the blank surface.

It was this, he thought, unable to write one word on the paper: it was all very well to make arrangements, and to go through life making arrangements. These arrangements constantly dissolved into the necessity for more arrangements, one was always ordering a previous ordering, and even if there were demonstrably some root error it was impossible ever to begin with—well, with what? With the materials of life, the blank wordless uninformed stuff of the thing. This was what could in no sense be reached again: one could if one chose speak of reform, but not of beginning over, or of making a fresh start; life was indelible but one could not either leave the page blank, there was the necessity to do something, the demand of the moment to eat or talk or solve the problem of the moment; and in the end, or at the middle—whenever one stopped to look back—one perceived not the deciduous errors, but a structure of errors, leaning, even toppling, but entirely one's own responsibility.

He had acted in this present matter to preserve the integrity of his family, and he prided himself still that so to act was with him an instinct, simply a drive to self-preservation on a larger scale than the lonely self, not unlike patriotism. Now he doubted if it might have been better to be less "instinctive" and more, say, "critical." The ironic temper was far from his

7 1

character, but he now felt, even so, guilty of being undeniably a romancer of sorts, of acting on traditional lines without respect for the situation, to the extent of allowing Leonora in some sense to usurp the place of his own son. Was that the integrity of the family?

With what amounted to nothing less than an inner illumination he perceived the possibility of Leonora's having acted from entirely discreditable motives, of her having wrenched the situation from true by describing it with herself as the center. Himself he saw as caught in a bramble of words, as though the lines made by a pen in writing should have assumed a new dimension and snared the hand that made them. Could one break free, at this date, by twisting the lines loose? Or would it be from now on a question only of drawing more lines always within the originals, and deluding oneself that this was a useful and even intelligent employment, until motion should have been strangled altogether? A cat's cradle, a complicity, a life.

With a very full sense of his inadequacy he wrote to Roger and described what had been done respecting Leonora. The humility with which he had found himself so possessed did not appear to great advantage on paper; the letter was entirely toneless. Only at the end did he hint at the bending of his all-sufficiency: "You may feel," he wrote, "that I am contributing to the wrongs of the world . . ." He had put this down almost without thinking of it, and was now at a loss for an answer or at least a way of turning the letter off to a close. He somewhat weakly concluded by inviting God to protect Roger in his course. Then with a sense of the most costly exhaustion in a doubtful cause he crawled into bed and slept reasonably well.

Mrs Boyne was unable to sleep for some time. She did not cry; tears had in her estimation a purely social value, were a means, like reason an instrument. Left to herself, she lay in bed and stared at the darkness. What shocked her most was the

7 2

sense of her son's freedom in a purely spatial way, the knowledge that he was out of reach entirely. She wondered what Roger was doing now, imagined him flying desperately through the night, surrounded by shining glass and metal objects whose significance was lost to her. This although as a matter of fact Roger could have been doing nothing of the kind, being, as a minute's thought would have convinced her, asleep. As she gazed into the darkness she saw the airplane fly on, in a queer silence, now through a rain storm, now in the brilliant night over snowy mountains. The wings shone in the moon. The airplane flew far, to China and to Herzegovina, never landed, never stopped. In the slow monotony of flight she saw the precise movements of Roger's arms at the controls. The arms were of shining metal, the fingers were little jointed metal rods, and on the third finger of one hand he wore a golden cog-wheel.

*I*N A PLACE called the Brotherly Club, Edmond was talking about love. The Brotherly Club, just off Atlantic Avenue, was the fourth such place they had visited that night, from the Friendly Café, the Club Little and the Amazon. The waiters and bartender at the Club Little were midgets. That was very interesting.

Everything, with Edmond, was very interesting, Susan found; you had only to look sufficiently interested while, like a Midas who turned everything he touched to decay, Edmond delicately pointed up the ironies at that moment on exhibition. He favored, especially late at night, places near the harbor and between North and South Stations where, under the aspect of a sad, salt and fish smell, you could hear the urgent noises of trucks outside, or the horn of a vessel hardly a quarter-mile away. When the wind was right, aircraft swept low across them to the Municipal Airport, their engines, throttled back to land, making a choking, desolate sound overhead.

This was the first time Susan had been alone with Dr Einman; on two other occasions since the party John Averist had come along. His behavior on both excursions had been similar; he sat in a dour silence consuming drinks which Edmond always and unprotestingly paid for; then, a little cheered, he made eyes at somebody's girl. Once they had got him out in time; the second time he had been warned politely by two sailors who escorted the corrupt-looking and snake-like girl (of about sixteen) to whom he had taken a fancy; upon his failure to regard the warning they had picked him up, set him on his feet and, disregarding the flailing of his arms, hammered him quickly through the street door. Dr Einman made no move. There seemed to be an understanding.

"He victimizes himself almost professionally," he said with sympathetic contempt. "He will eat the sins of the world." The sailors came back, apologized for any trouble, brought their girl to the table. Edmond bought beer all around.

In five minutes Averist had come back inside and sat down again. He and the sailors and even the girl got on very affably after that. The taller of the two sailors explained carefully the need for keeping your guard up, and not just lashing out anyhow.

But this time they were alone, or as much alone as anyone ever got to be in the Brotherly Club, with the juke-box right behind the booth, and the dancing couples scratching their bottoms gently along the edge of the table; and Edmond was talking about love.

Or at least "love" was the blank check Edmond always produced for conversational purposes: any value could be placed upon it, and it seemed valid tender at any bank on the funds of the Savior, the Life Force, the Buddha, Entropy and Entelechy (those twins that Susan kept promising herself she would look up).

But listening (or more likely not listening) Susan soon came to feel his talk was like the magician's cheap patter, the sharp obvious shooting of the cuffs which masked the slight motion that prepared the dutiful and trite miracle: either it was vast and general, dealing in epochal billions, or it was of what a woman had said when dying of uremia. (In these instances, Susan had a vision of cool, white corridors, white sheets, a magnificent organization assisting at the lonely and dirty death: Edmond generally spoke in the first person plural, and whole hospitals leaped into his background.)

As to what was this miracle in preparation, she could not or would not say: no return had been made to the theme of seduction, though Edmond always spoke most frankly about carnality, eroticism, lust-in-disease; and Susan was learning enough terminology to speak of their present relations as the period of incubation.

He was talking now about seaport towns, placing them in relation to those diagrammatic pictures of evolution which showed at the left fish emerging goggle-eyed from the eternal tropical depths and beginning the chain of progressively less stoop-shouldered types that trailed far up and away into the mountains toward an impossibly distant combination of the Acropolis and the Crystal Palace. But for Edmond the picture embraced considerably less space: we were still here at the shores, incurably riparian; and uncertain, moreover, which way to turn. In a fire, once, at Trevisum, people had been forced to drown themselves to escape the flames—more than forced, willing: they had jumped in while the fire was still a considerable distance off. A coastal tribe in Africa still sent "ambassadors" in their little craft far out into the ocean and they did not, so far as anyone knew, return. The sea was the mother, said Edmond, the mother.

For Susan the sea had always been the summer, the pure endless blue of the sky, the lighthouse at Cape Ann; or the gray days, unseasonably cold, when rain beat steadily at the windows of the sea-facing house, as steadily as the waves rolled at the gray rocks a few feet away. The Atlantic made her feel lonely sometimes, especially at night, and she had thought with a

7 6

purely physical chill of drowning out there, with no one by to hear her cries. But that the sea was or even might be the mother, she had never thought, and it sounded rather silly. Even though one had read Freud, and Mann, and a little Hölderlin, and Rilke, one was forbidden, she supposed, as much by one's birth and nationality as by anything, to take, except possibly as a gesture toward certain people, that European and rhapsodic view of Edmond's, biological and poetical at once, that ironical sentimentality that used capital letters, though it used them with a wry grin.

While Edmond talked Susan allowed herself to remember, to think vaguely and inconsequently of this thing and that thing. She started now with Arthur Charvet's attempted suicide, or rather, with the pallor of his face as his head lay in her lap. People came out of the nowhere perhaps to die in your arms, she thought, and you will never know (nor will Edmond) what they mean by it, what brought them to the point, what they wanted, where they went afterwards. She felt herself to be as one awakening to something, but uncertain of this new nature, though sure that the past would never again be solid. She wondered about her parents, and realized for the first time consciously that, though they advised, warned, directed and commanded, they were themselves as unaware of the meaning of their lives as she was of hers. It was always assumed that you were going some place, that this place was relatively easy to get to, or anyhow that the signposts were all up and newly painted, that despite common hardships it was necessary only to brush your teeth twice a day, stay clear of certain subjects in conversation, sleep regular hours, and you would get there. Mrs Boyne, for instance, had never let Susan go in swimming on a rainy day—evidently a metaphysical feeling about the ominous temperature, the color of the air. But later she had gone swimming on a rainy day and nothing had happened, though she had been strangely nervous. It was maybe this nervousness, almost a fear, that had opened her eyes so widely to the gray-green sky, made her listen to the least sounds, underneath the general surge, of the very waves that lapped against her body. In the midst of this, which she remembered as almost deadly in silence, she had known, she now thought, how lonely everyone was, and how no one knew what anything amounted to, at any time: there was the sea, and the sky, split once by a long crack of lightning, and there was yourself. Then came the storm. Later, with the rain beating on her upturned face, her eyes tight shut while she shifted gently with the waters, she had felt wonderful and cool and strong. And that night she had let a boy kiss her and touch her breast.

And that, in a way, seemed to have been all that had ever happened, in a separate existence far back in a remote march of time. The boy's name was John. The house at Cape Ann had been partly washed out in the hurricane in thirty-eight. She had gone back, for one day, since then, and there were the sea and the lighthouse and the great sky, as if preserved in the amber of time and waiting for her. But it had meant not very much after all.

Here was the Brotherly Club, with the signs about the walls: Fraternity. No Credit. You'll Feel Like Hell in the Morning. God Bless America. Edmond imperturbably talked on, not a bore exactly, but an accompaniment. Life was mainly stinking and choking, all in good fun, and sometimes it was hard to distinguish vomit and perfume, late at night. Susan gestured at the dancers.

"What is this for?" she asked. "Mightn't everything be entirely different?"

"Well." Edmond folded his hands neatly on the table. "Yes, I suppose everything might be entirely different, everything has been, in fact, is and will be, at various places, entirely different.

You mean sexual customs, habits of amusement, styles, manners—yes?"

Susan nodded. What I mean, she thought, is what am I to do with my life. Or why do I sit here with you.

"What should a person like me do with her time?" she asked lamely, meekly, surprising herself as much as Edmond.

"Why, what you please!" he was instantly all charm and deference. "You don't like it here? We go. Come."

No, no, she wanted to say (but was never given time), I will not be put off, I won't be given new toys, I am serious. But Edmond had already (one of the lesser miracles) discovered a cab outside, and they were going to the Ritz. A change of scene was prescribed.

Yet Edmond seemed to have understood something, for when they had got settled in the Ritz Bar he spoke rather tenderly and seriously, not quite of Susan, to be sure, but of matters that seemed to touch closely on what she had meant to ask.

"The trouble is this," he said once. "We know, or we feel, that there is a right rhythm, a pace, a tempo, a way for life to go—and the more we think of it, the less we seem able to find it, for everything we think, every judgment we make, seems to acknowledge and then disregard the fact that it is based on two incompatible premises: everything matters and then doesn't matter, we are right and at the same time we are wrong. We have reached the point of admitting in one breath that the criminal cannot help being a criminal, and in the next breath punishing him on the assumption that he could have helped being a criminal. The mind is, or was for a long time, a comfortable place, and these answers could be held in solution; and now for some reason, that is no longer possible. That the mental world is falling apart needs no newspapers to announce it—we can tell from the fact that we find no point of balance and rest but only a perpetual hopping about on thin alternatives. We live in a society which believes naively in the power of knowledge to transform the situation into something once more acceptable; but it cannot be; knowledge is forbidden by wisdom to make such a gross claim, and wisdom itself cannot change the conditions of the problem, but only professes to change ourselves." Edmond lit a fresh cigar, smelled at his brandy and leaned back; Susan noticed that a man and woman at the next table were hanging on his every word, and noticed too that Edmond knew this and was pleased by it.

"But what do you think a person should do?" she asked again, in a low voice.

For answer Edmond drew out his wallet and got a photograph from it; this he pushed across the table to her.

The photograph was of a fetus, whose head and body shone black with the patine of a statue in bronze. Its arms were folded in judicial and almost contemptuous posture, its insignificant legs were half-drawn up to its chest, and from the pit of the belly the umbilical cord curled away out of the picture like the signature of the artist.

But it was the head, erect and huge in comparison to the rest, which demanded attention. The brow was straight and high, though despite its black or bronze sheen two pronounced indentations at the temples had caught the light, as if they were the last thumb marks of a sculptor. The eyes, closed and recessed, formed pools of deepest black; and the mouth, with its straight lower and curved upper lip, seemed cruel and royal and full of sullen condemnation.

"It's beautiful," Susan said. "It's beautiful, but it's frightening too."

"You like it?" Edmond was pleased. "I give it to you."

"But surely," the girl cried, "surely you care for it too much to give it away."

8 o

"To me it is like a god," Edmond said. "I want you to have it."

"Thank you," Susan said with all sincerity, yet feeling somewhat absurd: thank you was either too much or not enough for this infant, however beautiful.

"What does it suggest to you?" Edmond wanted to know, and Susan looked hard at the picture.

"Intellect," she said finally. "Intellect and cruelty."

"No, more, more." Edmond took her up. "When you have looked at it often for a long time it will show you more. You are right, but there is more. Look at the mouth, at the eyes which seem to be watching you even while they are sunken and shut. To me there is a majesty—only in the head and the arms of course, and they will be reduced by life while the legs and trunk are aggrandized—a majesty, a contempt of the life which he enters, a sure knowledge of the death which will be the end, a—a feeling for one's own powers, a self-sustaining pomp or pride that is sullen because it is all-sufficient, yet a brooding quality, an inwardness. The whole expression concentrates, you see, between the eyes and back, back in the skull there, where the dreams are. Do you see?"

"Yes, I think I do," Susan agreed. She looked at the picture for a moment more. Intellect and cruelty, she thought again, contempt, and nothing, not a stick, more. "Yes," she said brightly, raising her eyes to Edmond's, "you're terribly right. Terribly."

2

CLAIRE had been several times before to the Catholic Poetry Society, and was thus accustomed to the respectful yet curious welcome she would receive. Her presence, she knew, had excited some suspicion that she intended to be converted, though she had said nothing; a week before, two women had at intervals approached her, pressed her hand in a meaningful way: "I hope you won't think it a liberty if I pray for you," one had said; and the other: "I shall include you in my prayers." Claire found this sanctimonious, but in a not unpleasant way; certainly she couldn't have, in politeness, refused.

The Poetry Society was directed by a Father Tumulty, a meager, gray-faced priest who smoked a large briar house-pipe, and who had not, at least while Claire was present, ever mentioned God or the Church. In fact the entire group followed his lead in trying, it seemed, to give the most secular and libertarian tone to the meetings; after the verses had been read, and coffee and sandwiches served, Father Tumulty's laughter was loud as any in the little knot of men and boys that told jokes in a mock-surreptitious tone over in the corner.

Tonight Father Tumulty brought with him another priest, whom he introduced as Father Meretruce. This individual nodded gravely to everyone and retired to a chair a little apart, where he sat, saying nothing, throughout the meeting.

Father Meretruce was young, perhaps in the middle thirties. His complexion was dark, his hair dead-black and smooth. His face was thin, handsome and, Claire thought, cruel; but in especial her attention returned again and again to his hands, which rested patiently on his knees during the entire evening. These hands were not long, but rather broad, with powerful short fingers, and quite hairless. The nails shone with a delicate pink luster that incongruously suggested manicure. The hands of a capable dentist, Claire thought, and took an immediate dislike to the man, imagining the spatulate, clean, rather moist fingertips, the voice saying perhaps, "If you will only be patient . . ."

From time to time she glanced at him quickly, as though to catch him off his guard in some expression of intellectual contempt, for the verse (which was frightful), for his fellow-priest

8 2

(evidently a less suavely plumed bird), or for the company. Claire's attitude toward the possibility of her own conversion had reached the delicate position of hypercriticism: just one uncharitable action, the idea was, just one, will see him damned. Her ideals for the behavior of others, especially Catholics, were at this time sufficiently lofty. But she looked in vain, nothing disturbed the calm and equal regard of Father Meretruce, he neither smiled nor frowned, and his utter immunity from conventional fidgetings made her nervous.

Once, long ago, Claire had asked her father what his religion was. "I am a Christian, of course," he had replied somewhat haughtily. "But I believe most of all in honesty and good citizenship." And on another occasion: "It doesn't matter what a man's faith is, so long as he leads an upright respectable life and serves his community." This had led rapidly to a discussion of the Municipal Planning Committee, of which Nicholas Boyne had been a member. There was to be a cement playground in Dorchester. It would keep the children off the streets. Claire had imagined the dirty paving, hot in the summer sun, the bleeding knees of the children, who would be dirty. "But do you believe in God?" she had wanted to know. "Of course," was the answer.

It so happened at this time that the person who was reading, a thin, ash-blonde girl with a wart on her chin, quoted as the epigraph to one of her poems the famous line: *Nunc per spaeculum in aenigmate, sed tunc facie ad faciem.* Father Tumulty beamed approval through tobacco smoke. The poem began then by considering a flower growing in the field, the poetess felt she saw God in the flower, in the generations of all the flowers. It was all awkward enough, and concluded with the rather badly wrenched lines:

> Earth is our mother, but God is our sire
> And their marriage shall be eternally.

8 3

There was a moment's silence. Most of the audience, the girls especially, looked enraptured, and doubtless sincerely were so. Father Tumulty clapped one hand delicately, almost noiselessly, against the other, which held the briar pipe. The other priest did not move, speak, or in the least change his expression. Claire knew, with a horrible quickening of the heart and a sensation of fear, that she was going to speak, that her words, already forming, would unavoidably issue. It was too late to stop; her intellect, and her education, had already betrayed her.

"That is a heresy."

The silence that now overtook the previous silence was one of confusion and massing of forces. The poetess crackled her papers uncertainly in her hands and looked as if she might cry. Father Tumulty turned to Claire with an ominous smile.

"Indeed?" he said softly. "Perhaps Miss Boyne will be kind enough to explain herself more fully, for the benefit of those"—his hand pointed demurely to his own breast, the smile broadened—"not so skilled in dispute. What is this heresy?"

A light, relieved titter went round the circle.

"It is the heresy of Averroes," Claire said stubbornly.

"And what is the 'heresy of Averroes,' please?" The rime was deliberately drawn out and emphasized.

"The *aeternitas materiae*, the eternity of the material world."

"A true scholar, I see. And now tell me, when did Averroes live?"

"In the twelfth century."

"Would you agree, Miss Boyne, that we are no longer in the twelfth century?" Father Tumulty was persuasively and malignantly Socratic.

This was too much, and as her departure had all along been the necessary consequence of her speech, Claire got up to go.

"I'm very sorry to have given offense," she said. "But I understood heresy to be heresy—according to my reading. It's very good to worship and have faith, I know. But the question does arise, of which God you happen to be worshipping at a given time."

Her coat was in a pile near the door. She took it up, and as she swept through the hall and out she heard Father Tumulty saying:

"Oh, come, I'm sure Miss Cattlet will forgive you. We all forgive you, if it comes to that." Claire slammed the door, imagining the priest saying of her that, like Pontius Pilate, she would not stay for an answer (in fact this was exactly what he was saying). Let him have his triumph, she thought. I won't stay to argue. "We are no longer in the twelfth century," indeed.

The door opened again, and Father Meretruce came out, wearing his overcoat.

"I shall accompany you to your home," he said.

"I would as soon you didn't," she replied, but he made no answer to this for a moment, until they were beyond question walking together in the empty street.

"Of course you were technically right about the heresy," he began then.

"I know that," Claire said, then fell immediately into temptation again. "It was for that belief, in a more subtle form, that St Thomas denounced Sigier de Brabant and Guillaume de St Amour in twelve-sixty-something."

"Of course," said Father Meretruce, as though she had mentioned the likelihood of snow. "Yet Sigier was later placed by Dante among the Great Doctors in the Heaven of the Sun, where by way of fair play St Thomas is made to introduce him."

"Yes, but his acquittal of the heresy doesn't make the doctrine of the world's eternity acceptable."

"Ah, well," said Father Meretruce lightly. "Here is the subway station."

"Of course," he said loudly, over the roar of the cars, "you were uncharitable. You should not have publicly accused a faithful if not very illuminated daughter of the Church . . ."

"I admit it."

". . . especially as you are yourself admittedly a follower of some form of the Lutheran heresy." His tone suggested clearly that it didn't much matter which form.

On the short walk home, he said more seriously: "You should not condemn the Church for the behavior of some of its members—you'll see, if you look, worse things than what you saw tonight, by a long way. You know that you look to the true Church of Christ for the personal profit of your soul's salvation. It would be foolish to be put off at the entrance for a reason accidental to that purpose. There are, it has been said, many mansions, and if it were only for that reason, charity would be invaluable and of supreme importance.

"I personally admire the intellectual ardor with which you seem to have begun the investigation of the faith. . . . That is an acceptable mode of access, but it is only a mode, and there are other modes. You must understand this."

Before her door he said: "I will visit you presently, if I may."

"Are you to be my—director?" Claire asked with a slight smile.

"If you like," he answered, "you can put it that way."

"Then let me confess—if you wish to put it that way—that my intellectual ardor, as you call it, has no very firm foundation: two courses in philosophy and a seminar in the philosophy of religion." They both laughed at this, then she continued: "And I am quite sorry for the way I behaved. But even so . . ."

"Ah, 'but' . . ." he said. "That's not enough."

And on this they said good night and Claire went in.

HE DAYS of winter con-
tinued. In Boston one awakened, after snow, to a glossy, brittle
city in which the sun was but an inferior reflection of the State
House dome, to days of glittering promise which revised themselves quickly into days merely of wet feet and red noses and
perhaps, at evening, a slight fever coupled with a sense of resentment, the feeling that something amounting to life had once
again proved evasive and undependable. Or else it rained, a
wintry rain that froze in the streets: one saw old ladies collapse
on the glassy surfaces while passers-by slithered in silent panic
to their rescue; automobiles clanked in chains, skidded into
lamp-posts, trees, or froze at night where they stood; elderly
gentlemen, the ferrule of umbrella or cane finding no sure hold,
appeared from a distance like little people possessed by pogo
sticks. Altogether life was treacherous or merely rowdy, depending on one's taste; and weakened muscles were sore every night
from coping with the situation.

The Boynes followed the simple routine of sensible people
during winter, a kind of active hibernation, no new thing being
undertaken. Mr Boyne continued to walk to his office each
morning, bundled up very warm and wearing earmuffs. Mrs
Boyne remained immured in the almost tropical heat of the

home, and expanded like a vegetable in the rich artificial culture; when she moved at all her progress through the domain could be checked by means of tea-cups forgotten beside every chair, on every table, on the windowsill of the stairway landing. In the evenings she discussed the possibilities of sickness, looked for symptoms, inquired about fevers. Friends coming to tea were messengers penetrating her fastness with news and rumors of flu, grippe, bronchitis, even pneumonia, all of which seemed to have reached epidemic prevalence when she heard of them. It is not surprising that she maintained stoutly a conception of the world outside her house as a place in which people were stricken while walking in the street, or fell down uttering dreadful, feeble cries before their very doors.

Briefly the family was like an organism which in severe times puts out one or two predetermined feelers in the direction of food and necessary activity; and even this with the slow certainty of a motion in sleep, whose object is not so much to accomplish anything in the world outside as to satisfy the dreamer that everything possible is being done to allow him to continue in sleep. It was a time also of moral recuperation, for there were no strong emotions that could deal with the weather.

It could have been for this reason alone that Father Meretruce was after a very little shilly-shallying received into the house and even entertained to supper by Mr and Mrs Boyne. To his first visit, made in late January, about two weeks after his first meeting with Claire, the reaction was sharp and immediate: representations were made to Claire. What did she mean by, how dare she bring into this house, did she consider—no, it was impossible. Claire answered that she would in that case as soon leave home as not. There the matter had to rest, and presently the parents, Mrs Boyne especially, discovered a delightful worldliness and sophistication about opening their doors to a Romish priest, particularly one of such quiet, cold charm as

Father Meretruce. She told her friends, as one imparting a great secret, that he was a Jesuit—"quite a somebody in the Society" —and went so far as to hint at political connections; this sufficiently deceived, among others, Uncle Fred, who preened himself on his intelligence in taking the hint, and was gravely polite to the priest whenever they met. In return he was met with a courtesy and condescension that made him feel as if he were undergoing examination, and led him to the quite far-fetched expectation of cutting in on the Irish vote in the fall.

Only Susan was, according to her mood, openly or covertly contemptuous.

"Are you getting the answers?" she asked Claire once, just after the priest had left.

"Yes, dear, I'm afraid I am," Claire replied with that diffidence which was her trial approach to charity.

"Very photogenic padre you've got there; I like the Valentino hair-do."

"I should much rather not discuss it with you."

"But if I should much rather discuss it with you . . . ?"

"Well?" Claire turned her back to the door and faced her sister. Susan looked at her steadily for a moment, then said, "You should be ashamed."

"Ashamed?"

"You're running out on life." This was too much for Claire, who smiled.

"We're not in the movies, Sue," she said.

"Dammit," said Susan, "will you please stop forgiving me in advance? Go and exercise your charity on Meretruce, that's what he's paid for. With me you may continue to be as sounding brass."

"Is that your considered opinion of me?" Claire asked.

"Ah-ah. Charity, remember." Susan raised a warning finger.

"Now that's enough," said Claire, and walked away.

"Does he think of you as a temptation in the desert?" Susan

called after her. "I don't know that you're spiritual enough," she went on. "You've got rather a pronounced rear end."

This and similar interviews did nothing to restore the sisters to their former intimacy. Soon they avoided each other, and met only at meals and over the infrequent letters that came from Roger, which took for the most part a professionally soldierly tone about the weather.

Susan too was at this time on the edge of a kind of conversion, though the change involved was as yet delicate, subjective and difficult to put a name to. She was as one holding his nose before jumping into a pool, not only because of the sinuses, but also because of the stench from the depths. Dr Einman had suggested to her, or at least by one of his indirections put the idea in her head, that one might have a vocation for lust, lechery, for viciousness and degradation of any kind.

"My dear Susan," he had said when questioned about this. "You can have a vocation for anything—for having a lingering illness, for selling automobiles, for jumping from a twentieth-story window—anything. Only the ritual makes the priest. I'm sure that whatever you do you will do thoroughly."

An odd intimacy, which was at the same time a kind of courtship, had developed. Edmond, Susan remarked, dressed better and looked a bit younger than he had when she first met him. He brought flowers, or had them sent several times in a week. Mrs Boyne was introduced one afternoon, regarded the doctor with suspicion and the flowers, after that, with fear and mistrust.

"You have an admirer," she said somewhat coyly to Susan. "He's a little old, isn't he? For you?" And later, looking sharply, "Promise you won't do anything without consulting me?"

"By 'anything,' Mother, do you refer to marriage, or to a life of shame?"

"Susan!"

But there it was, control had long since departed. Mrs Boyne had often thought with apprehension of the time when her daughters would choose and leave; but now that it came it was much worse and far more unnatural than she had ever dreamed. One went with a mental doctor (the prestige of "doctor" about cancelled out the suspect quality in "mental"; one had heard stories of this sort of doctor), the other "went with"—what else could you say?—a Catholic priest.

In any case, thought Mrs Boyne, and much as she hated admitting it, there was something vulgar about Susan, something common. A taint, she suggested delicately to herself. A taint. Her husband's father, of whom she had always stood in some awe, had run through three wives in a life of only moderate length, and was reputed to have been a rare bird beyond the limits of this curriculum. It was something, naturally, she would not think of mentioning to Nicholas, who had put on a hysterical display lasting for an entire week when the old Lothario died. But a taint, nevertheless.

Susan at this time saw nothing of her contemporaries, with the possible exception of John Averist, and was often alone. Aberrant and wakeful, she lived in a queer world of hesitant expectation, resisting sullenly the importunate suggestions of her family that she do something!—do something or get married (but not to Dr Einman) was the implication as one by one the alternatives were proposed—get a job, go to school, take up welfare work. Susan thought of the family's solicitude as part of a protestant fear of all inactivity, which to some extent she shared, but not enough to make her "do" something just for the sake of motion, of friction with the world. In her musings she considered "doing one thing" but this was as far as she got, for faced with the question of what thing would be alone worth doing her mind simply refused to deal in particulars. Without much thought at all she had reached the position of critical importance (a point which men, and most women, reach much later in general, and after great efforts in an outward, expressive direction) at which the possible, the multiplicity of life in potential, appears only as the more cheerful obverse face of the futility of life in particular, life as actualized by doing. She could not even know what she sought, for as soon as she believed she wanted an identification with some object or task around which she might harmoniously and attractively re-group the elements of her character, it became obvious that to want this was at the same time to wish to lose her identity, to give over, to depend. In some way connected with Dr Einman's proposal, which became more outrageous, forthright and attractive in memory than it had been in fact, she was aware now of life (sheerly, still, in the possible) as capable of infinite, improbable expansions: one might say "I am going out for a pack of cigarettes," and then for a variety of reasons never return. There was also the freedom to do nothing, which, exercised to the full, also became frightening: the tension set up by indecision itself might be decisive in time.

Meanwhile she spent most evenings with Edmond, and was gaining among other things, a casual experience of the depths of Boston, places whose existence she would previously have thought melodramatic and improbable. She was at first surprised and taken aback by the faces she saw, their expressions of open rapacity or furtive envy, their sneers, their sinister geniality; but upon making comparison of these faces with others, closer to home and raised by society (as they doubtless thought) above the possibility of such a comparison, she felt she knew that the smell of beer and urinals made the only difference.

Occasionally, and with a full and fascinated sense of helplessness and danger, she let herself be taken to Edmond's flat—his office, he called it. There, on a red leather sofa (disgustingly professional in appearance) she permitted tentative and experimental caresses. She rather enjoyed this, and admired the sordidness of the scene as much as anything; moreover these actions hardly ever approached passion or went beyond the amusing. Once Edmond had switched off the light, but Susan concealed her timidity with such a demonstration of coldness that even his confidence was shaken, and his laugh, as the lights went on again, seemed somewhat strained.

On the other side of the ledger, he once left her alone there with John Averist, pleading that he'd run out of liquor and would be back in ten minutes. When he had gone, John opened the bottom drawer of the desk and showed her a bottle of rye and one of rum, both mostly full.

"Edmond is pure scientist first and last," he said. "We are evidently an experiment."

"Shall we fall into the trap?" Susan asked, with what was meant to be a light laugh.

"I think not," John said. "He's probably standing in the hall. You're a nice girl," he continued, "and you shouldn't play with a horrible old man like Edmond. We could meet somewhere else."

"That would be nice," Susan said mockingly. "Nice, I mean, for a really nice girl. You watch your moral tone and I'll watch mine, brother."

"Have you slept with him yet?"

"Don't you know?" Susan affected surprise. "No, I haven't slept with him yet," she said, imitating his tone. "And what makes you so sure I will?"

"All the time in the world," he replied. "I can just see it coming."

"Sour grapes?"

"Maybe. A little."

He was rather attractive, she considered. She liked that thin face, with the high cheekbones.

Presently Edmond came back, empty-handed. He'd got half-

9 3

way to the liquor store (he explained) before he remembered there was some in the desk.

"See?" he invited them, pulling open the drawer.

Later Edmond took her home. He wanted to come in, but Hogan was standing in the front hall, and Susan quickly improvised a cold good night. I have definitely the soul of a whore, she thought, conscious as she passed that Hogan was making his own estimate of her possibilities.

Susan got up very late these mornings, and this was a source of constant displeasure, especially to her father. "You are learning bad habits," he said to her out of a clear sky one evening. "And I don't like the people I hear you're running around with. And see that you're up for breakfast. And try to spend an evening at home once in a while. Are you drinking?" Susan refused to answer and left the room. That night when she came home he was waiting up.

"You're still my daughter," he began in his most direfully civil way. "Try to remember that. You've been seen, you know."

"People do get seen now and again," Susan replied sweetly, but as she tried to walk past him he grabbed her wrist.

"Don't give me your insolence, Susan. I'm warning you once and once only. You can either behave as I think right, or I have means to rein you in, don't think I haven't." He let her go on this.

"Just think about it," he called after her as she started up the stairs. His voice trembled with control; he was very thin-tempered.

Susan went for long walks almost every afternoon, never in the direction of solitude but always toward the most crowded streets, and always with the inexpressible vague idea that something might happen, that circumstance would take the choice out of her hands. In the course of this stimulation of the possible, relating everything seen or heard at once to herself, at

94

once to what might happen to her, she collected in memory a scrapbook of scenes and occasions, sentences overheard, the sight of a strange face curiously resembling her own, a man who walked close behind her for a time in the early dusk. Seeing a rather garishly dressed woman whom she conceived to be a whore, she followed her at a distance symbolizing both fastidiousness and fear, and had the inconclusive pleasure of seeing her enter a respectable-looking brownstone house on Beacon Street.

No one can tell how long Susan's life might have gone on balancing and equivocating, or how long Claire might have hesitated at the threshold of the religious life; for the entire equilibrium was overthrown and toppled into action by a dislocation from an unexpected quarter when, late in March, Nicholas Boyne suddenly, in a day, went mad.

2

His route to and from the office—the same concrete track he boasted of having passed over day by day for so many years, rain or shine—led through Charles Street between the Common and the Gardens; and here, late one afternoon, he fell helplessly to the pavement and lay there while a crowd solicitously gathered. It must have been as terrible an experience as it was a ridiculous spectacle—the fifty-year-old man spraddled on the rutted and blackened ice, his hat, umbrella and portfolio lying about him like a strange heraldry; he meanwhile furiously conscious that he felt no pain but was yet unable to move a limb or speak. He saw the rude, kindly stares of men like and men unlike himself, heard their opinions expressed as from some distance: he had, it seemed, "sprained something," that was the consensus, though someone suggested a broken back: "You mustn't try to move him," this person officiously said. Then alien hands grubbed in his coat pocket to take his wallet; he saw it opened and heard someone read out: Nicholas Boyne, broker, and his home and office addresses and telephone numbers, all from a little card behind an isinglass screen in the wallet—put there, supposably, for just such an emergent turn.

A policeman came up and, kneeling, made some rudimentary gestures of diagnosis. He felt Mr Boyne's pulse, pronounced that he was alive. He touched thoughtfully all Mr Boyne's limbs and said they were unbroken. He smoothed the black pin-stripe cloth around the cage of Mr Boyne's ribs and said they felt all right too. "Internal injury, probably," he said then, and looked for blood, opening the sufferer's mouth to do so. Nicholas Boyne distinctly and bitterly tasted the white cotton glove. Then the policeman took out a notebook and pencil and asked questions. "Can you hear me?" he asked several times; but Nicholas Boyne's deliberate nod, or roll, of the head, must also have been internal, for the policeman asked again and again.

Presently, by whatever agency at last brings the right attention, in a crowded street, to such an accident, an ambulance arrived. Two orderlies brought a stretcher and put it down next Mr Boyne while they began a less cursory but rapid inspection for his injury.

Nicholas Boyne, all the while he was lying there, resented with terrible ferocity the idea that he was attracting attention, causing a disturbance, etc. His mind kept silently saying over and over: "I have never in my life asked you people for anything. Never." The speed of repetition, the agony of concentration on this formula made it all but prayerful: his mind blushed at the sight of himself lying so stupidly there and—this was the crucial thing—*depending* on others, strangers. "They are giving their time, their sympathy," he thought once. "They will expect to be rewarded." The revulsion he felt at being touched by these hands was multiplied by the fact that he could give it no expression; he was even incapable of shuddering.

But this internal tumult must have had some effect; for at the moment that the orderlies, in their white coats, were stooping at his either end to lift him upon the stretcher, Nicholas Boyne felt a sharp and exceedingly painful click at the back of his skull, as though two bones which had been locked together had suddenly sprung apart, grating in passage and smashing finally against the entire structure of his head. He sat up at once, and said rapidly: "I forbid you to touch me." Then, more fully realizing his public situation, he added: "Thank you very much for your kindness, but it was a passing fit, I am perfectly capable of going on by myself now." To prove that this was so, he got slowly to his feet. Hands handed him his scattered belongings.

It was evident that they did not want to let him go. The policeman looked dubious, the orderlies were ready to knock him down, if need be, to get him on the stretcher, or so at any rate it seemed.

Mr Boyne was inspired to lie.

"I have had these attacks before," he said. "I was foolish to go out today, but luckily I have escaped the worst effects this time. I'll call my doctor when I get home."

The news that he was already under medical care proved satisfactory to the official sponsors of his well-being; the lay public was not so easily shaken off, and Nicholas Boyne found himself escorted with some ceremony and deference by two fellow-citizens, one of them (he felt but could not be sure) the one who had diagnosed a broken back. This person seemed to feel he had found a friend, or at least that anyone who could fall down and lie for ten minutes motionless in the public street would be a likely and sympathetic confidant. He had, it appeared, spent some eighteen months in hospital, he was still occasionally subject to attacks, he wouldn't go back, though, not if you paid him. Mr Boyne was not listening.

He had a slight headache, but not of the sick variety; rather, the little pain was merely sufficient to emphasize a sense he had of vast spaces inside his head; a little feverish feeling also accented the possibility that his head was the entire world, or rather and better, the universe—expanding, contracting, what you will—but the universe, mysterious, echoing cold and broad, majestic and eerie, full of sighing spaces and corridors between brotherhoods of stars, both infinite and infinitesimal, all-encompassing and absolutely just. The voices of his companions were remote and pathetic squeaks to which he determined to pay no attention.

As a test, while they guided him, he determined to see Boston in an instant, in a moment of time. He shut his eyes and there it was: the State House, Symphony Hall, Back Bay Station, every blade of grass on the Common; Mechanics Hall, Harvard University, the Charles River, rack and shred, every brick and stone was there. He opened his eyes. He was satisfied.

They were quite near home when one of his companions affably suggested turning into the Lincolnshire Bar for a drink; Mr Boyne in his omnipotent daze did not refuse—I am above all this, he told himself, smiling a tolerant acquiescence—and was escorted into the hotel and up the stairs (the banister was painted orange, and this attracted him a great deal) into the bar, where he sat back in a deep chair and received a strong martini.

"Hey," said one of his new friends, when they had finished one round. "I don't know if he ought to be doing this. Shock, you know." He nodded his head with much seriousness.

"That's right," the other said, and leaned toward the patient. "How do you feel?" he asked.

"Splendid, splendid."

"Probably the best thing in the world for him," said one.

"Sure thing," the other said. "You don't want to take this doctor-crap too seriously."

I am the resurrection and the life, Mr Boyne hummed deep in his head. I am the Pole Star of the North. I am a tree of life to them that grab—no, to them that take hold, lay hold—something.

They had another round of martinis, and then declared it was time to leave. Mr Boyne became angry when they were unable to attract the waiter's attention, and he threw his olive at the man, causing a certain commotion which was nothing, however, to what he caused when with a grandiose gesture imposing silence he reached for his wallet and drew up nothing. It was as though he had unobtrusively brought his heart out of an inner pocket and then discovered it to have stopped.

"So!" he said to one, and then, "So!" to the other, fixing them in turn with a look full rather of conviction than suspicion. They for their part were quick enough to catch on and take offense.

"Waiter," Mr Boyne said imperiously. "Arrest these men."

His voice had been as loud as it was authoritative, and it seemed that everyone in the room got up at once. The headwaiter came in, the two companions tried to explain together, but had no success, the headwaiter was more interested in the tranquillity of the establishment than in justice.

"Go to the police," he kept saying. "To the police." While he spoke he was escorting all three of them to the door, backing them downstairs. Four waiters flanked him, and they all stood at the head of the staircase watching the three guests descend. Then the headwaiter lost his temper and rushed after them. He grabbed Nicholas Boyne's arm fiercely and hissed: "Don't you ever come back. Don't you dare."

In the street Mr Boyne looked at his companions. They looked at him. They both sneered. One of them shook his fist. They turned away, walking rapidly, and several times looked back as though to assure themselves that he was not following. Mr Boyne walked unsteadily in the other direction the two blocks to his home.

"Shame and injustice," he said to himself many times. When he reached the house he was weeping and snivelling quite freely and with no intention of stopping. Hogan let him in, and Mr Boyne, who had the intention of saying, "Hogan, I am going to take a bath," simply announced, "Hogan, my head will burst open." To illustrate this proposition he clasped his hands to his face, dropping meanwhile his umbrella and case. Hogan silently retrieved these.

Nicholas Boyne went wearily up the stairs, through his room and into the bathroom which connected his wife's bedroom with his own. He locked both doors, undressed, and got into a hot bath. This was so comfortable that he decided he would stay there forever. His head was spinning like a universe and he warned himself that if he fell asleep he might drown.

It was dinnertime before he was missed. Father Meretruce and Claire and Mrs Boyne were sitting in the library, Susan was expected down at any moment. Hogan announced dinner, and Mrs Boyne said she could not imagine what had become of her husband.

"He came in long ago, Ma'am," Hogan said.

"That's funny. Run up and tell him dinner's ready, Hogan, please."

Hogan returned looking pained and puzzled. Mr Boyne, it seemed, was in the bathroom and was never coming out.

"Never?"

" 'S what he said, Ma'am."

"But how silly. Never."

The following conversation then took place between Mrs Boyne and her husband, after which she knew that something was wrong with Nicholas.

"Dinner's ready, dear."

"What are we having?"

"Chicken. Fried chicken."

"I don't want any."

"Now, dear. You must eat."

"You can send some up."

"But you can't eat in the tub."

"Don't tell me what I can't do. Go away."

"Nicholas. Open the door."

"Go away."

"We'll have to have it broken down, you know, if you don't."

"You do, and I'll go down the drain and you'll never see me again."

"Now, Nicholas, you're too big to go down the drain."

"Don't be so damn reasonable. You know what I mean."

"But I don't. I really don't, Nicholas."

"I'll flush myself down the bowl. How'll you like that?"

Dinner, after this, was not an entertainment. Mrs Boyne had decided with what seemed to her exemplary firmness to say nothing, to pass it off lightly, to give the whole incident a chance to blow over; to this end she bent resolutely to her plate. But the empty chair opposite proved too strong for her.

"Father," she said after the main course, lifting to him her myopic and moist eyes, "my husband has locked himself in the bathroom and says he will never come out."

Susan, who had heard nothing of all this, laughed, and Mrs Boyne turned on her with sad ferocity.

"Susan, it's nothing to laugh about. I am afraid it's something quite serious." Simultaneously with this statement she realized, though, that it was in fact something to laugh about, something—if only one had not been concerned, if only it had been (for example) Mrs Emory's husband—far more richly ridiculous than plausible: "my husband has locked himself in the bathroom . . ."

Father Meretruce looked grave as he said, "That is indeed unfortunate." Susan here stifled a set of giggles at which Claire raised her eyebrows with the fixed stare of one who is determined to recognize the solemnity of a tragic accident in whatever comic circumstances.

"Have you called a doctor?" Father Meretruce then asked, seeming to resign his authority in this particular realm of consolation and remedy.

"But a doctor . . ." Mrs Boyne sighed windily, meaning probably that a doctor could accomplish little through a locked door.

"Well, what would you suggest, Mother?"—this from Susan —"a plumber?"

Mrs Boyne said, "I thought maybe the Father would go up."

Father Meretruce wiped his lips fastidiously with a napkin. "I will do what I may," he said rising, "but I suggest a medical man."

"Oh well, then," Susan said. "If you really want something done I'll call Einman."

"Susan!" Claire was only a moment before her mother. "You can't be thinking of having that man here at a time like this."

"That man? That man, as you so politely put it, is probably the only person we know who can help. And in the spiritual realm, for that matter, would not Dr Canbrode be more appropriate than your Roman?" Father Meretruce had by this time left the room.

In the end Susan had her way, a triumph somewhat emptied of content by the fact that everyone's way was had as well, the telephone being continuously employed over twenty minutes

to summon Dr Einman, Dr Tinker (the family physician), the
Reverend S J Canbrode (Episcopalian) and Uncle Fred Seely.

What presently followed closely resembled the contest on
Mount Carmel between Elijah and the prophets of Baal. At
the one door (or so it seemed to Susan, nor did the meaning
of the division escape Claire or appear anything but natural
to Mrs Boyne) were grouped Father Meretruce, Dr Canbrode,
Mrs Boyne and Claire, while at the other were Drs Einman
and Tinker with Susan. Hogan and Mrs Purse, ascended from
the subterrene realms, vacillated between doors until a sharp
command from the lady of the house established them firmly
on the side of comparative orthodoxy.

All began by beseeching Mr Boyne on grounds of common
knowledge and common sense, please to come out: you will
catch cold, you will do yourself no good in there, you can't
shut yourself away indefinitely, it will be better if you tell us
your troubles, rather now than later. All this received no answer.

For Nicholas Boyne had no troubles, or so at least it seemed
to him. Every few minutes he made the enormous exertion of
opening the hot water tap and bringing up once more the
temperature of his bath. When the place of his feet, just under
the faucet, became all but unbearably hot, he turned off the
water and hooshed himself back and forth in the tub to diffuse
the warmth. Then he lay back and listened to the soft lapping
of the waves against his flesh. It is possible, he thought, that
if I stay here long enough I will rot, I will flake away. He regarded his fingers, already pinched and white with wet. Why
had he not discovered this heavenly pleasure before?

The God in me was concealed, was in hiding until today,
he answered himself with grave simplicity. It gave him a certain
pleasure at this time to think of the war in Europe, of the Jews
dying under torture in Germany, of the creaking leather of
stormtroopers' boots, belts, holsters, of girls being brutally raped

in kitchens and yards and stables, of the dry stony powder which hangs in the air for so long after a bomb has hit a building, of young soldiers sweating coldly under fire, of the itchy discomfort of their stiff, muddy clothing and accoutrements.

Vive la mitrailleuse, he thought, and, pleased with the sound, said it aloud. "*Vive la mitrailleuse*." This caused the exhorters either side the door to multiply their efforts, for it crossed the grain of their uneasy suspicions with evidence that he was alive. Nicholas Boyne paid them no attention.

His imagination, he discovered, was brilliant and keen, pictures of the known and unknown displayed themselves with poignant clarity at his mere summons. The bath was celestial, full of sleep. He wondered why the water in a white bathtub should be green, when water in a glass was colorless, and turning on the tap again he delighted in watching the pure crystalline color hit the surface in a chaos of clear bubbles, then sink into this marvelous delicate light green. And the sea, he remembered, was blue. He held the green bar of soap like a vessel at the surface, then with a feeling of sad yet pleasant authority released it and saw it dive greenly between his knees. There, he thought. They have all drowned, perished deep down.

He remembered having been told in childhood that the world existed only upon the continuing Will of God, and that if the Author of the Universe should once relax his vigil, turn aside his attention, so much as blink, or (God forbid it) sleep, this planet would founder and fall into hell, or disintegrate and disperse in utter space. This theory now attracted him, and he determined to put it to the trial. I shall simply close my eyes, he thought, and when I open them there will be no world. Sleep, Omnipotent, Omniscient, Om. He closed his eyes and felt the beautifully clear, radiant light of infinity inside his head. He was drawn in to the streaming circles of all the planets' paths; he was Alpha and Omega.

At the doors of the steamy Turkish universe, pleading had become more elaborate, had begun to tap the rhetoric of more basic reasons (as, the rightness of Things, the comprehensibility of the Creation, that God is no Deceiver, and that medical science is *not wrong*) for having at any cost Nicholas Boyne out of there. Presently it came about that the beseechment developed into a florid style of vaunting from outside one door to outside the other, the words entirely skipping Nicholas Boyne in their passage through the bathroom. The prophets of Baal were at some little disadvantage, for, as Dr Tinker said to Dr Einman, and waved his stethoscope as he said it, "We can't get in to make an examination."

"Nonsense, examination," replied Dr Einman. "Haven't you ever wanted to stay all your life in a bath?"

"But you gentlemen are hired," Susan said sweetly, "to get him out of the bath. Personally, I rather think a plumber would have been the man."

The true prophets were not doing a great deal better, though they were not afflicted with doubt of the ultimate cause of Mr Boyne's action, or inaction ("*Accidia*," said Father Meretruce; "Sloth," affirmed Dr Canbrode), and matters were not much improved by the arrival of Uncle Fred, who at once began with, "Tell him he's got to take hold of himself. Here, I'll tell him. Nicholas, can you hear me? Pull yourself together, Nicholas." And so forth.

"That will do no good," Dr Canbrode said frigidly.

"Had we perhaps better try an exorcism of a formal sort?" suggested Father Meretruce.

"The Episcopalian Church, Father, does not believe, if you will pardon me, in dealing with Satan direct—or with his minions, either."

"There is much accuracy in the psychology of the evil spirit— it is not to be held in contempt by the modern research student." Dr Einman's voice came loudly through the two doors.

"The point," Susan remarked with equal clarity, "is not to exorcise the demon from my father, but my father from his bath."

"Has the medical profession any ideas?" inquired Dr Canbrode with what was perhaps a controlled sneer.

"Why don't you ask him in the name of God to open the door?" suggested Dr Tinker, with some seriousness.

"Or why doesn't God open the door?" Dr Einman asked.

"There is nothing incompatible between the conclusions of religion and those of science," said Dr Canbrode through the door, "but cheap cynicism is out of place in both fields."

Ultimately Hogan and the Church of Christ and Uncle Fred broke in the door, affirming a rather unspiritual victory. The daughters were hustled into the hall, "lest they see their father's shame," as The Reverend S J Canbrode carefully put it, and Nicholas Boyne was drawn up dripping out of his bath. He was fast asleep, or in a coma, and his head had drooped until his mouth, when they entered, was gently bubbling the water. He was dried with a rough towel by Hogan, dumped into a pair of pajamas and put into bed. His temperature was 103° and his breathing was somewhat shallow and harsh.

3

WHILE THE COMA lasted there could be doubt; but after midnight, when Mr Boyne came from the depths of sleep, fantastic as Lear with garlands, it seemed necessary to concede that whatever cotter pin or bit of wire had centrally for all but fifty years held him together, had sheared now or somehow given way.

Primarily, there was the point that he recognized no one but his wife, whom he knew, with great tenderness, as the Virgin

Mary, the Mother of God (he always used this full form of the title). When Mrs Purse brought a cup of hot bouillon he seemed to know her too for a moment: he called her Wallet. There was always the hope, as Dr Tinker pointed out, that this amnesia together with other phenomena of dislocation might merely go with and demonstrate a slight delirium—shock, perhaps, or even pneumonia. This "hope," Dr Einman said, emphasizing the word, was of slight probability: the patient's temperature returned to normal, so did his breathing, as he awakened from sleep.

Mrs Boyne wrung her hands and cried a little, and said to the Reverend Canbrode, "It is a sin for which I am being punished." The clergyman could not give her the comfort he wished to give; the presence of the priest made him forbear to express his belief, that "sin" was in any case too strong a word for a member of his congregation. Father Meretruce nodded his sympathetic understanding of Mrs Boyne's way of putting it, and Dr Einman smiled sourly and said, "God forbid some day I should have a wife who sins so that I go crazy from it."

Mr Boyne did not refrain from commenting intelligibly, during this period, that "Someone had better do something for the poor fellow." He entered quite authoritatively into the business of diagnosing his own ailment, with the sole exception that he did not seem to understand who was ailing, but kept referring to Uncle Fred, who for once was abashed to silence as though hexed.

Nicholas Boyne's affliction, from what the watchers at his bed could make out, consisted in two separate roles: he was God, and he was also a sinner affected by some unnamed and perhaps nameless guilt. These parts did not change by any defined phase of transition; rather they coexisted, advancing and receding, sentence by sentence. From his own point of view, everything would be well except for his fear, which was accentuated by all these people who stood by looking at him and talking about someone who was mad and might therefore do him some disservice. He fixed upon Uncle Fred Seely as the enemy, and not without cunning brought him too into the judgment of the company.

"I will punish that one," he cried, pointing at Uncle Fred, whose large egglike face was full of sorry reproach. "He is a pickpocket and a rapist and he has certainly knocked up, among others, the Daughters of Zion."

Statements like this had the effect of making the others scan closely Uncle Fred for a happiness that often madness hits on, that reason and sanity could not be so prosperously delivered of; similarly, whenever the patient spoke of God, Dr Canbrode with some facility proposed it as a sign of returning sanity. But since it always appeared presently that Nicholas Boyne was God, the clergyman's contention seemed insupportable.

Presently, declaring from their various points of vantage that whatever might be done could no longer be done that night, the gentlemen all departed, leaving Mrs Boyne alone at her husband's side.

Susan became Dr Einman's mistress that night. She was naked in bed when he entered her room, and fully awake. She had expected him.

At the same time Claire, in her room, was speaking in a low voice to Father Meretruce.

"It was three years ago," she said, "in the summer at Cape Ann. The man's name was John Innes."

"Continue."

"There's nothing much to continue," Claire said. "I slept with him."

"How many times?"

"Once."

"You loved him?"

"No."

"Then . . . ?"

"Then nothing. It was—whatever it was, it's over."

"Are you sorry?"

"In a way, I suppose. It wasn't pleasant."

"I mean, are you sorry for the sin?" Father Meretruce asked.

"I don't know."

"It is for the sin you must be sorry."

Claire bowed her head.

"Yes, Father. I am sorry."

BOOK · TWO

*B*APTISM and infant dam-
nation," Edmond said. He was speaking once more about the
photograph he had given Susan. "I can understand, sometimes,
that spiritual seriousness, that urgency, the setting of the seal
upon the newly formed vessel and saying to it, 'Go, die now,
you're one of us.' It would take back into the darkness the holy
energy, the best that life could give, the only thing, in fact,
the creature needed. They used, in old times, to baptize the
dead."

"I didn't know," Susan said shortly.

They were lying together in Susan's bed and in conjugal discomfort. This sort of long-term indiscretion and casualness had
been made possible by the departure, three weeks before, of
Mr and Mrs Boyne to a little place in the country; it was not
a sanitarium, not an asylum, Edmond had explained in recom-
mending it, simply a large home where competent medical care
was easily available, and where, moreover, Mrs Boyne need
hardly be separated from her husband, whose indisposition
whether temporary or permanent was hardly to be called violent
or dangerous.

Edmond had made all the arrangements and reservations,
had personally stood on the platform of the Back Bay station

and supervised the departure in two compartments of the Boynes and Hogan (who was to have returned in three days, but did not in fact get back for over a week and with no explanation). Edmond had stood by patiently while Mrs Boyne in a flutter between sorrow and arrangements reminded Claire and Susan that they must keep a budget, be firm with the servants, "Inquire about the price of everything *yourself*," not let Mrs Purse skip the *thorough* cleaning once a week.

"If anything goes wrong," she said some twenty times, "remember to call Uncle James in Dedham and he'll help you."

Uncle James was Nicholas Boyne's elder brother, a scapegrace who had brought grief to the family in his youth by becoming an author. However, it turned out that his books (of which there were now thirteen) were always so sedate as to miraculously turn literature into a respectable profession; besides, they made money on a reasonable scale, so that Uncle James seemed to have moved right through Bohemia into Boston again; his house in Dedham was filled with beautiful things.

A week after the exodus came a letter from Mrs Boyne. "It is lovely here, with many trees and beautifully kept lawns," she wrote in her overflowing hand. "There is entertainment in the evenings, and a dance on Saturday nights. The doctors say there is good hope for Nicholas, who seems very happy and has made several friends already!"

Susan's attitude toward her father's illness contained nothing of sorrow beyond a faint and abstracted sympathy. "It must be terrible to have something like that happen so suddenly," as people say in such cases, strangely implying that the speed and not the catastrophe is accountable, and that had it all happened slowly there would be no need to be sorry at all.

She had been, of course, deeply shocked; life could not, she thought, have chosen a better subject than her father on which to demonstrate an infinite capriciousness: her motto from that night forth was "Anything can happen." Nor (to give another demonstration) when she consented to sleep with Edmond, had she expected that this passionate and sinful beginning would so soon devolve into a domestic lubricity; with some still virginal part of her mind she resented fiercely the insolence with which Edmond began to claim rights, yet she hardly protested and still less thought of denying him and so re-establishing however tenuously some privacy.

The truth was perhaps this, that Susan had developed an overwhelming interest in *life*, which to her meant an interest in *the possible*, which paradoxically amounts to something the same as an overwhelming hatred of life. For life (as Edmond was at pains to show) proceeds by control, modification, adaptation, conflict of systems, grasping and letting go, systole and diastole; he was fond of quoting Nietzsche's remarks on this subject: "Evasion, love of irony, suspicion and joyous mistrust. . . ." Whereas what Susan wanted was crisis, passion, decision, fulfilment; she wanted, as he said to her once, "to tear everything in pieces." He was himself rather Epicurean; as with the meals of the aged and invalids, little and often was the device of all his pleasures.

And her complaint now, though as yet unvoiced, was that really nothing had happened. Life was, she thought, a broad river flowing with unobtrusive speed calmly: you might sink, swim, build a boat, try to drink up all the water, but this made no difference at all to the river, which continued to move and be still in its own time, and was the same and never the same. But her conviction that this was so could not in the least prevent her from trying to make life come to a decision, to take a final choice, to do (she said once) something *absolute.*

"Everything absolute belongs to death."

"I don't give a damn."

She no longer knew how to fill a day, how to pass the time. A day was so long, when one did nothing, when there was nothing one wanted very much to do. Left alone she would go, even in the morning, to movies, where she would sit in the dark and watch the images pass of desire, honor, ambition: all that millions of people were inspired to think was necessary, proper, attainable for the good life; and Susan, though she felt occasionally a flicker of interest in the monster faces and bodies on the screen, was sunken for the most part in apathy.

It sometimes happened that she arrived at a theatre just after it opened, and had as a result to sit in the prayerful, electric gloom of the auditorium with perhaps as many as eight or ten people, played upon by much-amplified, syrupy music. She was at such times filled with contempt, for herself and for these others, whom she hated because so evidently like herself they had *nothing to do* (the radical crime against society); they all seemed to be sinners of the most vicious yet abject sort, seated in the vast antechamber of a confessional and whipped into the proper mood by this sugared nonsense, doubled in octaves all along the line, the largest mechanical coupled with the smallest aesthetic effect, by which some weird and wealthy priesthood secured the necessary dissolution of the faculties. The golden, grotesque ornamentation of the theatre hung in gloom and distance overhead, with in one instance a roof painted to simulate the night sky with stars; everything, even Susan's shame and hatred of the place, had a cosmic vulgarity—not only pretending to be what it was not, but theatrically suggesting in its pretense that the real thing might be after all very little better, quite easily imitable and hardly more "real." The Kingdom of Heaven, the Garden of Eden, the Golden Age, all would resemble this rococo womb with its wooden cupids flaking bronze paint.

Then, with a fanfare multiplied in volume as the lights went

1 1 6

down, the curtains parted, swishing the first images into folds, and Susan was alone in the darkness with the public dream, the sub-erotic fancy which included the new black Buick, the large sum of money, the desirable virgin in her sacrificial costumes with her ultimate ambition of singing in a cabaret and having at the same time and on her own terms the handsome, woolly-headed, much-masculined lamb to whom a vestigial plot had umbilically attached her. The entire show was generally so inartistic as to be almost lifelike, and Susan wondered vaguely where all the actors went after the light faded, whether they were not condemned in punishment to continue in their hard-won and gimcrack fortune.

To come out, afterwards, to the brilliance of the daylight filled her with shame; she looked back on the movie house with dull horror as a kind of questionable narcotic therapy for some shameful disease of the soul; and she took the habit, at such times, of going to some quiet bar for a drink.

It seemed to her that under Edmond's aegis she had in a very short while, only a few weeks, grown from comparative girlhood by a number of easy yet sacrificial steps to adult customs and ways; the new freedom here implied did not correspond in any manner to maturation and discovery or to the evolution of some new law for her life; rather it demonstrated with something like enthusiasm or abandon life's seemingly infinite capacity and potential for regressing, putting away decision, allowing each fresh step toward novelty to open another broad vista in which the eye could find nothing worth the attention. She came to look upon the surrender of her chastity (putting it that way) as the price of admission to a wasteland. And she could no longer secure the exact sequence of feelings that had given her to Edmond, a middle-aged man who was no more, perhaps, than "interesting."

She was secretly ashamed to discover in herself an amazing

strength of lust, a sensual virtuosity of imagination that Edmond for the most part could more provoke than sate. He began to be, she noticed, just slightly timid of her now and again; her slight pleasure in this was offset by embarrassment and shame.

Since the departure of her parents, Susan was able freely to draw upon considerable funds marked for household expenses, clothes, etc. She was accountable for the time being only to Claire, who showed no signs of ever wanting an account. Susan remarked that Edmond was becoming ever so slightly more foppish and particular, and she suspected he thought himself, to however small extent, kept. She had indeed begun, as a sign of her new independence (or, regarded in another light, her new servitude), occasionally to pay checks for drinks or dinner. Edmond affected to resent this, really resenting perhaps the waiter's hardly concealed smile.

Ironically, the most unhappy times of all were those for which she had as she thought taken up this new life. Edmond regarded her bed, in his rather sybaritical and discriminating fashion, only in part as the haunt of fleshly pleasure; it was also, in somewhat larger part and like most any other place, a forum for the production of that all but incessant monologue which was perhaps his strongest attachment to life.

Now, as they were lying together, naked and somewhat sick of one another, for the moment at least, smoking cigarettes which they stubbed out in an ash tray between them (ashes scattered on the twisted sheets), Edmond continued to talk about death, in particular and in general as his habit was.

The baptism of the dead was, it appeared, one of the least curious death-customs he could draw up from some private museum in the depths: there were actually, it seemed, people who danced on their friends' graves by way of funeral ceremony; they did it to tamp down the earth. A tribe in Venezuela confessed that they buried their dead only to get them out of the way; an indifference shocking to Christian ethnologists, who would not dare to use (said Edmond) quite that frankness about their own dead.

But indifference to the body corresponded on the other hand to passionate concern for the soul, whatever that was. Among the Hurons it was the exact replica in miniature of a man; similarly with the Nootkas, for whom it is located in the crown of the head, where it must unsleepingly stand erect if its possessor is to continue in health. The soul is an egg, a wind, a white bird, a butterfly. Even better, your shadow is your soul, and terribly exposed too. The Basutos believe that crocodiles can eat the shadow of a man when it is cast on the surface of water; and many people even now cover the mirrors when death is in the house.

Susan yawned openly. Edmond's talk, so long as it could be understood as primarily attacking her virtue and only in the second place sowing information, had been acceptable enough, a flattering attention. Now, however, it became a bore.

"The Romans had the custom," Edmond said, continuing, "of making the heir inhale the dying breath . . ."

"Oh, damn these tags and scraps." Susan sat up. "Take me out of here. Take me some place where people look as though they're having a good time."

"Now?"

"Oh, no, not now. Next week maybe, when you finish the next sentence. Whenever it penetrates your skull that I'm bored."

"It's eleven-thirty." Edmond looked dubious.

"That's a good reason." Susan was elaborately sarcastic. "It's eleven-thirty. Life must stop because it's eleven-thirty. You can lie among the ashes all night if you like, but I'm going out."

"Very well, we go out." Slowly and in silence they began to dress.

There was a tedious routine they had for getting out of

Susan's room unobserved—one of their few concessions to caution. Susan went first to ascertain as casually as possible that no one was about in the upper hall or on the stair. Then she returned, Edmond went downstairs and let himself out; she followed in five minutes.

Tonight Edmond had the bad luck to meet Claire in the front hall. He said good evening with the utmost politeness. Claire coldly stared at him.

"Are you my sister's lover?" she asked when he had got his hand on the door.

"Certainly not," he said with the air of one who resents, who will bear tales, who *knows what to think* of such a gross imputation. "Are you mad?"

"I think you are lying," Claire said. He turned, came back and stood facing her.

"We know," he began, "that it is always a part of Christian virtue to think the worst—without the worst there could be no Christian virtue."

"Is that an admission?"

"It is not."

Claire turned away from him.

"I know you're lying," she said, standing with bent head and speaking as if to herself. "I don't know what I can do. You will make her very unhappy."

"May she not decide about that for herself?"

"Evidently she has. Are not you unhappy as well?"

"I?" Dr Einman was surprised. "No, I am not unhappy, not more than always."

"But unhappiness is not what matters," Claire said. "What you're doing is wrong. You can't defend it."

"Defend it? I have not admitted doing it."

"Please stop fencing, Doctor," Claire cried in exasperation. "I am not blind, and I have accused you rightly. You have seduced my sister, and I think it must have been because you hate not love her."

"A keen *apperçu*, Mademoiselle," said Dr Einman with a bow. "But bad luck—it is absolutely false." He drew himself up a little and with some dignity said, "Susan is my patient. This was to have remained a secret. Though I suppose you have a right to know, if anyone does."

"That is unlikely," Claire said scornfully. "How stupid—to try to impose on me with that. Every time you lie you hurt yourself more."

"These outmoded ethical psychologies." Dr Einman sneered. "Your primer-school observations are of no interest to me. I have told you what there is to tell. Perhaps if you continue to snoop here and there with great diligence you may also discover why your sister is in my hands for treatment."

"Now that will be enough."

"I should have thought it more than enough," Susan cried from the head of the stair.

In silence they watched her descend slowly and regally, like a person in a play. When she reached the foot she paused, then walked toward Claire.

"Now what is it you want to know about me?" she asked, with such precision of tone that Claire became somewhat abashed and even slightly frightened.

"Are you Dr Einman's patient?" was the way in which, after a long moment, she phrased her question.

"Yes." Dr Einman enforced Susan's answer by a somewhat important nod of the head.

"What is your—sickness?" Claire asked.

"That is my business, I'm afraid—and the doctor's." A smile came to Susan's face. "It's nothing serious, if that will reassure you."

"Susan," Claire said. "I must know."

1 2 1

"And why must you know?"

"Because I feel partly responsible."

"Because, you mean, you feel I'm a complete slut?"

"Susan! that's not so."

"I hope you don't imagine," Susan said, "that I didn't hear you quite distinctly from upstairs. If you didn't say 'slut' it was only from some innate delicacy of language—the sentiment seemed to be there." Her studied, exact, even mincing phrases contrasted strangely with the tension of her demeanor as she faced her sister; she stood rigidly, and her whole body seemed to shake with a suppressed trembling. "You may just as well make your little speech to my face," she concluded.

"Susan," said Dr Einman, raising a professional and warning hand. "You are not to excite yourself over this." He was becoming rather enjoyably frightened. A scene between two women could be, he felt, a most annoying scene; but he took at the same time a certain pleasure from Susan's dramatic and arrogant behavior in this situation.

Claire saw that her entire action was compromised by Susan's resolute countering; there was nothing for it but to go on.

"I asked if you were having an affair with this man," she said. "He has denied it in several different ways. Now I'm asking you."

"I'm afraid that too is my business, Claire. If you can't accept the word of my friend, especially as he's my doctor, I don't see anything for it but to drop the subject. Unless of course you'd like to apologize."

"Apologize. Oh, Susan, of course I'd apologize. If you'd just say one word . . ." Claire showed signs of wanting to cry.

"What word shall I say? You've been answered, haven't you?"

"Susan, I love you very much. I don't want you to hurt yourself."

"The Voice of Experience?" Susan inquired in a cold tone. "What you're doing with this man is shameful and wrong." "She who is without sin is now casting the first stone." "All right, then. I don't know what to do." Claire folded her hands together and wrung them as though twisting some invisible material. Her face looked tired. "You've hardened your heart against me, Susan."

"Please don't quote things at me."

"Ladies, ladies," said Dr Einman, ridiculously deploring with outspread hands in the manner of a bartender.

"Oh, you." Susan noticed him roughly, her temper overflowing. "Why not take me out of here instead of enjoying yourself so much?"

They left while Claire stood silently watching them. Later, in the dark corner of a bar, Susan began to weep quietly and hysterically. Edmond held her hand and felt helpless. She had several drinks without stopping her tears and inarticulate whisperings, from which the only speech that emerged was the reiterated question, "What do you really think of me? What do you really think?"

2

CLAIRE, when they had gone, went to her room. She had up there a prie-dieu, eighteenth century, French, which she had recently lugged from a corner of the library. As a machine of worship it was very efficient-looking, with pads for one's knees and a rest for the clasped hands, the bowed head. One got into position much as the pilot is strapped into the cramped kingdom of his power. Father Meretruce, on his latest visit, had smiled at the piece and said nothing.

Now Claire carried it downstairs again; she thought it a vanity. Returned to her room she went on her knees, choosing a bare portion of the floor away from any furniture that might provide support.

Prayer, Father Meretruce had said, was like the child's game in which you fall backwards and your friend catches you; a certain courage was implied, for falling backwards is an action calculated to elicit a great protest from the will. To be successful you must have faith in your friend, in his strength and willingness to save you from hitting the ground. In the case of prayer, however, you did not even look around to see if your friend was disposed to play this particular game, or even if he was in the room: simply you fell backwards. "Only by the knowledge of your safety, only by admitting you are in the hand of God, can you bring yourself to the difficult action of prayer."

All prayer paradoxically began with Hamlet's proposition: "Now I am alone" and proceeded, ideally, to the knowledge that one is never alone. Of the preliminary steps the focus of the mind was most important; the eyes to be fixed upon some object not necessarily of religious significance, the mouth to repeat and reiterate, not to discourse upon, some formula, the reason to cease from its work, the attention to be purely directed by love to God. "There is a certain edge which one passes over," the priest had said. "Until then the most of prayer is pain in the knees."

Claire was not long in discovering the truth of this statement; why it should be so no one knew, but it appeared by numerous witnesses that physical discomfort, even physical pain, aided in the way of perfection; that the effort not to regard such things was in itself a powerful incitement to the spirit.

What thing should we pray for? There was some question about this. Many had said that nothing could be found wrong with simple petitionary prayer as preached by the Son when he taught us to say: Pater noster qui es in caelis, etc. And to those who suggested, generally with a slight sneer, that to ask

1 2 4

for one's daily bread and so forth was to treat God as a shop-keeper, it might be replied that this showed at any rate more humility than that highly pious attitude of going down on the knees in the expectation that something important is about to happen, as a revelation, a vision, voices. There were fundamentally two kinds of Catholic (the priest was somewhat given to these epigrammatic distinctions): those who meditate on the sins of others, and those who meditate on their own sins. The former had, obviously, some affinities with the humanist heresies, since one prayed to God *for the purpose* of making the world a better place: which was a nonsense. The latter followed the way of the great mystics, of Saint Teresa, of Saint John of the Cross, of Tauler, of Eckhardt, of Saint Anthony—which was a way, also, fraught with the perils of arrogance, presumption, spiritual pride.

It would not be too irreverent, unhappily, to say that in prayer, as in other things, there were fashions and schools of thought: primitive, baroque (and even rococo), classical, neoromantic, modern, etc. On the whole it seemed best to say in everything: Our peace in Thy will.

One prayed, that is, for the power to accept.

Claire said now the Pater Noster; then chose a phrase: *So then it is not of him that willeth, nor of him that runneth, but of God that sheweth mercy.*

In some ten minutes time her knees and back began to pulse rhythmically with pain; she suited her words bitterly to this rhythm. Moreover, she had reached that phase of concentration intermingled with diffusion of spirit and senses at which it was possible easily (she had been warned, and knew already from her slight experience) to feel a perfect fool and break the whole pattern: for concentration is not reasonable, not discursively convincing, runs near (in fact) to idiocy and unconsciousness. If this feeling, that one was being merely stupid and silly, merely repeating an empty form of words (and one was), were a temptation from Hell, the Father had said, a minor and incompetent devil had been sent on the business; for the feeling would pass in a few moments if one sturdily disregarded it. It did pass.

Claire felt her heart begin to beat more rapidly; she did not know why; and heart-beat with the beat of pain set up a counterpoint which merged and divided in long streams through her whole frame.

So then it is not of him that willeth, nor of him that runneth, but of God that sheweth mercy.

An absolute of concentration could be achieved, Father Meretruce had said, but the whole effort here must be to deny oneself any expectation of it, any image, any surmise, any *idea.* Like a child's wish, if you thought about it you had lost it.

There was now no question any longer of meaning, or reason: the words of Paul slipped by like beads between the fingers, then fled silently by like a white road under the turning wheel. It was the purpose of pain at this time to absorb into its long curving waves all accidental, erratic feelings and reflections, to provide a thorough-bass of the whole body, to which divinity might, if He chose, write His theme in His own signature.

So then it is not of him that willeth . . .

Weariness and pain here passed away, as though she had in some small boat for hours taken the surge and beat of the open ocean to sail now into a harbor of which the water was like glass in sunlight and no wind was to be felt. A sweet and langorous exhaustion of the senses, a calm openness to what might be, on the new shore she seemed to approach.

. . . nor of him that runneth . . .

In the hushed glade, in the still dark hour that heralds the splendid rising of the sun, she seemed to kneel for a last age of seconds, with all about her the holy humming of the silence of God's approach; she knew now the cold, final lust for God that the purified heart holds, and knew as if she had most potently commanded it, the certainty of His coming. At such a moment, Meister Eckhardt had said, God in his omnipotence must bow His head and obey the soul's infinite love; He may not resist but must perforce stream boundlessly into the place which has been prepared for Him. The image appeared to Claire of Christ hanging upon the Cross: his head lolled shamefully forward, his brow bled under the thorns, she felt throughout her body the surge and strain of his weight, his life, upon the bloodied nails in his hands. The image had the duration of a moment only; resolutely she blinded her mind against all regret, turning the wheel of the Word.

. . . *but of God that sheweth mercy.*

The clear light of the Void, the Nameless and Imageless, the Father, The Son, the Holy Spirit—who could have said what appeared? For Claire it was the instantaneous spread of light in the center of her mind, together with impressions of tremendous majesty, a light so white and blinding that our earthly robes seemed by contrast tarred and defiled. In agony and love she saw this light glitter and gleam in brilliant flashes through her spine and head, unbearable in intensity, so that she wished and did not wish for the end. The light like thunder echoed in the circle of her mind, played in fitful coruscations among the gray, coiling masses of her brain, so that she seemed to see by flashes of utter radiance her own essence, that which slept and that which waked, its purities and its corruptions, the carbon and the many-faceted diamond.

Her love at this instant terrified her with its strength; she felt as if she were bleeding inwardly under a terrible pressure that would stop if she willed it, but she was powerless.

So then it is not of him that willeth, nor of him that runneth, but of God that sheweth mercy.

Eternity had endured for perhaps the duration of one phrase. She was staring at the crossed bars of her window, which seemed still to glimmer with the last fitful cadences of light; her clasped fingers were rigidly entwined, and numb. Pain flowed back into her awareness as if moaning through her limbs, as if threading her back through the outermost planets and into time again, into the circle of the clock's face and the dance which is our life.

She felt, primarily, the peaceful remembrance of peace, an ebbing of the tide of glory that sank past the rising tide of pain and painful fatigue; and felt too a vast consolation that touched and softened even the stupid light and the hard furnishings of her room.

In the last moments of her continuing consciousness, she thanked God. It would be easy, she knew, to live thenceforth in a world, a creation, of which the indestructible core was love; it would be easy (for in her unworthiness and abasement she had been given the proof) to accept the surfaces and the depths of life in holy charity and holy humbleness, for did she not know that all men were in the hand of God, that His power behind the thin screen of appearance buoyed up the world and life easily, as a father holds his child on his knee? And the marvelous strength and sweetness of that word, *Know*, which would make supportable every mischance, every doubt.

"I *know* that my Redeemer liveth, and will stand at the latter day upon the earth."

She had been on her knees for more than three hours. Soon now it would be dawn. Pain and weariness overcame her, for she was still kneeling. She fell forward to the floor and slept.

It was at about this time that Susan came home. She was alone, and sufficiently drunk. Hogan, who had apparently conceived it a duty or a potential pleasure, had waited up, napping in an oaken chair beside the door.

"It's very late, Miss," he remarked, not perhaps with insolence but certainly with some intent to infringe on the proper bounds; he had not, after all, been asked what time it was, or whether it was very late.

"I know," said Susan. She took off her coat and rather dejectedly began trailing it behind her as she started upstairs.

"Excuse me, Miss Susan," Hogan said, getting up and following. "I've been meaning to talk to you."

"About . . . ?" Susan turned on the lowest step and faced him.

"About your habits, Miss. About your habits and your hours. I know your Pa and Ma wouldn't like the way you go gadding out."

"Hogan, is this an hour for the trusted family retainer act?"

"No time like the present, Miss," Hogan complacently replied.

"And you want to call my attention to my fast life?" asked Susan in an edgy voice.

"You're not behaving the way any daughter of mine would."

"Well, as I am not by some providence any daughter of yours, Hogan, I should say my behavior was about ninety per cent my business and damnall of yours."

"I feel, Miss it's my responsibility to make it my business. If I was to tell your Ma this Dr Einman was just about living in your room, and when I go to make up the bed . . ."

Susan slapped the man smartly across the mouth.

"It's almost daylight now," she said. "Take two weeks pay and get out before the sun comes up." She began to look in her pocketbook for money.

"Now, Miss Susan." Hogan put his face very close to hers. "I didn't say I would have to tell anybody." He took the money she offered him and counted it. "It's not enough," he said gently. "Not nearly enough."

Susan stared at him.

"I'm goddamned if I will." She turned and started up the stairs.

"But you will think about it?" she heard him say from below, in a mock-pleading tone that carried a good deal of confidence. She did not answer. When she got into her room she locked the door. Undressed and in bed she pulled the sheets up over her head. This cannot be happening to me, she thought.

There came a knock on the door.

"Good night, Miss," said Hogan, who had doubtless seen illustrated in movies the efficacy of persistently haunting the proposed victim. "Sleep well."

Susan shuddered and nestled into the wretchedly crumpled covers. She felt something small, hard and uncomfortable under her shoulder. It turned out to be a twisted-up cigarette butt.

The sky began to gray. Presently the sun would suggest his pallid and shrill presence through the damp fog that had come from the Atlantic and now hung quiet over Boston. Susan would watch with dull eyes, unsleeping, for several hours.

*F*ATHER MERETRUCE was not much impressed. He sat with bowed head before the window through which the afternoon sun shone, and stared meditatively at the spot on which Claire had a few hours since knelt. Claire concluded her recital with the statement that she wished, now, to undergo the forms of conversion as quickly as possible.

"And do you wish to be canonized now," he asked with a certain deliberate vulgarity, "or will you wait?"

Claire was shocked. The possibility of such a reception had not occurred to her.

"How can you joke about such things? Don't you believe me?"

"And if I believed you," he imperturbably replied, "there is still the question (as you yourself once suggested, on the night we first met) of what, exactly, I would be believing. After all—a great light—thundering—love—agony: understand that, quite apart from whether or not you saw something—and quite apart, too, from the methods, stimuli, et cetera, by which you came to see—the fundamental thing for the Church is still *what* did you see. You will not, I hope, think ill of me for suggesting that the experience you describe could serve the turn equally well of Manichaeism, Buddhism, any number of tribal religions or that hotch-potch re-assembled by Richard Wagner which is now so prominent in Germany.

"The Church of Christ believes—or presumes, if you like that better—that its definition, its explicit and much refined definition of reality, is not merely mythoplastic, not merely a charming story—but simply and only the truth. It is the right representation by words, images, thought, of what *really is*, the *adequatio rei et intellectus*. And inasmuch as the truth is One, we beg leave to deny any other truth.

"There," he continued, seeing how disturbed Claire was becoming. "I mean to discourage you, you see, but not entirely; it seems sometimes, and may be so, that even the one genuine spark may produce billows of nonsensical smoke. You understand, don't you, how careful you must be, how this may be our old subtle foe's best weapon against you?"

"You mean the Devil?" incredulously cried Claire, whose upbringing had included the concept but not the person of evil.

"The Roman Catholic Church remains singular among Christian professions," the priest replied, smiling with some little malice, "not in recognizing the existence of Satan—for many do that—but in continuing to believe that Satan is evil, even after so many centuries during which it has been, as they say, 'proved' that he is merely 'interesting.' I do mean the Devil, and I ask you to consider the possibility with your best attention."

Claire was rapidly formulating the notion that the priest might be *jealous*.

"For example," he went on, "I see that already, since I have made bold to correct you, your demeanor to me has become notably unsubmissive—a not untypical reaction of the born Protestant to authority—and that when I tell you, as I must, that you stand very near to the deadliest sin of *superbia*, you will laugh in your heart and *think you know better*. To speak clearly, and as to a daughter, already, of the Church, let me tell you that the one is sin and the other is to aggravate sin; and you must chasten yourself to accept correction."

The priest looked at her steadily, and Claire abased her eyes. She was tired, looked worn about the eyes, and her temper was not of the best at this instant. Nevertheless, "I bow myself," she said in a voice hushed with reverence that tried unsuccessfully to compensate for the mocking character of the phrase. This struggle did not escape the priest's attention.

"As for your project of becoming baptized at once in the Roman Communion," he said, "let me strongly advise you to put this off until you have brought yourself to a real repentance and a real submission. I know this interview must have been a shock to your faith, and so I will accept for this moment your apology, without however pretending to be deceived. Think of this: that baptism, if your heart is purified, abolishes your past sins and constitutes you for that moment holy. To be weak in faith and after that relapse into some disobedience and into pride, would be a tragedy I am anxious to avoid."

How like a dentist he is, after all, Claire thought (that this wisdom tooth should become impacted is a tragedy I am anxious to avoid).

"In earlier days, many were so anxious to avoid such a fall from new grace that they refused baptism until they were on their death-beds, remaining catechumens all their lives. I do not recommend that to you, but I offer it as an illustration of the real danger in which you proposed placing yourself."

Is it real, or unreal? Does God exist? If He exists, must one subscribe to this church, this vast mumbling telephone exchange by means of which one communicates with God only through officious persons? Claire rebelliously asked herself these questions, and said nothing.

"Recognize your danger. Say to yourself: 'I have been proud, haughty, stiff-necked.' Pray for humility, submission and obedience. Put it to yourself that disobedience is spiritual unchastity."

There followed considerably more in the same strain, while Claire kept thinking: perhaps I'll feel differently tomorrow. For moments during the priest's exhortation she wondered: do I believe in God?

As the priest rose to take his leave he remembered something.

"There are two nuns," he said, "sisters of a European Order of Charity, who are now sitting on a bench in South Station waiting room. The diocese has no room for them at present— they arrived somewhat unexpectedly, fugitives from the Nazis. You have a large and all but empty house here, and I ask you, from the Bishop, if you would be good enough to put them up here for perhaps a week until we can have them moved."

Claire did not know what to say; in her somewhat compromised position she would not show a lack of charity; she acquiesced at once and with no enthusiasm.

"Good. The diocese will of course pay a nominal rent."

"That will not be necessary," Claire sadly replied.

"Ah, but it will. The Bishop does not wish to put himself in the position of forcibly extracting charity, especially from a non-Catholic."

"The charity is not forced but given."

"Ah? Ah, of course. May I use your telephone?"

There followed a long conversation, full of somewhat ceremonious phrases such as "How His Excellency will be pleased," "His Excellency has been looking for a place since this morning," "convey my respects to His Excellency." How unreal! Claire thought in a spasm of temper. Like a little monarchy.

"They will be here in half an hour," said Father Meretruce, turning from the phone. "I have never met them, of course, but you could not do better, I think, than *take lessons* in humility from the sisters of a charitable order." And on this, with a rather severe look, he went out the door.

Claire's mind was in turmoil. Her mystical or quasi-mystical experience, no longer, when she awakened, clear in her head (though that it had happened she could entertain no doubt), had not the effect of producing an entirely charitable outlook upon the world. She was physically exhausted still, and felt as though she had a slight fever. Her priest, moreover, had turned on her (she had in her prayer followed his instructions) in an inexplicable and seemingly unmotivated way.

And now these nuns. What would Susan say? Claire frowned, remembering Susan, who had come down from her room early in the afternoon and gone out, silent.

Claire went back to her room and read for half an hour, in Latin. The text was Richard of Saint Victor's, the subject, his regimen for monasteries. The brothers, he said, should not paddle their fingers in the broth, searching for meat. They should not wipe their fingers after meals upon their cassocks. They should not blow their noses into their cassocks. It was improper to spit in church, but especially improper to spit during the Mass, and a sin to spit in the holy water. Claire shut the book.

At five-thirty the two nuns arrived in a black Cadillac sedan, accompanied by a young priest with eczema, who sat stiffly in front beside the chauffeur, a lay person.

One of the women was about fifty, a frightful hag; the other was perhaps thirty and not unhandsome, though swarthy and with coarse hair which strayed from under her wimple. Neither had any luggage. Their robes were filthy.

"They seem to be under some sort of vow of silence," the priest told Claire. "It's not one of the rules of their Order, so it is probably penitential; they are very holy, I'm told. Of course it may be customary on a journey, though I can't think how they got tickets and so on. Anyhow," he said, "no one knows, as they won't say, when this period of silence will end, or for that matter what language they will speak or what part of Europe they've come from."

"Do they bathe?" Claire asked, but the priest only frowned. The two nuns, while he spoke, stood there in their black voluminous rags.

The priest gave Hogan instructions for their keep. "Yogurt and black bread *only*," he said with emphasis. "Those are the instructions that were forwarded to His Excellency from Lisbon."

The nuns were given one small room on the third floor. The beds and other furniture were removed, and two sufficiently thin mattresses were discovered in storage in the basement and provided with old blankets.

Susan came in for supper (the first time in perhaps a week) and Claire explained the presence of the Sisters of Charity, who had not, however, put in a further appearance.

"Jesus Christ, what next?" was Susan's comment. She seemed to have recovered some humor, some resilience, in however offensive a form (to her sister) this might be expressed. But all her animus against Claire seemed forgotten, and Claire thought she could herself do no better than likewise to forget, or seem to.

The nuns immediately proved rather a nuisance. Yogurt and black bread, it appeared, were expensive, and procurable only from a shop far out in Brookline, which promised however to bring supplies to the house for a slight extra charge. Then the sisters did not comprehend the use of the bathroom, and appropriated instead a large Chinese vase of a bad period which, when full, they deposited tactfully outside the kitchen door, where Hogan at once tripped over it.

It would be difficult, also, to provide them with a change of clothes. Their own, inimitably constructed more or less like a number of interwoven balloon-spinnakers, would evidently not last long and, moreover, were lousy. But it was beyond the patience of anyone in the house to convey to the sisters that they were to take these garments off and temporarily accept a less austere costume while Mrs Purse studied out and sewed, in blackout curtain material, the duplicates. It seemed that the sisters never took off these clothes, even to sleep.

Susan got out some port and with sudden inspiration offered it to the nuns. It was the first gesture they understood, and they accepted smilingly. The empty bottle was put in the hall outside their door some twenty minutes later.

That night they prayed antiphonally from ten till past midnight. The sound was not loud but it was audible through almost any part of the house. Mrs Purse told Claire that she was a religious woman herself, but she was damned if she could see that kind of stuff. "Them chants," she said dismally.

Of course it is not physically beautiful, Claire told herself. It has not the wretched beauty of the World—it is of the Holy Spirit, and the earth for them is a place of passage.

Nevertheless, though with some sense of shame and unworthiness, she bathed and scrubbed herself thoroughly before retiring, and searched the sheets for lice.

2

EDMOND was compiling facts. The eyeshade drawn low over his brows threw a green glare on the drawing board, on the white foolscap sheets along which crawled the neat illegibilities of Mr K——, Mrs O——, Miss B——, their lusts and fears, their trivial discoveries about the world, their unquestioned superstitions about contraception, about drinking coffee before bed, about the Holy Ghost, about stepping on lines or stepping only on squares. How so much contradictory junk could live together in one head was a never-failing wonder.

But it was Life. Edmond liked to delude himself as well as others with the somewhat alchemical notion that the answer lay somewhere within reach, that he was a man in a dark room fumbling for a light switch whose approximate location he felt he knew, that the next fortuitous re-arrangement of the elements, or the next but one, would flood the world with final light. He doubtless knew this for illusion, but it was the one on which he elected to proceed—it was the fundamental romantic gesture which made irony of everything else. Since he never really intended that the book, *Eros and Agape*, should be finished—for how could the Book of Life be finished—he had a beautiful patience with it and with himself, and no anxiety: he was at no time happier than during these hours of fastidious and careful annotation.

John Averist sat in the deep chair watching Edmond bent over the tilted drawing board. He generally seemed to derive some vague consolation from the spectacle; but tonight a supercilious half-smile, which deepened whenever Edmond paused or seemed about to look up, suggested that he wished to be noticed, and that if he thought of an opening clever enough he would interrupt. He wanted to talk about Susan, and was beginning to realize that Edmond knew this.

Secular nature of Agape, Edmond wrote. *The benediction of circumstances crowning effort. The bourgeois notion that the world meets one halfway. e.g., "There are plenty of jobs if you have the guts to go out and find them." But the Eros and the gut decay. Let Fortune turn her wheel, etc. The attitude of the man who neither spins the wheel nor falls under it, who knows his Karma to be no more than the sum of his mind, and what*

1 3 8

he really wants, therefore deserves. Equilibrium, and none . . .

"You're writing about Susan Boyne?"

. . . of this nonsense about passion, Edmond patiently wrote before replying: "That was a bad guess." In love, surrender accomplishes the assault and perfects the same; grace descends upon the issue of bonds, and makes possible the victory dinner, the prize for the best salesman, the gold watch presented with a speech. Vulgarity of success.

"What do you think of her?"

Necessity of partial success, necessity of tension; amusement derived from "situations." Edmond pushed the green shade up on his forehead.

"You are interrupting," he said.

"I know it."

"You mean you want to talk about this woman?"

"Yes."

"Go ahead then." Edmond threw down his pen in a gesture of studied impatience; it was characteristic of him that he had made, subjectively, the pace of life so slow—there was, for him, so much time—that no real impatience marred the conventionalized expression which was no more than a shifting of gears in his attention.

"Have you seduced her yet?"

"This knowledge is supremely important to you at this instant?"

Averist hesitated, uncertain how to answer.

"I admit it's none of my business, really," he said feebly.

"But . . ." Edmond supplied. "You are now on the threshold of making it your business." He turned to stare at the younger man. "Yes, I have been successful. Would you care for an intimate description, or do you merely wish to make remarks about my character or my age?"

"On the contrary, let me congratulate you," Averist said with a cinematic urbanity that could not disguise a slight tremor possibly of hatred.

"You have, maybe, some romantic feelings on this subject?"

"I have nothing," Averist replied.

"Only your envy, no?"

"I admit to a certain respect for your achievement."

"It was not hard," Edmond said with European modesty. "The readiness is all."

"I suppose now she will become more and more unhappy until she is a patient."

"Anything is possible."

"I admire the economy of your system," Averist said. "The patient becomes the mistress and the mistress becomes the patient—caught between the phallus and the caduceus the suffering ladies are rounded like butterballs, they confess on Tuesday to Father Einman that on Monday they sinned with dear old Ed, to the corruption of the body and the purification of the soul; dear Edmond, you are like a digestive system entire in yourself: you eat the dainty foods and you unflinchingly accept the filth to which you transmute them. The reversed alchemist: *per peristalsis ad rectum . . .*"

"John, please," sharply said Dr Einman. "Don't make dirty metaphors."

". . . saving Your Reverence." John Averist bowed slightly. "I was carried away by my enthusiasm. I am stricken with admiration," he went theatrically on, "and fiercely, as they say, desirous of emulation. Isn't there some final stunt whereby you convert them into virgins and begin again, or restore their lost youth, or resurrect the dead?"

"Very funny," Edmond observed. "I suggested, when I asked you if you'd like to live here, that you'd have to put up with my habits, which I didn't and don't intend changing. That policy worked for some time, and now it seems likely not to work much longer. Well. When my behavior becomes too disgusting for you to bear, let me propose you go elsewhere—there are enough women in the world, and you may treat them in whatever way you think gallant and proper, while I beg leave to go about my business as usual.

"I don't care that you do nothing whatever but drink," he continued. "Nor that as a private tutor you are so private as to have no pupils at all. I say to myself, 'He prefers it that way, and if I wish to have him around (and I do, John, I like you) I too must prefer it that way. In the same way, he must not interfere with me.'"

Upon this Edmond picked up his pen and, as Averist made no reply, worked in silence for some minutes. Once, with a sidelong glance, he said, "Of course, if you're in love with this girl . . ." but did not finish the sentence and continued anyhow to write.

Presently John Averist got up and went out. Twenty minutes' slow walking brought him to the narrow, shaded street upon which stood the Boyne house. Now, late in April, the green leaves, the sharp yellow of the lamps, the silent houses, made a melancholy and charming picture. But as he approached his destination he heard a kind of mournful plaining from an upper window, and this prayerful, not very harmonious or pleasing lamentation yet pleased him, though he could not know the reason of it, and struck him as poignantly appropriate.

It was the habit of his soul to wallow romantically. He was in love with Susan, he thought, and made of what he proposed to himself as a hopeless passion, together with her obvious accessibility at least to another, something rather special in the way of emotion: he felt at this moment lonely and desperate, yet had at the same time the close apprehension that Susan might open the front door and summon him in. He had the air of one who is giving Fate *one last chance*.

Averist had been a student of history, and one of those persons whom modern society seems to produce with such great regularity: brilliant, erratic and with a vast capacity for self-destruction, melancholy going over into sloth, rational despair, etc. Graduating a little too early from a small college in Maine, he had gone on to study history at Harvard, but left before completing his doctorate on the Jansenist controversy and the *Provincial Letters*. His parents were both dead, and his small inheritance had completely been spent on his education; when an elegant cynicism proved too thin for warmth and subsistence he dropped the elegance, only in this way distinguishing himself from a hero of Byron's.

The study of history, coupled with an extreme intelligence and a youthful hatred of hypocrisy, had produced in him a terrible and complex disillusion through which he lost whatever of poise and address he may ever have possessed; just as, economically, there had been no slack between him and the hard side of the world, so mentally he had no resilience or power of compromise to make even slightly acceptable the discovery that the best had perished, while the worst, which had survived, was continuously and authoritatively referred to in texts and in the mouths of lecturers as the best.

The time came when he felt choked with the dust and silt of the civilizations he studied; and quietly he moved out of the field. He realized, intellectually, that the extremity of his attitude was a luxury, but this knowledge seemed to make more imperative his wish to remain at extremity; for only by making his personal failure contingent upon the failure of the world (and that the world had, in his sense, failed he could have no doubt) could he find life further supportable. Instead of producing his evidence before learned bodies, he offered the same evidence in bars.

By the time of his meeting with Edmond, he had convinced

himself that he cared for nothing and no one in the world. This stance of mind, not very aggressive but surely defensive against society, had made him also, on the other hand, quite credulous and gullible, especially with women. Where another man with equally few scruples would definitively have entered into competition with Edmond, and quite prosily set about to get in the lee of Susan's virtue, Averist found himself unable to act in any direct and continuous way. In some sort he certainly preferred to lurk as he did now in the leafy shadow of the street and look at the house, whose black reclusive front door with its black lead portico flanked by glazed windows suggested to him the secret charms and possible lasciviousness which, like his mind, it guarded.

While he watched, the door opened and a man came out. He was dressed in black, and for a moment Averist thought him a priest, until he saw there was no clerical collar. The man stood for a few seconds in the light of the open doorway; then pulled to the door behind him and walked away toward Charles Street. Averist, between renewed jealousy and a quite groundless satisfaction that Edmond was unconsciously sharing the prize, debated whether to follow and make some attempt to identify the man.

While he considered, a light came on at the corner of the building, upstairs; and in moving over to view this better he lost track of the man, who must have turned the corner in the darkness.

The light streamed equally from two windows on the second story, the one giving on the street, the other on the courtyard at the side and its exiguous strip of garden, which bore one old and twisted apple tree, still hardly in leaf. Averist saw someone come to each of these windows in turn and throw them open; at the second window he became convinced this person was Susan.

He at once formed the wild project of visiting her by way of the garden wall and one secure-looking bough of the tree. Physically, he thought, it was not in the least infeasible, even for him; and once over the wall he would be well screened from observation.

His resolve produced in him an anxiety so severe he could scarcely breathe for some moments. He scanned the street up and down several times, noting the shy movement of foliage as it shifted the lights and shadows, half-convincing himself he saw people from the corners of his eyes.

What will I do when I get there? he asked himself. She will call the servants? Or simply tell me to leave? Never mind: the gesture will make her think well of me. Even if I am thrown out, entirely unsuccessful, she will find my action attractive later on.

Thus, for the prudent reasons a merchant or banker might have advanced—it will be a loss now, but a good investment for the future—he pulled himself up on the low wall, thence to the trunk of the tree. The mournful singing at this moment stopped, and all was still. He took this for a good omen.

3

THE CAUSE of Susan's comparative gaiety earlier that evening is easy to find but more difficult to justify. It consisted of a thoroughgoing rationalization which reduced Hogan to homuncular proportions, and an assertion of pride that one was perfectly capable of dealing with such a foolish and impotent threat.

First, there was the possibility that the scene with Hogan had not taken place: the hour, her drunkenness and the innate implausibility of the entire affair spoke for this view. One often, she argued, failed in such cases to remember what did happen;

might one not equally manage to remember what did not?

Against the occasionally intrusive suspicion, however, that *something* had occurred at three the previous morning (and that she could quite readily see herself standing on the lowest stair, speaking to Hogan, who was too close and smiling), she advanced the following: A servant became insolent, and I was forced to tick him off. I was effective, if not superb. Without losing my temper, I *did* put him in his place. It is something he'll not forget in a hurry.

About what did he become insolent?

God knows, something about money, most likely. Imagine it! You come in at three in the morning and this stupid man is waiting to talk about money. He should have seen it was not the time.

Did you give him money?

My Lord! I give him money? At that hour? Well, yes, it seems I did. Yes, I gave him two weeks in advance and told him to clear out by daylight. You see, I may be young, but I know how to deal with those people.

And he left?

Well, no. He didn't leave, but . . .

But?

Well, it's over. He asked for money, he got it: now he's pleased. You could see that at dinner this evening. Treat them well, and you get results. Anyhow, it's over, and there's no need to discuss it any further. Besides, it may not have happened at all. You know how I am when I'm a little tight. I imagine things. It's nothing abnormal, many people do it.

Through the cloud she was able to stir up, she still had dimly to perceive trouble, like a pike in a pond, lying at the bottom unmoving. But a still further possibility enabled her to dismiss the sight: she thought she might, if matters became disagreeable, and as the future gained the weight that would make it

1 4 5

present, move away. Quietly go. Say nothing. Live elsewhere. The thought was not frightening in the least; it was on the contrary rather fascinating. She would live in New York.

The fundamental axiom of her whole escape was this: such things do not happen to people like me. And the first theorem which hence proceeded: I shall know how to deal with this situation when the time comes. Theorem two: the time may never come. And the conclusion of the edifice, by proof as labored as any of God's existence, and iterated over and over again: there is no need to worry now.

Now she opened the windows and got into bed. When Susan was a child, her bed had magically each night become a sailboat, with a snug cockpit fashioned after that of a kayak, and extraordinarily secure against other people and the storms which on the world's sea raged all night every night. Tonight, as occasionally, she recalled this legend, and thought it might serve still. She considered Edmond, out there in the ocean; she considered John Averist, Claire, Hogan, the man who had bought her a drink that afternoon at the Lincolnshire. He resembled Victor Mature, and had wanted to take her out for supper, but she had put him off. Another person she considered was Leonora, who had also been at the Lincolnshire, alone.

Leonora seemed to have slipped, if such a thing were possible, considerably. She had been got up with her usual skill, which had, however, more short-comings to disguise than formerly: no amount of scarlet varnish, Susan had thought, could ever replace a good scrubbing of the nails; and when Leonora stood up, her stockings unforgivably wrinkled. She greeted Susan with the enthusiasm of the bore and gossip too long left alone. She was going, she said, to "her" psychiatrist; did Susan think that was too shameful—a psychiatrist, at her age? And she needed a drink terribly, to get her courage up.

Susan resented her sister-in-law's gushing no less than her

assumed familiarity, and replied that age was not the point; "many people go to a psychiatrist before they're thirty." Leonora smiled and said she heard Susan was well up on psychiatry these days.

Leonora, it appeared, had a neurosis. On going up a flight of stairs she received the impression that the banister she held was moving, and moving her along with it, at terrific speed; this sensation made her feel dizzy, so that she at once went to this psychiatrist, who helpfully dignified the situation by naming it (crise d'escalier) and referring it to the departure of her husband and consequent feelings of inferiority among her in-laws. Leonora was already considering what compensation the Boyne's might be brought to offer her for having "caused" this terrible disease; she had not yet stated the case (perhaps not even to herself) in dollars and cents; but she could not get over the notion (she told Susan) that someone owed her something. She would ask the psychiatrist that afternoon if he thought himself prepared to testify . . .

"If you want an expert opinion," Susan had said, "I will give you mine. I think (to use the jargon) that you are overweeningly libidinous about money. Are you running short on that nice allowance?"

Leonora became somewhat disgruntled about this, which was not more than the simple truth, and took her leave.

But now it was night-time, sleep time; the boat was about to sail, and outside the harbor were audible the noises of the storm: slight soughing of wind, the creaking spars of the apple tree at the window. The nuns, she noticed, had left off their incantations. One might sleep. Did Claire, she wondered, pray in her room alone? One supposed she did, but for what? What was worth praying for?

Susan turned out the light and tried to imagine herself praying. The moments before sleep were the most difficult, for then the rationales, the beautiful nervous gaiety, that were possible to maintain for long times during the day, entirely faded. And she was left with the clear sight of her life, which might really be, in the good old Victorian sense, ruined; left with the Hogan problem, which suggested, with academic simplicity, that no solution was to be had anywhere; and left with the knowledge that it had all, really, happened, and that time would not allow any of it to be erased.

Our Father in Heaven, she thought with little conviction. Zeus, Apollo, Dionysus Zagreus, Hermes, Trismegistus . . . Our Father in Heaven.

There came a slight rustling sound, a shifting perhaps of curtains, then a scratching sound, then the sound of breathing. Susan lay very still; perhaps it would go away.

"Susan." The voice was a whisper. "Susan."

She did not answer. Possibly, she thought, this was the secret; everyone, just before death, heard the light whisper calling intimately, calling by first names.

Again the voice whispered, more urgently.

"Miss Boyne. Are you awake?"

Surely Death would not fall back on the formal manner of address? Susan turned on the bedside lamp (the extinction of which a moment before had caused John Averist very nearly to fall into more than consternation).

"My God!" she said. "So it's you. What the hell does this mean?"

His face strained over the sill, at which his hands clutched.

"I've got stuck," he said. "It was further than I thought. If I take my feet off this branch it will swing away."

"Well—climb down again. Good night."

"I can't do that either."

"Do you think offhand of anything you can do?" Susan drew on her robe and came to the window. "I don't know exactly what to suggest," she said, by now rather enjoying the situation. "Are you getting tired?"

"Oh, not at all," he politely replied with somewhat strained sarcasm.

"If I hit you sharply on both hands at once you'd probably drop, wouldn't you?"

"Probably I would." His teeth grated together on this.

She looked at him thoughtfully.

"I suppose I could get you in," she said. "If you made a real effort, and jumped, and I grabbed you by the back of your coat . . ."

"Well then: one—two . . ."

"But I'm not sure I want to. You're very funny as you are."

"Thank you very much. Now will you stop this nonsense and give me a hand?"

"I think, considering the position, you might first apologize for entering my room?"

"I haven't entered your room."

"Oh, you were just passing through?"

"All right, I apologize."

"That's not good enough. I don't like your tone. You must say, 'Susan, I apologize for being a peeping Tom and a sexual opportunist.'"

"Don't be silly."

Susan tentatively began to bend back the little finger of his right hand.

"This may hurt just a little," she said.

"Susan, damn it, don't."

"Apologize."

He made the prescribed submission in full, and Susan clumsily helped him over the sill. He stood in the room sweating and pale.

"Here we are, on my terms," she said. "Now you can march

straight through that door and down the stairs on the left and follow your nose out of the house."

He sat down, or sunk himself, in an armchair, and Susan, with the air of counting the seconds, seated herself on the edge of the bed.

"Susan, are you in love with Ed?"

"With Edmond? Why should that concern you? And I think I mentioned the possibility of your leaving."

"I'll go in a few minutes. But answer my question first."

"You'll go now, my boy. You can write me a letter."

John frowned, but made no move, and seemed to be caught in some debate about his next words:

"Listen, Susan. I love you—very much."

Susan, even while she answered with light mockery—"Indeed, indeed?"—was thoroughly startled and a little touched. His statement, made in a serious voice and with the utmost simplicity (for which she would later a little despise him perhaps), was after all a very high card to be played for the purpose of remaining a few minutes longer in her room.

Dismissing then the merely tactical, strategic purpose must remain—e.g., seduction. Was this in fact the first move in a campaign to be conducted by means of promissory notes? It seemed unlikely.

"So you—love me?" she asked, considering.

"Yes. I'm afraid I do." His tone was horribly apologetic, as though to say: I do not wish to cause you the least inconvenience, but I must somehow have my case brought up and dealt with.

"I should like to marry you," he said, as though apologizing for his entire life. Susan laughed, but somewhat suited the laughter to the occasion: a gentle and slightly melancholy laugh, such as a European actress might use when she is about

1 5 0

to say, "You do not know, my friend," and lay her black-gloved hand across his hand on the café's marble table.

"Do you think I would make you a good wife?" she asked.

"I don't know," he replied. "Does that matter?"

"I suppose it must," Susan said. She was for the moment attracted, as much as anything by the compound of romantic and absurd in the situation, and felt for John Averist an emotion of sweet maternal contempt which would make any kind of equal meeting between them impossible as it would make impossible a permanent or even long-enduring relation of any intimacy; yet, flattered by his abjection, she was moved to some tenderness by her very appreciation of the mortal and fleeting character of her response, her knowledge that the love she might show him would be always the closest possible approach to disdain, and would have always prominent among its elements a slightly mitigated cruelty.

"Do you love Edmond?" he asked again now.

"No," Susan replied.

"Did you, ever?"

Ah, so he knows, then, Susan thought; and he is very anxious to prove that it didn't matter. He would rather think me a tart than a heroine of romance.

"No, I don't think I ever did," she said slowly.

"But you gave yourself to him?" The phrase made Susan want to laugh out loud, but, controlled and modulated, the impulse produced a melancholy and cryptic smile.

"Yes. I did."

Pale and unhappy, he looked at her in silence for a moment or two. It is love's axiom, she thought, that every admission is a place of concealment for some further secret: open sincerity is a sure sign of vile deceit.

"Who was the man who was here tonight?"

"Man? what man?"

"I saw him leave, Susan. I was in the shadows across the street and I saw him come from the front door."

"I suppose it must have been Hogan," she said thoughtfully. "It could only have been Hogan—the butler."

"Oh?"

"Yes." He is wondering if I have lied to him, she thought; he thinks at one and the same time that the man was not the butler, and that I have taken a servant for my lover.

"Could you love me?"

"I've no idea," she said. "If I let myself, though, I suppose I might. It would very much depend on you."

"How do you mean?"

"Come here," she said. "Sit by me."

Slowly he came and sat beside her on the bed. She took his hand and spoke.

"I don't suppose," she said, "that anyone has ever loved me before. I know that I have loved no one. I'm not sure what the word means, to me. Your climbing in my window at night was an attractive idea, and certainly flattering enough; I should be pleased that I have such a—a romantic value. But it was—if you'll forgive my saying so—unpardonably a failure, the whole enterprise. You were ridiculous and you are ridiculous, and while I was replying patiently to your inquisition I thought that it would make no difference to you if I had 'given myself to' the entire population of Harvard University, so long as you were at hand to receive my confession and pretend that everything would be all right. In short, I am not swept off my feet by your proposal. Of course I could 'love' you. I could 'love,' I suppose, anyone; I am reasonable to an almost commercial extent, and I hate to be vowed down to something because this word 'love' has some kind of power over your mind and because you think I am attractive and because therefore you have some idea you'd like to enslave yourself to me."

He made as though to interpose at this point, but she disregarded it and went on.

"Listen, I am in trouble. It's rather serious trouble, and I don't think much can be done about it except to let it work itself out. I am warning you of this as a suggestion to you, to stay away from me. If you truly 'love me,' as you put it, you'd be under the unhappy necessity of saving me, which would not be easy, and we would both probably drop into the mud together. I shouldn't like to think I'd done that to you. So why don't you just go home and forget it?"

"This trouble—is it with Einman?"

"No. Never mind what it is; you can do nothing."

"But Susan, I want to help. I do love you." He kissed her hand.

"Of course," she said, not without malice, "if you could help me through this—difficulty, you might expect to be—rewarded —after whatever romantical fashion you like."

She fell back on the bed and let him lean over to kiss her. After a minute however she pushed him away.

"I don't want you to feel you've been forced, later on," she said. "What you must do will require boldness and—above all— success. The gesture, you see, doesn't interest me. You must carry it through. And you'll have to decide first if I'm worth it to you. After all, as you seem to have discovered, I'm not exactly pure as the driven snow."

"Oh, Susan . . ." he tried to kiss her again. "Darling."

"Time enough for that, my dear prince, after the ogre has been slain. Now listen to me . . ."

When quietly, a few minutes later, she let him out by the street door, he was in the zealous rage of chivalry, albeit a little confused. Susan's manner of driving a bargain, far from cooling his fire, struck sympathetically some deep string of servility and

1 5 3

erotic abasement in him: he was her knight, the fair reward was promised and the task was set.

As a task it seemed difficult, yes; but not so much difficult as dirty, obscure, questionable; in partial service to the lust of others he was to expend the first of his presumably pure faith in his love, and from his casque streamed or depended, as the wind blew, not her silken scarf but the favor of a somewhat soiled yet emblematic dollar bill.

HE REST HOME of Monsalvat overlooked, from a high and lonely eminence in Virginia, the Atlantic Ocean. It was said, and it seemed likely, that the main buildings had been erected by one of the first American millionaires to have returned home after the ill-fated fourth Crusade. A man of vision, he must have seen that Gothic was through; a conservative man, he had not done away with the style entirely, but had satirized it by breaking up its tall lines and mingling with it the seeds of its decay in the shape of onion domes gilt or coppered, and numerous chimneys formed into squat arches from whose shoulders on a cold day the smoke arose. Also the boilers, furnaces, etc., were housed in a cube of red brick a little apart from the buildings they served, and this cube, like a college gymnasium, was a little larger than almost anything else in sight. Nevertheless, from a distance and from certain angles, Monsalvat achieved its effect; seen from seaward, for example, and against a sky lacquered, opaque, blue and set close after the medieval way, the group seemed fairly impressive. And on stormy days its height, on the sheer cliff, allowed it an ominous and sinister dignity.

Monsalvat was not, as Edmond had said, an asylum or sanitarium, but (on the surface at least) a Rest Home, and the forms of mental aberration to which alone it catered were rather philosophic than physical in manifestation. Numerous visitors suffered under the impression that they were God, just as did Nicholas Boyne; but all these gods were with each other equable and unaggressive. Only some of the physicians of the staff occasionally became somewhat queer in their behavior, as the ease and authority with which they controlled such a number of divinities went to their heads and threw them a little off balance.

Of course the successful management of such an establishment depended upon a good deal of discrimination, some of which may have been unfair. Medically, Monsalvat pretended to very little therapy beyond what could be given by fresh air, rest, tranquillity and comfort of surroundings, natural beauty, quiet service and permission to the patient for any belief, however extravagant, so long as it did not in any practical sense affect the community. In order, then, to keep a good record, Monsalvat closed its doors to the violent, the poor, those who extravagantly suffered or did so noisily, and of course to those already moribund from organic affects and deformations of the brain. Nicholas Boyne had barely made it; he might easily have been denied entrance but for the persuasions of Edmond Einman and the fact that he had practically "no history." To have a "good history" or none whatever was one of the first requisites for admission. Further, Mr. Boyne was very nearly not of sufficient age to be admitted into Monsalvat, which catered as much as possible to people over sixty and certainly not under fifty— since, statistically and for the record, it was necessary that as many as possible of those who died should do so for sufficient reason not connected with insanity.

The manager, Dr Ordway, was a fanatic on the subject of diet; he almost compulsively hated the physical deterioration that so often accompanies a pathological apathy of mind; so that he caused the patients, as far as possible, to gorge themselves on little cakes (a speciality of the chef's) which were served at every meal, including tea. Many of the long-term residents came to resemble skeletonless balloons, or the pale blobs of ectoplasm which, in photographs published by occult societies, issue from the mouths of mediums and assume a kind of generalized human shape. But many, despite this regimen, grew gaunt and hopeless-looking, as though the hundreds of fattening little cakes had simply fallen into a bottomless abyss of gloom and despair; these people were, by the patients who (as Dr Ordway said) responded to treatment, regarded with tolerant contempt, perhaps as occupying not enough space to merit the consideration of others who were fatter and thus happier.

Monsalvat may doubtless be accused with reason of catering to the appearance all but exclusively, and neglecting the reality; yet within its narrow boundaries it treated its charges with exemplary kindness and patience. The man, Ordway, was wise, humane, tolerant and absolutely uninterested in Hope; his sad, gray face always expressed a benevolent resignation. If he tried to fatten up the patients, this was not because of any therapeutic value he proposed from such a treatment; it was because he preferred, and thought his clients might prefer, fat moon faces to thin knife faces. "Kindness and harmlessness," he would say, "would ideally be both visceral and cerebral; considering the state of most intellects, both here and in the world, is it any wonder that kindness and harmlessness are entirely visceral virtues?" Also, patients of a certain age, having great bulk totally unsupported by any muscle, seemed to transmute their impassioned despondency into phlegmatic and motionless cheerfulness; and when they died it was quite likely to be through the fatty degeneration of some specialized organ, as the heart. This was not insanity.

Inasmuch as he thought of Monsalvat's regimen as a treatment, Dr Ordway considered it an indoctrination, a gentle introduction, to old age and a peaceful death. Few patients, in his long experience, walked away; most patients, on the other hand, were happy to remain. "Physically," he would tell his staff, "we depend on the slowing down, at the change of life, of the trophic function, and the consequent wasting which makes people easier to handle comfortably; and we follow nature by encouraging the restitution of tissues on a large scale by less highly organized material." He meant the little cakes.

Specifically on the mental side, Dr Ordway personally favored the practice of contemplation, meditation, the performance of yogic exercises calculated to emphasize the transient nature of sangsaric existence and the undesirability of a long continuation in the flesh.

"I do my patients," he said, "the service of keeping them unfit for this world; they can afford it."

He was very successful with the clientele of Monsalvat: he taught them the two chief Yogic postures, the various mudras, the arts of contemplation, and suggested that they employ their dream imagery in the drawing of mandalas which they might by day weave into prayer rugs. Nor did he fail to practice what he preached, and this with great austerity. On the fifth of July, 193–, he had attained the state, momentarily, of Sambogha-Kaya, and since then he had had at least three visions of the Nature of Things. One of these was of the physical construction of the universe. Staring for long hours at a pebble down at the beach, he discovered it to be composed of innumerable frogs seated at equal intervals from one another in the posture of the compassionate Avalokitesvara and making, each one in his turn, the mudra of fascination.

It was the custom for the more active members of the institution to play softball, about twice a month, with the team sent by a nudist cult some miles down the road. The nudists, who called themselves Nature's Own, dressed for these occasions in baseball uniforms with a large NO embroidered on the chest. They almost always and contemptuously won against the "fat boys" as they called the patients. But once Dr Ordway, in silent prayer, had levitated six balls in a row from the bats of his team far out to sea, where they counted for six home runs and were lost. He did not ordinarily, however, believe in performing miracles for trivial ends.

Mr and Mrs Boyne lived in a small and expensive cottage a little apart from the main buildings. They took most of their meals with the others in the dining hall, but breakfast was served to them separately in their quarters by a colored man named Boles.

Mrs Boyne found herself becoming somewhat perturbed by her situation. Many of the patients had the comforting presence of their connubial partners, the forms of their aberration being sufficiently mild to permit this, but it was not always easy to tell, in a given case, which of the couple was mad and which was being faithful: the expressions—of forbearance, humility, mystical resignation and a certain complacency—were on both faces exactly the same. And now she found it exceedingly difficult to reconcile the propositions, first, that her husband was "touched," second that they were living as they would at a hotel, third that he was not in any way segregated, or by any sort of treatment picked apart from herself.

In the beginning of their stay a certain chary caution had been exercised over the new patient: a tall, strapping fellow dressed as a waiter followed them around all day, served their meals, kept patiently inquiring if he could do anything for them —and Nicholas Boyne was at odd hours summoned away for mysterious interviews and examinations. Then, as the harmless nature of his affliction became manifest, these precautions were quietly dropped. Mrs Boyne had been impressed.

But latterly, she observed after a stay of only some two

months, much more had been dropped—a little too much, even. Young Dr Griffiths, for example, had absently one day complimented her: "You are a lucky woman, Mrs Boyne, to have a husband who will drop all his affairs in the world and stay to see this thing through, right by your side." Mrs Boyne had pointed out the error, and Dr Griffiths had apologized. In extenuation—he was not directly connected with Nicholas' case. Yet it was the sort of mistake that did nothing to inspire confidence. Also she found most of the physicians on the staff sufficiently queer: Dr Ordway with his sad tranquillity—he was "in charge of" Nicholas; Dr Rowley, a young man with crossed eyes and red hair who smelled slightly of gin at all times; even Boles, who evidently liked them very much, and had the habit of blessing their breakfast before he brought it in—she could hear the light mumbling of incantations in the hall.

The Boynes occasionally played bridge, generally with a Dr and Mrs Garball of Denver. He was a thin, famished and scholarly looking person with white hair and an appearance of such ascetic nobility on his face that Mrs Boyne could not believe him insane until one night when she cut the cards to him he simply sat there, unmoving, for over ten minutes— a not unusual thing with him, his wife explained (she was a fat, blowzy old woman who always had dirt in the creases of her neck)—and then put the deck together and began to deal as if no time had elapsed. It was only later she learned that Fanny Garball was the one undergoing treatment; Doctor Garball, Boles said with great erudition, had a little catalepsy— that was all.

Boles, for all his incantations, was a valuable friend to Mrs Boyne. She used to pass the time of day with him when Nicholas was in the bath, which was quite a lot of the time; and their little interchange soon developed into long conversations. Mrs Boyne had, she told herself, no race prejudice, and in any case

1 6 0

this was rather a special situation, instructive and enlightening. She felt intrepidly like an amateur ethnologist when Boles, pointing out to the blue Atlantic (and achieving suddenly a much stronger Southern Negro accent) would say: "My people live out dere beyon' de sea." He told her beautiful stories of tribal life: how Angka the lovely maiden was ravished by Mpo the great god in the shape of a crocodile, and carried into the green depths where she gave birth to the water spirits which shone on the river at night.

Mrs Boyne spoke with enthusiasm of Boles to Dr Ordway, who shook his head gravely and replied: "I had thought he was almost well again. Why, next month we might have let him go back to Harlem. But this . . ." He shook his head again, and said it was rather sad.

"You mean he doesn't come from Africa?"

"Oh, no." Dr Ordway took her out to the garage (a large converted stable) and showed her a huge black Rolls Royce, of which one significant feature was that the instruments were of gold and the interior ornamentation of gold inlay; each hub-cap had a small unostentatious diamond in its center.

"This belongs to poor Boles," he told her. And when questioned about Boles' status as a servant, answered, "He is learning humility."

Boles, it seemed, had struck a very reasonable though by no means permanent oil well on a small chicken ranch near Long Island City, back in 1925; at least it was said to have been an oil well, though maybe, as was possible in those times, he had struck merely the reputation of having struck an oil well; anyhow he had invested passionately and had somehow in his speculations got out before the crash. The triumph apparently went to his head. He and his Rolls Royce had been at Monsalvat for seven years.

"We could not have accepted him as a guest," said Dr Ordway, "because of his color. The other guests would have—you know. But Boles has real humility. I think he will recover himself one day."

Mrs Boyne thought steadily and seriously about Boles for three days, but could not work it all out; and when she spoke to him again it was with a faint embarrassment and with the supreme idea of distinguishing her sanity from his non-sanity or whatever indeed it might be called. Boles, thinking she had just noticed the color of his skin, was offended and cold.

Nicholas Boyne did not play baseball, and was otherwise distinguished from most of the other patients by a certain mature and quiet contempt he exuded in their presence, and by the fact that he grew neither fat nor meager but retained his pristine size and shape. He was provided with comfort and content in the form of a large green bathtub, into which he got every afternoon at two, remaining there until five; his happiness during these periods was sedate yet boundless. The skin of his hands and feet became gradually whiter than milk, as white as scar tissue—a disgusting sight. Pieces of the skin of his fingers could be peeled off easily, and this too gave him some pleasure.

He found himself able to take his bath at higher and higher temperatures, and procured a thermometer for the sole purpose of discovering when he had broken his record.

For the rest, he was not happy. Monsalvat, even in spring and summer, had more than its share of those gloomy and unseasonable days on which the sea threatens to transform the sky to its own sad color forever—days on which warm sweaters and scarves and even light overcoats became necessary. Nicholas Boyne's hot baths did nothing to accustom him to such a situation, and he began to suffer from most violent agues which corresponded exactly to the darker side of his ecstasies, the side on which the sinner predominated over the god. In the same way, the tabernacle of the god-self located itself ever more firmly in the green porcelain, the steam, the vaguely rippled reflections

1 6 2

and tropical climate of the private bathroom (Mrs Boyne, if she were under the necessities of nature at any time between two and five, had to walk all the way to the main buildings, rain or shine).

Dr Ordway noted and approved Nicholas Boyne's hot baths. "They constitute his only happiness; without them he would be in unalleviated misery," he reassuringly told Mrs Boyne, thinking the while that her husband more definitely each day entered the dire provinces of schizophrenia, but foreseeing also (he flattered himself) the eventual collapse by pneumonia or pleurisy.

One thing especially Mr Boyne found an ever-present threat to the security of his paradise: the bathroom door was thoughtfully deprived of its lock. He complained on grounds of objective indignation—decency, he said—but got in return only the cagiest smiles, from Boles, from Dr Ordway. He was to be permitted his divine indulgence—up to a point; and just where lay that point was a matter for the decision of others. An intolerable situation. Nicholas Boyne shuddered.

He became then more crafty, and less (to seeming) indignant. He gave the appearance of one who has let the question drop, who doesn't care, who has come to see reason. He was polite to Dr Ordway. And he furtively, behind the kitchen, cut a length of clothesline, with which one afternoon he lashed the doorknob to the towel rack. Behind the indulgent smiles of the staff members who got him out (the towel rack, being of glass, presently snapped) Mrs Boyne thought she detected annoyance and a mild consternation.

"You should have tied it to the steampipe," Dr Ordway said to the dripping offender. Dr Ordway saw no harm in this piece of information, he liked to show his patients that he had confidence in their ability to understand and cause no further trouble. "You won't do it again, old man, will you?" he asked kindly.

Nicholas Boyne, if he were to be believed, would not. He

was sorry, he was contrite. He suggested that a lock on the door might be the only real solution; but if not—why then, not. He appreciated the difficulty, was sorry for the trouble he had caused, thought he might try himself to control his dilection for bathing, exercise the power of his will, cut himself down (for a start) to two hours a day. Perhaps in the other hour he might (as some of the patients did) take up woodwork in the shop? Dr Ordway thought for a moment, then said he might.

Mr Boyne began making a scale model of the *Constitution*. It was a rather large project, being three feet long and fully detailed. On warm days he showed an astonishing aptitude for the work, but when the weather was cold he shivered so uncontrollably that he could not handle the tools. In two weeks he had shaped the hull and most of the deck equipment, however, and was ready to begin part of the work of assembly.

Three days later he had stolen a large can of casein cement, and lined with this powerful adhesive all the edges of his bathroom door, after which he went inside and shut the door. With him he had the unfinished model, to sail in the bath. It sailed beautifully and was an object, with him, of almost reverential pleasure.

Guilefully he had behaved so well for the past week that he got an extra half-hour's grace before anyone noticed that he had not yet emerged. Mrs Boyne tried the door; it would not move. She summoned Dr Ordway, who frowned and began reasonably to exhort the inmate. He got no answer. Nicholas Boyne saw no reason why he was not perfectly happy, no reason why he should not indefinitely remain so. The frigate *Constitution* now suffered a sea-storm, beaten up about the Scylla and Charybdis of his knees (whitened, he told himself, with the bird-droppings of innumerable centuries, and also with human bones). Hoosh-hoosh went the green water, while the vessel valiantly careened about. It was a worthy sight. But it would not do to try the frail construction too far. With a sigh, pitying and omnipotent, Nicholas Boyne thoughtfully stretched out his hand upon the waters and they grew calm.

Four men equipped with brace and bit took some time to get Nicholas Boyne from the bath. Dr Ordway did not consider it wise to have the water turned off, as "others, in that case, would suffer inconvenience." Also, if the water grew cold and the patient *still* did not come out, the probabilities of pneumonia would seem to have grown by the direct connivance of the authorities.

When the edges of the door were completely lined with small holes, they were able to smash the substantial panel in. It hit Nicholas Boyne on the head with some force. He had been in the hot bath for seven hours, and was unconscious for three more.

He did not return to work on the *Constitution*. An intolerable glass door was installed in the bathroom, and until the work was done he had as a punishment to go without his bath —a matter of more than a week. He sat about the lounge with a magazine, shivering even in this overheated room decorated with rubber plants in pots. He looked contemptuous and heroically sorry for himself, and he did not feel like a god.

Dr Ordway was displeased. "If he doesn't understand our language," he immemorially said after the fashion of authority all over the world, "we'll talk to him in a language he does understand."

*S*LOWLY time turned to summer and the nuns remained. Their vow of silence lapsed about the middle of May, and they began to talk all but steadily in a language which a small crew of priests sent by the bishop for the purpose determined was Hungarian. They also commanded a rather churchly Latin, with which they were able to satisfy, in an ecclesiastical drone, their small desires and still smaller curiosities about the new world. When the weather grew warm Claire brought them up an electric fan and showed them how to plug it in: "*ad refrigerium corporibus vestris,*" she explained sheepishly, and they with equal economy replied, "*gratias agimus.*" They continued to eat yogurt and black bread in surprising quantities, and the bishop caused Claire to be sent, each week, a check for one dollar.

No mention had been made of their possible departure, of any destination they might have short of the Kingdom: simply they stayed on, and Claire, her imputed arrogance of spirit returning upon itself, determined not to be the first, of herself and the priest, to speak. It would be unfair to say that the nuns caused very much practical trouble: they remained upstairs, they had ultimately comprehended the mystery of the toilet, they had let themselves be fitted out at last with new garments.

Yet their steady liturgical hum, which became the characteristic sound of silence in the house, like the buzzing of a refrigerator, occasioned a certain anxiety. You would think you had lost it; then as you opened a closet door there it would be, steady, slightly metallic with distance—now and again you would catch a phrase: "*lumen de luminis*" or "*virgo perpetua*," and you would realize with a slight shock that this hum, according at least to the opinion of some, was holding the tired, stupid world together, that the burning of most of Europe was contingent upon a noise in the woodwork of a house in Back Bay. It was, Claire thought, a secret beyond the imagination of G-men.

As for Father Meretruce, he seemed equally determined that if the question should be left to him the nuns might remain just where they were; or if the Bishop were busily creating a decision, he had not yet conferred with his servant.

"The Bishop has a great many things on his mind these days," he said once, answering, as he felt, an unspoken question. Claire received this news in silence, mentally picturing the Bishop as a kind of sales manager, with a boutonnière, walking between rows of glass counters; or as a thin-lipped adjutant behind a desk. Father Meretruce took advantage of the implicit occasion to compliment Claire on her patience.

"It is nothing," she said in a dry tone, determined not to seem to wish for a full discussion.

"Ah, but it is," he said with coy gravity. "There are not many who—umm." An idea seemed to strike him; and increasingly indeed Claire had felt that some rather large plan involving herself was being prepared behind the high candid forehead. "But you seem sad," he now went on. "Where you used to seem cheerful you now have this expression of melancholy on your face. Do not, please, confuse modesty and piety with unhappiness. If it is because I rebuked you—so long ago—do

1 6 7

not take the rebuke down into your soul. Do not harden your heart. The service of Christ is a joyful . . ."

"I do not serve," she said, still in the same neutral way. "I do nothing."

"Ah-ah," he said warningly. "They also serve, you know." Then, as though to recover them both from this platitude, he said more briskly: "But indeed there is much to be done—much."

That day he took her to a settlement house off Scollay Square. There children and old men, catechism and thin soup, were mingled in a hash that could have nourished neither body nor spirit. The dank, slightly furred brown walls of the place were of themselves sufficient to nauseate. Later they visited the charity ward of a hospital, where, though Claire felt she was being shown only the relatively presentable cases, she nevertheless saw enough to make her ill. Through it all, however, she most resented the priest's somewhat proprietary attitude toward suffering. He demonstrated his familiarity with the patients, calling them by their first names; he chatted with the doctors and nurses. All seemed to like him. But for Claire the expedition remained a kind of schoolgirl's treat, like those excursions made by parties of pupils to see ice-cream made. This comparison kept elaborating itself in her mind all the while that she accompanied Father Meretruce. "Here we have the raw suffering, which is economically almost useless; you can procure a good deal for a few cents anywhere. Here is the conveyor belt of sympathy, by which the crude suffering is molded and kneaded into shape by the soft podgy hands of workers chosen expressly for that purpose. Here is the assembly line of good doctrine where the suffering is made conscious of its high destiny; and here the room of frigid obedience where the now useful suffering, packed into blocks, is frozen to permanence and put into the delivery room for packaging and entrance to the world."

She readily admitted at the same time that she was being unfair. There was no getting around, she supposed, the fact that in the hospital, in the settlement house, people did something tangible and estimable for other people; the effect of slight religious blackmail (necessarily slight; there was little time, not enough labor, and the material had a certain rich resistance of its own) did not in the least so act as to cancel out whatever charitable thing (and though little enough it was not nothing) was being done.

"So, you see what the world is?" asked Father Meretruce, with the air of one who has just collapsed it all back into the hat. This tone of his alone would have destroyed the value, to Claire, of considerably more experience than their recently completed sightseeing tour.

Another time he took her to a meeting of certain holy intellectuals, in the wine-cellar of a rich and beautiful house in Cambridge, where an enormously fat monsignor, who had once talked with Joyce, discoursed on Vico, the Abbot Joachim, Berdyaev. The group met by candlelight secretly; its members were interested in a utopian situation which they called Catholic Anarchy, by which they meant that (with luck and a large amount of theory of history) the secular powers of the world would in the present war destroy each other, that there would be left at the end no unified lay authority, that Holy Church would devote Herself again to the foundation of a monastic life which would continue the world by prayer and learning. They were all, Claire considered, of the sort to profit by such an eventuality and by no other; their subterranean visages flickered with great propriety in the wavering light.

"I give Russia five weeks," a young man said as he looked judiciously at his watch. "Not more than five weeks."

"Nonsense," another replied. "America will enter soon, and then, if the Japanese side with Hitler, the military force of the

1 6 9

world will be in deadlock. Russia and Germany will destroy one another."

Father Meretruce spoke only once, intervening to establish a disputed point in the life of Saint Benedict; Claire uncomfortably felt that by bringing her to this place as well as to the hospital he was, a little, displaying his virtuosity.

But neither of these side-trips appeared to be the plan she became convinced he had in mind for her; it was as though he were showing her the terrain. And she saw him, at this time, infrequently—not more than twice in a week. Even while she appreciated his patience with her, Claire uncharitably thought of the priest, busying himself (she supposed) with other prospective converts, as of a traffic cop who must unload a certain number of tickets by the end of the month. She felt an increasing anxiety about committing herself to the Church.

Whenever she passed a Roman church, with its all but inevitable sign, so brightly colored and in such large letters— BINGO THIS FRIDAY NITE—she felt a twinge of disgust. The martyrs and saints, she said to herself, would not have played bingo, the apostles would not have played bingo. Odo de Bayeux was a bishop and had two wives, the latter being his daughter by the first, but he would not have played bingo. Or perhaps he might have. Roger wrote in one of his letters that the sergeant, when he fell out with the Roman Catholics for their Sunday church parade, referred to them invariably as "the bingo players." She was, also, disgusted and angry with herself for seeing at every turn in her way embarrassments of this kind.

The catechism bingo, the mass bingo, the body and blood bingo bingo. And side by side with all this, the accumulated and towering insolence of nineteen centuries, the secular brilliance, the etiquette, the protocol: His Eminence, His Holiness, the bulls, encyclicals, pastoral letters, dispensations and interdictions; the consistories and conclaves and diets and councils, the inquisitions and commissions in heresy. Remissions, unctions, indulgences.

Had her secular anxieties, political scruples, been all, Claire might securely have proceeded in her conversion on the epigram of Madame de La Mole: Priests are lackeys who are necessary to our salvation. But she had by no means the certainties necessary to the support of such a remark.

Since the night of the vision, and her subsequent rebuke, Claire tended more and more to relapse from prayer into reading, by which she had indeed been led to expect, according to the experience of others, that a period of aridity would follow the first revelation, which was more promise than fulfilment; yet the romantic and ardent character of her longing made her expect something more dramatic than what had now overtaken her. Subtly she rather willed the sudden and peremptory appearance of the Devil, bearing in his open hands the riches of this world: such a temptation she felt certain of her power to withstand. But no such thing happened. Instead she was tempted to nothing more luxurious than the idea of reading more and praying less, and thence to the not unreasonable idea that reading—the right kind of reading—was an acceptable surrogate for prayer.

"After all, to have had the experience is well enough; one must also interpret."

She committed the scholarly sin of beginning at the beginning which was not the beginning: she read in Cyprian, Tertullian, Jerome, Augustine. The New Testament seemed to her a little exoteric, a little well-known. If the truth about our life were there, these other huge folios would not have been written.

Occasionally she realized that the Devil's ultimate temptation occurs precisely when one says: This is too trivial to be a temptation of the Devil. Not this, but that other, would be temptation. But a compound of laziness and curiosity continued her in her course.

She wished to *know* (she said) if God existed; and in this determination she was becoming not a Christian but a student of history. Concerning the two nuns, she said to herself that she envied them their piety, and she almost but not quite fully appreciated the sophisticated contempt that this statement held.

"They are older—their lives are more fully decided. They have made their choice, and I have not made mine. There is time, I can afford to go carefully, it would be a shame not to know what I am doing."

She took the decision not to neglect the practical side of life. Thus she considered "the problem" of Susan, and she also began on the household accounts, which for some time past she had religiously neglected. "It's the little things that count."

The little things hereupon grew large with some rapidity. It was difficult enough in the first place to keep track of the household money, since neither Hogan nor Mrs Purse considered the itemizing of their daily expenditures, but simply asked for money "enough to cover" what Mrs Purse called "foodstuff and comforts." A large supply of money was kept in a cash box, of which Claire and Susan each had a key, in their father's former study. Sometimes Mrs Purse got her money from Susan, sometimes Hogan got his money from Claire, and sometimes it went the other way about, and no record was kept. Both the sisters were inclined a little to impatience with detail, and Mrs Purse especially, in her motherly way, cunningly exploited this impatience. Susan, she saw, never bothered about what was spent; so she used round numbers in asking Susan for money. "We'll need about fifteen dollars today," she would say, when the exact figure would have been both rounder and more accurate at ten.

Mrs Purse could always tell, too, by a tightening of the lips, a severity of brow, when Claire was going to question something, and she always came prepared accordingly.

"We'll need about fifteen dollars today, Miss."

"What do you mean, about?"

"Well"—and with a deal of fluster and confusion the shopping list was extricated from the old black handbag—"I thought we'd have the chuck steak at 79 cents a pound. Three pound, as the Father is to dinner, is—umm—$2.37. Then there's the lima beans, the potatoes . . ."

Before this litany of the concrete facts Claire had always given way. The curious thing was that Mrs Purse was not, really, cheating. Under Mrs Boyne's regime the house had been run with such strict understanding of the value of any particular product that there had never been, to use Mrs Purse's favorite phrase, "anything over"; and to have "something over" was her professional delight, whether this something were money or food, though money bore away the victory as being relatively immune to decay. Accordingly she now piled up, while she had the chance, "something over": it amounted to about eighteen or twenty dollars weekly, and she would not have dreamed of using it for herself, but it gave her a feeling of the greatest security.

But now that Claire was determined to find out where the money went, she resolved to hear Mrs Purse out, and one morning she did so. The twelve-dollar shopping list, since by experience Mrs Purse had limited the detail of her guile to six items, reduced itself despite frantic additions toward the end of several packets of steel wool and the repetition twice of butter, to eight dollars and fourteen cents. A pallid, humiliating figure. Mrs Purse stood there.

"I'll not have it," Claire pronounced with austerity. "You must submit to me every morning an itemized list of the day's expenses. If you do not, you will have to run the house that day on what you must surely have accumulated by now. If the list is extravagant or inaccurate you'll have to go." This last was

1 7 3

a piece of bluff which Mrs Purse felt she understood very well and knew how to deal with. The diet of the house, to Claire's great satisfaction and Susan's bewilderment, became for a few days very inexpensive and monastic in quality. Susan at the end of a week proposed dining with the nuns.

"Or bring them down here and we'll show them some real discipline," she said, staring in disbelief at the plate of cold liverwurst, the two hard little rolls, the green salad.

"And what's wrong with this?" asked Claire.

"Nothing, nothing," Susan said. "Perfectly delicious. You should run a snack bar. Or perhaps we're saving up to invest in munitions?"

"Perfectly good food, in sufficient quantity," Claire observed in a tone of cold annoyance.

"Perfectly."

A few days afterwards Mrs Purse asked Claire to order by telephone.

"The tradespeople," she said. "I'm almost ashamed. You've got to keep ordering, Miss Boyne, or they look down their noses. We've a position to hold up in the neighborhood."

"That is nonsense," Claire said. "Why should I be extravagant to please the butcher? But," she added, "when I asked you to itemize our expenses I did not mean to reduce us to picnic lunches. You may feel free to order as you did before, but be exact about the price."

Thus in another week the household worked back to the position as before. Times were getting harder, Mrs Purse complained. The butcher, the grocer became minor deities to be placated and propitiated with little gifts against present shortages and those to come.

But in any case Claire had found a new area in which to worry. There remained a considerable sum, each week, that for no accountable purpose disappeared from the cash box. She asked Susan about it, and Susan said she could not imagine what became of this sum, amounting, as far as could with accuracy be made out, due to the turmoil of other accounts, to more than forty dollars weekly. Perhaps, Susan suggested, she or Claire had left a key lying about. Hogan, possibly? Claire repudiated the idea.

"I've had my key with me," she said. "Anyhow, he wouldn't dare, would he?"

"I have really no idea," Susan answered.

This sum of forty dollars aggravated Claire terribly, for she quickly began to suppose that Susan was giving this amount to Einman every week. Since their scene of a few weeks before, Einman did not any more come in the evening or stay in the house late at night. This seemed to Claire a clinching argument of guilt. Susan, instead, went out—to him, Claire supposed— and came in very late and often drunk.

But Claire was horrified to think that she paid him money.

The subject was difficult of approach: to accuse directly simply invited a denial.

"I suppose you know," Claire said, "that we're missing a considerable sum of money each week."

Supper had been cleared away, the whole polished expanse of oak lay brilliantly between them, marred only by two miniscule lakes of cream.

"I do know," Susan said. The two sisters faced and fixed upon one another the blank regard that is equally prepared to wait a long time for the truth or quickly to devise a lie. But as neither had known they were about to enter this contest of looks, their facial expressions were completely unpremeditated, and they both had a partly paralyzed look. It was like that moment in a word association test when, meeting with unexpected and terrible resistance over what had seemed a purely negative word, the will wrestles in silence while the seconds tick audibly by.

Hogan entered and removed the two spots of cream. As he bent over the table he became aware of the silence, felt the fixed stares passing through his head; with an apologetic word or two (disturb, Miss) he rapidly left the room.

(It is that moment out of time, the moment somehow unprovided for in the script, carefully studied out as that may have been. The next line exists doubtless, but at the end of a long catalepsy now masquerading as intense emotion. The prompter has confidently gone out for a beer, the conductor discovers an old page or three or seven pages of something else bound at this point into his score, the orchestra, a heavy truck stopping on a highway at night, lurches into silence. Grand pianos groan as they are pushed through the storage warehouse. And old documents rustle drily in the green strongbox near the attic window.

The intense litigation of two wills without a word between them: it degenerates into waiting, an impure exercise. The two faces for each other fade and focus by turns. Papers blow in a dusty street, white sails immortally spank off Gloucester, with a noise like a popping of paper bags, the dew is fresh on the very green days underfoot. Eyelashes quiver, portentous blinks are delivered, on a golden stormy day the heliographs flash at sea. They are flashing in a foreign tongue.

They say it is just this moment, exactly, however long or little it may seem to last, about which nothing can be done. The pulses beat, the hearts beat, the blood journeys around, hair and nails continue to grow, saliva forms and is disposed of, respiration goes on working, but time has stopped and the public buildings of the world lie in ruins at our feet and the bad, muscle-bound murals are a heap of vari-colored dusts. At this instant the guilty are confounded, and so are the innocent; that hoarsely-breathing, perhaps slightly asthmatic and quite mortal machinery by whose means the future is manufactured in general at such smooth speed, has given way somewhere in its gut, the flywheel rocks twice and stops. In the metal silence of cooling steel, black oil drips on the tarmac.

By circumstances nicely concatenated two lives lock into one another, and then it becomes impossible to say anything. The charges and accusations, courts-martial of the heart being here convened, can by no means be hurled; the large house has become a single room, of which the walls have been collapsed one against another. And how honesty resents it! But no questions are going to be asked tonight, for we know where our breed is bettered, and know in that moment how we have subsisted and will continue to subsist only on the huge hypocrisies and municipal conveniences with handles for flushing that belong to no one and are not our responsibility: Hoosh! and all has disappeared.)

Benedictus qui venit, began the nuns sweetly to sing, *qui venit in nomine Domini.*

Tears formed at the corners of both sisters' eyes, from too much staring and a great determination not to blink. It was as though their eyes were strung on the same tight silver wires that ran through the brain and anchored equally to the walls of their heads.

(It is easy to imagine the other worlds that might be. One, for example, of a delicious lubricity, indiscriminate and always pleasant copulation à *la Thélème*, and every nymphomaniac there remains sixteen for always and always but is an intelligent conversationalist, charmed by poetry and good music, who can repeat to you word for word the entire *Book of the Courtier*. There on Urbino's windy hill, where blows Castiglione's wise and sexual beard, the sun varies in color from a bloody incandescence in the morning to a dusk of lavender, heliotrope, pale rose, and a few ruins by Piranesi delicately accent the small cumulus clouds artistically piled at one corner of a sky which is not too large.

Or nuns, in white robes, like stalagmites in the gloom of a cathedral, raise their ardent voices to the Father, Son and Holy Ghost. Their icy happiness modesty conceals, but it burns in their eyes which are lifted up to the cross. The cathedral is made of stone, but seems encrusted with ice, keen thin spines formed partly by numerous candles, partly by the ornamentation our eyes supply, as if we had thrown over all a glaze of chastity and devotion to life in death.)

2

ON THE NEXT MORNING but one Father Meretruce appeared, but not alone. With him came a contingent comprising the Bishop, an interpreter of Hungarian, the Bishop's secretary (a layman dressed something like a waiter) and two nuns. Claire had expected only Father Meretruce; nevertheless, concealing her surprise, she received the party and offered them tea.

"Afterwards we should be delighted," the Bishop said, raising a hand. "But first we have business with you."

The business in its preliminaries took the form of an inspection, of the nuns' quarters mostly, but also and by the way of the entire top floor.

"And this is the solar and this is the playroom." Father Meretruce, ducking slightly at each phrase, opened doors that the Bishop might look briefly in, grunt something or nod, and move on, Claire placed just behind his elbow.

The Bishop did not correspond to Claire's preconception of a bishop. He was a small, lean and even athletic-appearing man of perhaps sixty, with a strong jaw and bright blue eyes that served more or less to focus an expression otherwise of vague and unattending benevolence.

"And is this all?" he asked, when he had been shown five rooms.

"All but the Hungarian sisters, Your Excellency," replied the priest.

"Ah, let us see the sisters."

The Bishop, through his interpreter, formally asked the nuns' blessing and for their prayers, then caused them to be summoned downstairs with the rest.

"We should like to take our tea now, please," he said graciously to Claire; and one of the visiting nuns, who had up to then been silent, tugged at Claire's sleeve and whispered, "His Excellency means that he should like to have tea served now."

Downstairs in the library the tea service had been already set out; Claire sat behind the urn and poured, while the Bishop and the interpreter conferred apart with the Hungarian nuns, and Father Meretruce handed about a plate of cookies. His Excellency's secretary failed signally to balance his cup of tea against the writing pad he also held: the tea went on the floor and the cup rolled under the harpsichord. Hogan was called in to mop up.

"We have come to confer with you," the Bishop then began very directly to Claire, "about the possible establishment of a charitable *asile* . . ."

"For the reform of ladies of the night," mincingly interjected Father Meretruce.

". . . for the reform," said the Bishop, staring at the priest, "of whores. I find too many instances, incidentally, of this prissiness of language among clergymen—a delicacy for which the fathers give little or no authority. And why? We should not call blasphemy a sin for the reason that it offended against taste— why then, this set of carnal euphemisms which I hear on everyone's lips these days?"

"Pardon, Excellency."

"Do not think of it, Father. To resume, then—the reform of whores, many of them young and but lately corrupted, no doubt as much as anything by the vast increase in the numbers of the armed services that is now taking place." His Excellency produced and lit a cigarette, which he smoked in a very distant fashion, that is, by holding gingerly the cigarette between thumb and forefinger and applying it frequently to the exact center of the mouth from which in the intervals (as in the comic strips) floated round, well-spaced pieces of smoke.

"I realize the magnitude of the imposition (you may well take it as an imposition), and wish at once to emphasize that you have no obligation of even the most socially attenuated sort, to this diocese or indeed to Holy Church Herself. Even had you at this time formally professed the faith there would be no obligation. The world is what it is—we know that well —and you have in the secular sense every right to cite against us the number of wealthy Catholics in this community, many of whom have done, are doing, and intend to do, exactly nothing comparable to what we ask of you—say rather, suggest to you. I need hardly point out the reasons that dictate our choice of yourself: the spacious quarters, respectable neighborhood, and the fact especially that you are faithfully disposed to the Church and would presumably be willing to serve personally in at least the secular manage of the place.

"Before you answer," the Bishop continued, "let me outline a little fully the prospect before us." He smiled suddenly, and whistled a few measures from Boyce's ballet of that name. The secretary dropped his pencil and looked offended. The Hungarian nuns smiled and the American nuns frowned. The Bishop went on, summarizing points on his fingers.

"First—living expenses, cleaning, and so forth, together with the undeniable costs here and there of minor litigations, defense against cries of 'abduction!'—these will be paid by the diocese. The girls will be expected to live a life of somewhat severe comfort, with instruction in religion a little, and in needlework a

1 8 0

little. Second—the diocese will also provide furniture of a sufficient austerity to house, in the five upstairs rooms, some twenty women. Third—we have considered the hire of a suitable psychiatrist of not too downright anti-clerical prejudice"—the Bishop here smiled again—"and about this we have not finally decided; but in any event the funds of the diocese would be applied against this charge. A priest will visit the women daily; we propose also that two nuns—Sisters Catherine and Terese here —live in the establishment for its more convenient regulation.

"This brings us to the question—so important—of the kitchen. Here we run into a certain amount of trouble; for this is the only point in the plan at which the religious establishment must enter the secular one. The difficulty can be lessened by the provision—the diocese will see to it—of electric burners upon which breakfast and supper of a light nature may be prepared, leaving only one large meal at midday to be dispatched in the kitchen. Is this a possible arrangement?"

His Excellency came to a full stop, though the secretary continued to write busily for some moments.

"The practical side can be managed," Claire said. "Of course you understand that my sister must be consulted in this."

"Of course." His Excellency bowed slightly from his chair.

"But the practical side is not all, Your Excellency. Are you convinced either of the validity of your scheme or of its practicability? Further, can you convince me? Even should the plan work—twenty women are not very many, and surely in such a good cause enough money should be available for a larger scheme?"

"My dear child . . ." Father Meretruce was shocked. "It is not for you to question His Excellency. You were simply asked . . ."

"Father," said the Bishop in the smooth style of a knife interrupting butter, "please remember that Miss Boyne is not a child except before God and His Son. It is not impossible that many adults must resent—at least in purely secular arrangements—the browbeating implied in the possession of such a number of fathers in the priesthood. We are not Santa Claus, Father, and we are not here to threaten Miss Boyne with our paternal and astringent love, but regard her as an equal with whom we may reach an understanding."

"But the entire matter of obedience . . ."

". . . is not in question here. I'm afraid, Father, that you are speaking of that kind of obedience which results in the taxation of the poor by a Church conceived in holy poverty as to the riches of this world. We are not, if you follow me, ever in a position to extort the private goods of others, and Miss Boyne, if she come to her Canossa, kneels before God and not before ourselves or for that matter the Pope."

The Bishop turned to Claire. "I am not accusing you of pride," he said. "I merely became a little enwrapped in the figure."

"A dangerous doctrine, Excellency," said Father Meretruce, glowering. "And not unconnected with liberty of conscience."

"That's as may be—but some of you priests with such Rhadamanthine ideas of your position should get it into your heads that the Church is no longer capable of (or, we hope, interested in) the secular enslavement of the world. We will discuss this in general at another time.

"Let us return then to Miss Boyne's question, which reduces itself, I should say, to this: what reason is there for helping twenty when millions are in need of help? May I say, Miss Boyne, that I think you are perhaps too impressed with the modern way of dealing, with the mass-production of remedies for all? That way would begin like this: we wish to prevent—for reasons, say, of taste, public health, and so forth—the indiscriminate copulation, the trade in vice, the corruption of young daughters and the consequent disease and disorder in individuals and in society. First, we raise up a grandiose edifice —on paper—designed for the segregation of million from million, we select important people to administer the vast funds at the same time being collected: we run our ethical action, in short, as a modern state is run, and with the results generally achieved by modern states—that is, quite reasonable when directed at bacteria, floods, fire; but not so reasonable in dealing with people or enabling people to deal with themselves. In that, the police power is called into play, because the democratic state, almost as much as the fascist state, holds man in contempt.

"We hold, on the contrary, that ethical action begins with one—the One above and each one below. Without quoting to you 'there is more joy in heaven' let me ask if you do not feel it better to do what you can, than to wait upon the proposal of the next temporary utopia?"

"I agree, Excellency," Claire said. "And I do feel you've made my question look absurd, even uncharitable. I am, myself, in great uncertainty, not only in this but in other matters of, you may feel, more importance, and I feel—if I can put it this way —culpable enough about my life to wish to help all I can. You see, you can't avoid, as you probably know, some sort of spiritual blackmail."

"I know," the Bishop said, smiling gently, while the American nuns pursed up their lips in the silent disposition of a Bronx cheer.

"Good morning, ladies and gentlemen," said Susan from the door. "If you're discussing blackmail, go right ahead. Quite a gathering you've got—all you need is a Pope and the odd bishop."

"We have at any rate the odd Bishop," Claire said coldly. "This is my sister Susan, Your Excellency." The Bishop rose halfway to his feet as Susan made a slight curtsey.

"I seem to have made the first error," she said. "I hope to

be pardoned. I thought you wore a miter and ornamented robes and looked arrogant—I have an entirely novelistic education in bishops."

"I wanted to be like the young one in *Le Rouge et le Noir*," His Excellency unexpectedly remarked. "Instead—only what you see here." He pointed to his own breast with a kind of mocking reverence.

"Sufficiently impressive, anyhow," said Susan, quite charmed.

"Thank you."

"His Excellency has a request of us, Susan," Claire said, determining to get this over quickly.

"Yes?"

"He wishes to employ our top floor for a charitable purpose—that is, for the rehabilitation of"—Claire glanced sidewise at the Bishop—"of whores."

"Not, surely, a training center?" Susan's eyebrows went up.

"That remark is irreverent and full of shame," said Father Meretruce, and the Bishop signed him to be still.

"I couldn't care less—if they don't get in our hair," Susan said. "We have enough space, God knows. And it would be rather interesting to meet a professional; Boston is so full of enthusiastic amateurs. Where do you find these—whores?"

"They would in many cases be the results of police raids upon their places of work," said the Bishop.

"Well—I hope you won't embarrass us by bringing in too many of the people we know socially."

"Susan!"

"You think it unlikely, Claire? I'm sure the Bishop will tell you that vice is not peculiarly confined among the poor. Quite, quite the reverse, I think. However." Susan turned back to the Bishop. "And that's all you want of us—the upstairs rooms?"

"Just the space," agreed the Bishop.

"And your sister's time," added Father Meretruce.

"Just our time and space, then," Susan said. "Why not, why ever not? For what is time, and space, what? This may reverberate slightly around Boston. Back-Bay Mansion Turned into Home for—what will be the euphemism? I know—Women of the Night."

The Bishop grinned disconcertingly; then suddenly achieving his feet he made the sign of the Cross over Claire, who bent her head; and over Susan, saying, "Don't wince, it isn't poison."

At the door he stopped amid his retinue.

"The beds will be secured immediately," he said. "We may be able to begin our operations within a week or so. I think I may send my interpreter here to give the Hungarian sisters a few necessary words of our tongue: *food, bath, toilet, flush, pray*—I shall make up a list. Good-bye. Good-bye."

"Oh, yes," he shouted from the street, while the chauffeur held open the car door. "One room must be consecrated. I'll have some holy water and a priest sent."

Dignified in a jumble of black, the six religious piled into the automobile; the chauffeur sealed the door with a blob of black wax, climbed into his place, and away they went.

3

Hogan was vain, clever and rather timid; this last factor, far from mitigating his admiration for himself, increased it. He thought he saw in himself a resemblance to an aging yet still popular movie hero, and every evening he strove to further the resemblance by brushing back his iron-gray hair one hundred times with a pair of military brushes. This gave him the opportunity of remaining for several minutes in front of the glass, where also he imagined himself in various kinds of dramatic scenes, giving commands, winning victories, exulting ruthlessly in so many ways; meanwhile, he knew, his selective service number gave every assurance that he would be called in a short time to serve in the large-scale and personally profitless crusade that, it seemed to him, was even now being blown up. With acute realism he imagined himself a cook in a filthy galvanized iron shed set down in the middle of nowhere and called an Officer's Mess, and he thought possibly it was time to seek out a doctor and prepare some excuse against such an eventuality; perhaps Dr Einman (a man, obviously, of little conscience but great expedition) might be laid personally under contribution.

The sum he got each week from Susan amounted to forty dollars in addition to his pay. These payments had been going on for many weeks now, and even while he congratulated himself, Hogan worried. Susan had evidently a capacity for paying with a smile which gained with each payment in sinister implications: he would have welcomed some slight hitch, some sign at least of anxiety on her part. It was not right, he put it to himself, for a thing like this to go so smoothly. The world, for Hogan, was composed of money, which flowed in his dreams like water or blood, and Susan, to him, was paying for her pleasures; himself, he exacted a justice which was at the same time profitable. Curiously, he did have moral objections to her behavior, but it would have been impossible for him to express these except in connection with money; like the church militant, Hogan lived in a finite and explicable world where sin could be evaluated and penances accordingly imposed. She has chosen expensive amusements, he said to himself.

But the real cause of his anxiety, which each week gained in force, was the silence imposed upon him as the condition of his success. He felt nervously that Susan was organizing counter-measures which would be the more severe according as they were longer delayed. He had never attempted blackmail before except, in a small moral way, at high school, and what most impressed him was the secrecy which equally enveloped Susan and himself in a relation whose very exclusiveness gave it a subtle and distant erotic tone. Half-consciously, Hogan now realized, he had conceived the enterprise as leading gradually and with delicious slowness to a climax in which he commanded, lordlike, Susan to his bed and she obeyed—a pleasure of uncertain value, and dangerous, but having a heroic insolence, surely. This idea, hardly so much as an expectation, hovered between the ambitions of dream and waking for a long time.

But once expressed it could at once be seen as false. For one thing, no climax was possible precisely because no development was possible. Forty dollars was forty dollars, and would go on being, week by week, forty dollars. Suddenly to raise the ante was an action he scrupled to take, for it could lead as easily to debacle as to debauch; and though the amount, forty dollars, had fixed itself automatically by what Susan had given him on the night she told him to leave, Hogan had come by some curious logic to the view that it was an exactly measured price not lightly to be departed from. Yet without some such step as a peremptory demand for more (by which, he had read, criminals always eventually gave themselves away, the lesson of society being that rapacity should in one degree or another suffer curb or control) it seemed unlikely that anything further could be expected, unless indeed both he and Susan, conspiring silently, gradually let the whole matter lapse—an absurd conclusion. Yet how else to conclude? Reason suggested that forty dollars, even for the rich, became in time something of a burden; ultimately, even if she had not already, Susan would have to take steps. What these might be, Hogan's not very full acquaintance with the world failed to inform him.

The forty dollars was placed, each Monday evening after supper, under the bust of Plato which stood on the harpsichord in the library. Here, when all was quiet, Hogan collected it. The location was Susan's choice, for she refused to give him the money directly, and Hogan felt obscurely that the figure of the philosopher attempted to convey to him some snide remark in symbol and silence, but he could find in the encyclopedia nothing to justify this suspicion.

Hogan noticed himself becoming increasingly nervous. In the curriculum of the amateur blackmailer enough descriptions were included of how the victim became white and drawn to convince him that something, somewhere, had slipped; for Susan seemed on the whole to be bearing up considerably better than himself, and he had taken to sitting up nights reading mystery stories until a very late hour, after which he generally found it difficult to sleep.

These mystery stories, which represented for Hogan the advanced literature of his subject, and which therefore he assiduously studied for a description of the criminal world into which he seemed definitely to have entered, presented a uniformly somber picture of his activity.

For one thing, the cases were few and far between in which the criminal escaped with the profits of his crime—few indeed in which he escaped at all. The authors exercised fantastic ingenuity and cruelty in turning the perpetrator's deed back on himself: A murdered X just two hours before, as was subsequently proved, X would have given him a check for a million dollars; B became accidentally immured in the fresh concrete he had thoughtfully prepared for the disposition of Y; Q discovered himself not to be the beneficiary of the insurance for which he had chopped up A in a bathtub. A thousand contrivances of plot and technique hammered home the same point: crime may be fun at first, but is profitless except to that rare person who robs only from the rich and gives all to the poor, and what profit was there in that?

But worse still was to be considered. Hogan was impressed,

even shaken, by the number of murdered men who turned out to have been blackmailing someone. The ringing shot on page one, the slovenly corpse with gray spats pointed up on page two (no one liked him, and his face showed it even in death) and the steady outward flow (page sixty-four) of checks made out to cash—all these remorselessly proceeded to the discovery that the slain man had been blackmailing everyone in the book, from dear old uncouth Uncle Steven (who made his fortune through a rather unhappy episode in the Australian bush—or was it brush? anyhow, marooned there at the age of ten he slaughtered his older brother) right down to beautiful couth young Lola, who should have retained the negatives of those photographs.

Moreover, many authors had the custom of stepping for a moment personally into the stream of their narratives, for the sole purpose of excoriating and condemning the practice of blackmail; not even murder elicited so purely vengeful an indignation, and the blackmailer, if he lived to the end of the book, did so under a terrible scorn, censure and retribution. Hogan, looking at the literature from the point of view of the active practitioner, could not quite comprehend what all the anger was about, but found no less plausible than terrifying the exposition of so many possible fates, all unkind. It became his habit, after reading, to consider; and after considering, to go out to a nearby café for a beer—seldom more than one, he had little head for drink—of which the taste, combined with the sweet night air, produced a satisfying drowsiness.

One night he realized that he was being followed. Turning about on suspicion, he thought he saw a furtive wavering of shadow along the dark line of buildings; and as he resumed his way footsteps began to sound, with no effort at concealment, a little behind him.

On turning a corner he craftily went to the wall and waited.

The footsteps clicked in the narrow sidestreet, then stopped. Hogan stood still, his heart beating loudly; then noticed with some chagrin that he had stopped so close to the corner of the building whose shelter he wanted, that the street lamp, set a little way along, threw his shadow distinctly in the path of the pursuer—tactically a piece of foolishness. On the other hand, would it have been so wise in any case, had the ruse succeeded, to confront danger in an empty street? Hogan abandoned the position and hurried on. The footsteps took up again behind him.

By the time he reached the café-bar, which was called The Salutation, the effect of clandestine shadowing had become a formality; the stranger was perhaps ten feet behind, and Hogan did not dare to look around.

She has hired an assassin, was his thought as he scurried downstairs into the lighted and smoky room. He might have expected this—so it always turned out. You pushed the victim's patience too far, you did not know when to stop, you would be found, one gray dawn, lying with your iron-gray hair in a pool of mud that gradually was becoming red. By your side was the strange oriental weapon—yataghan or kris—that did you in. He felt the explosive blow in the back of his head.

Yet here for the time being he was safe. His pursuer had not followed him in, but was presumably waiting outside. Very well, one might call a taxi. Pleased with this idea, Hogan got himself a beer and went to an empty table. No sooner had he sat down, however, than he was confronted by a tall, thin young man with black hair, who leaned across the table and said:

"I want to talk to you." He pulled out a chair and sat down, but his eyes never left Hogan's. He must have come in while I was at the bar, Hogan thought. Yet what could happen in this place? This interview would necessarily be a warning then, and in the future one had better be more careful about going out alone.

"Talk," he said to the stranger, speaking in the laconic tradition of the hard-boiled style. Then, "Have a beer." (This was bravado.) The stranger nodded, went to the bar and brought back a mug of beer. He sat down again, looked with a tentative seriousness at Hogan, who returned the tone of his look as exactly as possible—as the novice, playing against an unfamiliar opening at chess, will duplicate his opponent's first moves.

A protracted silence began here. John Averist had no conception of the correct line of approach, or rather, the definitive nature of his conception was embarrassed by many circumstances. He was armed with various instruments of aggression —his hands, for one, for another, a check for a substantial sum together with cash to cover a journey by rail as far as, say, East Peoria—but he had no possible way of insuring the finality of any results these devices would procure. There was no tangible evidence, no papers, photographs, material indiscretions to change hands, no guarantee that one would not be made a fool of. On the other side, Hogan had not either any proof; therefore the whole matter lay disgustingly open to debate and would probably be gone into fully, doubtless in terms the more salacious for their descriptive neutrality. He was in the position of defending an honor that only in the most dubious sort existed, and defending it to a servant who would have a full realization of what Averist stood to gain.

The two men sipped cautiously at their beers without disengaging their glances. Hogan's mind for some reason could think only of the most glaring irrelevancies both defensive and counter-accusative, which welled up from the past. No, it kept nervously saying, No, I did not steal Arvid Fino's history notebook. No, that is not my handwriting, Margery did it, I wasn't in the room at the time.

"You've been blackmailing Susan Boyne." Averist had chosen the direct approach.

"What have I been blackmailing Miss Boyne about?" asked

Hogan in a rising voice; this was a good question, it laid open the way for all sorts of resentment, generous indignation, resistance, prevarication and evasion.

"I don't think we need go into that," said Averist haughtily, yet with a sinking feeling as he knew very well they would go into nothing else. "I'm not interested in denials or protests, or in discussing the matter," he continued. "I am here to tell you it's going to stop." Surely that was definite enough?

"Surely that's definite enough," he added.

"You seem pretty sure of yourself, young man," Hogan said.

"Sure enough, anyhow."

The two men drank more beer, then Hogan said, "Supposing someone were blackmailing Miss Boyne for some reason, how would you go about stopping it?"

"That would depend entirely on someone's attitude. A stubborn man could get his face beaten in. Someone more pliable might just have money enough to go away and forget the whole thing." Averist put his large hands flat on the table. "But I'm not discussing someone," he said. "I'm talking about you, and it will be just the way you ask for it."

"I haven't admitted anything, young man."

"No one wants you to admit anything. I want you out of it, Miss Boyne wants you out of it, and there's a certain distance we're prepared to go to get that result."

"We . . . ?" Hogan narrowed his eyes in what he felt to be the approved style, then opened them wide and lifted his brows in naive wonder. "We?"

"Miss Boyne and I." Averist steadily met the other's look. Both drank a little more beer.

"Young love," Hogan observed noncommittally, and again there was a silence.

John Averist secretly regarded Hogan with something near horror, inspired with more or less relevance by the resemblance between Hogan and a professor of history at Harvard; that man had been full of aged cleverness, irony (it was Averist's habit to regard the irony of others as a dirty trick) and something like hypocrisy—he represented (and Hogan came now to share the representation) the operation of time, its morally neutral and inexorable tendency rather to evil than good, the automatic shove it gently gave one toward the easy, the relaxed extreme of choice, away from all rigorous criteria. Averist felt strongly now that the man across the table would somehow defeat him, in this as in everything, for the simple reason that time was the grave into which all fell, and Hogan had fallen further than himself. There were (he thought) so many devices for winning if only one *didn't care* and *didn't scruple*. Hogan, like the history professor, had graying hair brushed smoothly back, had a broad forehead, a thin mouth—had the same suggestion of confidence and of knowing what he was about—and looked, in a word, though shabbily and in need of refurbishing if not of actual repair, *distinguished*: a word in which Averist was accustomed to sum up the entire score against the more successful products of society.

Hogan on his side feared youth, strength, the nervousness of pride untempered by any success or by time. Without phrasing it so to himself, he feared Averist for a wild impetuosity and decisiveness like that of a fierce beast whom one might hope however to confuse and bewilder by the slowest possible tempo, the certainties of evasion.

"Young love," he repeated, and shook his head slowly and with melancholy wisdom. Then, brusquely changing pace, "You spoke of money?"

Averist brought out the check and held it up for the other to see.

"That's a very nice sum," said Hogan. "A good sum of money it is." He smiled, and the guile of the smile did credit to all those detective stories. "Of course," he went on, "it would have to be in cash. I wouldn't put my name to anything."

"Even if it were in cash," Averist said, "we should have to have your signature on some sort of note. We must protect ourselves as we can."

"No, no," Hogan said slowly, and sighed. "I'm afraid I can't let myself be tempted."

"Brother, you had better get yourself tempted but quick," Averist said.

"What good would my note do you anyhow? You wouldn't go to the police."

"It would make us feel ever so much better—put it that way. And I'm sure if we had the note phrased just right we would be in a position to deal with the police. After all they can't be entirely without experience in this kind of thing."

"I'm sorry," Hogan said. "I can't deal with you. Anyhow, a nice sum each week . . ."

"There won't be any nice sum each week."

"We'll see," Hogan remarked. The two men sipped at their beers. There fell another silence.

"Young man," Hogan said finally. "Let me give you a piece of advice."

"I'm waiting."

"Don't fool around with that young woman. She'll just make trouble for you."

"Is that the advice?"

"Don't get all on edge. I'm going to be quite frank with you. She's bad right the way through. I'm just a servant, I know . . ." (the humility here was appalling) "but a servant has chances to look around him, if you see what I mean. . . ."

"How could I fail to see what you mean?" remarked John Averist, maintaining a precarious civility. "I think that's about enough, though," he added.

Hogan spread wide his hands with an effect of candor and simplicity. "What can I say then?" he asked. "You look to me like a good, honest kind of young fellow—worth any six of her every time. You're poor, she's rich. Here right off she's got you out doing her dirty work. That's no way." He nervously cleared his throat. "As a matter of fact," he went on, "I'm glad this matter has come up just this way, because there's no one I'd rather discuss it with than a man like yourself—direct, straightforward, and so on. I like your looks and I want to put my cards on the table."

The transparency of this last, the kind of remark most often made by someone about to put on the table strength amounting to perhaps a pair of fours, made John Averist smile slightly. Hogan advantaged himself of this clemency with the speed of a man who wishes to sunbathe between two storms.

"There," he said, "I knew you'd hear me out. You've no idea how happy I am to have someone to talk to about all this. It's the keeping still, keeping everything to yourself, that makes the trouble—every time." He looked sharply at Averist. "Remember," he said sternly. "I haven't admitted anything."

"All right, then. Come to it."

Hogan appeared for a moment to debate his course.

"It's not as if this Einman was the only one," he said, setting out the remark carefully yet as though it were inconsequential. "Now wait a minute . . ." he spoke with surprising authority, and held up his hand. "Don't jump on me, but be sensible for a minute and listen.

"I don't take much belief, myself, in this love business. You might say I'm more interested in the value of it, the price people are willing to pay to carry it on—you'll thank me for this one day. Now you, on the other hand—you're giving her something for nothing, isn't that right? What you've got is promises, and deep in your head you know you're being a little stupid, you know that if she doesn't feel the way you do—the way you think you do—she'll promise anyhow. Promises don't cost—you know all this as well as I do. She's given you some kind of story and sent you out to be a hero, and now I'm telling you the story is not true. You're a little mixed up, because you had an idea it might not be true—and now you're not sure if you ought to beat me up, which wouldn't change a thing, or maybe take my word for it and begin to change your mind about her.

"It wouldn't be much of a change, would it?"

Averist did not reply, having envisioned well and helplessly, if rather in the abstract than the particular, the appearance of some fundamental irony that would make ridiculous the nature of his action. The divisive and subtle brilliance of his mind brought him to realize at once that though Hogan was working in the dark desperately he might also be telling the truth, or something nearer to it than Averist had got in his brief interview with Susan.

"With others, you say?" he asked.

Hogan promptly nodded: with others, yes. He did not trust himself to fill in details, names, cases, but—after all, one had eyes, one looked about: the others were in evidence.

"Let me buy you another beer," Hogan offered, and Averist, who was not listening, made no objection. His vanity lay so close to the surface that the mere possibility of his having been made a dupe was almost sufficient to cause a complete veer in policy: the nature of his romantic attachment (he told himself) was suitor-like, one-sided, by no means contracted for: let her be surprised, it would be only what she had bargained for.

The thought, the image of her, hurt him; a wanton sweetness assailed his mind, considering her corruption which but made her the more poignantly attractive, envisioning a supple and lecherous insanity in her slightest and most graceful gesture—when she took his hand, when she lay back, as though to surrender, on her bed. Why could he not have, then, taken more convincing action? Why had he let himself be put off? It was possible (as in the fairy tales, where the hero must perform no action more heroic than the asking of a simple question—but it must be the right question) that she had at that time, at that very instant, been trembling with lust, and would think of him with mockery and contempt for having lost the occasion.

And was she, with it all, lying, putting him off while strengthening by the same gesture his attachment? It seemed even likely that this was so, and even while he bitterly resented and envied he felt an almost consolatory sense of the lostness of his cause; for he was, after all, attached. The delightful intellectual freedom by which he criticized her, and which would make him, in a moment, easily accept Hogan's version of the situation, was consciously powerless against a deep abjection, a romantic and sensual desire to give of himself (having nothing else) more and more until he would so evidently be merely throwing this self away—in her face? Possibly.

"The thing I've learned"—Hogan set down the beers and resumed his place—"is that everyone is really a s—. That's my philosophy of life."

And Hogan? To deal with Hogan would be about as effective as to slap at a mosquito while you were dying of thirst. Yet it was probable that people did slap at mosquitoes in the last moments no matter what they were dying of.

"Everyone can be bought somehow," Hogan continued, developing an ethic perhaps better suited to richer folk. "Everyone wears a price tag on some part of their anatomy."

Like a fig-leaf on the statue? Might one not knock down this villain, this *plein-air*, obvious and inept villain? But what would be the use, what would one do afterwards, where would the action have its effect? To say "Do not speak of my beloved's price-tag, fig-leaf, or whatever, in that tone of voice" would be a statement uncompromisingly worthy of a laugh.

"Now as it happens," Hogan said, "I've got an idea I'm in a

position to buy you. If I offered to cut you in with about twenty-five per cent—that's ten bucks a week payable right here over a friendly beer on Monday nights . . ." his voice trailed gently off the edge of this suggestion and disappeared. He looked with tolerant curiosity at Averist's shabby tweed jacket, the black knitted tie which desperately in poverty turned out its Brooks Brothers ancestry at the world.

Suddenly, in the midst of the motion of anger, the thing became simply funny. Of course one would accept, for "has not everyone his price?" Perhaps with his ten bucks he would pay Edmond a small rent, and Edmond might one night take this rent from his pocket and place it on the marble counter so that he and Susan might spend the night in a nice hotel. And one would say to Susan, "I have seen the criminal and I am his. We decided on a merger. I have become his agent and am to scout around for new prospects." Surely the experimental attitude—the one Edmond so theoretically and Susan so practically (it appeared) held in favor—was the only one remotely satisfying, at all amusing, and one which might be, in a world so full of connections, circles, cycles and dark designs, actually prepotent for the successful manage of life . . . if, of course, one could hold to this decision—or to any other—for as much as five minutes.

He took in silence the bill which Hogan held out, folded and between two fingers in the best capitalist tradition. "You are a very funny man," he said glumly. Hogan nodded and smiled.

$\mathcal{T}$HE WHOLE activity of her life seemed now to Susan to be carried on in the midst of an intolerable silence, without direction, impulse or criticism; as one standing in a desert and somewhat dizzied with the heat she saw the world sway and turn this way and that about her, and saw most of all that she was alone. From the two secret and related aspects of her life—her meetings with Edmond and the money she paid week by week to Hogan, putting it impersonally in a previously determined hiding place whence he later took it (once she waited in concealment to watch him do this, and got from his furtiveness and evident timidity a vague feeling of triumph)—she had gained an impression of herself as one who desperately and obviously disguised a complete covert, an entire underworld of which others were quite aware. This was untrue: her life was for the most part spent in ways as innocent-seeming as and duller than those followed by most of her contemporaries, her unemployment that of a tragedian without a visible tragedy. But if one suspects oneself, suspicion is everywhere. So she angrily carried through the hot summer a sense of desolation, waste, futility which she aggravated by continual thought. The nature of her assertion had fully procured for Susan perfect freedom, and there was nothing to do.

Freedom and apathy—they went mockingly hand in hand, and when the world bestowed freedom the self answered with apathy, so that still nothing could be done. Her life was becoming, as she powerlessly realized, dangerously dreamlike, losing the crisp and decisive nature which it should have gained from choice, from commitment which could not be managed. In her mind she saw all things as remote, as though blurred by waves of heat in the fever of some private dream. Out of this dream one thing clearly emerged to alarm her, and this was the face of Uncle Fred Seely.

As election time drew on, this face made its appearance at the most incongruous intersections of the world and the imagination. (It is an argument against the reality of life itself that this world is so liable to the production of absurdities, non sequiturs, dream pictures of all kinds: advertising is primarily responsible for this duplication under natural conditions of the most fantastic and anarchic reveries—the moon face chomping a cigar, for example, that is likely to appear around the corner of any street or corridor, and be accepted, moreover, not only as a reality but further as another proof that the world exists, when logic and propriety both strongly inform against the idea of its existing with such things in it.)

In election year, and beginning about now (August) one saw all over Boston, in the subways, the lavatories, on public buildings and decaying fences, ruins and excavations, vying for attention with recruiting posters, advertisements for cosmetics, automobiles, clothing, with public health warnings on the subject of venereal disease, the smiling face of Uncle Fred, strong, benign, empty. *Elect Fred Seely* (the poster never said to what office, but seemed to refer to a secret agreement among the voters): *The Right Man for the Job.* The photograph portrayed in Uncle Fred the essences of spirit, determination, courage and candor which, staring at an endless succession of tramcars, pedestrians, automobiles, or surveying across a tiled room a long battery of pay toilets, seemed to say that nothing, nothing whatever, was beneath the concern of the candidate, that, like Jehovah, he regarded and weighed (or was ready to fight about) the fall of a sparrow, the drop of a hat, the click of a turnstile.

The fashion prevailing in political photographs demanded at this time what may be called the objectless regard—the candidate looked *strongly* and *cleverly* at nothing, or at whatever happened to be going by. This was unfortunate for Susan, who gained the suggestion that Uncle Fred was, from a hundred public places, watching her. The sight of that mean-spirited and furtive face, its eyes here retouched to a forthrightness which even their owner might have found unrecognizable, she saw not simply as revolting but as an accusation, also, mechanic and implacable and the more terrifying as proceeding from such a source as Uncle Fred: it seemed the acknowledgment between them of a common corruption. The saving American grace of a sense of humor did not come to her aid either: the anguish and shame were real if their occasion was not, and the distance between them was terrifying in itself, as in some strange music of which the voices are by so many octaves separated as to produce in the listener's mind the resonance of spaces too empty to be borne.

It was in those spaces, it seemed to her, that she spent her life. She was struck by the strength of her own convictions against all her courses, by the intensity of a guilt and self-loathing for which she had not suspected her capacity, and at the same time by the helpless absolutism with which she continued in these courses. She was aware of how her absurd secrecy and isolation strained her, but there was a cavity the tongue could not leave alone, and the feeling of the abscess communicated itself by a rapid contagion to what had been healthier parts of time, so that wherever she might be she carried in mute comparison the image of Edmond's room, to which she was still compelled to go, hardly so much for pleasure as for the reason that this attachment was the only real result in her life.

Edmond conveyed to her the impression of a sickly and despairing charm, an equivocal evenness of temper which suggested that any enchantment in their relation had somehow been passed by, but that he was willing for the moment at least to continue. She found his sexual powers more satisfying now in bitterness than previously in amusement, and his fancy in this matter more varied and provocative: the savage gratifications they achieved, though occasionally, and not without a mute anger liable at any moment to petty and spiteful fulmination, were the landmarks to bring into momentary focus the desolate plain on which she was.

It became clear to her that she was not, whatever she was, a person who had, or was satisfied with, "a good time." She was capable of a passion and finality that her world, her circumstances, by no means would support, a seriousness that the triviality and absurdity of things as they happened could not attenuate. Thus, since meeting Edmond she had cut herself almost entirely free of the society she previously had frequented, and free in general from people of her own age, not to mention what used to be called—and may as well be called so still—station. This had had the effect of intensifying the strange silence about her, in which she often passed a whole day without speaking to anyone. Now she occasionally found attractive the idea of returning to her friends, of refusing to see or communicate with Edmond, with John.

Yet the return, though viewed secretly as a measure of protection—as, almost, the equivalent of a retreat from the edges of life—must be accomplished as though freely and triumphantly, with style. It was not her way to creep back apologetically, or to suggest by the least hint of demeanor that scars existed to be shown; and at the same time there might be, she thought, a not unpleasant feeling of duplicity in renewing the comparison between what she regarded as fully two lives, from the standpoint of what would become, regarded in retrospect, a richer experience. It would be something comparable perhaps to the occasional retreat, so popular in past centuries, of ladies of fashion to a nunnery, no more to gloat than to meditate, yet with a fairly precise sense of the close relation between these activities.

But she discovered that this could not be done. She met, one afternoon, Mathilde and Eileen, accompanied them while they shopped (shopping seemed by their talk to be all but the whole occupation of their daytime life) and then to the Ritz Bar. Susan was bored and rather irritated by everything and very ill at ease.

"We've missed you," said Mathilde. "Where have you been?"

"You're very thin," said Eileen. "And nervous. What's the matter?"

She was indeed nervous. She could not resist, often, clenching her fists so hard that her arms trembled, simply to relieve an unendurable tension.

"You don't look well," Eileen said.

It was impossible, they bored her, and more, they suspected some weakness. Worse still, she found in herself a pathetic impulse to say something forbidden, to hint, to give information, to confess. The two girls, without knowing it, exacted a sufficient retribution for Susan's opinion of them.

This meeting, and one or two others like it that occurred by chance, simply confirmed Susan in her isolation but in addition made her suspect more strongly than ever that all her concerns, her inadequacies, were immediately visible to everyone. She experienced now among people the strain of control which had to be consciously exerted. It happened that she would feel an impulsion to scream or to weep at the very moment, perhaps, that she was smiling or speaking; and this, however easily she might repress it, frightened her simply by its presence so close to the surface, so ready to break out. She also began to be subject to attacks of nausea, which overtook her for the most part in public places, especially where, as in a theater, no escape could be rapid enough. These attacks were, like nightmares, unreal: that is, they had no physical consequence, she never became actually sick and moreover she knew she would not be sick, yet the sensations of stifling, choking (and meanwhile preserving some kind of quiet countenance) produced sometimes the most terrible agonies and fears.

She began to think about death. It struck her for the first time that one day she must die; her impression of that day was suddenly immediate and forcible. "I will not be any more; where I was there will be nothing, and the world will go sailing on the way clouds sail over trees, but I will not be there." There was something in this that a little pacified her mind, and she often thought of it with a double feeling of pleasure and horror. "It might become necessary for me to take my own life," she told herself. "Would I be able to do it?" It appeared to her that she possessed, by the mere contemplation of this extremity, an ancient virtue and courage, and under the spell of the thought she did a strange thing. She took a sharp knife from the kitchen and, hiding it under her jacket, carried it upstairs. Alone in her room she examined it closely.

The knife was part of a carving set; with its sharp point and edge, short triangular blade, and handle of horn, it suggested rather the hunt or the sacrifice than the pantry; at the same time there was something silly about it, as about all useful and highly polished objects, it was so very shiny.

Susan made herself imagine plunging it into her own breast;

the result was that she felt faint, the room blurred about her, it was as though she were indeed dying. But a strange feeling of shame prevented her from returning the knife, and she put it instead in her bureau drawer, under some silk scarves.

"I could never do it, at the last moment I would always draw back." But the idea remained full of fascination, the sense of which led her, one evening, to telephone to Arthur Charvet who, on the grounds of a long though not intimate acquaintance, was easily persuaded to invite her out. She desired in her misery and self-disgust to hear from this person, whom her strength had despised, what the feelings had been which led him to attempt his own death, and to learn whether any decisive change had occurred in him as the result of his failure.

The interview was neutral and toneless in the extreme. Arthur Charvet had, now, a girl. In taking Susan out he was celebrating, in mild imitation of a rake, those playgrounds which would soon be closed. One thing worried him: ought he to marry when he might so soon have to go into the army? And when Susan forced her subject on his attention he blushed.

"It was a silly sort of thing to try," he said, as though speaking with slight pride of a precocious son. "I used to get depressed." Urged further, he became curious of Susan's motives, looked at her strictly and issued a piece of advice.

"You should see a good psychiatrist," he said. She laughed.

"I do," she replied. "I do."

2

"If our relation should change," said Edmond slowly, "that is, if you were to become my patient and we succeeded in dropping our past—familiarities (for that is what you seem to wish), you feel you might begin to clear up certain personal difficulties that beset you, yes?"

"I want to know who and what I am," Susan said. "And what I should do. I want to decide." This theme she had been varying during half-an-hour's discussion. They had been out to lunch; now they sat in Edmond's office, drinking little glasses of whiskey. It was early afternoon of a very hot day.

"To decide. Very good, you wish to decide. This suggests to me, naturally, that you have already decided, and wish to make the decision public, or wish to get some outside support for the decision. No, don't speak for a minute. Let me show you.

"If you became my patient, I should insist only on two things. Consider yourself. Consider the world. Do these things methodically and do them well for a long time. For there is no invariable condition of health; cases are imaginable in which the bite of the adder is a blessing and the sickness unto death a great relief. In my own way I am nothing more nor less than those beautiful quacks, the writers of books explaining with much enthusiasm that you have in yourself 'deep reservoirs of power,' 'untapped resources' and so forth. But my explanation is far more amusing than theirs. You have—everyone has— these untapped resources; so has the world, of course, and this must be considered. Further, the state of our knowledge is so absurdly bounded that we know, in one direction, what we can accomplish, without knowing on the other hand if we wish to accomplish it.

"Decision and self-destruction—identical. The whole construction of life is designed to prevent decision, and if it can only hold out for maybe seventy years, that is a fault in the mechanism. With only one nervous system you could hurl yourself at the grave and arrive there perfectly happy within a week; with only the other you would curl up and die. Both ways seem decisive enough. So that my studies direct themselves simply at describing the narrow limits between which can subsist the given mediocrity by which life operates.

"You can see the extraordinary difficulty life has provided for itself in the shape of self-consciousness; that is, an apparatus for imagining that things might be other than what they are. It cuts down at once on the possibility of all happiness or satisfaction, and we are taught at best to moderate our discontent, to rephrase our passion in art or science, to evolve enormous objectivities in which, as in a game of chess, we know at least how we may move, though we may not know the right move.

"But your decision was that of passion, was it not? You would tear up life by the roots solely for your own pleasure. With two results: the pleasure, you find, is finite; and life's roots go very deep. That is to say, in the largest sense, nothing that you do can ever matter in a visible way to life; you may provoke or excite a vast change beneath the surface, but it will not be known by your name. Only in martyrdom and blood sacrifice, only where the pleasure passes into pain (which is not finite), only where your self is overgone and lost and where the last breath is doleful and anguished, is any great thing achieved. You do not understand that?"

"No," Susan said. "A few things in the early part sounded familiar. But I lost you when you talked about pain."

"Let us try another way, then." Edmond leaned forward urgently. "As I am a doctor, you might reasonably say, mightn't you, that you have come to me to be cured?"

"Yes—though I know from your tone that that must be the wrong answer."

"Well—no one can tell if it is or not. In matters of the mind it is impossible to say (except in the picayune nonsense of 'adjusting to society') if the operation that performs the cure is removing a tumor or a child. Consider the magnificent conceptions formed by madness, which psychiatry must in so many individual cases have transformed into mediocrity, meanwhile congratulating itself on having achieved a cure.

"But you come here, let us say, to be cured. And I ask, of what? How do you suffer? And you say, make a diagnosis. So I ask you questions, intimate and detailed; you describe the symptoms and tell me once again of your great desire to be returned to the ordinary world where nothing hurts except with reason. What am I to say? That the whole business of 'psychology' is a way of flattering society by hindering the development of the extraordinary wherever it appears? No. You have come to be cured, that is, to be like everybody else again, and you don't give a damn if your pain is extraordinary and significant for the further development of the human dream (which maybe seems to you doomed to unsuccess anyhow)— all you want is not to suffer.

"So I exercise my highly skilled mind to discover an appropriate ritual which will allow you to retch thoroughly into my notebooks without feeling ashamed; and when you have brought up the cigar butts, hair-shirts, rupture appliances and too-much-used handkerchiefs on which you have been gagging, and feel decently empty again, if a bit exhausted and weak, I show them to you and say (with my best professional laugh), Look, they are only hair-shirts, old religious works, pieties of irrelevance, things which for a moment in your dreams resembled other things. I laugh again, you laugh, I put your money in my pocket, you go home and eat a good dinner, I go to Locke's and eat a good dinner, I am the psychiatrist, you are the patient, we are both still laughing and everything is hotsy-totsy. But what has happened? What has happened?

"Nothing has happened except that between us we have amputated or at the least atrophied another limb of humanity— you. Another place exists in which power was and now is not. From mere humanity we have created another civilized and amusing person who knows how to get on in the world: no charge could be more damning.

"Now suppose instead that I am not a laughing psychiatrist, with bound volumes of *Imago* and Freud's *Gesammelte Werke* all over the place to give the patient confidence that I already know what's what (copies of *Time*, also, would be in the waiting room). Suppose—and you can easily imagine it—I am a criminal and irresponsible fraud, an unholy, impious fake—as I am."

Somewhat complacently—for an unholy, impious fake—Edmond began to suck on a small cigar. The afternoon sunlight fell aslant through the window, touched the two glasses of whiskey and splayed itself across the floor, while Susan thought dutifully and without difficulty of Edmond as a criminal and irresponsible fraud. Edmond now lit the cigar: the match's little spurt of heat and light in the midst of heat and light resembled furtively an insult. Susan found herself to be trembling slightly. It was the heat, and drinking too soon in the day. She took a sip of her drink, and leaned back on the red leather couch, which was hot where the sun struck it. She smoothed the skirt down over her legs.

"So I say to myself," Edmond continued, "that I know nothing about society and its needs, nothing about the sort of behavior that 'goes,' as they say—I know only, if I am intelligent and studious enough, the kind of powers that belong to my patient; and I don't see any kind of logic that lets me suppose for a moment that the individual's peculiar gifts are bound to be—or even likely to be—those which his group demands and approves. A businessman, for example, has a certain talent for hallucination. Nothing morbid, he merely sees things. Oh, no, says the psychiatrist, that will never do (the businessman agrees, of course): you must have blinders put on, to make the grindstone more acceptable, and paradoxically we put on the blinders by what we call 'opening your eyes to reality.' So the patient, with his eyes opened to reality, goes back and speculates on the market and ruins himself in two weeks, neither with nor without necessity, and has not even hallucinations for a comfort. An aviator enabled to overcome a sudden overmastering fear of flight, goes up and is killed in a crash. You think I must be joking? It happens, this sort of thing, just as it happens, farmers say, that the barn you insure will be the one to burn. There are connections, then, which are referred to superstition because they are not understood, and because they are not understood, no one has investigated the large body of cases in which such connections between powers and sicknesses, even between will and the body of fate, have a most reasonable appearance."

Smoke wisped and curled about the straight lines of sunlight. Susan felt drowsy and wished he would talk more about her, or more directly about her. Edmond pulled toward him and opened a book, covered in brown paper, that lay on the desk.

"The science of psychology," he said, "with its mechanical classifications of this and that variety, I find such a mess that I've turned with great pleasure to a work which seems to have a far closer acquaintance with the minds of human beings. Its categories, though arbitrary and mechanical also, are vastly more complex than usually the simple-minded theorist permits himself, and they leave room, in good hands, for the operation of a good deal of insight—which is more than can be said for those works which so pompously study man by means of the activities of rats. I found here this passage which you may agree has something to do with yourself. I read:

" 'Here one finds men and women who love those who rob them or beat them, as though the soul were intoxicated by its discovery of human nature, or found even a secret delight in the shattering of the image of its desire. It is as though it cried, "I would be possessed by" or "I would possess that which is Human. What do I care if it is good or bad?" There is no "disillusionment," for they have found that which they have sought, but that which they have sought and found is a fragment.' "

Edmond peered at her through a fog of smoke. "A fragment," he repeated severely. "What you are seeking and what you will find is a fragment. What does that mean? It means, I think, that your anxiety for decision, your wish to make things clear and to choose, is at once an act of exclusion—simply because when you begin to look very hard at this thing you are no longer looking at that thing or all those other things. The psychiatrist would want you to relax, sit back, become expansive, 'develop a broader outlook,' and so on. He would resent the suggestion that the fragment, regarded with intensity, might be of more importance than all life looked at with apathy—that the particular gains great strength simply by being itself and not everything else.

"But if you would choose, you must choose, passionately elect. You shilly-shally like an innocent, as if you were awaiting instructions from the world. But the world seldom or never gives instructions, or if it should, these would be equivocal in the extreme.

"I know—I knew weeks ago—that we were through, you and I. So I watched for your decision, for your arrival at the point of crisis, the point where one grasps the world and is swung far out and far away. But you make the mistake—all this from now on is guesswork, but good guesswork—your mistake is that you wait for a sign from outside, you don't bank on yourself heavily enough. Your proposition reads: I would willingly become a whore—but only if I were certain of being the Whore, herself, of Babylon. You're wrong: the world will not put you in the position of being unable to choose anything else. You are the only one who can do that. Do that, then—and take your chance on what the body of your fate will provide. Give yourself away, as it comes to pass in the old stories, to the first beggar you meet: it is only *after* the gift—and could it be without the gift?—that he becomes Christ, Dionysos, the Black Prince, Pan, Tammuz. And you? you make yourself irrevocable, and that is your happiness. And that will be your only happiness."

"And you," Susan asked with drowsy insolence, "what have you become? Pan? Dionysos? Christ?"

Edmond, a little out of breath, poured them each another drink.

"I am out of it," he said at last, slowly. "Thank you for the gift which I was not able to take advantage of. Look at me, I'm an old man with a dirty body to carry around. I'm dying, Susan." Two large tears coursed down his ruddy cheeks; he pulled sighing at his cigar. "I don't want to talk about it," he said, and two more tears followed.

Susan looked at him with amazement; it struck her that she had never in her life pitied anyone. There had been at most the conventional expressions by which pity is demonstrated, and these served as acceptable disguises for a strange embarrassment and revulsion. She saw now in Edmond's weakness the use and realm of pity—it was the star which the lost and ship-ruined mariner would momentarily take for a light on shore.

"My darling," she said in a low voice, helplessly. He was not, of course, and could not be, dying; there are predicaments that calculation will not admit. But the idea of death produced in her great tenderness and strength of feeling, and this idea in turn had been, must have been, produced in him by sentiments she felt had been hers alone and had therefore hated: it was as the vehicle of an unearthly fatigue that she received his statement, and they had, looking at one another, a moment of recognition such as two strangers might have in the doctor's reception room or outside the confessional. Susan, after this, said:

"Must I believe you?"

"That's as you please."

"You are sick?"

"I don't wish to talk about it."

If he were dying, it could only be of disgust. We live, she thought, only so tenuously in the world that its whole solidity may dissolve in a bad dream, a victory of the imagination which now so frequently passes for conscience. Or was the solidity a matter merely of appearance? not the thin ice of the adage but the baked mud, maybe, at the shore of the boiling lake? Passion, tenderness, pity—she saw in her mind a spider scuttling on a wall—were suicidal extravagances of the will, the image of whose desire was really the white silence of the hospital room, the cool sheets, the bloodless redress of these grievances. And love (as one reverently called it, the very syllable a breath, an apologetic sigh, of weariness) tended that same way too.

She got up and walked around the desk; Edmond did not move. In an access of ardor that had in it something brusque and wrathful she, standing behind him, pulled his head to her body. She said:

"My poor darling, how we've wasted one another."

"Ah, no," he said. "There was nothing in me to waste. But you had every choice still to make."

Susan resented this: it seemed to deny her all effect, making her move in a weightless and ghostly world. Here then, she recognized—so far at any rate as concerned herself—was the sentiment of love in its purest state: its interest in pleasure, in happiness, was of the slightest, it had waited but to seize upon the moment of misery and have its whole exaltation in glorifying that; it fastened and fed on crisis and loss, its melancholy charm lay in disillusion which when it could not provoke it would invent. By this agency two people manufactured choice from a world of chance (which included their own meeting, their first tentative nods and curtseys) and so committed themselves irrevocably, each to the mystery behind the other's forehead. Irrevocably, yes, though neither always nor necessarily in time—but that made no difference to the choice, which remained, like an abscess in the fabric of things, unaffected by what one did afterwards: one was then a heretic inescapably engaged to trial by a justice in which one no longer believed.

Surely now, this moment, was the time for thinking briefly and with regret of the wide world of chances, of possibilities, of atoms raining widdershins in time; of that juvenile universe where meeting and parting, which were but images on a screen, lacked weight and one entire dimension; that early world we bear inside us so rich in diverse and exotic fates that choice blushes at finding itself among them. It is only the flower one picks that must die—the rest in the garden, so great that riot and disorder of unfailing fairness, seem infinitely renewable and infinitely, in dreams, to be expended.

Susan's awareness of this was brief; it seemed to her that in the pathos of their situation she at least found her first and eminent happiness, her first (and not fragile) *connection* in the world. This pathos, it was true, founded itself on a fiction—which they would necessarily keep up while it served—that someone was, as a matter of moments, of days perhaps but hardly of weeks, dying, so that a choice was made which at the same time fully assuaged one's feeling for the temporary and the various, one's feeling, in short, for one's own youth. There was, too, a feeling of shame, secret and thrilling, in the evocation of a childhood fantasy where one nursed the dying hero and in this licentious relation had the advantages of death with those of life. How those scenes were seductions, she thought, to intimacies one regained only now, only imperfectly, as the actor but also as the remote and amused critic of this first night. But this too belonged among the proper exigencies of love: Edmond's obvious imperfections for a heroic role, his being in every way but one (his having been irrevocably chosen for the part) so absurdly and farcically miscast, were precisely what had in the first place evoked as so strong a response this tenderness so nearly grievous, by whose compulsion she now, hardly aware of it, placed her hand over his eyes as though to give him, for his last qualification, blindness.

"So this is what it comes to," she said. "I came here to get free of you."

"It was clear enough," he said.

"Do you love me?"

"Yes."

"Ah, you should have said no." She smiled. "I would have pleaded with you, and you would heroically have refused to be a burden to me. You would talk about my youth, my future, and as fast as you put those things in the scales I would throw them out again." She paused and then, with her hand still over his eyes, said: "What should we do?"

"You, at any rate, should go away."

"Yes, there's my gallant man. And when you were on your deathbed—finally—it would come about that I saw your stethoscope hanging in the pawnshop window, found out your address and arrived for the last scene. I would press your fevered brow to my (by then) ample and matronly bosom and cluck soothingly while you failed. No, my sad friend, that will not be the way. We're already beyond the beauties of renunciation."

"What then?"

"We'll marry." She took her hand from his face. "I mean to hold onto you."

He looked up at her. "There will be, you know, objections."

"As I foresee. My sister will be righteous, but I will persuade her you have achieved a swift repentance. You will come to live with us."

"You can't manage that, Susan."

"Not even if it's put—as I shall put it—that you've come to die? Dearest, and my old, old gentleman, we shall do well. You must imagine, if you don't know, that what I wish, now that I have wishes, I will provide." She gave a little laugh. "We'll be a Christian household, forgiving each other daily for everything. And as for my family—it's a strange world, let that be their comfort."

"And if, by some final irony," he asked in a courteous and distant tone, "I should have been telling the truth, a moment ago?"

"I do believe you," she said gravely. "But, like yourself, I'd prefer we didn't discuss it."

BOOK · THREE

CHAPTER · ONE

*S*UMMER was ending, the days when they were hot were so with the concentrated quiet heat given out by the embers of a fire. On one of the hottest of these days the Church invaded the Boyne house. At eleven in the morning the Bishop arrived, bringing with him the two American nuns, Sisters Catherine and Terese, who carried little black suitcases containing presumably all their worldly possessions.

"Inauguration day," the Bishop briskly said to Claire. He beamed. "I cannot tell you how happy I am, and how grateful for your help." He became for a moment thoughtful. "There is one thing," he said. "I've drawn up a small agreement—you see, we must have something to show the police; to demonstrate our responsibility for what you might call our captures—eh? It's no very complicated document," he went on, drawing a paper from his hat. "It simply attests to the fact that this program of ours is entered on in your house by your full consent and agreement. See—it has already been notarized."

"Surely not without my signature?" Claire looked over his shoulder at the foolscap sheet.

"Ah, well," the Bishop said. "I was able to get it done. If one is trusted, you know . . ." Claire thought of a tame notary in a wire cage, dutifully stamping what was put before him.

"Where do I sign?" she asked. On being told, she went to the desk and signed all three copies; whereupon His Excellency looked doubtful.

"Perhaps you ought to have read it first," he said. "One shouldn't sign what one hasn't read."

"Oh—but trust," said Claire. "Trust."

"No," the Bishop replied. "Simply sound business sense." This maxim was issued in a rather brusque tone; however, he brightened again quickly enough and turned to the nuns, who stood quietly sweating by the window.

"You know Sisters Catherine and Terese—you've met before," he said.

"Hullo," said Sister Terese; Sister Catherine nonchalantly saluted with drooping hand.

"They are to stay with you," the Bishop went on. "We hope to start operations in a few days now—the movers will be here with the furniture today sometime. Any questions of conduct and discipline may be referred to the sisters. But"—he signed to Claire to withdraw with him a little, that they might not be overheard . . .

"The situation may seem somewhat—ambiguous, now and again," he whispered.

Claire was shocked.

"Your meaning?" she inquired in a voice of great asperity.

"I mean," he said, not quite whispering, but in sufficiently low tones "that I cannot be around to keep an eye on things. I have a whole diocese, I must delegate—in short, I mean that I am surrounded by people I do not trust. Or no, perhaps that is put too strongly—the whole question of ecclesiastical discipline—the lifelong recruitment and war of the Church is— well, say rather this: that discretion may sometimes be the same as secrecy—if you take my meaning. One can't keep an

eye on everything; *curious things* have been known to happen."
His Excellency was whispering again, and seemed very nervous.

"I do not understand you," Claire said. The Bishop drew
himself up.

"Please understand this," he said, or rather announced, in
a tone whose severity hardly suited with the fact that it was
almost inaudible. The two nuns, at a distance, looked boldly
on. "Understand that I would not have permitted this venture
had I not thought its result would be, *on the whole,* good." He
looked Claire in the eye. "I hardly know how to make it clear,"
he said. "Have you, by the way, a cigarette?"

Claire produced cigarettes in a silver box, held a match for
the Bishop, who then said:

"I am going to speak to you in *general terms.*" It was as
though he announced the intention of turning water into wine,
so firm an emphasis did he give the last two words, with which
also he raised his voice again to a normal volume.

"The world is fuller of evil things than you imagine," he
began by assuring her. "This city of Boston, for all its moral
hauteur, is filthy, is riddled with filth. And the Church, to
combat that—it is a war in which there are no front lines.
You see? We recruit from the depths of the human soul—a
perpetual vigilance, an espionage, even, is necessary—and impossible. We have to trust, to *trust,* mind you—such people
sometimes—you would not believe . . ." Claire had the impression he nodded his head ever so slightly in the direction of
the two nuns at this moment. She could not be sure. "No, don't
speak to me," he continued, "of monastic reform." She had of
course no intention of introducing this subject. "Ah," he cried,
"we are—we must be—founded in filth, *super cloacam ecclesia,*
we fight temptation by subjecting ourselves to its worst—by
subjecting these, these others. You understand me?"

"You don't speak to me very openly, Your Excellency," Claire

2 2 1

said. The Bishop drew heavily on his cigarette, inadvertently blew the smoke in her face, smiled a vague and nervous apology, put the cigarette out in an ash tray, bit his lip twice, and said:

"It's all political—political." He muttered something of which Claire caught only the word "Rome."

"Do you mean—I have something to fear? Do you intend me to understand that?" she asked, also inclining her head toward the nuns, but so slightly that he would notice it only if that had been his drift. He did not, however, choose to take the hint.

"When we oppose evil with good," he remarked, "we have a turmoil; we do not *know* who wins, but we believe good must win. If we knew, it may be that they corrupt each other? That is not something I am saying, mind you"—he shook a finger at her—"I'm merely pointing out that in a secular sense, a moral sense—we don't know." He sighed. "We must forgive," he said. "We must forgive—everything."

It seemed an intolerable burden, for immediately after this he sat down, fanning himself with his hat.

"But seriously," he went on after a moment; Claire wondered if he considered his last remarks frivolous. "Seriously—you're not to worry. All is in responsible hands, really. I meant nothing more than that you should not expect—perfection. We are bringing, after all, evil, viciousness, into your house; but only as the doctor receives the sick. The risks of contagion . . . ? They are there, yes, but they can be kept down." This statement seemed to cheer him, and he said: "Ours is not—is it?— a fugitive and cloistered virtue."

Claire saw no reason to reply by more than a nod of the head to this piece of encouragement; her understanding, in the most "general" terms, of the Bishop's apprehensions had already decided her on a course of suspicion and wariness. But he seemed to have argued himself, at least, into a state of satisfaction on whatever the subject had been—one couldn't be certain—that so concerned him. He got up again and said, with the energy of relief:

"And your charming sister—where is she?"

"Not yet arisen, Your Excellency."

"Ah?" The tone was not so much of reprobation as of disbelief; he glanced swiftly at and away from the clock, which showed eleven-forty. Then he asked if they might not, before he left, have a look at the Hungarian sisters. Claire led the way upstairs, and they were followed by Catherine and Terese, who, however, did not for a moment relinquish their luggage to what might befall it in a strange, rich house they evidently mistrusted.

The Hungarian nuns were praying at an almost breathless speed. They were knelt down near to and facing a wall to which they addressed a continuous muttering. They rocked slightly back and forth, and swayed a little from side to side; the flow of their words was interrupted only occasionally for a brief instant in which one of them would gulp back from the corners of her mouth an excess of saliva, or swiftly wipe her lips at the wrist of her garment. They paid no attention to the opening of the door, or to the group standing there: it is probable that they had not noticed.

It was for Claire, this spectacle, like the sight of an exhibit in a zoo or a museum, where one looked at another way or another order of being, and turned away wondering uselessly what it would be like to be an ichneumon, an Etruscan warrior, a monkey, a seal, a Sioux squaw—how one survived, say, the pressures of the Tonga trench, or flew by night like the horned owl, whose skeleton, she recalled, for all the enormous fulcrum of its breastbone, so resembled that of a homunculus. She was oppressed with a sense of ages past and irrecoverable, of the number of the dead which now so far exceeded the number of the living in this world, this valley of dry bones of which the stars were the reflected phosphorescence.

We see them praying, she thought with sudden simplicity. We know what they are doing, they are praying to God. Supposing we didn't know, we might regard this activity as we do that of apes who without embarrassment scratch where it itches —but we *know* they are praying to God. That these mumblings and spittings, these consonants and vowels, rise up through the weather, the troposphere—the stratosphere and ionosphere, yes, and anything else we care to put in their way—and beyond the stars they go to the great face of this ancient dream. That face which is everywhere the wall of the world. We live in the skull of God.

It was exceedingly hot in the little room, and the buzzing of a number of flies could be heard threading its way through the stream of prayer. One of these flies alighted on the forehead of the younger nun, who however did not acknowledge its presence by any slightest interruption of her devotions; presently the fly went away, but was soon followed by another.

They might be already dead, Claire thought; what do they say to Him? Her own experience of prayer did not tell her, that entire event had discreetly faded from her recollection except as she considered it a kind of illusion, a device of "psychology." In truth, she had fears of once again entering that strange realm and being, possibly, committed beyond the denial of her will to the invisible and absurd, whereby one became, like these nuns, reduced from the sense of the many to the nonsense of the One. How many prayers had gone up, and the smoke of how many candles blackened the faces of how many images? But the seals of the door remained as they were, unbroken; and back there behind the stage of the world granma and nuncle and coz might be sporting together on clouds and playing harps (forgotten then the cancer, the bankruptcy) or might be giving one another the cut direct in the cold solitudes of hell, or might be not at all. Nothing. Finished. Behind the cardboard castles, the fluffy factories, the entirely fluid munitions plants, there might be not so much as an idea, and one prayed to nothing, *néant*, *nada*, *niente*. In this case one was, neither beautifully nor nobly, a fool, no?

Sister Terese coughed, as it might have been in a desperate protest against oblivion. The Bishop frowned and turned from the door, looking, Claire thought, unhappy. On the way downstairs he said:

"That is the inward life—we must not equivocate or pretend there is something better." Sisters Catherine and Terese, ahead on the stair, turned so abruptly at this that his Excellency bumped into them.

"Please!" he said irritably. And then, "I'm sorry, sisters."

At the door, before leaving—the nuns having been shunted into the library—he spoke again.

"That's the way of it," he said as much to himself as to Claire. "Martha, Martha, Martha, no Maries anywhere. One mustn't complain. What am I, after all, but an executive?" He then formally gave Claire his blessing, shuffled uneasily for a moment, said, "Remember what I told you," and took his leave. She stood watching his back for a little time, asking herself just what it was she ought to remember, then—with a discouraged mind—returned to the nuns, who stood primly, like girls returned from school, by the harpsichord.

"Won't you sit down?" she asked them. They sat down. Claire offered to have tea sent for. They accepted. Tea was sent for, and presently it came. The sisters watched Claire steadily over the rims of their cups.

They seemed neither of them to be much older than Claire, and this accentuated the discomfort of the situation—there was evidently no authority on either side, but there was a good deal of suspicion and the two wimple-pinched white faces seemed peculiarly suited to expressing it. Claire wondered what they were like, and if (for example) Catherine and Terese were their real names—Lois and Iris being on the whole more likely—what their homes had been (in Somerville or Allston or Belmont, with the orange and blue chromo of the Holy Mother of God dripping tears—five tears—on the world), how early and for the reason of what vicious innocence they had veiled themselves, whether they liked it, and if they sometimes thought with horror and self-loathing of what they had put away from themselves, and if they imagined themselves to be, as the phrase went, brides of Christ. With a start of chagrin, she realized herself to have been looking at them with an expression that must legibly have been of pity—they did seem, in this extensive room full of the pillage of Christian civilizations, the pathetic children of a bad idea, from which already they had derived a certain smugness, condescension and air of being always intolerably in the right: the intransigent pity of their kind, with whose outward sign they now looked back at her.

So then, she thought, we pity each other. And pity is the most terrible of the emotions, because it involves no exchange, no reciprocation; unlike love, it can survive disregard, contempt, anger. We come never to any composition of our several pities, but go on in the arrogance and miserable pride of the thing forever. And people may be pitiable for anything—for their successes, their failures, virtues, vices, powers and weaknesses. It is that legacy which Christianity has given us.

"I suppose you know," she said to them, "that your room won't be ready until the Bishop's men bring the furniture? I'm sorry," she added.

"That is perfectly all right," Sister Catherine replied. "We are quite comfortable here."

"Please do not put yourself out," said Sister Terese.

"If there is anything at all I can do . . ." Claire helplessly said, knowing that with this acceptable last maneuver conversation formally ended.

"Nothing at all," both sisters assured her with the same dour half-smile.

Claire asked herself on what sort of footing it was possible to get with these people, who could not be treated as servants, as friends—perhaps as nurses? Their very presence suggested an invisible sickness in the house, and one was in every offer made to feel one's bungling and incompetent amateur standing against the curt economies of the merciful profession, the technical sympathy, the cheerful courage in the face of another's death. It was obvious that they were, these nuns, as uninterested in as incapable of the luxury of feeling beyond the strict and necessitous pity which called in question everything worldly about the room they sat in: to see the place through their eyes it was necessary only to draw a great black X through almost everything—the heavy velvet hangings at the windows, the Mabuse—a copy—on the wall, the harpsichord, the books, the thick patterned rug.

But this was perhaps unjust? Nonsense, look at them, at those bloodless faces from which the life has been in so few years so fully pressed, at the pale power of death that looks out at you from the eyes of young girls in all its repressive vulgarity. Their faith had rejected the world for them, and now they held the world as if reasonably in contempt, in a destructive and unkind pity.

And I have brought them here, into my house, she thought with pained realization. They have arrived bearing the Invisible with all its inexplicable demands which are so much more excessive than any the visible and sensible can make. These black

2 2 7

bundles will possess the corridors of the house, coming and going on their urgent and incomprehensible errands.

This was for Claire a moment of extreme nervousness, the moment at which the grand idea began to take on its displeasing flesh (or at least its very voluminous robes) and show itself for what it was—a vast deal of bother to which one had rather too casually exposed oneself. She felt she had been deluded, and more—practiced upon sharply. What had appeared so plausible and commendable in theory, this *practical* charity, had turned in fact into Catherine and Terese and whatever in the way of the exotic their presence here was certain to evoke.

One must have more enthusiasm than that, she told herself sharply. Everything is in competent hands, surely. But this she could not quite believe. Thinking it over, she found a good many details on which there was no direction. Surely, for example, these girls were a little young, a little—inexperienced, considering what it was they would have to do? The women who were brought in would be, would they not—some of them at least—hard, cynical, full of their own manage? Claire had not much idea of what a whore might be expected to look like; the movies were her sole source on the subject, and she imagined the movies, when they dealt with it at all, rather overdid it. But surely their own inherent viciousness—they were, presumably, vicious—and the difficulty of their lives (it must be, she thought, a difficult trade) would soon teach them to make a mockery of any such establishment as this, conducted by (to put it at its worst) a post-debutante and a couple of convent schoolgirls.

At this moment Susan entered, wearing a gray-silk nightgown and short robe. She carried a cup of coffee, a pack of cigarettes and the morning paper. After saying good morning to Claire she briefly noticed the nuns.

"Aha!" she said. "*Ça commence.*" Hereupon she took herself

off to the far end of the room and at a distance of thirty feet (the distance at which one is comfortably absent yet present) sat down. The nuns looked sidelong at her from time to time, thinking doubtless what thoughts it was given them to think, until Claire spoke:

"These women," she said, "who will be sent here—have you had any experience of this kind of thing before?"

"You are nervous, aren't you?" said Sister Catherine.

"Yes, I am," Claire admitted. "For instance: what's to prevent them from simply walking out? Why would they stay?"

"It will be a refuge," Sister Catherine said. "They won't have to earn money. Can't you imagine they'll find that some relief, and be glad to stay?"

"To be perfectly candid with you—no, I cannot."

"Then, too," Sister Terese said with engaging simplicity, "it's either this place or the jail. There's hardly a choice, is there? I mean—such a nice house." In just this way, Claire thought, the nurse too assures you that you have a nice house, with lovely things in it, only the tone of her voice making the slight reservation that there is typhus here.

"Yes," said Sister Catherine. "The police, you see, take their names."

"And then," Sister Terese observed, "if they don't like it here, there is always the women's prison."

"It's too simple, really, isn't it?" Susan remarked from her corner.

"That's not fair, Susan," her sister said. "There must be some authority."

"Unfortunately," added Sister Catherine.

It seemed for a moment as though there might be some composition of friendliness between all parties, but with this brief exchange the conversation stopped, exhausted. Presently Susan went up to dress, and when she returned they all four had lunch. The meal provided at least the essential break in continuity after which it was possible for Claire to excuse herself and go upstairs, leaving the nuns again in their places in the library.

She had hardly time to lie down for a rest before there was a knock on the door, and Susan came in.

"I have something to speak with you of," she said. "It's quite important to me."

"Yes?" Claire sat up on the edge of the bed. She felt apprehensive of Susan's confidences, the more so because of Susan's own marked uneasiness, and wished it were possible simply to lie down, to shut her eyes, turn her back on what was proving a thoroughly disagreeable day. Nevertheless, "Go on," she said.

"I feel I should apologize to you. I don't think you like me very well any more, and I can see why—I don't care for myself so much, either." These words were difficult for Susan to bring out; she intended them sincerely and openly but could not avoid seeing what this interview, as she planned it, would reveal as their tactical meaning.

"You've no need," Claire said. "Don't feel you must make things right with me."

"But if I must . . . ? I've acted the fool. One can't forgive oneself, it isn't enough. I've made myself unhappy, I'm not the sort of person I thought I was—pride can't take that very well." She clasped her hands in a demure and charming gesture of whose value she was not unaware. "I've come to be forgiven, Claire."

"That's very well," Claire said, "and if it comes to that, of course I forgive you. But can you simply erase what's been done?" This was, she felt, necessary if ungracious. "When I've forgiven everything I may—forgiven what concerns me—what of all the things that remain over?"

"I'm coming to that. But first, say you forgive me—we'll be friends."

"I do forgive you," Claire said gravely, wondering at the same time just what was the extent of what she forgave, and in what respect, after all, she had been injured. "I'll always forgive you, Susan, if it's what you want. I don't see, though . . ." she smiled a little wearily. "No matter," she said. "It's all over. We'll never speak of it again."

"Ah, but we must," Susan said.

"Then it isn't simply forgiveness you've come for, but a kind of indulgence?"

"You're very quick."

"And you're not so very subtle, after all. Tell me, now, what forgiveness includes."

"My marriage to Edmond."

Claire was silent for a time, then: "Has this taken place?" she inquired. "Are you handing me the *fait accompli* and inviting me to make the best of it?"

"No. I'm not married," Susan said. "But I intend to marry Edmond—that is, isn't it, the approved way of righting these wrongs?"

"I see," Claire said slowly. "You are forcing me, isn't that it? You want the connivance of some Christian principle at your wedding. Some principle—or makeshift, anyhow. Susan, how can I agree? He's old, he has no money, I don't think him an honorable person. I think him despicable," she said softly.

"Honor?" asked Susan, just as softly.

"Ah, I know," Claire said. "It is approved, it is right, he is doing the right thing, as they say. We should be grateful, Dr Einman is doing the honorable thing—by marrying his whore."

"That was not necessary," Susan said. "In charity you must . . ."

"In charity I need do nothing. Nothing, do you understand me? Why should you make me carry the imposition of your—your dishonor?" She shook her head. "I'll not say I am happy for you, Susan—whatever you may decide to do."

"I have decided to marry Edmond."

"He is too old for you, he is an opportunist, a cynic—he is using you to recruit his fortunes."

"The suggestion of marriage did not come from him."

"From you, then. And that, I suppose, makes it better?" Claire pressed her lips together, looked at her sister, then said decisively: "I think it unsuitable, and I'll oppose it. You can't love him—a beautiful and young girl like you. Why will you condemn yourself?"

"I think your revulsion's a little excessive," Susan said. "No one is asking you to sleep with him."

Claire laughed angrily.

"So this is what forgiveness amounts to," she said. "A weapon for blackmail."

"Don't think," Susan said, "that your permission is an absolute necessity to me. I would like to have it, but if I can't it doesn't matter. You have no authority over me."

"How true! Nothing has authority over you—except your own sweet will. And, evidently, that of your lover."

"Why be so outraged?" asked Susan. "Why pretend that everything counts so heavily? It's only my life," she added after a moment.

"Which I am unwilling to see ruined," Claire replied.

"Oh—ruin—what a word!" Susan sat down in the chair by the window, facing away from her sister. "You have," she said, "this strange idea that life is so beautiful and good if only one doesn't ruin it somehow. It's an idea you can't possibly maintain about your own life—which God knows looks a ridiculous mess! —but you have the comfort of applying it very strictly to mine. In that life everything is clean and aboveboard, isn't it? The girl is beautiful and virgin, sufficiently religious and yet worshipful of honor and a good match. Many dangers lie in wait for this fair young thing, but if she obeys the book of instructions that comes with every set she can avoid them all, and achieve whatever mysterious result is ideally desirable for her to achieve—make a marriage, I suppose, which will be a model for the statistician."

"You don't understand," said Claire. "I'm talking about *this* marriage and *this* situation. You're the one who insists on generalizing."

"That's just it," Susan answered heatedly. "Just what I object to—one feels that if it were a theoretical marriage you wouldn't mind discussing the most wildly improbable misalliance—with Hogan, for example. But it's *this* marriage"—she imitated Claire's tone and emphasis—"that you can't stand. And as it happens, this marriage is the only one I have any interest in."

"But you don't—you can't be in love with this man."

"You mean that you can't understand it—in your mythology these things don't happen, or they happen to other people, and thus stand as a dreadful warning—like the noblewoman in Swift who became infatuated with an old footman and suffered him to beat her. You have a pride you can't maintain—your piety forbids it. But you expect me to maintain it (yes, even despite my many lapses and failings you expect that) while you juggle about with nuns and priests and the reform of street-walkers. And you hate decision, and hate change: my marriage and your conversion are acceptable to you if you regard them merely as possibilities, but when the moving-vans arrive and people—real people, mind you—arrive to cause inconvenience, you begin to dislike everything. You disliked those two stupid girls downstairs, didn't you? They made you nervous?"

"Please." Claire lifted her hand as though in defense, then passed it over her hair. "Can't that be another question? Must everything connect—so violently and so speciously?"

"I think it must—it does," Susan said. "Because life isn't beautiful and good, and there aren't any new leaves to turn over. My life is what I can salvage from the wreckage of its first collision. You think differently, I know," she said heatedly. "You think one goes to the store and gets new equipment—starts afresh, as they say. But even better, one avoids the collision, one commits oneself to nothing. Look what it's done for you—when you can't make up your mind you read the desert Fathers. Your faith is a graduate school and your God is a sociologist—and you can't even believe in the sociologist." She paused, then added: "Can't you see that life is what happens, what one does? One *is* that. Not what one may decide tomorrow."

"Admitting all this," Claire said after a brief interval, "are you precisely the person who ought to be saying it? Even to me? What have you done that's so wonderful? You've fornicated with a middle-aged and reasonably unattractive person, whom you have to keep on money which is partly mine—don't interrupt now, for I *know*, you see—and then you take the tragic view that as you have ruined your life you may as well marry the man. Love or not, I don't know. But what in the world is so extraordinarily passionate, courageous, convincing in all that? What gives you the right to talk to me about God? You must be so certain, anyhow, that He does not exist."

Susan said: "I do not give Edmond money. Please believe that."

"Will you tell me what I ought to believe? The money is missing. I don't take it. You have the other key."

"I do take the money," Susan sullenly said. "But it doesn't go to Edmond."

"Where, then . . . ?"

"I mustn't answer that."

Claire was silent; there was nothing she could find to say to this new illumination except, finally, the obvious: "You're in some trouble."

"But I'll solve it," Susan said quickly yet uneasily. "Don't worry. It'll soon be over." She wished she could believe that, and determined to speak with Hogan soon. What she would say to him she did not know.

"What's the good of our talking together?" said Claire. "I haven't your confidence. Whatever we may be, we're not good friends. You'll do what you please after all the talk—I can't stop you."

Susan said:

"I've asked Edmond to move in here."

"What?"

"Please don't look as if you didn't understand—Edmond is going to move in here."

"I won't allow that."

"If you mean by that that you won't be happy about it, I quite agree. But he is moving in." Susan got up and put her hand on Claire's shoulder. "He's sick," she said. "He needs care."

Claire did not look up. "Why don't you go and live with him then?" she asked. "Why bring him here—into this house?"

"Because it is what I choose to do," Susan replied.

So far as concerned result the interview ended here, as it had to do on the making of such an assertion, which was not reasonably to be defended and had, even in Susan's own eyes, little more virtue than the fact of its assertiveness could give it. Yet this was something, after all, a gesture at positive and unequivocal action, a deliberate affront to whatever real recalcitrance existed in Claire's reiterated statement that she would not—could not—allow it. At the same time she recognized that the conversation had really solved nothing, though it committed her to much that lay, possibly, beyond her strength.

But it is not the way of interviews to end simply because the impasse has been reached and the definitive statement made;

conversation resembles love in that neither party will accept an unequivocal expression running counter to his own wish, but must still be producing reasons. So Claire now referred her opinion away for support to that of the world, of other people in general and in particular. "What will Mother and Father think?" she asked at last. Susan shrugged her shoulders, this was something she could not consider: what had been left out of account would simply have to remain out. She said, after a long pause, that she thought Edmond was dying; whereupon Claire became reasonably full of renewed objections—did that, she wanted to know, make things any better? How did she know? Of what was he dying? Of some contagion? Susan in sullenness rested upon ignorant conviction.

"I don't understand you," Claire said. "I don't understand what you want."

"Neither do I," Susan replied. "I can find out only by wanting something."

She had to admit to herself, though, that the whole cogency of her new attachment to Edmond rested suspiciously on something like a sympathy for death: that was the feeling that made the argument and gave to her wishes such a decisive character. From the resignation of the condemned she gained the desire and the momentary power to insult the judging world.

Returning to her own room she stood by the window. The heat was all but stifling, though thick, dirty clouds rapidly overspread the sky and a darkening greenish light foretold a storm. Over the huddled red roofs of houses a faint wind hurried wisps of chimney smoke and produced black stitches of squall on the river beyond, where several little sailboats were out. Their sails took a sharper whiteness from the deepening weather, and every object she could see was now as if etched and deeply cut from its surroundings, so great the clarity, the distinction, even the loneliness of a sail, a gull, the shallow dark arch of the bridge against this sky that seemed to be lit by mere reflection from these things.

Susan had kept—as much out of an inability to throw away papers as anything else—the photograph Edmond once gave her of a fetus, and she took it now, somewhat crumpled, from a handbag on her dressing table.

The picture too seemed to shine, to glow inwardly, as though the black flesh—so ironlike, or like bronze—were powerless to stop the show of some secret fire. The infant here portrayed had, for all its ridiculous posture (arms in a grave and judicial manner folded, huge proud head, legs like afterthoughts trailing away), a certain solemn, grotesque and not a little repulsive majesty—Susan thought of a line of verse: "If a star were confined into a tomb" . . . and of another: "Dear, beauteous Death! the jewel of the just!"

It appealed to her obscurely that there was, between the homunculus of the photograph and the world outside the window (paralyzed, even as she looked up, by the first wide flare of lightning), an intimate connection as mysterious in itself as the elements that composed it were clear. The very roofs of houses, slanting, and bright now with the first rain, had a quality of revelation, though as she regarded them with abstracted and musing mind she could not have said just what of the secret and impressive they revealed, what tomb they opened: rather they revealed, all simply, themselves, in a clear and lovely absence of meaning. There are visions of the interior and the depths, but there are also those outward and of the surface which, when the mind relinquishes for a moment its secular grasp on things, displays itself as if newly created, a world tranquilly and not arrogantly superfluous, made for nothing but thus to be gazed at.

She looked again at the photograph, and found there that same soulless innocence, that freedom from complexity and inwardness. Edmond had spoken of this majestuous child as of a god, referring to some central depth (where the dreams are), its expression of slumbrous contempt, and she had then in part agreed, finding there intellect and cruelty that shocked and did violence to the plane on which one lived, or tried to; yet now, under the aegis, as it were, of the storm which at this moment fully broke, she looked on the glossy paper with delight as at a stone in which she had found some peculiar richness of texture—a stone which caught and intensified the light so as to seem coldly on fire.

It was nothing more than a stone, and the world too—a stone that coldly and sacredly burned without being visibly consumed. If one could watch it, watch it in this way—with the eyes as though misted over with the purity of sight—forever, for one's whole life, she ardently thought, standing there while the rain blurred the glass, one would know a peace beyond anything that life can give. Every moment which stood thus separate, without past or future, every moment in which one didn't think, was infinite. All the houses were both sacred and solid, as the mere appearance of things should be, in the wet afterlight of the rain.

Now we shall see a rainbow, Claire thought, in a sky of brass. The storm had given her no relief; she found it oppressive, simply a continuation and intensification of the heat itself— and when it was over the heat settled in again as though nothing had happened. She had a physical sensitivity to pressures in the weather, and electrical storms generally made her feel a slight headache. She had felt sickened enough by her talk with Susan —a talk so entirely appropriate to an afternoon of heat aggravated by a storm—and it was with great difficulty she brought herself to remember that the two nuns would still be downstairs, that the movers would doubtless be bringing the furniture very soon: in short that there were, as there always were, and not as a mitigation of earthly troubles but as their last emphasis, adding insult to injury, things to be done.

She made an effort and went downstairs, to find gathered there a congregation of doubtless efficient and certainly officious persons: two movers, extremely dwarfish swarthy men in leather aprons; an indeterminate number of priests of various descriptions, as blue-jowled or white-faced, anxious-looking, calm, severe—she had seen none of them before, and wondered why so simple and material an operation as furniture-moving should evoke such a sanctimonious body of inspectors. They were wandering, a few of them, in aimless anxiety from room to room —they hadn't wished to cause any disturbance, two of them simultaneously tried to explain, but they hadn't known exactly where things should be placed (they indicated the pile of camp-beds in the hallway) and the movers were being adamant about their time and its value elsewhere; having moved so far, the movers seemed to be contending, they had moved far enough and would now remove themselves. The clergy objected to this high-handed economy, very naturally inasmuch as it would leave them under the necessity of carrying the beds upstairs—the beds and that huge pile of beaverboard for partitions (it had come as a last-minute decision from above that the fallen sisters were to have an elemental privacy).

Claire took the situation in firm but unavailing grasp, spoke to the movers who heatedly in Italian ridiculed the priesthood and heatedly departed. Then she turned to the priests; it looked, she said, as though the fathers would have to be so good as to lend a hand. . . . There was some grumbling at this, and talk of mismanagement, but at last all fell to and began at Claire's direction to carry things. Hogan brought hammer and nails, and somehow someone botched together the necessary screens.

While the perspiring fathers vigorously wrestled with such various conveniences as bedding, ancient and rickety commodes, a picnic table, edifying pictures and even one or two ash trays, Susan came downstairs.

"God," she said in a sufficiently loud voice, surveying the scene. "The Lateran Council, as I live and breathe!" Several priests looked up from their work at this, and Susan said pleasantly, "I hope you're not scratching the banisters."

"I hope you don't imagine you're being amusing," Claire said, her anger obscurely intensified by the fact that Susan seemed to have got over the afternoon's crisis quite easily.

Finally the job was done, such as it was. Several rooms had been partitioned off by screens into what their size if not their shape suggested were to be called cubicles: they looked rather like wedges in pies. One room, on which a gaggle of fathers had spent some dispute, behaving (as Susan said) like interior decorators, had been made into a kind of commons, with the long table (that looked stolen from a picnic ground) in the center flanked by benches, with chairs in the corners and ash trays on the chairs. On the walls were several representations of religious subjects, prominent among them a nativity which might have done very well on the cover of the *Saturday Evening Post*. Susan looked in and called the place the Divine Rumpus Room.

CHAPTER · TWO

*F*OR a week Edmond hesitated; in this instance of which the decision had somehow been taken for him, upon his advice and therefore presumably with his consent and even his enthusiasm, he did not see why he should deny himself the pleasure of vacillation; a purely speculative pleasure, since the small equipment of an easily portable life was in the main assembled on the floor about his feet, and there was no doubt, to put the thing at its most extreme statement, that he would move into the Boyne house, become as in some fantastic fairytale the husband of a beautiful young girl, and, at some indeterminate time not far off, die. The ease with which this had been settled, had seemed to flow logically as consequence from the superior generalities and profundities of his conversation, proved a little frightening; he entertained doubtfully the hope that in the capacious hospitality of that house he might become, for some little time at least, misplaced and forgotten, or remembered as merely another object of a charity which appeared, from what Susan had told him of her sister's reformative designs, munificent, eccentric, experimental and probably of very short duration.

The whole course of events was proceeding, he reflected in some irritation, from his own inability to forego a scene or miss the play-like charm of a situation; this gift for the dramatic, or this susceptibility to it, was for him the source of life's pleasures and its embarrassments about equally: he never resisted the temptations of crisis, and hardly ever kept an enduring responsibility to the feelings crisis evoked. A more or less continuous annoyance he had with himself was thus interfused with a more or less continuous pride.

How accurate in certain dramatic respects, how full of deep propriety, had been his assertion! "I am dying." It had been the gesture, respectful yet instinct with virtuosity, with which the honest jeweler demonstrates the glass-bead necklace to be composed of pearls, and had brought as if naturally from the girl a passionate and tender possessiveness of which he was the object; it had given, he thought, a suggestion of danger to their common enterprise. The assertion was not, moreover, a cheap or contemptible trick, for the mere appeal to death was at the time obvious, suggestible to the most adolescent flair for hidden and disguised relations between feelings—no, it succeeded, and could have succeeded, only by the utmost sincerity, spontaneity. To have honestly, bitterly, wearily and foolishly meant it, that was the achievement and the measure of its meaning, for the moment. And, now that the moment was over, what? The crisis of the spirit, by whose means alone one was brought to saying something decisive, brought in its train the secular complication that now caused luggage, somewhat sloppily packed for the most part in cardboard boxes tied with rough, splintery string, to be strewn confusedly over the floor. In the midst of all this—the detritus it seemed of some nine lives, all of them small and addicted to the ownership of talismanic bits of brass junk, ash trays, pipe-stands and other things which could only in their evident uselessness have served as cult-objects in a forgotten rite —Edmond now sat before his desk (he was leaving the furniture) and turned his gray felt hat around and around. A heavy walking stick lay before him, its provenance unknown beyond the time, a few hours before, when it had fallen on his head from the upper shelf of a closet: it had seemed better to carry than pack the thing, now that it had made its appearance with such dramatic and inopportune insistence. The things one owned, the things one kept! They formed the materials for a paleontology one no longer had patience with, but they never got thrown away, they continued (that signed photograph of Mme Schumann-Heink, for example; where had that come from?) to await the rearrangements of some disinterested scholar.

Susan was coming at five to call for him, he was to be introduced to the new life under her direct auspices, for what they would accomplish, and shown (she said) immediately to his room, there to rest until supper. He had been taken in charge, given over already to what could be sustained between them of formality, and there was now less than an hour remaining, of a gray, smoky afternoon full of the first suggestion of autumn, for the enjoyment of speculation.

There remained only to call the taxi, to go to South Station or even to the harbor, thence to entrain, embark, leaving behind all one's packages or perhaps taking them along for the sheer delight of dropping the greater part over a taff-rail, and liberate oneself at once and forever from anything that had been said. Edmond had not managed to convince himself to the point of action. He saw himself in the taxi, in the train or the boat, he felt in his chest the full delightful expansion (with sea air by preference) that permitted the most exhaustive sigh of relief, but he saw also the grotesque struggle with a dozen packages between which one vainly attacked an inner pocket in the hope of wringing money from it, he saw the putting down and the picking up, the impossibility of getting any intelligent assistance, the insolence of cab-men, porters, conductors, stewards, he saw himself in tears on any concrete platform; bored, sweating, disgusted, he watched himself sitting on the hard and inappropriately curved bench of a waiting-room: *the departure for hell.* These and other inconveniences could perhaps be overcome, if one had a destination, a direction, a clear purpose; even the weird and wonderful obstacles placed in one's way by people who presumably had contracted to take one from A to B would be as nothing, would fade away before the clarity with which one viewed the objective. But where to go? And what to do on arrival?

His assertion, then, had had after all enough of truth in it, enough to keep him. Regarded in one way, it was the expression of the ultimate, sad charm about two people, invoking the disastrous vows of poverty, the magnetism of failure; but in another reading it stood for the mere inertia of middle-life, in which one's boredom and fatigue were but the acceptable functions of a desire for establishment, permanence, comfort.

I said that I was dying, he thought, because I wished to die. What a comedy! This deep and on the whole puerile longing for stillness and rest has the effect on Susan of the last provocation in sensuality, the delicate turn whereby an outworn and tedious lust is changed in an instant to *love,* on a "higher plane," pale with suffering and sorrowful thoughts. And the mystical outcome of all this is to be a marriage. How womanly and firm the reasoning of it: since he is dying (she says) why should we waste a death? Let him also be a sacrifice.

Thus he felt he had been, not without treachery, committed by time itself to a kind of permanence, to a decision. All he had experienced of life as, so to say, a figure of dance the whole attraction of which consisted in the hesitant and tentative, the one step up, engage, bow and courteously step back one, was not and had never been enduringly relative or all-variously measurable, but rested on an energy which, as he well knew, ran in one direction, ran out like sand through the hour. And at that crucial instant the energy which remained had said, referring to that which had already gone, "I am dying." No more recognition was required than this to make him (aging as he was and momentarily persuaded to an all but religious condescension toward his flesh) a vessel of the spirit. And such a vessel he didn't want to be, he emphatically rejected in his mind the bizarre sanctity with which the mere idea of death had endowed him—as though Lethe already had washed away the body with its follies and foulnesses.

But it was no longer a question of what he didn't want but rather, as time appeared to be demonstrating, of what he was prepared to accept; even now he could not feel himself deeply and thoroughly committed to more than the quiet enjoyment, for a few weeks, of whatever placid malady might be attributed to his appearance of pallor and fatigue—those at least were real.

But I might of course marry her, he thought now. What would be so strange in that? The more he thought of the situation the more its rich and diverse treasures of irony exposed themselves. Of course in that way, he told himself, one chuckles and chuckles—intelligently—and then suddenly it's too late: *it*, whatever *it* is, has happened.

He had not irrevocably severed himself from the material conditions of his life as it extended beyond Susan; John Averist would keep the apartment, with its furniture, to his own use for the time being; the patients had been informed—with a fine disregard for whatever degree of transference they might have achieved—of Dr Einman's indefinitely to be prolonged absence, and advised (in a footnote to the same sign on the mailbox) not to try to communicate their troubles by post.

To John Averist, Edmond had announced at first simply the intention of going elsewhere for a short or a long while, leaving to John the rooms together with some little money, enough to allow of his staying on if he cared to. This proposal, though, struck John as altogether too liberal to be innocent; he suspected, and said as much, some dark and unclean design; he expressed with peculiar vigor two contradictory theories of the position: that Edmond was going away with Susan, and that Edmond, having got Susan with child, was going away from her. To all this, many times repeated, Edmond listened with his usual imperturbability, making only the most reasonable objections.

"I can't be doing both, can I?" he asked, spreading his hands as though to weigh the two courses of action. "You must make up your mind what it is I'm going to do—and accuse me of that alone."

"Nothing would surprise me," John Averist angrily replied.

The temptation, here again, to counter with the right, the inevitable and dramatic revelation, was too great to be resisted—and in any case, as Edmond experimentally put it to himself, what was the advantage of secrecy? He said then that in a few weeks' time he and Susan would be married. The forthrightness of the statement, its honest flavor coming from his own lips, pleased him; he felt for a moment the calm security of decision. "Married," he repeated somewhat complacently, savoring the idea as though for the first time.

John turned very pale, and could say nothing. What recondite hopes he had entertained of some obscure twist in the affair by which he might suddenly have been projected as though automatically into success beyond the power of his own mismanagement to thwart had now to disappear at once and be replaced by mere vacancy or—what was worse—outright recognition of a total and permanent disappointment. The violence of his own feelings convinced him afresh that he loved Susan, and he realized with fierce shame that her shame was what he had built his hopes on—the furtiveness, the guilt, the criminality almost, of her former relations with Edmond had been for him the guarantees of fortune's inconstancy, promising him that the mere varying of the wind should find his sails filling while those of his antagonist slackened; yet now, the bitter thought came to him, he alone of the three of them bore the shame and punishment of what he called their *sin*—he who had hoped to take the profit without the sourness of it—while they escaped into an exclusive honesty where he could not follow. That this marriage was his fault he fully believed: from lying, from playing for time, from trading in terms of feeling— from everything that was opposite to the passionate intransigence he should have maintained against Hogan—came his present predicament; he was the trimmer trimmed, and in his own eyes his punishment fitted his sin as exactly as a homily would have it do. It was myself that I sold, he thought, and a mute, miserable rage shook him.

Edmond was made uneasy by the protracted silence, the last thing he expected or desired from John.

"It will seem strange to you, I guess," he said after a while. "I mean—that I am not young . . ." he stopped in some dismay; it is not right, he thought, that I should apologize—an apology may be in order, but not to him.

John Averist made a small, stifled sound which might have been a sob, a cough or a grunt, expressive possibly of sorrow, anger, deprecation or disgust. Edmond was again helplessly lured on into the silence. . . .

"I am sorry for you," he said, and it seemed to him that this succession of sounds was as ambiguous, evasive and yet full of meaning as the grunt, cough, sob or whatever which had preceded it. In his embarrassment he continued, developing an eloquence out of the energies of relief as he led away from the immediate subject and toward more general aspects of the sorrow, the pity, he had pronounced for his young friend. His young friend was, it seemed, in a bad way—a way which got worse with the development of each rather flourishing period in Edmond's unleashed style. The drinking, first; there was too much of it; it passed beyond pleasure and bore the aspect of a punishment. With this went hand in hand a variable and inconstant temper, the lack of an interest, a profession—an aim in life, Edmond finally and fatuously said. One might mock (he went on) the bourgeois ideal—the convention, rather—of moderation, temperance, industry, thrift; but these virtues did, after all, exist; they were not mere fantastic nonsense which one might dismiss at will. No, there was, and John would find it out—was in effect finding it out now—retribution, a kind of watchful justice one held, actually, over oneself; the body had its limits, so did the mind: excess brought its own scarcity. He (John) might say what he liked, but he (Edmond) was convinced of it, that there did operate in human lives a metaphysical hangover, as it might be called, which ruled according to fixed and unchangeable laws—these might vary in the individual case, but . . . Edmond grew not only eloquent but even angry, a little, as he fervently persuaded himself of the existence of a moral law by the demonstration that John was breaking it.

John Averist heard out this strange tirade in a silence which might have been scornful or totally submissive; at its end he said, in neutral, lifeless tones:

"What should I do about all that?"

If irony could have survived the dullness of that voice, Edmond chose to disregard it; he suggested, in the most general way, remedies: a healthful life, a regimen, something definite to do each day, even a moderate amount of exercise—long walks. In the midst of this obfuscation of any issue that might exist between them he broke off as suddenly as he had begun.

"We are not talking about what we are talking about," he said.

"I love her," said John.

"Ah—love," Edmond agreed, waving vaguely one hand. John's statement, its unequivocal naked simplicity, annoyed him; it was shameful, he considered, to show such weakness. For that, after all, was what it was—weakness, not a challenge but an admission.

That conversation had ended in evasion and indecisive generalities. John Averist had spoken very briefly of his "hatred" of having charity held over his head. Edmond had courteously invited him to please himself about that; to this John had sullenly refused an answer (suggesting that he would stay on if nothing better turned up, but refusing the obligation of acknowledgment) and Edmond in a momentary flash of temper had accused him of having "a perpetual adolescence."

Unsatisfactory, ridiculous—yes, all of that, he now thought. But what was one to have said? What did this great moon-calf want of his life? Edmond was, really, quite impatient of equivocation: one might indeed desire one thing today and another thing (quite possibly exclusive of the first) tomorrow, but the desire itself at any moment must be clear and clearly seen— precisely, he reminded himself, what his own desires, if he had any, were at this moment not.

Susan came promptly at five; she wore a white linen dress that Edmond thought very attractive; there was aroused in him a slight, surprised sense of possession.

"The cab driver will come up in a minute to help with your things," she said, after having briefly kissed him.

She was amazingly adaptable, Edmond thought, as they busied themselves by moving the luggage to the door. Already she treated him with a brusque, friendly affection that must have been reserved to things placed and accounted for; now their demeanor with one another spoke of an established and even a happy marriage, her immediate anxieties and the numerous particulars of her nervousness were penetrated already with a tone of tranquillity. Also, the mere possibility of his being in fact ill in some serious sense was taken by her with a peculiar tact and charm which, while preventing the subject in any explicit question or hint from being brought up, set the mode in which she treated him as one of prevailing though gentle caution and concern.

"I'd like, when we get to the house," she said now, "to have you lie down and rest for an hour before supper. I'm afraid," she had to add, "that my sister will want to speak with you some time this evening. That won't be agreeable—but if you are firm, clear . . ." She did not finish the sentence, but said instead, "Don't worry about it now."

They held hands in the taxi, Edmond leaning back with closed eyes. He was quite unexpectedly happy. As for Susan, leaving Edmond's rooms, with him, had been set in her mind as the final closing of a door (which reason denied it could be, since one had, quite conceivably, the hem of one's garment caught in the jamb) and the opening up of a new scene. "It may be possible, after all," she said gravely to herself, "to be happy." This new vocation of happiness was much strengthened by the ride in the cab, despite her apprehensions of whatever in the way of a scene might be mustered for their welcome home; she had not allowed herself to believe fully, during the past week, that they would get even this far.

"Are you nervous?" she asked as they got out of the cab.

"A little, but not so seriously," he replied.

She could have spared her own anxiety, for Claire did not appear. Hogan alone, with an obsequiousness verging on insolence, came out and busied himself about Edmond's packages.

A room had been made ready on the second floor, at the opposite end of the corridor from Susan's and just beneath the abode of the Hungarian nuns. The room had no view, giving as it did on a blank wall at a distance of some three feet, and this was unfortunate, but otherwise it looked extremely pleasant, and a cool breeze circulated in it. It was ample, if not ducally spacious, and had been provided, in addition to the usual bedroom furniture, with a desk for Edmond's use.

Edmond found it attractive enough, but the cleanliness of it made him a little nervous and he privately thought the ceiling far too high for his own comfort. He was impelled by his nervousness, which Hogan's servile courtesy increased, to dig in his pockets and give the man fifty cents—for all the extra work of carrying my things, he told himself. He was dismayed when Hogan offered silently to return the money; Edmond refused to put out his hand to meet the offer, and the butler, after a second's hesitation, put the coin on the bedside table and walked out.

Perhaps I did wrongly, he thought, but all the same that was a very cool way of letting me know.

He complied with Susan's wish and lay down on the counterpane, having first removed his shoes, coat and tie. He had been there only about ten minutes when Susan came in, bringing him a Scotch and soda. They drank together, then she left, saying she would call him in sufficient time for dinner.

It was very pleasant, Edmond decided as he was falling asleep; it was like a Mohammedan paradise. In such a situation one could acknowledge the real extent of one's weariness, admit at least to oneself how extremely comforted one was by being thus maintained; at the same time he had, through his lassitude, a tense impression that this was mere preamble to some theme that would inevitably compel his attention and his anxiety. But he soon fell asleep.

CLAIRE had arranged to receive Edmond in her father's study, and she went there some quarter of an hour before the appointed time. It was twilight, and the room lay in blueish shadow that deepened away from the window; the stained, ancient surface of the desk gathered the light as though on smooth water. She did not immediately turn on a lamp, but after walking indecisively about for a moment sat down at the desk. She had the intention now of thinking for these few moments seriously and consecutively about Edmond—the "problem" of Edmond, as she put it, blaming herself for having by so much neglected her responsibility, turned a blind eye, as to have let him enter the house as its guest. What, though, was she to have done, and how could she effectively have interfered? Insistently, despite the resolution to serious and consecutive thought, the problem of Edmond deepened with the falling darkness and became the problem of Claire. The depth of her uncertainties, and her unsuspected capacity for indecision, were surprising enough even if she did not add to them the great and increasing extent of the gap between what she believed, or hoped to believe, and what she would and did acquiesce in. These nuns, she thought now in some exasperation—they are responsible to love alone; everything else has been taken away. I am responsible to every stick of furniture. Happiness consists solely in decision, it would be the whole decisiveness of one's life, as though that were but a moment. Instead, to be strangled by a wealth of obligations, as I am—to have such a *heavy* soul—that's impossible.

God, she said within herself, God—God. It was not a prayer, but a struggle to *think* God, and it evoked, as she had known it would, only the most random and doubtfully relevant associations: the towers of Notre Dame de Paris—pigeons in the sunlight of a public square—some sort of tall monument with a figure on its top. God, so far as this moment seemed able to tell her, was the Grand Tour. Where were the well-known peace and the much-advertised consolation?

With a long sigh, of which the rather dramatic quality made her ashamed, alone though she was, Claire rested her head in her arms on the desk. It was almost totally dark now, at that time of evening which is so beautiful because it is sad—the hour at which, doubtless, self-pity was invented.

A knock on the door was followed, before she had time to reply, by the entrance of Edmond, who, believing perhaps that Claire had not yet come, searched for and found the light-switch.

Claire quickly raised her head; the room had sprung into brilliant illumination that placed, in her estimation, a heavy accent over every line of its somewhat tawdry and overdone manliness. Above the mantel, on which stood a jovial beer-mug bearing the arms of Harvard University, a fox's head, collared in a mahogany plaque, stuck through the wall as though to ask a silly question: a kind of sneering eagerness about this animal's mouth suggested some implacable force had halted it and struck it dead at this point in its flight (of terrific velocity) from the next room—its hind-quarters, one felt, might be sticking out the other side of the wall.

Edmond stood as though in apology at the door; Claire looked at him closely. She had had at dinner the impression that the man was ill—an impression she felt, though, that she owed it to Susan to have; but now a more searching inspection gave a like result. He was older, she thought, than her recollection of him had told her, though not more than a few months had elapsed since their last meeting, and he had no longer— if he had ever had it outside her imagination—a certain arrogance, a humorous power that had formed in her memory the key to his appearance: she now thought him vaguely and for no very particular reason pitiable. The hair perhaps more thoroughly gray, the wrinkles perhaps slightly more pronounced—these things perhaps, and perhaps not; it was, if anything, the whole cast and set of the face that had changed, loosened, relaxed, as though the will behind it found the effort no longer worth while.

"Please turn off that light," she said, switching on the desk lamp. "We'll have this one instead. Will you sit down?"

When he had established himself in the armchair, facing her, with the shaded glow of the small lamp warming the space between them, they sat in silence for a few moments, both of them feeling uncomfortably the nature of their meeting as official, as an interview, with everything that idea held of suspicion and unease. But at least, thought Claire, that animal's head has discreetly faded back into shadow. I must be kind, she told herself, I must not presume to judge. Yet for what other reason have I asked him here? She began with a sufficient coldness and hardness: "My sister tells me that you wish to marry her."

"Ah," Edmond noncommittally said. Claire waited, but this seemed to have been the whole reply.

"I don't wish," she went on, "to be officious, or to let myself be prejudiced by—by anything that has happened. And I realize that the decision must belong to yourself and Susan at last. At the same time I can't pretend to be glad that this has come up. You must recognize my position and my right to an explanation."

"What you wish," Edmond said. "Whatever you wish."

"Then let me ask—what is your motive in this affair?"

Edmond thought for a long moment.

"Can't I offer you the motive which is usually acceptable?" he asked. "Is it forbidden to say simply 'I love'—an answer which would stand in your thoughts for whatever darkness and evasion you liked—and so pass on to something else, something more—limited?"

"Ah," she said sadly. "I shall always be played with—I can't force you to answer. You're older than I, you know more. But can't you," she cried in sudden outrage, "can't you say one thing with honor and certainty? Why should you ask me what answer will be most pleasing? You must say what your heart wants you to say."

"My heart?" Edmond was candidly puzzled and incredulous; this was a terminology of which he had not the skill. Claire herself felt baffled by his bewilderment; she might as well have been discussing the calculus with a Bantu.

"Your heart," she repeated. "Don't you ever—clearly—feel anything? If you truly loved her, wouldn't it strike you that you couldn't, in this situation, say anything else but that?"

"No," he said. "No—and that wouldn't satisfy you anyhow. You would still have to ask, after that, about money, position, suitability, many other things. You are deeply involved—your feeling does you credit. But, if I may ask a counter-question, why are you so deeply involved? Doesn't it seem as though, through your words, you were referring to a slightly different question?"

"And that is . . . ?"

2 5 5

"The possibility," he replied, "and the necessity even, of someone's indeed entertaining the tender feelings you speak of—but toward yourself. Isn't that really and recognizably the source of such urgent demands for a declaration?"

"Oh, that is your mystery—you have the advantage of me there," she said with a somewhat bitter lightness. "I'd forgotten that in the new psychology there are no simplicities of feeling, but everything is also its own opposite—that's why," she added, "you strike me as so fundamentally dishonest. There's nothing clear about you."

"That's the second time in a few minutes that you've used that word 'clear,'" Edmond observed. "Doesn't it sound a little as though you're saying your own name, using it as the epitome of all desirable qualities? You might almost be suggesting I think less about Susan and more about clear Claire—at least that's what 'psychology' would say," he finished in some little amusement.

"You have a disgusting insolence—in addition to your many other virtues," she sarcastically replied.

"I don't insist on it," Edmond said. "I merely mention it—as an observation."

"Please spare me your observations," she said, "and let's go back to the question."

But despite this brave renewal of the attack they had to sit there in silence—she expecting an answer, he wondering exactly what question was intended—for several minutes. The stillness, the warm lamplight, seemed the travesty of some intimate scene: the pair of them might, from their appearance, have been old friends. At least old friends, Claire angrily thought.

"I'm told you are ill," she said at last. "Is that true?"

"I suppose it is."

"You suppose! That's not very decisive. Can you give me a clear answer—to anything?"

"Now, please listen." Edmond sat up straight, and spoke with surprising earnestness. It is not—as you put it—*clear*. I am sick, if you like—of the world, of the necessity for choice, decision—sick, perhaps, of this entire demand for clarity. That is something I think you have already experienced, young as you are: how one doesn't know what to do, and doesn't know what to do, until one finally wants to do nothing, at least commit oneself to nothing. Can you understand that?"

"Yes," Claire said in a low voice.

"Well, then—whether I am sick or not . . . ? Organically, physically, not. But who knows what susceptibilities may not be developed, if one sufficiently doesn't care? Or what secret flaws may open up?"

"You've answered my question," she said. "You don't love her."

"Love," repeated Edmond. "Love. I've reached the point of wanting pity. I'm afraid of being left alone."

"And you'd sacrifice her to that?" Claire asked.

"What shall I say?" He shrugged his shoulders. "That I am her weakness as she is my strength? What is there to say, if you accuse me?"

"And I do accuse you," Claire said. "What sort of man are you? Doesn't there ever come a day, with people like you, when you renounce, when you sacrifice one desire instead of someone's life? You speak of being sick of choice, but all the same you'll end by strangling her just as if you'd chosen to."

"That's too dramatic," Edmond said, but she gave him no heed.

"I know you'll think me meanly cold," she went on. "You'll think I can't understand the depth or warmth of feeling you want me to believe is there—in yourself and in Susan. But I've —wanted things, in my life; I know the feeling. There are times when it must simply be put by, even if that is painful."

She spoke quietly, yet with a slight exaltation that made her speech rapid and forceful. After a brief pause, she asked him: "Do you believe in God?"

This question so suddenly delivered caused an expression of surprise—something between amusement and concern—to travel over Edmond's features before he could reply: "My marriage has extremely metaphysical extensions, hasn't it?"

She impatiently waved this aside. "Can you answer that?" she demanded.

"But of course—I do not think I believe in God."

"You show a noble caution," she said derisively.

"I believe in life," Edmond said, horribly conscious of the blatancy in this. Her silence was the certificate of his being held in contempt along with his reply. Finally, though, she said: "Then you have no responsibility to anything?"

Edmond glanced over at her, at the compressed severity of her lips, the fine poise of her head, held very high and framed in pale golden hair which the light seemed hardly to warm, at the rather melancholy intransigence of her whole expression; it is a real question for her, he thought with some surprise at his own surprise.

"Claire," he asked, calling her by name for the first time, "have you any friends?"

It was her turn to show surprise, hearing in his voice a mixture of tenderness and mockery out of which she most fully understood and resented a certain condescension implying that the sad answer was necessarily contained in the question, which could not otherwise have been asked.

"Why?" she said, half to herself. "Why?"

"Because I should like to be your friend," he said simply.

"I don't see how that can be," she answered, "how you can wish such a thing or how I could accept your friendship."

"You're very unhappy, aren't you," he said. "Poor Claire."

That was it, she thought—the ultimate count of the indictment, what we all finally accuse one another of. To be unhappy, that is the weakness fullest of shame; that we are unhappy is the thing we dread most to be told, unless we dread still more the idea that another can think us unhappy.

"I'm not sure I would like to be what you'd call happy," she replied.

"But that isn't an answer," Edmond insisted. "Is it?"

"I suppose not."

The look she gave him now was both puzzled and miserable, was full, it seemed to him, of the most delicate equivocation of feelings which could not be balanced for long; he expected some outburst of temper or else some kind of admission, but as the moments passed without any result he grew at once impatient and fearful of having overstepped the limits of his position with her, so that he said resentfully: "I see. You don't believe me. When I say I'd like to be your friend that means nothing to you."

"I believe you," she said resignedly. "It's not that. The question is, what I am offering to believe. I can't think my friendship valuable or necessary to you—all it would mean would be my submission to your judgment, my backing up your wishes. I won't agree to that."

"And if it meant more than that?"

"No, no. You mustn't joke with me." Claire put her hands to her face; she felt as though stifled, yet excited by the oppressive potency of this instant, of what it was within her power now to let happen.

"You've no need of me," she said in a low voice. "I can't believe that. Go—go marry, or don't marry—what do I care? It's nothing to do with me. I don't want your—tender feelings, as you call them."

Edmond was not a little surprised at the intensity of this

2 5 9

development from what he had regarded as tentative maneuvering for position; the strength of Claire's response aroused his curiosity, which was with him a kind of inquisitory, experimental passion. He got up and, leaning over the desk, took her hand, which she violently withdrew.

"I think then," he said, "this is the end of the argument, no? You consent, you rid yourself of the bother."

"I suppose so," she said dully, and she too stood up.

"Why do you withdraw in this way?" Edmond persisted in asking. "Are you afraid? All you accomplish is to embitter yourself."

She had her head bowed, but now she looked up at him with such a concentration of bewilderment and unhappiness as to arouse in him some timidity, the shame to be felt before some inadmissible and pathetic piece of candor.

"If I could be certain of your feeling," she said slowly. "If I could persuade you to give up your—project. . . . Ah, no. I could never trust you."

"And if you could . . . ?"

"You might be sure, then, of my friendship," she concluded, and added, walking to the door, "of my gratitude, and affection."

Standing by the door, Edmond took her by the shoulders, and she did not resist.

"Please," he said. "Trust me." He drew her closer and kissed her softly and without haste on the cheek, then on the throat. He felt her hesitate and relax slightly against him; she was shuddering in his arms, and when he looked up he discerned that her eyes were wet. He kissed a tear as it rolled down her face. She kissed him quickly on the mouth, then disengaged herself, but gently, and dried her eyes.

"Leave me," she said. "Go downstairs. I'll be down in a moment."

Left to herself she stood for a time after the door had closed, savoring the complexity of bitterness and relief. *What* have I done? alternated with What *have* I done? and the last few minutes seemed capable of opposite disproportion, as too much or, after all, too little, all but nothing.

It seems I have a friend, she at last said to herself with half-humorous anger. A friend, *un ami.* She went to her room and looked at herself in the glass; a strangely sorrowful expression, a white, unhappy face, belied her lighter feelings.

"Dishonor in everything," she said aloud. "In everything."

As for Edmond, he reflected, walking downstairs, that he now felt more his old self and own man; there was nothing like emotion—of any sort—for toning up the system. But who would have thought there was such a kick in it? He had been surprised and, a little, touched. She was attractive, there was a violence under that austere manner. It wasn't impossible— but of that later. The point now was that new complications, new possibilities, existed, and that was always good. One felt younger.

In the hall downstairs he saw Susan in what seemed to be earnest conversation with that man, that butler—Hogan. Edmond felt vaguely resentful. But as he walked toward them the doorbell rang and Hogan left to answer it.

"How'd it go?" Susan asked.

"Quite well," Edmond said. "Not bad at all—we're quite to be brother and sister now, Claire and I. I hope so, that is." Susan squeezed his arm.

"Good," she said. "I'm glad." But she was conscious as she spoke of doubt as well as relief; it seemed, to say the least, unlikely that an interview of such great and predictable diffi- culty should have so easily resolved itself, that attitudes at such obstinate extremes should have collapsed at the mere touch, in half an hour. She would have asked for a more detailed sum-mary, but that the opening of the door now concluded the possibility of conversation.

2

FOUR WOMEN stood in the entry. Beyond them, on the sidewalk across the street, which reflected the street lamp with a hard starlike glitter, stood four men, of whom one was a priest and another a policeman; the two remaining were dressed in evening clothes. All four intently watched the women in such a way as silently to suggest a concentration of superior will that had dictated the crossing of the street, the mounting of the stair. In a moment, however, the women being within, Hogan closed the door, shutting out this strange scene, but not before it had impressed on Susan at least its quality of remote and silent intensity, as though (she thought) it were an advertisement for a dream.

Of the women, who now stood in the hall, looking about them with eyes expressive of nervousness and mistrust, one was very beautiful and well-dressed. She stood apart from the others, tapping an impatient foot and making as evident as possible the contempt of the superior person—as an officer might do, who, captured in nondescript uniform and bundled together with private soldiers, relies dubiously enough on "background and breeding." So this girl held her blonde head very high, tapped loudly with her foot and looked about her scornfully.

The other three by contrast huddled closely together—two young girls under the protection of an old woman—clutching their pocketbooks and the edges of their coats as though they feared the drastic and immediate removal of all that was theirs, by some magical violence in this strange place.

The young girls were probably, in their own milieu, pretty; here, however, their scared pallor emphasized the bravura (inexperienced and at the same time professional) with which their makeup had been put on—there is a cosmetic art appropriate to a certain distance from the street light—and this gave to their features a clownish and masklike appearance.

But it was the old woman who, in this situation, commanded most attention.

It was hard to tell, impossible to tell, how old she was; her face seemed to have been a thousand times shrunken and overlaid by powders and rouges and creams which now had little organic relation to the contours beneath but had of themselves and with the aid of time formed a mask like those which savages compose about the skulls of their enemies. In the fixity of this aged monument a muscle would move, the lips would move, the bright eyes would move, but every movement signified only the threatened cracking of the surface. For all this, absurd and unpleasant as it was, this old face had about it something decisive and powerful which displayed itself despite the poor artifices at its disposal: a cruelty which demonstrated an existence beyond that one which served for the mere purpose of being sold, obviously, at any behest, unguents, lotions and ointments that withered and dried at the lightest touches of time or the weather. There was about the old woman a certain birdlike alacrity, a nervous quality of—as it seemed to Susan, at least—evil, of a life built wholly on sinister intention that no travesty of fashion could entirely conceal. Her eyes were deeply sunken over the cheekbones and so heavily shadowed as to give the appearance of existing in little umbrellas; her hair was battle-gray with blue tints here and there in it, curled and plastered to the skull with great precision, surmounted by a little hat whose decorative accent was a bunch of cherries which had evidently been stewed before being placed there; they were of a bronzed color. In her hideous likeness to the symbol of American motherhood as seen on boxes of candy, this old

2 6 3

woman might have served as the trademark of a firm producing poisoned chocolates.

Hogan was sent to fetch Claire, but Edmond and Susan had simply to stand there watching the women in silence (for no one had anything to say) and being watched by them for a considerable time. During this interval the voices of the Hungarian nuns began to be heard droning from far away, and at this the women started slightly and looked around them more apprehensively than before; nevertheless they did not speak, having apparently resolved in advance on a sullen and minimal submissiveness in the face of whatever authority over them happened to exist in this house which they had been compelled to enter.

Now that the theoretical proposition as to the existence of such women, who sold themselves for money, had been replaced by their presence, here, in the house, Susan was surprised to feel hatred and loathing of them rising in her mind. It is not enough, she said to herself, to know that such things can be. When one sees such faces . . . And yet the young girls did not by any means look depraved or anything other than demure, poor and frightened. It was something else, some quality of tedious and routine excess, which she was incapable of analyzing, and so she concentrated her attention fully on the more beautiful and richly dressed girl, whose appearance of strained haughtiness provided a more acceptable object of dislike. I can see beneath that, she thought, to the softness, the loathsome softness of that life. But then she began to feel that this revulsion, this obscure shame, attached rather to herself than to anyone else, and she refused to look at the girl, but looked down instead at the floor. I too am like that, she thought.

Claire came down the stairs, flanked by Sisters Catherine and Terese and followed by Hogan.

"Good evening," she said to the women in a pleasant, though official and matronly tone. "You are the . . ." she stopped; the struggle between the priestly derision of the word advocated by the Bishop (to which she had grown more accustomed than was perhaps necessary) and the sense that this word would be exactly the one least appreciated by those to whom it might with most justice be applied, produced a sudden silence and loss of command. This hesitation was not overlooked by the women, who gained from it a little confidence. The old woman stepped forward and offered her hand to Claire, who could not avoid shaking it.

"I am Amelia Fosker," she said, showed her false teeth by a broad smile. "Mother Fosker, as they call me. This is a nice place you have here, a real nice place." She pushed the two girls forward. "These are two of mine," she said. "Nolly and Jane. I don't know about the other one. Do you work for an organization, dear?" she asked, turning to the other girl.

"I work for myself," the girl replied in a cool voice of gin and milk.

"Ah, that's too bad." Mother Fosker pursed her lips and shook her head in a melancholy way. "I know what it is to be an independent—one trouble after another. And you don't really earn more if you add it up in the long run. You need a manager, dear, someone like me—yes," she seemed to consider for a moment, then, decisively, "yes, I think I could find you an opening in a little place I'm developing. . . ."

"No, thanks," said the girl.

"Ah, well. If you're sure—no need to answer so hasty," Mother Fosker said, and returned her attention to Claire. "A real nice place, as I say," she repeated. "I'm sure we'll be very happy here. As nice a house as—do you know the Saint Ambrosius Home for Decayed Gentlewomen? *That* was a nice place, if you like. I stayed there back in thirty-two for a few weeks, when the big vice purge was on. I was glad to be out of Boston then, I can tell you that. I can remember Molly Horsner saying she'd try to stick it out, and you know what happened to Molly Horsner—seven years, and when she came out her whole business was gone, gone, and she never did get started again. I always say you've got to be more philosophical, ride with the administration—know what I mean? A little holiday, that's what I tell my girls, take yourself a little holiday."

Claire interrupted here to say, with what was perhaps irony, that she was glad Mother Fosker could see her way to being happy in these circumstances. "Although this is a—house of correction, I suppose," she said to the girls, "I want things to be as pleasant as possible for you. Within limits, of course. I expect your co-operation, for your own comfort."

"You'll get it," Mother Fosker said, glancing somewhat grimly at Nolly and Jane, who looked both serious and unhappy. "Nolly and Jane will co-operate, won't you, dears?" she said coyly. "Nolly and Jane got in a little trouble tonight from not co-operating—they thought they could scout around after working hours and save themselves my percentage. So they got arrested—on the corner of Tremont and Park, of all places." Mother Fosker smiled again, thinly. "I don't favor private enterprise, unless it's my private enterprise," she said. "Just remember that, girls, will you? Stick with Mother and you'll get along all right."

Claire felt that if this were not the kind of co-operation she meant, it was more and better than she had expected. The submissiveness of the women pleased her, as did also the calm efficiency of the nuns, who presently shepherded their first charges upstairs without incident and presumably oversaw their going quietly and in part contentedly to bed.

So that's all there is to it, Claire said to herself when the house was settled and she had gone to her own room. Here they are; they don't make any fuss for they know we have the law on our side. We treat them decently—like human beings—and in return they will behave in a quiet and orderly fashion.

She even felt a slight resentment at being able to credit herself with good works at so little cost, and determined to exercise her charity toward the women even beyond what was necessary—to do them little favors, which they would repay by an honest regard for her as having pulled them out of the horrid life which had formerly been theirs. I must have tea with them in the afternoons, she thought, and gain their confidence—though that old one is a frightful chatterbox.

3

It was late at night; far upstairs the nuns had long ago left off praying, the time for argument was past, another day had gone. And now, disencumbered of human activity, the house itself came into its own and seemed by a number of slight indications to draw breath, the unregarded breath given by the generations, which in the dark spaces of the night cautiously expressed itself. Cushions in these hours uncrumpled themselves—almost silently but not quite—and that silken whisper was penetrated by the occasional sudden expansion of a couch spring, the sound of a mouse scratching in the wall, the creak of a floor-board, the drip of a tap, the low mumbling of pipes. In the kitchen the refrigerator buzzed, groaned, stopped and began again as though in uneasy sleep, and the pilot-lights of the old blackened stove wavered and shed a wavering light.

Upstairs, the corridors were darkened through which Hogan went to Susan's room. He heard the ticking of a distant clock, the slight shuffle of his shoes, his own breathing and his rapidly beating heart, but his nervousness was so great he fancied himself everywhere spied upon and thought he detected ghostly motion in every angle of his way. The light bending of a white curtain before an open window at the end of the hall caused him almost to suffocate of fear. But there was in his mind no question of not going.

Susan had bid him come to her room when the house was still; there had been no time, in their brief meeting downstairs, for explanations, and indeed she had seemed disinclined to give any. He recalled the set, intense pride of her look as she gave him, in as few words as possible, this extreme command which was capable of having, after all, but one meaning.

No, there was no question of his not obeying—obeying in order to conquer, as he put it to himself (though not quite explicitly). He was frightened, but his fear was tactical merely, for he held stubbornly to an idea which his years as a servant should probably have taught him was inadmissible—the idea of his destiny, which one day would take him and lift him up.

The society which Hogan occasionally frequented on evenings off was a strange one, composed exclusively of what used to be called "upper" servants, Martin, the chauffeur of Mrs de K——, Harris, the butler of ancient Mr Q——, Emerson, the valet of the old bachelor Mr R—— who was related to the house of Bourbon-Parma. These men regarded themselves no less than their employers as the last representatives of a dying order, and their political views accordingly were conservative to a degree, to that degree, in fact, at which death itself becomes the error of a radical regime. But in proportion as they felt themselves threatened by the death of the master, which in each of their cases was reasonably imminent, they were given to discussing the future, lugubriously but with vehemence. From these men, who rather suffered him as an interesting *parvenu*, Hogan had gained some ideas about history: these ideas were curiously like those held at the time among educated men and "liberals."

His impression of history was that it consisted in equal parts of events and great men, whose conjunction always produced Opportunity: thus at a certain moment in European History events had so arranged themselves as to produce, granted the birth of Napoleon and certain other obscure but necessary factors in the stage-setting, a most remarkable and unpredictable success, a career full of blood, grandeur and reward. But since Hogan's acquaintances in their disquisitions had neglected to provide any adequate notion of what greatness might be, his idea of history was finally imaginable as a billiard table in whose composition Opportunity was a movable pocket which might be placed at any moment in the path of any ball.

In times of decadence—a word which from the speed of its being bandied about had gained an enormous centrifugal force—Opportunities were multiplied (the billiard table became full of pockets) and, as could plainly be seen from the careers of Hitler, Mussolini, X—— and Y——, success was possible to the most obscure men (there was no longer a billiard table but simply one gigantic pocket) with or without "greatness." These companions of Hogan's possessed and had endued him with a nearly heroic gift for self-deception; they each carried, side by side with their apprehensions of being left thoroughly in the cold, fabulous expectations from the end of their servitude—money, a chain of cheap restaurants in Ankara, the Duchy of —— near Naples. None of these old and on the whole likable gentlemen really expected the fulfilment of any such dreams, but they were fond of using such counters in their conversation, and demonstrating to their own and each other's satisfaction how close they had come, in their lives, to success, eminence, leisure—as a man who is the double of the King of England or of a fashionable actor may derive from the resemblance a higher opinion of his personal qualities than his fortune will give him warrant for.

2 6 9

None of them, though, had ever spoken of such a means of access to better things as now seemed to have appeared before Hogan—and that is surprising, if one considers that in history, of which they were all so fond, the bed-chamber has always stood in the closest relation to the council-chamber. Each of these servants seemed to have, embalmed in a long career of fidelity and discretion, one episode, complete with dark stairway and the rustle of an expensive, perfumed nightdress, which could at the appropriate moment be brought out, though always in a low voice as if the evocation were meant to be overheard rather than heard; but these were sweet souvenirs precisely because they hadn't been anything else and had led to no permanent improvement or revision of life; Hogan fancied his position to be somewhat different.

From the moment of Susan's invitation, earlier that evening, he had begun to regard himself as ruthless, and to look upon this moment as the crisis during which he must seize power; characteristically he thought little or nothing of any pleasure he might derive from the rendezvous, but had for two hours already been looking beyond it to a nebulous conception of himself tomorrow and the next day and all the days after that, a man (somehow) of position and authority. According to the paradigm of history, as Hogan understood it, the Boyne household was passing through a period of decadence, an interregnum consequent on the abdication of the supreme authority (Mr and Mrs Boyne), the over-running of the domain by barbarians (whores and nuns), the dispute over the throne between two princesses, of whom one was swayed by the Church and the other was accessible to lust: the erotic and the political were in conjunction and in favorable aspect, and Hogan's star was at last, by some means not entirely clear, to rise.

He stopped before Susan's door, uncertain whether or not to knock; finally he decided not to knock but to let boldness show his mastery of the situation, and he opened the door. It was with inexplicable relief that he discovered Susan to be fully dressed. She sat in an armchair facing the door, a single lamp shone from behind her, illuminating her hair and the line of her shoulders but leaving her face in shadow.

"So we don't knock at doors any longer?" she said coldly.

"You expected me," Hogan replied. She looked at him, then gestured a little wearily with one hand as though to dismiss the subject.

"You know why I've asked you here," she said, placing the matter between question and statement.

"It would be out of place in me to say I *know*," he returned, "and I don't want to guess."

"So I must tell you," she said. "You want that too."

He was silent and stood there before her because he had not quite the security of insolence necessary to let him sit down without being invited. As for Susan, she looked at him in a long moment of contemptuous inspection, then: "This is your cheap triumph," she said.

"Maybe while you're still a servant," she presently added, "and just before you become a hero—you'd go down and bring us something to drink."

Hogan relished neither leaving the crisis in its present condition nor making two extra trips through the dark house; nevertheless, he complied.

Susan smoked a cigarette until he came back. What she now required, she told herself, was a violence of feeling, even of anger, to support her decision. She had not realized that there existed between Hogan and herself so many opportunities and, more, necessities, for explanation, mediation—for words. Blindly she had resolved on a decisive scene, on one liberating action; but in this blind resolve she had not foreseen that there would be, first, as there always must be, conversation. The nature of what she proposed had seemed to her so bestial, so shameful to all feeling, as to be acceptable only as the act of a beast, without talk, above all without talk. Talk relaxed the will, talk obscured the moment until the moment was over, and most of all to talk of the decisive was to take away everything decisive in it. But miserably she recognized that there would be talk.

Hogan returned carrying a bottle and two glasses. Susan swallowed at once the drink he gave her.

"I can't pay you any more money," she said. "I refuse to. I want after this to be absolutely free of you. Do you understand?"

Hogan smiled and raised his eyebrows, trying to show a confidence he did not feel. The idea of being "absolutely free" had singularly little charm for him, and he thought she proposed paying a high price for such a vague benefit.

"Well, must I spell it out," she said impatiently. "Do you accept?"

"Sure." Hogan continued smiling. He felt miserable and knew too that he was trading something for nothing. As in chess, it had been better to hold the threat than to use it, to cash it in for the slight advantage it was giving.

"Well, then . . ." Just before she turned out the light he saw her open with one nervous hand the clasp at her throat.

TUESDAY

DECEMBER

28

1948		DECEMBER			1948	
SU	MO	TU	WE	TH	FR	SA
. .	. .	. .	. .	1	2	3	4
5	6	7	8	9	10	11
12	13	14	15	16	17	18
19	20	21	22	23	24	25
26	27	28	29	30	31	. .

*T*HIS is a world in which, according to the first tenet of poetry, the spiritual and the material reflect and interpenetrate one another. Spiritual things are conceived and spoken of as embodied, material things however commonplace are imbued with and expressive of idea, spirit, desire. Consider, as exemplary of the general proposition, even so ordinary a thing as a door, which becomes when regarded in this light a subtle and significant demonstration of the human spirit, and even, in respect of its ambiguous nature, a miraculous invention.

Anciently the guardian of gateways was Janus, whose two faces, though they gained him a reputation for irony and deceit, were merely the image and denomination, as honest as possible, of the crucial situation expressed by a door: that it had to do with inside and outside and represented therefore the entire possibility of human society, which without this distinction could not have existed. It is the door which stands in the mind for the scenic setting-off of the private from the public, the secret from the well-known, the intimate from the available, as we see from the example of the little pig in the cartoon, who presses himself in terror against the locked door of his house which has meanwhile been blown down by the wolf; nor do various metaphors and metonymies in common speech fail to illustrate the power of this symbolism. To honored guests or conquerors we give the keys to the city, secret meetings take place "behind locked doors," people have or have not "the entry" to certain areas of society, opportunity knocks on one's door, in beginning some public activity we "throw open the doors." Samson expresses his contempt for the Philistines by carrying away the gates of Gaza to the top of Hebron Hill, the everlasting doors are lifted up at the advent of the King of Glory, it is the doorway of Hell which so decisively marks, in Dante, the change of state from hope to despair, as it is in the same poet the locking of a door which occasions Ugolino's crime. Society, like death in the old play, "hath ten thousand several doors."

Doors express a certain independence, hardness, coolness, and even snobbishness; they pose a distinction few would willingly do without, yet are capable of emphasizing that in some instances the distinction is more valuable than in others: the doors of rich houses, the gates of castles, the guarded entrance to a block of expensive apartments where one must submit to being judged by appearance alone. The guardianship of doors, together with the primitive (doubtless deliberately primitive) means of communication between inside and outside—the bell, the buzzer, the knocker, the servant, the telephone guaranteed to disguise the voice; all those means by which the will, with urgency from outside and obscurantism from within, seeks to make itself felt through a thickness of wood—forms a vast subject in itself. Yet the mere mention has been enough, has sufficed to draw attention to the real problem of doors, their relation with the will.

Between the unequivocal opening of a door and the unequivocal leaving it shut, matter has failed to be as variously and subtly conformable to the hesitations and vacillations of the spirit as could be wished; it is as though the nature of things were only to a certain extent patient of man's shilly-shallying, and after that wished to enforce upon him a choice: the door must be opened or left shut. Expedients have been tried, ranging from half-doors and sliding panels to many secretaries and the chain of command, but no door has yet been devised which infallibly will admit the right people and as infallibly exclude the wrong ones; philosophers will note with satisfaction the complex ramifications of this problem in the domains of purpose, of functional as against organic reality, of the apparent and the actual—a detestable person brings you necessary information, a good friend arrives and unconsciously prevents a meeting with your mistress.

The ownership of a door, then, does not pre-emptively assert the possession of silence and solitude. The door is but an instrument of the spirit; much depends on the will. Times of interior crisis are likely to produce feverish activity also in doors; of which the final example is perhaps the funeral followed by the auction.

In the house owned (in a rather remote sense at present) by Nicholas Boyne, the laws governing the spiritual function of doors operated as inflexibly as anywhere else, and expressed by merely opening and closing the manifold uncertainties, conflicts and deep requirements of the multiplied spirit within. This was true not only of the front and back doors, but with respect also to doors within the house, designed for more subtle distinctions of privacy and segregation, confusion and uncertainty began to be felt.

The week following the arrival of Mother Fosker and the other women was marked in particular by the departure of Mrs Purse, so that there was now no cook in the house and, in view of the expanding situation, little chance of getting one. Mrs Purse, having made up her mind to leave, acted decisively, staying not to argue or be temporized with but simply packing her belongings and sneaking out the back way. She left a note, of which only the words "impossible" and "too much" were legible, standing out in block letters from a wildly cursive script. Claire was inclined to agree with Mrs Purse, and found herself repeating under her breath at critical moments (of which there were, that day, several) "impossible" and "too much."

Hogan found the note and brought it to Claire in the early afternoon. He brought also troubles of his own.

"Miss Susan wishes me to leave your service," he said with great humility, through which Claire thought she detected an undeniable smugness.

"Did she give any reason?"

"No, Miss. She just sort of blew up in my face."

"Well, I'll look into it. You can't leave us now, that's one certain thing."

I shouldn't have said that, Claire thought when the man had gone. I should not have committed myself one way or the other. Now he thinks he's been promised something.

She called Susan and repeated the butler's words.

"I can't fire the man without a reason," she said. "He's been here—why, as long as you have, almost. What has he done that's so terrible?"

Susan began to cry, though she made every effort to repress her feeling; and this choked whimpering which would at any other time probably have evoked Claire's most tender feelings had now the effect of making her lose her temper.

"Now listen," she said. "I run this house; I take it all on myself. I'm not complaining. But I refuse to make things any harder for myself for no reason at all. If the man has done anything wrong, tell me about it. I want to be just."

There was no answer. Susan, still sobbing, left the room. Claire called after her: "On the other hand, if you simply lost your temper with him over nothing, I think you ought to apologize. I can't afford to be left without a servant in the house."

My God, Claire thought—this place, this madhouse! She retired to her father's study and locked the door. She stayed there all afternoon. Her intention was to think, primarily and supremely about finding a replacement for Mrs Purse; but this problem, local and practical as it had seemed, could not be kept apart in her mind from the responsibilities of the house as a whole. Everything she thought of appeared to involve everything else in a terrible confusion.

First, the presence of those women—the nuns and the others had become equally "those women." The Bishop's thoughtful prevision of electric burners to be used upstairs had not extended to the provision of such burners, and it had already become a common feature of life in this house to have women in various kinds and stages of dress going like sleepwalkers with arms extended and clattering trays through the halls, up and down the stairs. That alone put the services of an employment agency out of the question. One could imagine the interview: "You will have to cook for a mere dozen people, more or less— but of course that number is expected to increase during the next few days." It was laughable but that did not improve Claire's humor.

Well, then, she thought. I brought those people here, they must be fed, they are my responsibility. What to do?

It was unfortunate that her thoughts arrived at the practical question by precisely this path, for what she now turned to thinking of was the meaning of her having brought "those people" into her house, and this not only deranged all her sense of the practical and urgent but also involved her in a disagreeable examination of conscience.

This examination referred ultimately to two things: her feeling for the Roman Catholic Church, and her feeling for Dr

Einman. But that did not at once become clear, the route between the surface and the depths was, as usual, devious and hidden.

The women were here, in the house, they were the victims, or the patients, or the beneficiaries of a scheme which was supposed to have both interior and exterior results—it had all seemed so plain and simple once. In a guaranteed if temporary freedom from the exigencies by which alone (it was presumed) such entire collapses of chastity occurred, the women were to have the opportunity of repentance, of strengthening the will to virtue before being exposed once again to temptation. That was all very well, but was it working? How was it working?

In the material sense it was not working very well: the women were both lazy and slovenly, and Sisters Catherine and Terese either did not sufficiently care or were unable to exert sufficient control, more likely the latter. It was really Mother Fosker who kept her girls in line, and had that very beautiful one quieted down as well. The beautiful one, whose name was Amy, had made a great fuss over being made to share common quarters and meals—"I refuse to be put with this riff-raff," she had said with vigor and a splendid freedom from embarrassment. "I want a room with bath." Upon being refused she had tried to bribe Sister Catherine with twenty dollars. But since Mother Fosker, with a sly expression on her old face, had taken her aside for a few moments, Amy gave no more trouble. Mother Fosker was in effect a blessing: if those girls made their beds and even swept up a little dust once in a while it was because Mother Fosker told them to, and not because of anything the nuns might say.

But Mother Fosker was of course a blessing only in effect, only materially; theologically considered—and it was essential that she be considered that way—she, being a bawd, was more reprehensible than all the others taken together, was corrupt in herself and also the occasion of corruption in others: any alliance with her had about it a taint, a hint that one traded with the enemy. But already the idea of conducting the enterprise without her co-operation—since she was here—seemed unthinkable. She had ingratiated herself easily even with the nuns, to whom (as to everyone who would listen, in fact) she chattered incessantly about her life, her friends, how things had been when her husband was alive and they owned a little club in Somerville.

Now the slovenliness, the laziness, could not be called entirely the fault of these women, whose whole occupation had, after all, been suddenly taken away. The day was long, there was little for them to do; and for that reason among others they could not be kept apart from the rest of the household. Nolly and Jane were fond of exploring, and had twice been discovered after prolonged search in remote reaches of the house; Amy, with quiet assumption, made use at opportunity of any room in which she thought she would be left alone, and there read books which she borrowed from the Boyne library. This was all innocent enough, and Claire would have thought herself uncharitable had she been more severe; but she could not help noticing already the implication of a rather proprietary freedom which included the whole house.

Father Meretruce came every afternoon and was closeted with whores and nuns together for one hour; what did he say to them at these times? Perhaps (Claire thought) he read to them from the scripture, in especial from the horrible page of Isaiah, which began: "Because the daughters of Zion are haughty, and walk with stretched forth neck and wanton eyes, walking and mincing as they go, and making a tinkling with their feet: Therefore the Lord will smite with a scab the crown of the head of the daughters of Zion, and the Lord will discover their secret parts." She thought with a certain disgust and fear of the slow surgery conducted by the priest's voice in the dissection of lust: "And it shall come to pass, that instead of sweet smell there shall be stink. . . ."

She was appalled at the sense of these words, and even more at the sense of her own loathing for them: "and instead of well-set hair baldness"—that was peculiarly repulsive: the Lord God would scalp you, snatch you bald—"and burning instead of beauty." And she called to mind those medieval pictures in which the sufferings of the flesh were depicted with such an evidently sensual delight: *La Chute des Damnés*, where the bodies of the sinners male and female, refined almost to emaciation for the better emphasis of their sexuality which was at the same time pitiful and sordid, were devoured by monsters with radulate teeth; those other paintings which so thoroughly illustrated an obsessive and perverse pleasure in the imagination of marble-smooth and youthful flesh being pierced by sharp instruments, by nails, spears, arrows, huge bloodied thorns: the crucifixions, the Saint Sebastians, the massacre of St. Ursula and her friends, the impaled and squirming Martyrs of the Thebaid.

Did she believe in it? It seemed to her now that she had lost the sense of the wholeness of things; what had she seen, and what felt, on that evening—it was not so long ago—when her prayers had been answered, or had for a moment corresponded with the undeniable existence of something? God was love—it was written so, and Claire had felt that it was so. But again, what were the feelings which that word love excited? As she could remember them, those feelings had once to do with something cold, icy, exalted and chaste; a distant music sounding in spacious, invisible corridors, a wind like a silver sword, a silent flash of blue-white lightning. Love was, in a mystical phrase she had so easily accepted as a piece of superior knowledge, the sighing and trembling of the universe before its creator. Yet now she so strongly felt that love was something else again, and had to do with those paintings of destruction, with the women Isaiah excoriated, in fact, with Mother Fosker and her girls as much as with anyone else, with Susan, with Edmond, with herself. As the "sighing and trembling of the universe" threw molten lava from the depths of the earth, so love might be a rumbling in the bowels, a sickness of the flesh, a soft lasciviousness as well as a hard chastity, a cruelty involving blood and pus and lymph, the trembling of the body before pain and death and decay. She imagined that many must have witnessed with hot pleasure the Son of Man writhing on the Cross, which pleasure might in some subterranean change after his death have been the motive of their conversion. They feared, perhaps, the vengeance of the dead, not because they had killed Him but because He bore away into death the deepest powers of their lust.

The idea of love revolted her; it was unclean. The whole of her extremely moral nature resisted the belief that she could have been created sinful and utterly dependent from the beginning, that both the sin in its original and its forgiveness were beyond her power to choose. "I have not committed murder, I have not stolen; am I not better than a crook in prison, better than a whore in the street, better than a swindler, a Fascist, a pervert?" But believing herself at least to this extent and in this negative way honorable and virtuous she nevertheless detested the belief, for she thought it immodest.

Closer to home, there was her relation with Edmond to be considered—that friendship which she had conditionally offered him. Their first meeting in private had been followed by a second and a third, during which she had thought it proper to encourage him in virtue (that is to say, in giving up the idea of marrying Susan) both by exhortation and by the renewal of such evanescent intimacies and tendernesses as might amply be covered by the idea of friendship and sisterly feeling. Or perhaps not amply? Claire resented but could not avoid the idea that she was striking a bargain with Edmond, permitting slightly more than was proper in exchange for a certain agreement which as yet she had to presume in him; he for his part insisted on expressing a feeling for her of sympathy and understanding of which the visible and not quite innocent signification was a kiss—chaste enough in all conscience—or his hand on her shoulder. For this sympathy and understanding she admitted a need; it was something of which she deeply felt the lack in her conversations with Father Meretruce, who in a doctrinaire way treated her not as a person but as a complicated assortment of virtues and vices built into a kind of atomic structure. "Chastity," he would say, and "Pride" and "Obedience," with the absolute assumption that these words referred to things recognizably and isolably part of her which might be taken out and tinkered with and put back. With Edmond it was different; she had for him something of the feeling she wished she might have had for her father and she greatly desired his friendship on the understanding that this, with his other relations in their house, would have no permanent issue; but had she, in consequence, raised his hopes (as the falsely modest way was of putting it) or suggested to him any progressive admission to greater things? And thus sought, with whatever virtuous intention, to replace Susan?

That was unthinkable. "If that were so, all human relations would be like blackmail." "If that were so, I should be no better than a whore." It was better put, she told herself, that, understanding what was good, what was right, she acted so as to secure her sister's happiness—"even at my own expense; I would sacrifice myself but that nothing like that is necessary in the case." They are all wrong, she thought, the religions and the psychologies together, all, with their extravagant notions.

One must simply do what is right—there is never any excuse.

And meanwhile it was getting late, supper was to be considered, and the problems of provisioning for the future. The days stretched out before her, each with its three meals, and she sighed.

Susan during this time quarreled with Edmond. After leaving Claire she went to her room and stayed there until she could stop crying, which was some few minutes, then washed, changed her clothes and went to his room. He was not there.

She found him downstairs in the library, taking notes of the conversation of Amy, who was evidently telling the history of her life; when Susan entered she was speaking of having been educated abroad.

"In a convent-school at Lausanne," she said, giving the place-name full value as "Louse Anne." "Before father lost his money in the Crash."

Susan was in temper enough to make her dismissal curt, and Amy went off upstairs throwing angry looks backward.

"She has been lying to me for twenty minutes," Edmond said. "A very interesting girl."

Disregarding this, which she thought was intended for a provocation, Susan sat down next him and began to speak, more urgently than he had heard her do before, of love. Edmond recognized from the suppressed intensity of feeling in her voice and the repetition of certain phrases, that some extraordinary force was demanding a declaration, a full reassurance. Partly amused and partly annoyed, he did not acknowledge the demand, so that she was at last compelled to speak out: she wanted him to go upstairs, pack a few things while she did likewise, and take her away; they could be married as soon as possible.

"If we don't go away," she said, "I don't know what will happen." As he was silent, she looked at him closely. "You don't love me," she said calmly enough, with pity in her voice. "You don't care for anyone."

"Ah, love," he said, taking her hand; he was embarrassed by this necessity of having strong emotion always available; nevertheless he objected rather coldly that he loved her. He saw that her face was pale, and guessed she had been crying over something; she smelled slightly of soap, a hygienic and depressing odor which a little offended him.

"Something has made you unhappy. What is it?" he said.

For a moment Susan was on the point of telling him; it was not shame that prevented her, strong as her shame was, but the feeling that she had made herself ridiculous. Love, she thought, was a game the strong could play together, weakness on one side would be treasured up to be laughed at on the other. She repeated her demand.

"You're wrought up about something," he replied. "Let's not speak of it all now."

Susan had determined before he spoke that these words were to represent his final opinion, beyond which she would not demean herself by pleading further; but she could not resist one more move.

"Is it Claire," she asked, "who has caused this change?"

He smiled, and denied it, and further denied that there had been a change; Susan took her pride in her hands and left the room. Their quarrel had been for the most part conducted by their silence rather than their words, but it was inescapably there. She had the impression that she had finally rejected him, as he had her, and that by doing it without explicitly saying so she had obscurely scored a point. She passed Hogan on the stairs, but they did not speak.

In the afternoon mail Susan received a letter from John Averist. He, too, spoke of love (it was a fashionable thing, she observed, to speak of), implored her not to marry "this man," as he several times referred to Edmond, expressed for herself his feeling, which was one of passionate regard if the marriage were not taking place and of ideal longing and refined self-pity if it were; finally he asked to be allowed to visit her once more. Concerning the matter in which she had asked his assistance—here the letter grew vague and inexpressive—he had, perhaps, failed or done worse even than that, but he would explain this to her face if she gave permission, and he would (again) do anything to demonstrate the depth of his affection, the constancy of his feeling, etc.

Susan was very far from being touched by this letter; nevertheless she telephoned a wire to him setting a time next evening at which he might call. There was, at least, someone whose desire exposed him to any cruelty and humiliation.

Toward the end of the afternoon arrived Father Meretruce; he generally contrived to time his appearance so that the hour of edification would end near the hour for dinner, to which his invitation, when he was present, was assumed. Today he went first to see Claire, to whom he confessed a certain impatience and anxiety over her conversion.

"My feeling is that you have been ready for some time," he said. "I hope we are not in danger of losing you." He glanced at her searchingly.

This was for Claire the last aggravation. She began an explanation of her delay, the coolness of her faith such as it was, her lack of assurance in the Church—and inextricably confused this account with the tale of her domestic difficulties which by now almost wholly occupied her mind. Father Meretruce smiled ominously.

"What a tragedy! to lose one's faith and one's cook in a single day."

Claire was in no temper for epigram.

"I can't help what I feel," she said. "I've changed my mind.

I honestly do not wish to enter the Roman Church." Exasperation had in a moment produced this decisive statement after months of vacillation.

"You put us all in a very disagreeable position," said the priest. "His Excellency, myself, and . . ." he gestured largely toward the ceiling, including the nuns and possibly God.

Claire said that she was sorry for this; but added, however, that she had not understood her salvation to be implicated in the social embarrassments of anyone whatever.

"You needn't fear," she said. "I recognize my obligations and I don't intend to withdraw from them."

"Ah, that is for us to decide," returned Father Meretruce. "We have entrusted these women to you . . ." he stopped as though to indicate his sense was obvious.

"I don't in the least see that you've *entrusted*, as you put it, anything to me beyond the mere feeding of these women— and that, I assure you, is my major concern at this moment."

"But there are, nevertheless, spiritual values in the case."

"There are, admittedly, spiritual values."

They glowered at one another for a moment, then the priest got up.

"My child, I am thoroughly sorry for you—heartily sorry." He went toward the door, then turned back. "No. I cannot leave you like this. You have natural doubts, you are confused. Surely you will change your mind—your heart?"

Claire took this as an accusation of an accepted inconstancy, as in fact the diagnosis of a critical point in her conversion rather than of her total disaffection.

"If I should change," she said with a slight smile, "I suppose the Church will still be there?"

The priest had no recourse but to leave the room, which he did after imparting to her a perfunctory blessing with the wish that God's grace might be hers.

"About the practical side of the matter," he said, "we'll continue for the moment as though nothing had happened. And I will speak with His Excellency."

So saying, he went upstairs, where he spoke with infuriated eloquence for three-quarters of an hour concerning the foolish virgins who took no oil in their lamps; Nolly asked him how ten virgins could possibly go to meet one bridegroom.

"It is an allegory," the priest replied heavily, and prepared to explain.

"It's bigotry in this state," Nolly said.

Almost everyone in the house was angry.

At about six o'clock a police wagon appeared in the street; with a quite unnecessary clangor of its bell it drew up, and, while inquisitive faces peered from the windows of every house, some seventeen women were driven through the Boyne front door.

These women were of all ages, types, stages of repute and disrepute. The Bishop had spoken to Claire of "whores," but the rough honesty of that word proved in the end misleading, since it suggested that the women to be dealt with would be of one kind: poor, easily recognized, docile and stupid. Here were seventeen women of very varied degrees of advancement in the same general profession, the youngest being perhaps twelve, the oldest about fifty. Except for five, who had been taken, evidently, in a raid upon a single house, and were still dressed in the sleazy but diaphanous kimonos and pieces of curtain material through which they exhibited their charms to prospective customers, none of these women displayed any single common characteristic by which their disgrace might be known. One was a thin, elderly and sour person dressed in black; she wore pince-nez, and resembled the Platonic idea of a high-school teacher of French. Another, who wore a short mink jacket over a very modish light suit, possessed that fresh, early-morning loveliness that is the trademark, in advertisements, of the expensive and desirable American girl. Nothing was more obvious than that there existed, as a factor of the first importance, differences of style, class and especially income, which prevented these women from showing for one another the sisterly recognition of a common mystery that they ought theoretically to have shown and which would have made them quietly amenable to being thus lumped together. These distinctions were apparent by the way they grouped themselves in the front hall according to barriers of caste: from the worn-out veterans who could no longer command a greater price than perhaps two dollars (and that seldom), through the common occupants of houses, the union and guild members so to speak, to the nervously insolent beauties who maintained "decorated" apartments and maids and were on call to a select list capable of renting such charm. Among these last was Leonora.

Some little time after Roger's departure to Canada she had been forced to give up Gerry Landis, whose attentions she found personally displeasing and financially unwholesome; she had then been for a short while the mistress of a professor of political economy at Harvard. In the society she inhabited, however, availability was everything: she found it impossible, having given herself to one person, to deny her favors to his friends—it would have been thought snobbish and affected. She had attended parties whose object was to produce the maximum number of permutations among the guests; this was gay, but expensive and unprofitable: one too often in a moment of madness paid for the taxi or casually added a bottle of Scotch to the common stock. Leonora determined to reform, and with this object began to charge for her services. In this way she quickly alienated her set, but not before a limited and respectable reputation had been gained. She was handsome, provocative and abandoned, but had a very strict attitude about money, and this added to her charm a certain moral strength. She lived quietly and successfully.

The superintendent of her apartment amply noted her way of life. Fascinated by her looks as well as by her accessibility he applied to be one of her clients, but, having got so close, was repelled by a tariff he deemed excessive. In a fit of chagrin he turned in her name to a society whose work it was to guard the public morals, and this society persuaded the police to tap the wires of her telephone.

When they met now, Leonora displayed less embarrassment than Claire.

"What have you done with this house?" she whispered when they had all got upstairs and she found herself for a moment alone with her sister-in-law. "You'll never get away with it for long."

Claire did not reply; indeed she did not understand that a large number of the women shared Leonora's view, and were looking on the Boyne house as a rich and well-organized brothel into which they had been shanghaied, an opinion which certain circumstances made credible.

In the first place, here was Mother Fosker, whom most of them knew either personally or by reputation. Secondly, the luxury of which they had a glimpse on the way upstairs spoke to them of extravagance and pleasure. Again, so many girls as were here could not have been collected for another purpose.

Against this they remembered the police, the arrests, the appearance before the magistrate; and here also were nuns (that was puzzling) and a priest. But of course one always heard rumors that prostitution was to be legalized and even operated by the state; perhaps this had happened, and the nuns might be nurses who were to give injections. Or something like that, some of them thought, reducing, dismissing or explaining whatever did not fit with their first idea.

They had been allowed to stand too long, cackling and whispering, while beds were assigned and other arrangements debated. Suddenly the rumor was current among them that they were to be shipped to an army camp—in Louisiana, some said, others said it would be Fort Devens. The choice ones, the young ones, would be given to officers, the others to enlisted men; but all would have to wait on table as well as everything else. They set up a frightful bickering and wailing at this, which could not be quelled for some minutes. Father Meretruce then spoke to them severely and, as he imagined, unequivocally; but he had made the essential point, that this was a house of correction, in his first sentence, while a good deal of confusion still obscured what was said: many had not heard him there, and others were certain only of his having said "This is a house. . . ." The rest of his talk, divorced from this fundamental definition and employing such vast terms as "society," "virtue," "the faith," and "rehabilitation," left an extremely general and vague impression.

Owing to a miscalculation, there were not beds enough; so that four girls (the cleanest, as it happened, and most fashionable in appearance) had to be distributed through the house as might best be managed. Two of them occupied Mr and Mrs Boyne's room, another was put in the room that used to be Roger's, another went to a guest room. These girls naturally did not conceal from their colleagues that such luxury and magnificence were to be found on the floor below, and a good deal of anger was thus occasioned.

In all this, Mother Fosker was of far greater assistance and tact than the nuns and the priest put together. Talking incessantly, smiling, she moved among the women (several of whom recognized her authority as the only properly constituted kind in such an establishment), directing, commanding, soothing and issuing hints that all would be well. By this means she at once gained the liberty of the house, which she kept by her amazing capacity for appearing everywhere and knowing everything.

She knew already, through Hogan, with whom she had struck up acquaintance—"a lovely man, Mr Hogan," she told Sister Catherine—of the defection of the cook, and in this crisis she saw an opportunity of being serviceable to many interests at once. When the women were somewhat settled in, then, Mother Fosker appeared before Claire and announced that a cook could be easily made available. Moreover, she insisted, the greatly increased population of the house made more help necessary; she would be glad if Claire would accept the loan, the temporary loan, of one or two servants whom she, Mother Fosker, would telephone at once—these people could do the necessary shopping on their way to the house.

"You're very kind," Claire said doubtfully; she feared incurring an obligation to the old woman. But Mother Fosker saw this.

"Don't worry about me, dear," she said. "I'm not asking any favors—it's enough if an old lady like me has a place to put her head at night. But I can see you need help, as you don't know what a business this kind of thing is, and how much work has to be done to keep things going smoothly. Let me get you some help—it will be a pleasure for me to make you easy in your mind."

She talked in this strain until Claire was glad to accept the offer. Mother Fosker then retired and made several phone calls. She had gained the position of servant, which in all the more dubious areas of life is the position of supreme power.

Meanwhile, however, sandwiches were ordered from a delicatessen and distributed through the house in lieu of supper.

Everyone without exception commented unfavorably about this.

The house seemed dangerously overcrowded, as if it were under siege. Claire expected the walls to bulge under the concentration of such a weight of humanity; neither could all this bulk contain itself in quiet. At every moment, especially through the upper floors, a door would open or fly shut, always there were women walking in the corridors, several quarrels broke out during the early evening, and when the Hungarian sisters began their evening prayers in a room apart they could be heard only with difficulty through and against the general imprecatory babble to which were now added shouts and wails of protest and recommendations of the most obscene kind.

"There is no discipline," said Sister Catherine to Claire. "It is disgraceful." She came downstairs, or sent down Sister Terese, about once every fifteen minutes, simply to say something like that.

"There are too many of these women," Father Meretruce said. He sat in the library, rapidly eating sandwiches. "I think someone has made a mistake." He tried to telephone the Bishop, but Mother Fosker was fully occupying the upstairs extension and he could not get through.

At eight o'clock the servants came in. Besides the cook, a grim giantess of a woman with gray hair and four gold teeth in the front of her mouth, there were not one or two but five tall old men. They brought with them in a truck a quantity of food, and brought also suitcases from which they produced and donned tuxedoes of a burgundy color, their livery. Thus attired they would speak only to Mother Fosker, who took them aside, smiled reassuringly at Claire and gave them directions which must have been sharp and specific in the extreme, for in less than twenty minutes the house was reasonably quiet.

"In this business," Mother Fosker told Claire, "you have to have organization."

"There are so many servants," Claire said, somewhat dazed by the speed with which order had been established.

"A firm hand," Mother Fosker replied.

2

MOTHER FOSKER had occasion to speak again that night of "a firm hand," and this phrase occurred not once only in the course of a long conversation she had with Hogan.

The Boyne house was built, as has been noted, around a little plaza, stone-flagged and bordered by arched columns; in its center stood a fountain that did not work. The area of the plaza extended upwards to give an effective view of the corridors on the second floor, but above that the corridors were enclosed and smooth plaster walls led to the top of the house where a skylight covered the extent of the enclosed court. Here walked Mother Fosker and Hogan, long after the other inhabitants had retired under the extraordinary stresses of the day.

It was late. A sallow moonlight came through the glass above and gave a grayish uncertain light on the flagstones about the fountain; the night was cool, too, and both people had coats hung cape-fashion over their shoulders as they steadily paced, with heels that but slightly clicked, around the court. There was in their demeanor the hint of steady rhythmic energy, tending to speed up if anything, that characterizes the movement of people on a confined path such as the deck of a boat. In the interests of their conversation, which had been going on for some time, they had fallen into step, and this gave them something of the appearance of officers who, before the troops are formed up for review, pace the side of the parade-ground, talking in low voices without diminishing the effect of their military bearing. In fact they a little resembled the parody of a pair of generals, with their coats flapping grotesquely over their backs, and their shoulders hunched a little forward; and their talk, like that of generals, had in a short while reached the level of grand strategy, at which it was often indistinguishable from questions of policy and even philosophy.

It was Hogan who had the subordinate position, that of an aide, of a staff-major who perhaps holds his rank only because he has traveled in the land under attack and knows something of its people. Having informed Mother Fosker of the condition of the house, the attitude and relations of its inhabitants, he kept silence except as he was asked a question. The old woman impressed him greatly; he had never met with a mind so certain of itself, so acute and so limited.

"There must be no force," she now said. "Or very little— but a firm hand, that there must be. Co-operation would be the most desirable thing. The younger sister, you say . . . ?"

"Susan, yes."

"And their sister-in-law, the brother's wife?"

"She seems to be on our side."

"What we want," said Mother Fosker, "is an entering wedge. It is the Church I'm worried about. What to do with the Church? You can't hold up the Church at the point of a pistol."

They walked in silence several times around the fountain.

"If I may suggest it," Hogan said, "we must hand them the thing on a platter."

"Certainly."

"They must be involved."

"I know that," the old woman replied impatiently. Then, "I think I've got it."

"Yes."

"A party, simply a party."

Hogan said nothing; he was ashamed to show that he did not understand, so he tried to look knowing and nodded his head several times, pensively. But the old woman did not explain herself, she was already occupied with tactical directions.

"You must go at once to my printer," she said decisively. "The invitations must be delivered in the afternoon mail. Oh, he'll get out of bed, never fear. He must work all night. Mother Fosker's *selective* mailing list, tell him that. *Selective*—remember that. I don't want a lot of college boys and I don't want the dregs of Boston."

"I'm afraid I don't see," Hogan admitted.

"Ah now, never mind that, Mr Hogan. You do what Mother says, Mother sees a pot of gold at the end of the rainbow, Mr Hogan. But we must hurry, we have so much to do." She smiled at him. "There's nothing quite like a party," she said.

And Hogan, taking the address of the printer, hurried away.

The old woman did not go to bed; she needed very little sleep and the night was her time for the most acute wakefulness. Night is the time for evil only because night is the time for trust; when people of a moderate honesty go securely to sleep, then the witches are able to work. She paced in the cold court, around and around as if under a spell, until she heard noises in the front hall. She went there, thinking it was Hogan returned, but silently, as she considered it too early for that if he had been successful.

Peering around the corner of the dining room door she saw two men in uniforms and greatcoats. The uniforms were blue —not, fortunately, the dark blue of the police, but a light slate blue which was unfamiliar to her. She cursed Hogan for having left the front door on the latch, then she saw that one of the men had a key in his hand, which he now carelessly returned to his pocket. Caught between fear and curiosity she withdrew her head but stayed in the dark dining room to listen.

"Christ, I'm drunk," said one voice.

"Too true you're drunk," the other said.

"I've never been this drunk."

"No, I don't guess you've ever been."

Both voices were whispering with exaggerated caution but very audibly; yet there was some distinction of tone, the first being plaintive and, as it continued to announce, drunk, the second deep, remote, amused and somewhat less drunk.

"Pappy," said the first voice. "You going to put me to bed, Pappy?"

"You show me where the bed is," said the second voice (pronouncing it "baid"). "It's your house, so you say."

As Mother Fosker began to guess, this was that Roger Boyne of whom Hogan had told her. He was in the Royal Canadian Air Force; that explained the uniform. His wife, she mused, his wife was that thin blonde one who had been put—where? In a guest room? She debated with herself what could be made of this situation.

Roger and his guest, Pilot Officer Hannan, who came from Alabama, were quite newly commissioned. They were on a brief embarcation leave from Halifax and, being fighter pilots who had never fought, were full of that arrogance (known in the service as *piss and vinegar*) which is thought proper to their state. The rail service between Halifax and Boston would have driven older men to drink, but these two had not waited to be driven: they had killed a huge Canadian quart of rye on the journey, and were well along with another.

Pilot Officer Hannan was taller, huskier, older than Roger; though not so intelligent he was far better versed in the world, to which his card of admission was a smile which lit his handsome face with the slow cruelty of a bully conscious of his power and of little more. He had, by offering his protection against a rough society, made Roger his sycophant; they had contrived to stay together during all their training. Roger loved and worshipped Hannan with the unquestioning devotion that military life inherits from the school playground, and called him Pappy. Hannan called Roger Sonny, or Boston, and held him in contempt and affection.

Both officers now took off their greatcoats and flung them on a chair, displaying the bright new wings stitched above their hearts; they both wore the top button of the tunic undone because that had been de rigeur for fighter pilots in the Battle of Britain.

"This way," Roger whispered. "Get up them stairs." He giggled and, being drunk, missed his way in the shadows at the back of the hall. He hit his knee on the newel, and swore.

"Don't you even know your way around your own house?" Hannan asked.

"This way, Pappy," Roger repeated. "It's all right."

Mother Fosker stepped out of the dining room.

"What can I do for you, young gentlemen?" she inquired sharply yet affably enough.

"What can you do for me?" Roger turned and peered at her in the half-light. His eyes did not focus very well.

"This is a private house, you know," said the old lady. "And it's a hell of a time of night to come calling," she added.

"Say, what is this?" Hannan asked. "This is your house, isn't it?" He too looked closely at Mother Fosker. "Well, who's this —your mother?"

"I've never seen the woman before," Roger said.

"I'm afraid I must ask you to leave. Either that or I call the police."

"The police?" Roger shrilly echoed. "But this is where I live."

"I'm sorry." Mother Fosker was courteous but firm. "You've made a mistake, and no surprise either, in the dark and the pair of you tight as ticks. This is my house."

They looked at her.

"It's just like my house," Roger said. "Funny, isn't it?" He laughed uncertainly.

2 9 7

"How come he has a key?" asked Pilot Officer Hannan. "It must be his house, he's got the key."

"I'm not going to argue with you—let the police decide whose house it is." Mother Fosker crossed the hall to the telephone. Then she turned about, assumed what she could of an ecstatically motherly expression . . .

"Why, bless me," she said. "You must be Roger Boyne!"

"Sure I am," Roger said with indignation.

"I'd completely forgotten about you—your sisters did say you had the extra key. I remember now—it was the day I rented the place. Imagine your coming home without knowing! What a surprise!"

It was indeed a surprise; the two officers goggled at her for half a minute.

"Of course," she said, "I couldn't dream of turning you out. You must stay the night at least, you and your friend, poor, tired boys."

"Where have my sisters gone?" asked Roger.

"Ah—that I'm not sure of. They did say something. But, an old lady like me, you know—the memory." She tapped her forehead several times. "Was it the North Shore? The Cape? I'm sure I knew once. But no matter. Maybe I'll remember in the morning." Suddenly she said, as though inspired: "But I know what you boys will want—a drink. A drink before bed, isn't that the thing?"

They agreed that was the thing, and Mother Fosker went to the sideboard in the dining room and prepared two highballs.

"You won't mind it without ice?" she said, and led them into the library, where she pointed out comfortable chairs.

"Hm, same furniture," Roger muttered, sipping at his drink. He undid the belt of his tunic, loosened his collar and tie, and made himself comfortable.

"You boys are pilots?" Mother Fosker asked Hannan.

"Yes, ma'am."

"Wonderful, wonderful," she said. And she asked him a few flattering questions. When they next glanced at Roger they saw he was asleep.

"Poor child," Mother Fosker said. "He's not as strong as you, is he?"

"No, ma'am, I guess not."

"I suppose you're as fit as a fiddle after coming all the way from Canada."

"Oh, I'm all right." He looked at her steadily. "It's very queer, isn't it, his not knowing you'd rented the house."

"Oh, dear me, these things do happen, though, don't they? But come now, you'll be wanting your sleep—the other one might just as well stay right where he is, he looks so comfortable. I'll take you to your room."

On the way she stopped to make him another drink. Then, at the foot of the stairs, she detained him and, looking him straight in the eyes, said:

"You wouldn't like a girl in your bed tonight, would you?"

Her smirk led Hannan to suppose this weird person was offering herself, and he withdrew a few steps.

"No, dear," the old woman said smiling. "A pretty, young girl—you'd like?"

"Say, what is this?" he asked.

"A perfectly straight offer," Mother Fosker said. "If you're not interested, just say so."

"Well, hell." Pilot Officer Hannan began to laugh. "A cathouse," he cried in glee.

"Please!" Mother Fosker said with frightening dignity. "Please!"

"All right," he said. "How much?"

"On the house, dear," said the old woman. "A favor for the armed forces. How about your friend?"

"Oh, let him sleep." Hannan became ever so slightly confidential. "He's not much interested in women anyhow."

Then she conducted him upstairs, after first warning him against noise. Outside Leonora's door she whispered to him:

"If I were you I'd pay the little girl, though. If it were up to me I wouldn't care, but she'll make a fuss."

Mother Fosker watched him through the chamber door, and watched it close. Then she walked downstairs and turned out the lights in the library, where Roger slept.

It was no matter about the money, she thought as she resumed her pacing of the court, waiting for Hogan's return. No matter—for here was the entering wedge.

$\mathcal{U}$NCLE FRED SEELY
was dining out with certain political acquaintances from whom
he hoped to gain personal as well as official approval. They had
taken a private room at the R—— Restaurant, where both
during and after the meal they drank heavily. It was to Uncle
Fred a measure of the wealth and importance of these men, to
whom only his candidacy gave him the access, that they drank
more and better than what he was used to. As he pulled now on
the excellent cigar he had been given by the waiter he considered
that he was in part—the official part—accepted by these gray-
haired, eminent men who had questioned him so closely about
his opinions. He had been coached, he had known what to
say, he had given the impression of a safe man, his campaign
had won support. He might have been satisfied.

But as the talk by barely perceptible turns veered from the
political, and as their attention correspondingly drifted away
from him, Uncle Fred began to feel somewhat isolated and resentful; it seemed to him that having been used he was now
regarded as little better than a servant of a discreet kind, before
whom these dignitaries were not embarrassed to speak—a little
obliquely to be sure—of certain pleasures, past and proposed.

As the guest of honor he sat near the head, just on the right of the chairman, a person who had become vastly wealthy through the manufacture of air-rifles for children. But this privileged position turned out a disadvantage when, with the shift of the conversation, chairs were hitched down nearer the other end of the table, where a little knot of men bent their heads together and occasionally marked the pauses of their low-voiced conversation with a burst of laughter; Uncle Fred and the chairman were as far as possible away from this pleasant conspiracy, but after a few moments the chairman without a word of apology simply dragged his chair down to the other end, where he too joined in the hushed buzzing.

This was intolerable, and Uncle Fred accordingly took his boldest course; had he been sober he would not have dared. But now he got up and boldly intruded on the group, leaning over between two men on whose shoulders he placed his friendly hands.

The conversation stopped for a moment, and several white cards which had been lying on the table were stuffed back into their envelopes and hastily returned to pockets. There was a brief interval of constraint on both sides, and Uncle Fred was about to apologize and retire in bitterness of heart when the generally convivial mood of the group reacted in his favor, and someone said:

"What say, shall we let Seely in on this?"

There was a confused murmur in which a couple of voices of doubt and assent were clearly heard.

"Could we work him in, do you think?" another person asked.

"Why not? Our word ought to be good by this time." There was a laugh at this.

"There are a few things he ought to understand, if he's to come along," said the chairman, and with agreement from the others he took Uncle Fred aside, to a little table in the anteroom. A waiter brought them fresh glasses of Benedictine.

"There's to be an—entertainment," the chairman said, fixing his eyes closely on Uncle Fred and evidently choosing his words with care. "A little gathering in a private house—at which a certain license is permitted—indulgences of behavior, you understand." Without being greatly particular he contrived to let Uncle Fred gain an idea of the kind of indulgence he meant. Uncle Fred thought, however, that he was to be taken to a common brothel, and wondered what all this secrecy could have to do with it. The chairman's next words therefore puzzled him.

"You may find you know a good many people there," he said. "But—discretion. Do not mention any names, either while we are there or afterwards." Then he added, "It will be quite expensive—you have money?"

Uncle Fred nodded rapidly, signifying his excited assent to everything.

"Not only will you have to pay for a few little things while you are there," the chairman said. "But also your name will be known, and you will receive a bill by mail in a few days, covering your share in the evening's entertainment." He paused and stared very seriously at Uncle Fred. "It is advisable," he continued, "to pay this bill at once by check to the name and address you will find printed on it. It is—very advisable to pay at once. As you can understand." This seemed to conclude his instructions, for he stood up at once, only adding with a little laugh, "I guess I don't need to tell you the bill won't be itemized."

They returned to the others.

"All right, boys," the chairman announced. "Seely's in."

There was laughter and applause of an ironic sort. Uncle Fred felt pleased and happy, and after another quick round of drinks the gentlemen went downstairs and called for taxis.

They arrived in darkness which could not, however, disguise from Uncle Fred that the house was familiar to him. A feeling of bewilderment which he suppressed while they stood outside, telling himself that he had made a mistake, that it could not possibly be *that* house, became overwhelming when they entered and he discovered himself beyond doubt to be standing in the entrance hall of the home of his brother-in-law, Nicholas Boyne.

There had been some changes, to be sure, most striking among them the presence of a table extended the length of the hall and serving as a bar; this, like the other functions of the house, was attended by footmen in costumes of a deep red, like wine. One of these men sat at the end of the table nearest the front door, where he received the invitations. Under the sponsorship of two of his new friends Uncle Fred passed by this guardian; no one had spoken his name aloud but it had been written down, with his address, on a register kept by the servant, which he was required to sign. Just beyond this administrative office, and across the hall from it, a little antechamber was used for a cloakroom, and here it was possible for the gentlemen to purchase silk masks—not only possible, but evidently desirable, for everyone bought one and Uncle Fred did not in this refuse to conform, though the masks were very expensive. One simply watched the person before one and, like him, put down ten dollars, which was after all not such a great price for shuffling off one's identity. And then one passed properly into the community of that house.

In the plaza, which was strung with Japanese lanterns, a trio dressed in bright pantaloons and sashes and white silk shirts of the flowing sort played sentimental gypsy tunes on stringed instruments. Uncle Fred noticed with surprise and a feeling of desecration that the fountain here had been repaired and was playing up a bright jet of water which splashed at its stony base; he recalled that his brother-in-law had once hated the sound of that fountain and refused to allow it to be restored to service.

In the rooms beyond, in dim and intimate light, gentlemen and ladies, all in masks, conversed, walked together or sat decorously in corners sipping at drinks; a very few couples— three that he counted in the first moments—were dancing. They would dance but a few steps, lean together for a second, then resume their seats. An air of polite depression pervaded the place. All the men he saw were gray-haired, there was not a young man in the gathering. The ladies, on the contrary, appeared young and beautiful of form. Uncle Fred thought he could recognize several men with whom he was connected professionally, but remembering the chairman's warning about names he felt too embarrassed to give them a greeting, and the party had by no means as yet reached the stages of conviviality at which one speaks easily to strangers. He returned to the bar and got himself a drink. This too was very costly. He wandered into the library again and sat down in a corner by himself.

What could have happened to this house? To his relatives? He had seen no one among the women resembling either of his nieces, but he thought they must surely be there. The only plausible interpretation he could reach was this, that Susan and Claire must be the operators of a high-priced call house which occasionally gave such a party as this for its clientele. At this thought he was wrought up to lecherous indignation—how dared they? It outraged him to think of Susan especially, whom he had always considered very attractive but far out of his reach by reason of her youth, her innocence—and now it appeared she would have all the knowledge necessary, all the knowledge and all the inclination, had he but known. He resolved to look about for her. He got up and began a progress through the rooms. In one place he was accosted by an old woman who smiled toothily at him from beneath her mask.

"Have you no sweetheart, love?" she asked in a grating voice. "Don't the ladies please you?" And she summoned from the side of the room a young woman in a black evening gown that chastely covered even her throat and arms yet outlined her body so closely as to be more suggestive than nakedness. Uncle Fred was impressed and excited; this, after all, was what he was paying for, and he began to see that such a party might have the greatest attractions, combining as it did an undoubted satisfaction with the pleasure of putting it off for some little while in an atmosphere so rich and elegant and full of the erotic tension that went with a kind of play at courtship. He took the arm of the lady, who smiled up at him with full, very red lips, and led her into the bar for a drink.

It went well, Mother Fosker thought as she turned away. Slowly but well. The house was getting crowded, you could feel that the temperature had risen a little as an effect of so much humanity in comparatively little space, and this intensified a slightly acrid yet not unpleasant (rather provocative, in fact) odor of well-groomed and perfumed bodies.

. That it went well (though slowly), that it would in time go well indeed, was an effect of Mother Fosker's undoubted genius. She had given such parties before, though never before in a house so magnificent, so well calculated to furnish the necessary impression of freedom, adventure and intimacy. She appreciated fully the essential lesson of her trade, by which less imaginative bawds might well be edified, that the act of darkness in itself, except as performed between proficients of very full acquaintance with one another's possibilities, is likelier than not to be dull, disappointing and productive of a bad smell; what is required is imagination, the manufacture of illusion and suspense to put a romantic gloss on the tedious mechanics of the mere event; and this romantic gloss was what Mother Fosker expensively and brilliantly labored to provide.

For lust is inextricably tangled with love, and is more satisfied as it may more highly value the object of its fleetingly aroused attention. The worst excesses return to the conven-

3 0 6

tions of honesty and the imitation of a virginal passion, by which the blasé are more stimulated than by the sight of flesh, upon which they have too much fed; the ideal is to collapse the blushing renunciations of a long engagement, and the final excitement of the marriage, into one evening; so that at ten o'clock the man of forty becomes the lad of eighteen, chooses his partner and courts her by dance and conversation until, having exhausted the resources of his fictive passion, he puts out the bedside light at two and rises in the early dawn a man of forty once again, who wonders what has happened.

The essential illusion in all this was that of free choice—choice, that is, which not only appears to be made in freedom but appears also to leave one free after it has been made. Thus anonymity, and thus the wearing of masks. That person, that tedious person, oneself, with whom one had lived so long as with a nagging and unlovely wife, might here be discarded for one night which had the cadence, the rhythm, the rise and fall of one's best years; one might fall in love and marry, it was of the greatest importance to do so, in fact, and yet it was utterly without consequence.

To bring about such a desirable result certain conditions had to be satisfied, and Mother Fosker from long study knew them all. Her selective mailing list, built up over a period of years, employed three criteria: wealth, social position and age. One had to have men who were, to say the least of it, mature—who knew what they wanted and, being of a somewhat limited potency, were willing to prolong their engagement by the exercise of manners, deriving perhaps more pleasure from the process than from the result but certainly not less. They had to be men whose position would guarantee their discretion, men who had everything to lose: for despite all private gratifications here achieved, Mother Fosker's parties were social functions. Whoever might have scruples, or might feel himself to be committing a *sin*, would quietly be enabled to recognize among his fellows people he respected, people more wealthy, more powerful, more important than himself; one's own guilt and anxiety were absorbed by one's society. And not only so with the men, but it was rumored too that a few of the women who attended these affairs were not (not ordinarily, that is) call-girls but of a very different station; there were stories of men who had had most unexpected encounters with their own wives, and, in fact, the marriage of a prominent couple was said to have been saved from divorce by the charm of just such a meeting.

Finally the gentlemen had to be wealthy, and free with their wealth. There was no use in running off such an event as this in the circumstances of poverty or among even the least visible hints of a necessary parsimoniousness; everything had to flow as from a tap. There was a great danger always present, that the essential sordidness of the occasion would somewhere show through, in anger, in drunken temper, in perversion or sickness, of which the results might be laughable, pathetic or disastrous but would surely be disturbing. Once an aged judge, who had repeatedly been warned by his physician to avoid such entertainments, had suffered a heart attack; happily, friends took him home and the consequences were not fatal. Again, a celebrated author had been disposed to make a terrible furor over the loss of his woolen vest, which had, he claimed, been stolen.

Such things were always possible, but money, a great deal of money, could in one way or another generally prevent either their occurrence or at least their more serious consequences. The atmosphere provided had to be that of a country club which should be the scenic equivalent of the Abbey of Thélème.

For the same cause, the girls had to be young and pretty. Mother Fosker had not depended entirely on what chance had thrown her way in the Boyne house, but at the last moment summoned recruits from other parts of the city. The rest—the old, the poor, the insufficiently plausible—were kept upstairs as a reserve force; they were told that late in the evening they might come down and ply what trade they could.

As for the girls who were here, downstairs and actively engaged, they were in the flowering of their excellence and youth; such a party as this was not to be undertaken cheaply or meanly, but only with the most desirable equipment. Mother Fosker was proud to watch them go through the evening, some of them coquettishly, with the smiles of attraction, others with heads held high and the charming affectation of a chaste, cold spirit, but all well-mannered, lovely and of a sufficient pretension to culture—a necessary element, the last, because so much of the effect depended, after all, on conversation.

By this time the general tone had improved, the pace had quickened. Those who were uncertain now gained in confidence, drinks were being passed around in great plenty, there was more dancing, more bold whirling of long skirts, louder conversation, much laughter. Here and there caresses, as yet a little awkward and quickly withdrawn when noticed, were attempted which the girls put off, whispering "later" in such a way as to increase their gentlemen's ardors; everywhere glances full of deep intimation were exchanged. All were behaving beautifully, that is, predictably, and Mother Fosker watched with cool and artistic approval the performance of this symphony whose orchestration at least was her own. She felt at the same time a cynical pity, not for the girls (who supposedly knew what they were about) but for the gentlemen, who so quickly and ardently embraced not so much their partners as in them the illusion of their own powers. All thought of money—the grim absolute upon which so much delightful relativity was founded as life is on death—had obviously faded from their minds and been replaced by a strong impression of personal vigor, represented by the blood surging in the head and blushing in the cheek, that was so easily exerting a force on another, a stranger who would have seemed inaccessible in any other place. Mother Fosker's complex mechanism here succeeded in bestowing the final illusions of seduction and personal compliance.

It went well, she thought again, and laboriously began to climb the stairs.

The others, the victims of this palace revolution, had been confined since four-thirty that afternoon in the bare, dismal commons which Susan had called The Divine Rumpus Room; this place, as it had but one window (and that giving on the enclosed plaza where the gypsy trio now played), formed an ideal hall of detention. The prisoners were twelve in number.

Leonora, Roger and Pilot Officer Hannan were there, among whom existed a rather complex situation. Leonora, wakened from a sound sleep the night before to find a stranger in her room, had been not so much surprised as angry, and at first treated Hannan rudely enough; however, she finally allowed him to have his way. There had followed a dispute about price, which was settled neither satisfactorily nor amicably at one-half the original demand, and in Canadian dollars at that, which Hannan had neglected to exchange. Only then had Leonora noticed his uniform, and naturally asked him (with that easy assumption, made by outsiders about all organizations of whatever size, that everyone knows everyone else) whether he knew a Roger Boyne.

"Certainly," Hannan had said. "He's downstairs."

"How funny!" Leonora replied. "He is my husband."

"He is my best friend."

The embarrassment of the situation was quickly overcome; they explained to one another in how many ways it didn't matter. They ended by finding the coincidence utterly delightful and funny and, as they discussed it while lying naked in bed, one thing led to another in the most natural way; presently they fell asleep.

They were awakened by a violent discussion. Several people —Claire, Roger, two nuns and the little old woman who had conveyed Hannan where he was—stood in the room. The old woman was speaking vehemently.

"And this is what goes on," she said. "Under the very nose of the Church itself." She winked at Pilot Officer Hannan as though in signal that he should be quiet. "I thought there was something strange about this set-up." She went into this in some detail: who could tell, she complained, but what there might be a man in every room. She had been prepared to co-operate, and had instructed her girls to do the same, but this —it was not only shameful, it was shameless, and also unprofitable. "Not only that," she cried, "but to give this young gentleman a pair of horns at cost price, as I might say. . . ." She turned to Roger, whose silent grimace of anguish referred not so much to the situation as to a severe headache; however, it was enough.

Mother Fosker thereupon continued her speech, which developed into a violent harangue directed for the most part at Claire. Claire must not be surprised, the old woman said, at anything that happened from then on; she, Mother Fosker, had begun to realize what kind of hands she had fallen into. Say what you like (she continued) about herself and her girls, at least they did not pretend to be better than they were, nor affected to cast out the mote from another's eye without having first cast out the beam from their own—in short, there were factors in this ménage which suited very ill with its pretensions to piety and reform. Here were Claire's sister and that doctor openly living in sin; and not only so, but had Claire realized that this same sister, that so-pretty and so-innocent-looking Susan, had also, not more than a night ago—Mother Fosker knew it on good grounds—summoned to her bed, her insatiable bed, honest Mr. Hogan, who had given way to the temptation, as what man would not? To say nothing of the fact, so apparent in this very room, that it was nearly impossible to pick up a girl in greater Boston and be certain she would not turn out a relative of the Boynes; Mother Fosker here nodded at Leonora with great contempt, and sniffed.

These charges, inasmuch as they were not only absurd but in part true as well, were unanswerable; their mere recognition would have been a defeat. Claire left the room. Mother Fosker directed her notice to Sisters Catherine and Terese; she was shocked, she began, that all this—she waved at Leonora and Hannan, who had not moved in some minutes but sat upright with the covers drawn to their chins—that all this should have taken place as if under the auspices and authority of the Roman Catholic Church, which must have at the very least winked an eye at what went on; but then, she was not surprised, it was what always happened, the rich were indulged in any vice, while the poor, who were but vicious for their daily bread, suffered the most rigorous penalties. She said such things then about nuns and monks and the cenobitic life as it was well-known (she said) to be lived as caused the sisters to stop their ears with their fingers and finally to run from the scene. They came to Claire in her room, where they began to blubber and weep: everything, they lamented, was dissolving in their hands, there would be no discipline, no authority—the beds would not be made. They kept recurring obsessively to these beds which would not be made, and in the intervals between bursts of tears allowed Claire sufficiently to know that it was all her fault. The father would come that afternoon, they cried, and take them away—they could not be expected to live in a house of shame. Claire, who had begun by offering what comfort she could, which was little enough, hereupon referred briefly and with acerbity to their namesakes the saints—would Catherine of Siena have snivelled in this way? Would Teresa of Avila have objected to the dirty work in the vineyard? No matter. That was different, Sister Catherine said through her tears—that was in "the olden time."

From that moment everything had got out of hand, and if Claire did not appreciate the fact until later in the day, it was because she did not apply herself very strongly to control; she was like a person driving very fast who suddenly suspects that the steering-gear is no longer connected with the wheels but nevertheless holds tightly to it and does not dare turn it to find out.

Despite the great crisis over Leonora, the day seemed to go on without much more difficulty than the day before; there seemed to be, after that one scene, no overt rebellion, and it was only slowly that Claire realized the invasion had taken place and she was a prisoner in her own house. Mother Fosker's servants, those tall old men in their ridiculous burgundy suits, kept unobtrusive watch over the doors and the telephone extensions—indeed the telephone seemed always to be in use. Claire suffered no indignity from these persons only because she never risked any by offering an objection or making a demand. She justified her timidity by the thought that Father Meretruce would come during the afternoon—"and then we shall see." It was with difficulty that she kept herself from fully realizing what had taken place—and yet, apart from these signs of a kind of police surveillance, nothing very extraordinary seemed to be happening; even the Hungarian nuns could be heard as usual at their prayers and for the rest the house was reasonably quiet. "What more can I expect?" she asked herself, but she did not turn the wheel to find out.

As the consequence of this policy here she was, here they all were, shut in a room and guarded by Hogan. Through the one window they could hear the melancholy yet sugary scrapings of stringed instruments, the sound of voices, the splash of a fountain and, through all this, a steady undertone made by the shuffling of numerous feet and the clinking of ice in glasses.

There were present in this room the following: Leonora, Roger and Pilot Officer Hannan, who sat in a corner as far away from everyone else as they could get and carried on in low but intense voices a discussion that had been in progress all day; Sisters Catherine and Terese and the Hungarian sisters, who sat in the other corner; Susan, Claire, Edmond, John Averist and Father Meretruce, who sat around the picnic table on the hard wooden benches and had the corporate appearance of a board of trustees for a shady venture.

Hogan sat on a chair by the door. He held a large black automatic, and could not keep his eyes from it. He had never seen one so close up before, and it was for him a *fact* of the utmost importance. When Mother Fosker assigned him to this duty, one of her servants had given him the gun, together with instructions about its operation.

"You pull this," the man had said, indicating the trigger. Then he added, "But for Jesus' sake, friend, don't shoot anybody."

So Hogan sat there with the gun in his hand; everyone else had long ago ceased to be nervous about it, but he was in a kind of trembling ecstasy of the imagination and would probably not have noticed, at this time, had they all got up and left. The weapon was his starting point for what is clinically called a very rich phantasy life. His lips moved slightly as he silently issued commands and threats. His thumb had discovered the safety catch (which his preceptor had prudently left at safe) and was absently twitching this back and forth.

It had been a matter of no great difficulty to entrap all these people in such a fashion. As in the large so in the local situation, their concerns were interior and this betrayed them. They thought of conscience when perhaps it would have been as well to think of policy. The Hungarian nuns were invited with smiles and beckonings, and they went. Catherine and Terese were told that Father Meretruce awaited them, and they went. Claire was told that the sisters were having trouble, and she went. Edmond was told that Claire wished to speak with him, and he went. And so on. By ones and twos and threes they were shut in the room. Father Meretruce came at five o'clock and with a certain pompous assurance mounted the stairs to his imprisonment; John Averist came a few minutes later announcing he had an appointment with Susan, and he too suffered himself to be led upstairs and put away. Only Roger and Leonora and Pilot Officer Hannan had to be pushed into the room when it became apparent that their bickering could not be stopped in time for Leonora's services to become of use during the evening.

Susan had very nearly killed herself that afternoon. She had all but reached the end of her endurance, and had come anyhow to that point at which her own self-loathing was no longer a matter of scruple and nicety but was physically a sickness and a burden. Moving about her room in a state of inconsequent agitation—that state in which one has literally nothing to do, picking up such objects as ash trays, books, and putting them down again at once, she had come as though by accident on the knife.

It lay in the drawer where she had concealed it with some scarves after taking it from the kitchen; it appeared to her significant that the scarves had been shifted somehow so that the blade of the knife lay in full view when she opened the drawer, and she could not feel that this was accidental; it was as though her aimless-looking motion about the room had in effect been a kind of search and this was the reward of her thoroughness.

315

"It has been lying here," she said to herself, "waiting for a moment like this." And she accepted the sight as an omen, or even as the expression of a wish on her part or a recommendation on the world's.

Her mind refused to come near the idea of Hogan, but she could not avoid suffering what was worse, the imagery, the sensations, of that encounter—the nakedness, the soft hairiness, the peculiar smell of the stranger brought so close. And the absurd combination of intimacy with hauteur, as though the bodies rather lustlessly plunging on the bed merely happened to be in the same room with a lady taking a high tone before her servant—it reminded her suddenly of a dirty joke long forgotten: "Any more familiarity from you, young lady," said Colonel Higinbotham, "and the f . . .'s off." With a feeling of horror she stood, having picked up the knife, while her memory helplessly regarded its buried treasure: the locker-room of the high-school gym, lines of lockers and benches like the foundations of a ruined city, the sharp smell of sweat, a kind of shame about nakedness before other girls, the queer, nasty conversations of discovery.

"How much there's already been time to forget!"

But of course, as one was told, one forgot nothing; everything that had happened was there, was still there, and not dead either, but alive and mysteriously moving, the crawling corruption of the past by which one bred the future. Every cigarette butt with every word, and the fall of the sparrow not unregarded, one's life was at every instant complete, finished. Out of the depths, de profundis, I cry unto thee, clamavi ad te; but the depths one cried out of were within, were the thick smoky blackness she felt in her mind, the filth of the body as of a deep cesspool; and one cried, also, to no one, or to oneself.

She then lay down on the bed and held the point of the knife to her side. She had little enough idea where to strike so

3 1 6

as to be sure. But the symbolic propriety of the place and the position struck her as contemptible and operatic, so she got up and took the knife into the bathroom, whose white and hygienic brightness she imagined her blood as already soiling. The clean, impersonal likeness of this room to a hospital filled her with a tranquil courage, but her hands were shaking as though feeling already the shock of the wound. All at once she conceived the idea that cutting her throat would be the quickest and best and, hardly thinking, raised her head and saw her face in the mirror with the knife a silver line across her neck. With a cry she flung the knife away; it clattered in the tub and Susan fell down fainting.

Yet when she came to she considered her resolve in essence unchanged and undiminished. Only not now, she would not do it now. She made to herself the excuse that she was exhausted—as though one had to be in the top of one's condition in order to die, as though it were an athletic event.

Instead, she would write a note explaining her deed; she sat down at her table and got out paper and pen. But this was perhaps more difficult than dying: what did one say? How explain? What was there to explain? This was to be her last word to the community of all the living, was to be the concise, final illumination, the chance to say without regret, explanation or any reasoned diminution or mitigation of effect, exactly what she pleased about the entire accident of life. And what she found herself to have done was doodle—a series of swift parallel shadings at the top right corner of the page. Angrily she put the pen to the paper and wrote the word "hatred" and wrote it again several times; it became reminiscent of practice in penmanship.

At this moment a servant—one of those aged men in red—came to say that Dr. Einman wished to see her upstairs. He offered no explanation, naturally, and Susan followed him into the dismal room where now they all sat, hearing the syrupy music and seeing without intention or interest the gaudy cheap prints—the Nativity, the Flight into Egypt, the Kiss of Judas, a Crucifixion of which the artist had evidently enjoyed painting the blood—that hung evenly spaced upon the walls.

The strangest thing about this gathering was that no one present had expressed alarm or fear, though there had been much indignation. One would have thought that being in a house commandeered for criminal purposes, being shut into a room against their will, being exposed to the show of violence, would have summoned from these people a furious timidity; but no such thing. Their appreciation of themselves, of "the kind of people" they were—intelligent, well-bred, of a certain position and estimation and gentility—made fear a difficult emotion in such civil surroundings; they greatly preferred what remonstration reason and pride would let them make. Whatever was going on downstairs—and most of them had formed by now a fairly unequivocal impression of what it must be—had to end soon; police would arrive, the evildoers would be put where they could not offend, or at least not visibly offend. Meanwhile —dignity! And one made one's position known, clearly defined one's attitude, spoke generally and with authority.

For they were divided among themselves and much inclined to blame one another. Each wished it to be known that his or her actions had been conscientious, purified of self-interest, etc. There was, however, a good deal of half-acknowledged suspicion that "the situation" as it stood proceeded as much as anything from the peculiar moralities assembled in this room, or some of them; that the public contretemps downstairs was but the world's reciprocation to an interior wish, a personal guilt, the private treachery of the heart.

"Of course," said Edmond with heavy irony, "from this proposal to reform whores what else could you expect?" This remark was simply tossed without preparation on the table.

"Nothing was wrong with the project considered in itself," the priest replied after a silence of some moments.

"Nothing is wrong with a whore considered in herself," Edmond observed.

"That remark appears to me to be perfectly meaningless," Father Meretruce said. Edmond made a little gesture of indifference with his hands, and the priest went on.

"The trouble, if I may put it without mincing matters, lies not in the plan, which is a good one and a charitable one. The trouble lies in a misunderstanding of the seriousness involved in such an action, the trouble lies in a certain libertine attitude of 'I know best' instead of a proper submissiveness and obedience. As I have several times remarked to the Bishop, the choice of this house was by no means a happy one. . . ." He looked severely about him.

"If that is without mincing matters," Edmond said, "I think we would be very impressed to hear you mince some matters one day—it would be a performance."

"Father is referring to me, I'm afraid," said Claire. "To me and my 'libertine' attitude. I can't help saying that if this house has not proved a happy choice, that doesn't change the fact that the Church seemed rather pleased with the opportunity of making itself at home here."

"That is precisely what I mean," said Father Meretruce. "There were certain presumptions, agreements—promises, even —which were made evidently without the least intention of fulfilment. There was," he said sententiously, "a want of sincerity."

"Thank you," Claire returned. "That was kind. All the same, a want of efficiency and intelligence may also be noted, just in passing."

"But there," Edmond said. "We're all inefficient and unintelligent people sitting in a little room, while downstairs— downstairs listen to the love."

"And that is another thing," said the priest. "The shame

that we can all hear—the pretty scandal which is proceeding downstairs—it could not have come into a Christian home where a certain sympathy for it did not previously exist. Shall I speak more plainly? The seed has fallen on fertile soil, on ground already prepared."

"Not plain only, but also elegant," Edmond said.

"I refer to you, sir," the priest said angrily. "To you and your drab, there." He actually pointed, like the picture of a prophet denouncing, at Susan, who did not even look up.

"Please don't say anything like that again," said John Averist violently.

"Ah, but that is his job," said Edmond. "Seriously, though, Father, you must keep that kind of thing for the flock; here it is not good. We're all in a mess together, and we must, as you people are so fond of putting it, love one another."

"You cannot know what love is—you oughtn't to take the word in your mouth."

"Perhaps. But then, I have certain empirical data on the subject which you haven't bothered (if I may be so indelicate) to collect."

In this tone they continued and in a very few minutes were engaged in a philosophical and exalted slanging-match concerning the nature of love; like children quarreling, they deliberately misunderstood one another for the better maintenance of their two tempers, and the idea was inescapable that both priest and doctor were more pleased than not at having connected their situation firmly with the laws they supposed it to illustrate. And Claire could see, for her part, that there must be much satisfaction in any view of life which let the believer treat his own imprisonment (for example) as a heroic and dramatic demonstration, as representative and significant rather than as here and now, in such a way as led finally to the position which said the world itself depended on one's belief, that one's imprisonment in this very room was no more than the symbolic extension of what had been said in heaven, in one's dreams, what had been dictated by the fallen state or the death-wish.

Father Meretruce spoke feelingly of the Triune Sun, light-giving, life-giving, heat-giving; of the "benevolence of the holy spirit, in fervore qui totum calefacit"; of the love which streamed without cessation from the godhead through the orders of being. Edmond sneered and said "Plotinus," fairly spitting the word. Let there be no Jesuitical misunderstanding, he said of the mis-understanding he was helping to propagate, he and the priest were speaking of the same thing when they spoke of love, they were speaking of the dark violence, the fertile chaos of the human soul, whose unpredictability and irresponsibility had seemed to the ancients the thing in man most worthy to be deified. It was to that darkness, he strongly implied and at last said, that Catholics "really" prayed.

That, said Father Meretruce, struggling with the apoplexy that goes with having one's words and one's sense deliberately perverted, that was the worst, that was more Jesuitico if you liked, but without responsibility to the truth; it was that clever schoolboy trick of learning a few terms and using them to ob-scure all distinction. He had heard such things of so-called psychology before, but he would not have believed anyone capable of sinking so low as simply to take over the words with-out their signification; he accused Edmond of being profession-ally jealous of "the lucidity and order of the Catholic mind," and did not allow him to forget what the fool was proverbially recorded as having said in his heart.

Edmond replied that in centuries of existence the Church had certainly accumulated a good deal of rhetoric; whether that was wisdom or not must be, he said, a separate judgment. He in-vited everyone present to consider the Mass, that sacrament whose savage, tribal and cannibalistic affiliations it did not require the mind of Freud to point out; they would recognize in the ritual slaughter and ceremonious.eating of the totem animal . . .

That the Savior, the Light of the World, should be called a *totem animal*, said the priest, and by a crackpot witch-doctor of the new school, at that, a practitioner of hideous mumbo-jumbo in a darkened room, was typical, he called them to witness, typical of the modern tendency toward the degradation of man, typical of that pseudo-science which replaced the old wine with new vinegar and invited all to drink of it.

It might well be so, Edmond agreed, he was not one (he said) to oppose magniloquence to reason. But if they examined the evidence, drew the parallels that were there to be drawn, they must inescapably conclude with a clear similarity. Moreover, if they went on to the external and aggressive purpose of that barbarous agape, to wit, that the Lamb of God took away the sins of the world, which was a good thing, but that it was all the same a bad thing to have killed the Lamb of God, so that the impulse for the killing had to be displaced and projected on the Jews—if they noted that well they could not help somewhat extending the comparison to a civilized as well as to a primitive savagery: to "the mechanized totem-feast" of the Nazi State.

Yes, love, he went on, love indeed licensed the Catholic, the truly faithful, to the commission of wonderful deeds—the rack, the thumbscrew and the wheel were among the instruments by which love entered the world. If Father Meretruce wanted his Catholic heritage he must take it all, he should never mention Aquinas without also mentioning Conrad of Marsburg or the *Malleus Maleficarum* or Chaucer's nasty propaganda story about little Hugh of Lincoln. And that significant delight in deep Hell, in burning flesh both here and hereafter—that should not be forgotten either.

Very well then, the priest said in a quiet but hardly a chastened voice, might the company be entertained with Dr. Einman's own definition of love? After which, he implied, there would be much to say on his side.

Why not? Let them think first—as "a firm basis for discourse" —of, say, the huge copulations of Gargantua and his bride, which Rabelais' first translator Englished, if Edmond remembered aright, with the striking phrase about "frotting their bacons together." Would that do? As a kind of reminder of what must be considered in talking of love?

"So that is the whole dignity of man?" the priest ironically observed.

"I make no claim for its dignity," Edmond said.

The others heard this dispute in various moods and degrees of attention; the Hungarian sisters, who understood nothing but occasional tags of Latin, nevertheless followed the exchange with expressions of interest, looking from one to the other side like spectators at tennis. Sisters Catherine and Terese seemed to have understood only what disgusted them. Leonora observed that she had never heard such a stupid lot of talk about a perfectly simple matter—what difference did it make what people believed? She held Pilot Officer Hannan's hand in hers and played with the fingers; to this Roger seemed to have no objection, it was as though the three of them had reached some sort of triune understanding.

Only the entrance of Mother Fosker, however, at last interrupted the debate; she stood in the doorway, a strange apparition in the most genteel black dress with lace at the neck drawn together by a cameo of an ancient color like a nicotine stain, and, withal, an incongruous mask of green silk. She chuckled.

"You're talking of love," she said. "You should see it downstairs. They've just chosen the queen of the May, so to speak, and she has to bathe in the fountain. Strictly in the nude, of course—the gentlemen won't have it another way." Here she cackled pleasantly. "They're having such a good time," she said.

"Madame," Roger suddenly burst forth, standing up. "I've no idea what's going on here and I don't very much care—I've been lied to, deceived, cuckolded and coerced, to say nothing of having been argued with and told it's all for my own good. But there is this one thing: Pilot Officer Hannan and I must leave; our passes are nearly up, our train pulls out of North Station in less than an hour, if we are not on it the authorities will make trouble for us and we will take the greatest pleasure in making trouble for you. Is that clear?"

Mother Fosker now pushed the green mask up on her forehead and with a dainty handkerchief taken from her sleeve blew her nose loudly.

"That's right, dear," she said approvingly. "That's the sort of honest talk I can understand. You and I can come to an agreement, I bet. Of course," she added, "we're just down to rock bottom here and there's absolutely no security except personal trust. I've got to trust you, and I don't know if I can do that." She shook her head in melancholy puzzlement.

"If we give our word of honor," said Roger eagerly, "as officers and gentlemen . . . ?"

Edmond and John Averist guffawed simultaneously.

". . . that we'll get on that train without saying a word to anyone, that we'll forget the whole business . . ."

"Roger!" said Claire. "If you get out of here it's your duty to get a policeman."

"Don't tell me what my duty is," Roger said. "I don't know what it is you've been doing since I left—you and Susan both— or what all these people are or how they connect up. But I do know I'm not interested and I'm not responsible. I want to go back to the war where it's safe and people know what they're doing." He took a deep breath.

"I solemnly give my word as an officer and a gentleman . . ." he began.

"Save it," said Mother Fosker. "I accept, but you won't mind if I send one of my boys along with you to see you off? And what about your friend, does he give his word?"

"Yeh, sure," said Hannan. "It's no skin off my ass," he added thoughtfully.

And so it was arranged. Roger, before leaving, made a little speech comparing military virtue and civilian vice, in which occurred the words "manly comradeship," "world of tomorrow," "clean living, clean thinking, clean dying."

"You may think it ridiculous," he said at last, "with your talk about love. But look what you've got yourselves into, and laugh that off. When I think of the world we will be fighting to defend . . ." etc.

"*Molto onor, poco contante,*" Edmond said as the door closed behind Roger and Hannan. "*La gloria militar.*"

"As for the rest of you," Mother Fosker said, "you don't want the police, the last thing you want is the police. I would spread you all over every newspaper in the country. Just let things take their course, why don't you? Be more philosophical. Sex exists. You've got to face it. After all, you're just as responsible for the set-up as anyone else—if you hadn't been a pretty sexy crew yourselves, or if you hadn't behaved like such a bunch of nincompoops—no, don't tell me. You've got yourselves to blame. Just imagine it"—she ran her hand through the air to show the size of a banner headline—"Clergy, Debutantes, Run Backbay Hotspot."

"Priest indicted in fertility rites," added Edmond. "Claims it is all a mistake."

"I suppose," Father Meretruce said, "you take this woman's side?"

"Hardly," Edmond answered. "But I can certainly see the joke."

"That's right," said Mother Fosker. As she left the room she stopped to pat Hogan gently and affectionately on the head. "Don't let them put anything over, Mr. Hogan," she said. Hogan waved his gun in the affirmative.

Downstairs the party had accelerated its pace and originality. The gypsy trio, at a sign from Mother Fosker, now played "Goodnight, Ladies," and packed its instruments to go home: if it is true, as it is said in the Symposium, that music is the knowledge of love in harmony and system, the merrymakers no longer required its instruction.

The lights had progressively been turned down until now they burned few and far apart; in a kind of livid air thus provided, smoky and hot, one could see the heltering to and fro of those few lively spirits male and female who still delayed the consummation by keeping to their feet. These people were of that sort which is never content but must always be devising new pranks, such as applying to a bare foot the flame of a match—they took a giggling pride in doing this at a crucial moment. Because of this there began to be a little unpleasantness.

Uncle Fred had even time to wonder, as he dutifully nuzzled his nose into the naked breast of a fat, rather dirty girl with whom in the chance and change of things he had been partnered, whether he was having a good time. He decided he had liked his first companion better, not so much because she was more beautiful as because he had not, finally, had her: a little mystery, a little chastity, a little clothing—they might arrange these things better, he thought.

How charming it had been at first, in the first darkness and the air tense with perfumes, to hear the whisper of silk, the scratch of satin, the somber hiss of velvet, to feel the kindly touch of flesh that was smooth as marble, warm and dry; and, not either to be despised, the happy communal sense that one did what the others did. Yet in so short a while how this paradise had changed. Uncle Fred felt wretched, and took moreover a certain pleasure in feeling wretched, as though his wretchedness guaranteed in some way that he had had a good time. He coughed because the smoke in the air tickled his windpipe, and the cough brought a little taste of bile into his throat. But far stronger than the smoke or the odor of alcohol was that peculiar smell of sweat and semen which to many people is the spitting image of reality and at least as unpleasant as what they mean by that word. This, together with the truly vile stench of various perfumes, unguents, ointments, powders, oils, greases, pomades, friends to daintiness and foes to underarm perspiration, which, having not a little gone off, overpoweringly resembled the poet's "lilies that fester"—all this produced in Uncle Fred a considerable nausea, which he was, however, able to control. Others had not been so strong, and from somewhere not far away came the final odor, like a solo instrument outsoaring that orchestra, of vomit. The sound of heavy breathing, like distant waves, went up and down in the room, and a few people were snoring. The grayish-green tones of flesh reflecting the dull little light there was suggested rather the battlefield than the pleasure dome; it was like a human abattoir.

Uncle Fred wanted to go home. He wondered how he would go about finding his clothes, his trousers especially. The thought discouraged him, and he fell unsoberly asleep on the acquiescent breast of his whore.

But some people were still not at rest. The pleasures of the flesh are simply insufficient and no ingenuity can altogether conceal what must come ultimately to the tedious repetition. But here, having exhausted by now the amusements afforded by exhibitionism when it caters to voyeurism, these happy few began to take an interest in pain, and had devised a little party of which the essence was whipping with curtain wires, which were torn from their sockets. The heavy drapes of brocaded stuff lay on the floor, and one snoring couple used them for blankets. The indefatigable dancers danced on, whipping one another cheer-

3 2 7

fully with the curtain wires and stumbling from time to time over the bodies on the floor.

Upstairs, they were talking again, largely and generously, of love. The priest used phrases like "the intellectual love of God" and "the annihilation of self in love," and Sister Catherine somewhat shyly said she had often pitied those who could not feel that blessed love. Edmond spoke of "libido," of "drives," of "energy" in what he claimed was Blake's sense of the term. John Averist syncretistically pointed out that the concept of libido was not a new one, the Middle Ages having distinguished two such forces in addition to the sexual one intended by the modern use: the *libido dominandi*, the *libido sciendi*, the diseases of Faust. To which Edmond replied that the term was old but its content new. The Hungarian nuns were becoming restless; it was predictable that they would soon get down to praying.

Susan had said nothing all evening. Her face was pale but composed. Internally and almost physically she wished to die. The voices raised in argument around her roused her mind to a remote exasperation. Occasionally she raised her eyes and regarded Hogan, who looked terribly bored even despite his possession of a gun.

Downstairs the music had stopped, and they could hear plainly, even with the window closed, voices speaking lewdness.

"We speak of love, yes," said Claire in a tired voice. "But isn't it after all love which has, one way and another, produced this situation? To me it's quite clear: I am shut in a room in my own house and watched by a man with a pistol—simply because of love and its mysterious ways. The quantity of *love* in this house," she added, giving to the word "love" with each repetition an increasingly sarcastic emphasis, "must have been, tonight, quite enough to drive a rocket to Mars. Father *loves* humanity. Edmond *loves* Susan. Susan *loves*—herself, is it? The nuns *love* God and God *loves* us all and even the whores do what they can. Having granted all that—look at us all. And laugh."

"But there is no doubt," said John, "that love exists."

"Exists, exists. Of course it does, or something does, whatever you want to call it. But do we want it? Couldn't we substitute something else—minding our own business, for example? What *love* seems to have done in this instance is to have involved everyone with everyone else in a peculiarly sticky way; we're a nest of vipers who poison one another."

"Beware," said Father Meretruce, "lest you reject the hope of salvation."

"He means don't throw out the baby with the bath," Edmond helpfully said. "I think I agree with him, though. Without love, one is nothing."

Father Meretruce raised a hand to stop him.

"What the apostle said was not so vague as 'love.' 'If I have not *charity* . . .' that was his word. When you speak of 'love,' you may mean anything, anything at all."

"Pray do not be so easily scandalized, Father," Edmond said. "I think I am acquainted with the distinction. I deliberately used the word 'love' because it is accurate—the thing named is as irresponsible and ambiguous as its name—and also because I did not wish to make a finicking and pedantic substitution for the term commonly accepted. The world proceeds by love. That is a statement on which I hope we can agree. I would not agree that the world proceeds by charity."

"Verbal maneuvering."

"Not in the least. There is a real distinction. In the word 'love' we may include—as we must in any account of our world —violence, growth, generation and death. We cannot do as much with charity, which is rather one manifestation than the principle itself. By the word 'love' let us distinguish the essential, desire."

3 2 9

"It seems to me that we love because we are alone," said John Averist.

"Let us admit," said Edmond, disregarding the interruption, "that we don't know, beyond desire, what love is or what its consequences may be, what is right or what is perverse. But there is a power in things that continuously is creating love, which is desire, which is life."

"Ignoble and vague," said the priest. "But we have the revealed truth which enables us to control this power of love according to the law of its Creator, the all-just and all-merciful God in heaven, whose only-begotten Son Jesus Christ took on flesh and because of love bore away the sins of the world and caused Hell itself to tremble with love. Of course, there are many who do not accept this fact but continue whoring after knowledge as though knowledge were still to be gained on the one subject of utter importance, man's salvation, concerning which the Scriptures fully direct us. And what can they expect, who will not have the truth at any price?"

"There is only one objection—you make it sound as though Catholics are better than other people, a fact which observation will hardly persuade us of."

"But that's not the point," Claire said. "Look at our behavior here. Is it that of people who in any sense at all love one another? I think not. We talk of love, we tell ourselves how vastly important it is, but really it's just a kind of rubbing together for warmth, isn't it? And sometimes it makes us happy, other times the rubbing creates friction—but that's all the same to us, we call it *love* when we marry, and *love* when we hold an *auto-da-fe*, and *love* when we decide how other people should live. It's not love which is our trouble, it's only dishonesty."

"I can't agree," John said. "Dishonesty, yes; we are dishonest —but that doesn't affect the one, main thing, which is our feeling for someone else, however we may dodge and be devious and finally make a mess of everything." He looked at Susan, who had her hands spread flat on the table and was staring at them. "I feel, myself," he said shyly yet somberly, with the evident intention that his words should be meaningful to one person and cryptic to all others, "that I've lost everything, so I don't hope for gain. But I do love. I realize how alone one is."

"So do the people downstairs," Edmond observed.

"You all take it so seriously," said Leonora. "Haven't you ever thought it might be fun—just going to bed, I mean, without the trimmings? There's something about meeting someone that way, you know. Ten minutes ago you're strangers, and then—there you are. You just know in advance how good it's going to be, but you can still be surprised. Anyhow," she concluded, "it seems to me when there's this much talk there's probably damnall else."

Edmond bowed mockingly across the table.

"A clever thrust," he said, "and doubtless we deserve it. But as we are growing old it becomes a point of honor."

"An invitation?" asked Leonora, smiling. Edmond bowed again.

"Must this be part of our argument?" the priest wearily and disdainfully asked.

"Certainly," replied Edmond. "On what else does the argument rest?"

Susan raised her head now and spoke.

"On what else indeed? Good old love. When you pay your nickel you may use the public toilet; no one asks what you put into it."

"Susan!" Claire cried, and Father Meretruce said, "That is an insufferable remark."

"I'm very tired," Susan said.

"That doesn't excuse what you've said. You cannot say things like that." Claire drew herself up stiffly. "I think you must apologize."

"Let me finish. I said I'm very tired, and I mean it. There will be no apologies. I've told you the truth, quite simply, and you don't want to hear it. After all," she said in a kind of muttered aside, "we know by now what evil is, evil is what smells bad.

"I've listened to you all evening, and it's clear you all live in a world I don't live in—you have enough words, all of you, to keep the horror out. But why not ask Hogan about love? You haven't yet got his opinion, the good word according to Hogan."

Hogan, hearing his name mentioned, came suddenly awake (he had all but dozed off) and pointed the gun straight before him; he tried to look serious, attentive and dangerous, and wondered what was demanding his attention.

"Yes, you should indeed plumb the fine ardors of Hogan's soul," Susan went on. "Or mine. Hogan and I have pretty thoroughly explored the nature of love, the ruling passion. It causes the beasts of the forest to couple in their season, and the beasts of the town . . ." She shuddered, and tried to smile. "Forty dollars a week," she said, "is the whole nature of love—and then the darkness and the especially dirty loneliness in which you're never quite alone."

She turned to face Edmond.

"I've done something decisive, you see," she said. "And I want you to know, I feel a great contempt for you. And for all of you," she added, rising. "Dislike and contempt. But nothing to what I feel about myself."

Susan walked toward the door; Hogan got up and, standing in her way, leveled the gun at her. Had he been less of a novice he might have found some less extreme solution to his problem, but the gun in his hand appeared to him the supreme, almost magical factor of power, the only one worth considering, and he held it carefully on her. She, however, walked calmly and directly up to him and reached out to the weapon.

Beyond this no one could say who caused her death, whether Hogan in an access of nervous panic had fired or Susan had simply pressed his finger back on the trigger; only it was certain that, whatever the original impulse, he was still firing as she fell. The gun went off several times. Susan was slammed against the wall by the impact and was thus partly supported so that she fell quite slowly. The explosions resounded and died away around the room.

She was dead before anyone had moved; two bullets had smashed her spine and a third caught her hand upflung in falling.

Father Meretruce eventually took the gun from Hogan, who surrendered it without a word and without even looking at it.

No one spoke.

Edmond bent down to the girl and felt for her heart. She lay on her side, and all could see the wounds large and bloodied in her back; the cracked end of a rib stuck through her clothing. Still no one said anything. There was about their faces a quality rather of embarrassment than horror, as though they were more affected by Susan's last words to them than by her death which had made those words irrevocable.

Father Meretruce at last spoke.

"What a terrible death."

"I suppose you mean," Edmond said, looking up, "that she should have forgiven us first."

"Yes," said the priest simply. "I do mean that."

"Please, don't," Claire said. "Don't let this, too, be something we talk about."

"If she could have forgiven she would not have died," said John Averist.

And they looked stupidly into one another's faces, while Father Meretruce held the gun on Hogan, who of them all was the first to weep.

Downstairs the sound of firing had a huge effect. Sleepers rolled and stirred uneasily, then climbed from the floor; it was, in the early light of dawn, as though graves were opening and pushing forth their tenants. No one knew clearly what was happening, but all took alarm. There were low-voiced, hurried quarrels and even fights over clothes. A rumor started that the police were in the house, and all those fled who were capable: the scene was like sunrise on the Bröcken, at the dispersal of the hags. Nevertheless many remained whom perhaps the trumpet of doom would not have awakened at this moment.

Mother Fosker and her servants, with the women who were dressed and not drunk, were out of the house before the shots had fairly stopped sounding. It was as though they had never been.

Claire, Leonora, Edmond and John Averist came down and entered the library, with Hogan before them. Edmond held the gun. The religious remained upstairs with Susan's corpse, over which a blanket had been spread. The mechanical yet eloquent muttering they kept up in the presence of death could be heard distantly down the stairs.

The library was devastated, its curtains torn down, ash trays spilt or overflowing, sleeping bodies, several of them, on the floor.

"Le Mort de Sardanapale," said John. He flicked a cigarette from the veneer surface of a table, where it had left a long, stained burn.

Many drinks had been spilled, broken glass was in a number of places. From the torn upholstery of the couch white stuffing ectoplastically protruded. Claire sat down here and put her head in her hands and began to cry. John gently put his hand on her shoulder and she shook it off without looking up.

"This is absurd," Edmond said, waving the gun in vague indication of three people, a man and two women, who were asleep under the harpsichord. Their breathing was hoarse and loud, racked occasionally by what seemed a communal cough.

"I didn't do it," Hogan said. "I swear I didn't—she did it herself."

"Think what you'll get just for having the gun in your hand," Edmond said. "You might as well take the whole works."

"It was awful," said Leonora. "She wanted to die." Leonora walked slowly and in a preoccupied way about the room. She affected not to notice the scattered and corpselike sleepers that everywhere threatened to trip her up, but when she came to an ash tray she absently took it up and emptied it into a waste-basket, then put it back where it came from; the air of the room had the pale gray smell of cold ashes.

Uncle Fred Seely just now rose up from the floor, where his lady still lay naked and unconscious. Recognizing Claire and Leonora he made his hand serve for a fig-leaf, which gave him the posture of a nymph on an ash tray. He had an agonizing headache. Claire looked up at him.

"Susan was killed just now," she said. "Get dressed and get your friends out of here. We must call the police. No, there's nothing to explain," she said as his mouth opened. "Go home."

Uncle Fred picked up and put on a pair of trousers which fitted him fairly enough. He then began to kick the other sleepers, who indignantly sat up and had the situation explained to them. While thus engaged he stepped on a piece of broken glass and his foot began to bleed; he put on his shoes anyhow. Without the least embarrassment but in the cold ebb of life that comes with morning, all silently watched the late-lustful companions who with trembling hands were putting on their underwear.

"I will stay," Uncle Fred said. "It is my duty to stay." He looked appealingly at the group.

"Please, don't be fatuous," Claire said. "Go home. We have trouble enough without you."

"You're sure you don't mind?" he asked, being already at the door. "I mean, I had nothing to do with it. I was—you know that. It might be better if." He disappeared. The other celebrants, having arranged themselves as they might in what clothing came to hand, at last also departed. Leonora went with them.

"It's not my affair," she said, with that firmness that had made her what she was. "I don't see why I should be dragged into it."

Claire and John sat on the couch, regarding Hogan who leaned back in a deep armchair; his situation would not previously have allowed him the use of an armchair in this room, but he had dignified himself at last. Edmond walked aimlessly about, scarcely so much holding his weapon as twiddling it. From upstairs could be heard the cool babbling of prayer making its usual recommendations. There was a heavy tread on the stair. Father Meretruce entered the room and sniffed with distaste.

"I have grave fears for her soul," he said pompously and with the authority of one who brings news of the greatest importance. "I am not at all certain she did not take her own life, using this man only as the merest instrument in her own hand."

"She's dead," said Claire. "Can't you leave her alone?"

"We all must die, that is not the question. But the soul goes to judgment."

"She wasn't a Catholic," said John. "How she would have resented this proprietary interest."

"I fail to see," said the priest, "how that can make any difference now."

"Doesn't it occur to you all," asked Edmond, "that this is a nonsensical discussion?"

"On the contrary," said Father Meretruce. "I was about to ask you to pray with me, for her soul. You have seen, now, what life can do—I should have thought you were ready to kneel."

"I could not," said John. "I feel I helped with her murder—I am as guilty as that one, for I could have helped her and I did not." He looked somberly at Hogan. "Did I somehow wish for her to die?" he asked at large. No one replied.

"I too am to blame," Edmond said. "I did not understand that kind of seriousness—nor do I understand it better now."

"I must have hurt her terribly," said Claire. "But how could that be known except now?"

To all of them Susan's death had the certain appearance of suicide whether it was so in fact or not, and this had the strange effect of making Hogan, in their eyes, less culpable than themselves. Hogan, however, was now nerving himself to speak; it seemed to him of the greatest importance, and also inconceivably difficult, to say simply:

"I slept with her too."

John Averist, who had up till then remained impassive, shuddered at this and began to cry. Edmond pointed at Hogan with the gun.

"But here is the villain," he said gently, and with a little smile. "The law does not trouble with our silent wishes, but wants the hand only which did the murder. Only the hand can meet justice, isn't that so? But look at him—in the cold morning light. What profit of villainy? He looks so pale, so tired, so unrewarded. I wonder, then, why one is villainous."

They made no reply, and he said to John and Claire:

"As for you two, you dear, abject failures, complicated timidities for whom I confess affection—I should think you might take the lesson, and go marry. Cultivate the solid and the virtuous. I give you to one another, for whatever good may come of that."

Edmond now gave the gun to John and went out to the hall. They heard him telephoning to the police. Father Meretruce sat on a hard chair and put his hands on his knees and yawned widely. Claire got up, and, without looking at Hogan or John or the priest, went to the harpsichord. She sat down and began to play, inattentively at first but presently with more care, a little piece in fugue. The instrument was out of tune and not only that, but broken glass tinkled on some of the strings, but it seemed not to matter. The morning light seemed to clear the room as the voices in a minor key steadily moved to and from one another, showing an inexorable confidence in their not quite harmonious world.